THE BOYS IN THE CHURCH

A JOE COURT NOVEL

BY
CHRIS CULVER
ST. LOUIS, MO

First paperback edition April 2019

First eBook edition April 2019

www.indiecrime.com

Facebook.com/ChrisCulverBooks

Contents

Chapter 1

P aige had ivory skin still unblemished by time, brunette
hair that flowed down to her shoulders, and the long,
muscular legs of a dancer. Her eyes were her only flaw. Hazy
and vapid, they belied the sharp mind that lay within. In his
younger years, Glenn would have made a fool out of himself
to impress her. Now, that was no longer an issue.

He slipped the mask over his face and sauntered down the
concrete steps. With the first couple, he hadn't worn a mask.
Unfortunately, they had watched enough television to know
what that meant. Despite his best efforts, he had never been
able to develop a rapport with them, because they knew a
man who let them see his face would never let them go. Ever
since then, he had worn a replica of a seventeenth-century
plague doctor's mask. Its long, pointed beak drew and held
the sinners' attention until the end.

Grit crunched beneath his shoes as he descended into the
gloom. Helen followed a few steps behind him. Though
she was capable of many things, Helen hated manual labor,
leaving Glenn to carry the cattle prod and cooler himself.

When he reached the bottom step, he put both items down and flicked on the light switch.

Paige and Jude shielded their eyes but otherwise didn't move from their cot. The room was a simple storm cellar divided in half by a heavy-duty chain-link fence. A light bulb hung from the ceiling in the center of the room. The air was damp and held a whiff of mold. Glenn had tried to make the space comfortable by putting in a cot, mattress, and pillows, but he couldn't mask its nature.

Nor did he want to.

"Good morning," whispered Glenn. "I hope I didn't wake you up."

On previous visits, Jude had jumped out of bed and run to the fence as soon as Glenn and Helen stepped inside. Some days he had begged for Glenn to let him out, while other days he had threatened and screamed at the top of his lungs. Now, he didn't even look up. Paige drew in a breath but didn't otherwise move.

"It's time," said Helen. "They're ready to give in."

"I think you're right," said Glenn, glancing over his shoulder at his sister.

She wore a blue pencil dress with a cream-colored bow around her waist and a matching blue masquerade mask. A red hair tie pulled her straight, brunette hair from her face. Though her outfit and simple makeup, made her look like a lawyer or accountant, Helen didn't have a job. She lived with him, and he provided for them both. She needed little, so Glenn didn't mind. He loved his sister, but more than that, she had helped raise him after their mother died. She had earned her place in his home.

"Who are you talking to?" asked Jude, his voice scratchy.

"My sister," said Glenn. "You've met her before."

"There's no one there," said Paige, her voice wavering as she sat upright. "There's never anybody else there."

Glenn looked at his sister again. She had disappeared into the shadows. Helen was a beautiful woman, but she felt insecure at times. Their mother had died when they were young, so no one had taught Helen to put on makeup or to dress for her body type. She had to learn that all on her own, and she still didn't always like the results she achieved. Glenn tried to tell her she looked beautiful and had nothing to be ashamed of, but Helen preferred to stay in the shadows when others were around. She didn't like it when people looked at her. That was her choice, and he respected it.

"You don't need to see her," said Glenn, turning to his two young captives. "How are you two lovebirds feeling? Hungry?"

Neither Jude nor Paige said anything. Jude's skin, like Paige's, had grown paler in the past few weeks, but the most visible change had been to his cheeks. They had grown hollow and more pronounced. Even on his best day, no one would have ever called him handsome, but after weeks surviving on scraps of food, he now looked gaunt, almost ghoulish.

Jude and Paige were the sixth couple he and Helen had taken. This was his life's work, the highest, noblest thing he had ever done. It was the only way to right the sins of his past. His sister had taught him that. If he lived to a hundred, he could never thank her enough.

"I have something for you," said Glenn, reaching into the small cooler he had brought with him. He pulled out a Ziploc bag containing half a ham sandwich. It wasn't much, just a piece of processed meat between two pieces of cheap white bread. It didn't even have mayonnaise on it. Jude sat up and stared as if he had taken out the most delectable cut of meat in the world. Though Glenn gave his captives as much water as they could want, both had lost a significant amount of weight, and they moved slowly. They were weak.

"Will you stay on the bed if I open the door?" he asked. Both nodded, so Glenn walked to the cell's gate and unlocked the padlock. Four weeks ago, he wouldn't have done that. Now, they'd be weak enough to do as they were told. Still, he picked up his cattle prod in case Jude tried to play hero.

"The sandwich is for Jude," said Glenn, holding out the bag. "I've got another half in the cooler."

Jude hesitated and then looked to his girlfriend.

"What does Paige get?"

"The sandwich is for you," said Glenn, allowing a gentle smile to form on his lips. "I suppose you can do with it whatever you want. You've got to be hungry."

Jude licked his lips and stood. Only then did Glenn see the way Jude's shirt hung off his once athletic shoulders and the way the bones of his wrist protruded beneath his skin. Some people could survive months on a starvation diet as long as they had enough water, but neither Paige nor Jude had come in with excess body fat. Unless they ate soon, he doubted they'd have much time left.

Jude snatched the bag from Glenn's hand as if he feared it would disappear at any moment. Then he smiled as tears formed in his eyes.

"Thank you," he said, opening the bag and sitting beside his girlfriend. Paige never took her eyes from the small bit of food in front of her. Glenn watched and prayed, hoping today would be the day. Jude took the sandwich from the bag, tore it in half, and held a part toward Paige. She cried tears of joy, but Glenn's shoulders slumped. He sighed and lifted his cattle prod before either took a bite.

It was too early.

He shocked Jude first. Paige yelped and dropped her food as she scurried away, but Jude tried to shove the sandwich into his mouth. Glenn kicked him in the face so he couldn't. Then he shocked him again, this time holding the prod against his neck until Jude's body convulsed on the ground.

Glenn grabbed the remnants of the sandwich from the cot and stabbed Paige in the gut with his cattle prod to remind her how much it hurt. She screamed and curled into a ball.

Neither fought back. They had learned the consequences of fighting with him weeks ago.

Glenn hurried out of the cell, swearing nonstop under his breath as he locked the gate. Then he threw the sandwich down and gripped the chain-link fence. He trembled with rage and frustration, and he screamed an animalistic scream. Paige and Jude looked at him as if he were the crazy one, as if he had turned down the sandwich. He wasn't crazy, though. He was angry.

"Calm down, Glenn," said Helen. "They're not ready yet, but they will be."

"I'm tired of waiting," he said. The kids both wailed louder upon hearing his voice, so he glared at them and snarled. "Shut up."

Paige and Jude held each other on the bed. They quieted down, and Glenn took two deep breaths.

"He loves her and thinks he needs to take care of her," said Helen in her soothing, singsong voice. "It always takes time, and you always get impatient at the end."

"Simon and Jordan took four weeks. Andrew and Nicole took five. No one has taken over six. Something is wrong. They're sneaking food somehow."

Helen shushed him and then left the shadows to put her arm over his shoulder as she led him out of the cellar.

"Did you see them? They don't have secret supplies of food. They're starving," she said. "Every couple is different.

This one is stronger than most, but we haven't failed yet. We won't fail now. Have patience. We're closer than you think."

He knew his sister was right, but the need still burned inside him.

"What do we do?" he asked, after drawing in a deep breath.

"First, you turn off the light," she said. "If we leave them in darkness, they'll break faster. Second, we go to Winfield. There's no reason we can't handle two at once."

He flicked off the light.

"Don't leave us!"

The voice was so panic-stricken, Glenn couldn't even tell whether it was Paige or Jude. He turned and screamed over his shoulder.

"Shut up!"

The voices quieted, and Helen rubbed his shoulder. As they climbed the steps, he came back to his senses. She was right. Three more days—a week at most—and Jude and Paige would give in to their animal natures. They simply needed more seasoning.

He and Helen left the cellar and emerged into a beautiful, early summer morning. Birds chirped in the trees, and insects buzzed around the wildflowers at the edge of the clearing. A rabbit darted from the abandoned building behind him.

"You sure we should go to Winfield?" he asked, pulling the cellar door shut to the protests of the people inside. He locked that with another padlock and walked to his car. Helen kept pace over the uneven ground despite the high-heeled shoes she wore.

"Hunting would do us both good," she said. "It would take our minds off things."

Glenn had driven a black Kia that morning. At one time, the car had belonged to John Rodgers of Hannibal, Illinois, but with John's death many months ago, it now belonged to him and served a purpose far higher than ferrying a teenager to and from school. Glenn never drove his own car to the dungeon. That would have been foolish. Upon reaching the vehicle, he put the cooler and cattle prod on the ground and opened his trunk. He hadn't gone hunting in almost six weeks. He missed the rush.

"Let's pick up Peter and Mary, then. If they take six weeks to break, we might as well start now."

Chapter 2

I got to my station at a few minutes before eight in the morning. My stomach had butterflies, my mouth was dry, and my fingers couldn't stop drumming the steering wheel of my old Dodge pickup. I had spoken during the morning briefing dozens of times in the past year alone, but today was special. Today, we had guests from the FBI.

Since the station's lot was full, I parked on the street about half a block away and hurried toward my building. St. Augustine wasn't a wealthy county, so we didn't have the newest equipment or fancy squad cars, and we could have doubled the number of uniformed officers on staff and still been shorthanded. Nobody complained about our headquarters building, though.

At one time, it had been a Masonic temple, but the county had purchased it when the Masons left town. Most of it needed renovation, but it was a gorgeous building. The county promised to remodel the second and third floors eventually and give us a modern forensics lab and enough private offices for each detective in the department to have his own place, but I knew how government worked and wasn't hopeful that would happen in my lifetime. Still, I appreciated what we had.

I opened the heavy oak front door and walked inside. Trisha Marshall, the day shift's dispatcher, sat behind the front desk. She nodded at me.

"You're late, Joe," she said, smiling. "The boss is in the conference room. You'd better hurry."

"On my way," I said, knocking on her wooden desktop as I passed. When the Masons built their temple, they had put an auditorium with three hundred seats in the middle of the building. Upon purchasing the property, the county pulled out the seats and the stage and put in cubicles. It was now our bullpen, a purpose it served well.

I walked through the maze of desks to the conference room. A dozen uniformed officers had gathered around the open door to listen to that morning's briefing. It was two minutes before eight, but already Sheriff George Delgado's voice carried outside as he read the previous evening's arrest reports.

I whispered apologies as I slipped through the crowd. The boss's eyes lingered on me once he saw me. My ego wasn't big enough for me to believe he had started early to make me look bad, but he seemed to enjoy glaring at me all the same.

I mouthed an apology, but Delgado rolled his eyes and looked away. Half a dozen unfamiliar men in suits sat around the conference table. All of them looked bored. In addition, someone had wheeled in whiteboards and tacked maps of the local area to the wall.

When he finished the daily briefing, Delgado looked around the room and drew in a deep breath.

"I know most of you hoped for an update on Paige Maxwell and Jude Lewis. You won't get one."

Several uniformed officers grumbled, but we needed secrecy on a case like this. I trusted my colleagues, but the more people who knew about the case, the greater the chance we'd spring a leak. The local community was on edge already; we didn't need to push them into a panic.

"This isn't a democracy, so you can stop bitching now," said Delgado. "If you've got an assignment, go to it. If you don't, go home."

The room emptied. The crowd almost carried me out, too, but I slipped past my colleagues so I could stand near the head of the conference room table. An unfamiliar man stood and held his hand toward me.

"Bruce Lawson," he said. "I'm the special agent in charge of the Bureau's field office in St. Louis. I'm heading up the task force. You must be Detective Court."

I shook his hand and nodded. Lawson was in his early fifties, and he had neat brown hair and a clean-shaven face. A navy-blue suit coat and white shirt hugged his torso. His long, thin fingers wrapped around my knuckles as I shook his hand. Despite the massive size of his hands, he was only an inch or two taller than me, so most of his agents towered over him.

"I'm Joe. Nice to meet you, Agent Lawson."

"From the reports I've read, you did good work on this. I look forward to hearing this in your own words," he said, nodding toward the head of the table. "Have a seat, and we'll get started."

The butterflies fluttered in my gut once more. After my colleagues had left, Delgado closed the door and walked to the table.

"This is your show, Bruce," he said, pulling out a chair. "Floor is yours."

Agent Lawson flashed him a tight smile.

"First things first, thank you for letting my team camp out in your station, Sheriff Delgado," he said, looking to the sheriff and then to the other men around the table. "We're here because the FBI's Behavioral Analysis Unit believes we have a serial murderer in the region. Before we start, let me clarify that we wouldn't be here at all if it hadn't been for the work of Detective Joe Court."

I crossed my arms so I wouldn't feel so exposed. Lawson smiled before focusing on the other officers around the table.

"Before we get into BAU's findings, I'd like Detective Court to tell us where we're at and how we got here," said Lawson, nodding toward me.

I hesitated before standing. Every eye in the room turned. I fought the urge to wave at them and kept my hands laced behind my back as if I were reciting letters at an elementary school spelling bee.

"Okay, I guess I'll get started. About six weeks ago, my station received word that two young people had gone missing—"

Agent Lawson cleared his throat, getting my attention. I looked at him and raised my brow.

"Details," he said. "Don't hold back. Who called it in, how old are the kids, and when did they disappear?"

I cleared my throat and looked down to give myself a moment to think.

"The girl was named Paige Maxwell. She was a senior in high school, and she was seventeen. Her boyfriend, the missing young man, attended the same high school and had recently turned eighteen. Paige's parents contacted us on March 14. Jude Lewis's parents called us the next day. I talked to all four of them and then typed up my interview notes afterwards. They should be available on our department's server."

One of the FBI agents looked up from a notepad and leaned forward. He had black hair cut close to his scalp line and acne scars that pockmarked his cheeks. His brown eyes were small for his angular face, while his pointed chin was large for his frame. He kind of looked like a cartoon version of Dracula.

"You said Paige was seventeen and Jude was eighteen. Why are we using the past tense? Are we sure they're dead?"

13

My eyes flicked to Agent Lawson before focusing on Dracula once more.

"We're not positive, but I can't imagine they're still alive. They disappeared six weeks ago, and neither has contacted his or her family or friends, neither has used credit cards or tried to access their bank accounts, and neither has shown up yet. We also found Paige's car in the woods. The backseat had hair, sweat, saliva, and seminal fluids—the kind of stuff you'd expect in a teenager's car—but someone had cleaned the front seats. You don't clean and dump a car that deep in the woods without a reason."

Agent Lawson nodded, but his eyes looked distant.

"Where's this car now?" he asked.

"The State Highway Patrol has it," I said. "We're a small station. They've got access to resources we don't, so we handed it over to them."

Dracula looked at Lawson. "For the time being, I'd suggest we assume Paige and Jude are still alive. Until we discover this guy's pattern, we can't assume he's killed them already."

Lawson nodded and looked at me. "Agreed. Go ahead, Detective. After you learned Paige and Jude were missing, what did you do?"

I wanted to tell Dracula I didn't simply assume Paige and Jude were dead, but this wasn't an interrogation or a critique. They were there to gather information. We were partners in this case.

At least that's what I told myself.

"I tried to track down their cell phones, but they were both off; I checked out their finances and discovered that both Paige and Jude had withdrawn five hundred dollars each from their bank accounts; I talked to their friends to make sure they didn't know where Paige and Jude were; I searched their rooms at home to see whether I could find anything interesting; and I called the State Highway Patrol and put them on notice to look for Paige's car. I also called a couple dozen hospitals to make sure they hadn't shown up."

"What did you do after you couldn't find them?" asked Dracula again.

"I kept the case active, but I wasn't worried at first. Paige was a minor, but she had a car and a job. She and Jude were also dating. Paige fought with her parents often, so I figured she and her boyfriend disappeared for a few days to take a break. I thought they would come home again after blowing through their savings."

Dracula wrote a few things down before considering me. He didn't seem impressed.

"What happened next? Did you make any follow-up inquiries?"

"If there were inquiries to make, I would have made them," I said, leaning forward. "We kept the case active, and I kept in touch with their friends in case Jude or Paige called. I also kept track of their cell phones and bank accounts. If they'd used their debit cards, or if they'd turned on their phones, I would have heard about it. We're a small department. As much as we wanted to, we couldn't drop everything to search for two missing kids."

"No one's criticizing you, Detective," said Agent Lawson, leaning forward and flashing me a tight smile. "We're just trying to gather the facts."

I forced myself to smile. "Of course."

"I've heard there's something interesting with a map," said one of the other agents. He had gray hair, and his skin had the tanned patina of a lifelong smoker. His voice was low, and his gray mustache bounced as he spoke. He looked like the Marlboro Man. "Can you tell us about that?"

I opened my mouth to say something, but Lawson interrupted.

"Instead of telling us," he said, "show us."

He nodded toward a large map of the Midwest taped onto a rolling easel. I took a marker from the easel's well and eyed the map so I could orient myself.

"We're here," I said, making a dot over St. Augustine. It was the center of the map. "On May 13, 2017, Olivia King and her boyfriend, John Rodgers, were reported missing in Hannibal, Illinois."

I made a large dot on the map over Hannibal.

"On July 15, 2017, police officers in Kennett, Missouri, received a report that Tayla Walker and her boyfriend, Matthew Bridges, had gone missing."

I made another dot over Kennett.

"Two months later, Amy Hoffman and her boyfriend, James Tyler, disappeared in Decatur, Illinois. Two months after that, Jordan Fitzgerald and her boyfriend, Simon Fisher, disappeared in Mountain Grove, Missouri. Two months after that, Nicole Moore and her boyfriend, Andrew White, disappeared in Sturgis, Kentucky."

I marked the spots on the map before turning around. My stomach still had butterflies, but I felt stronger. The FBI agents got it now.

"All the victims are between sixteen and eighteen, all attended high school together, and all were dating. They disappeared at two-month intervals. The pattern repeated in every case. The children withdrew money from their bank accounts, they filled up their gas tanks, and then they disappeared. In all cases, the original presumption was that the victims had run away from home or disappeared so they could have sex without their parents knocking on the door."

Everyone around the room took that in. Several nodded.

"Now connect the dots," said Agent Lawson, glancing from me to his colleagues. I walked back to the board and put my marker on Hannibal. From there, I drew a line to Kennett, Missouri and then another one to Decatur, Illinois. Once I had five lines drawn, several of the assembled agents gasped.

"It's a pentagram with St. Augustine in the center," I said. "Once we found the pentagram, we knew these weren't random disappearances. Harry Grainger, our former sheriff, called the US Attorney's Office in St. Louis. They called you."

For a few moments, nobody said anything. Then Lawson took charge. He nodded.

"Have a seat, Detective," he said, before focusing on his team. "We've run the details by Behavioral Analysis. Our murderer appears organized and detail-oriented. We believe we're looking at one individual, but he might have a partner. Either way, he's evaded capture or detection for at least a year. In that time, he's abducted at least twelve victims. That is troubling."

Lawson opened a folder on the table and pulled out a stack of papers.

"We know a few things already," said Lawson. "The victims are all white, which means our killer is also probably white. Serial murderers rarely cross racial lines. Statistically, our killer is male. Furthermore, his ability to remain hidden tells us he's likely intelligent. What's more, we know he had the PINs and bank cards of all his victims because he withdrew money from their accounts. It's possible he works in a bank, but it's more likely that he talked his victims into giving this information out."

As Lawson spoke, I wrote his conclusions down.

"Is it possible our killer knows his victims?" I asked, glancing up from my notepad. "It might help explain his ability to talk them into giving him their bank information."

"We need to figure that out," said Lawson. "We also need to discuss the elephant in the room: the pentagram. Since we've not found his victims yet, all we can do so far is speculate as to our killer's motives. The pentagram is an ancient symbol used in dozens of religions, including Wiccanism, Christianity, and Bahaism. It also adorns the flags of Morocco and Ethiopia. Our killer isn't choosing his victims at random, but we don't know what this symbol means to him.

"This case has the salacious details that make reporters excited, but we don't know how our killer will react to seeing this on the news. Because of that, no one talks to the press without my explicit say-so. Questions about our media policy or anything else?"

Nobody spoke, so I leaned forward.

"There's another point you didn't mention," I said. "Our male victims are Jude, John, Matthew, James, Simon, and Andrew. They're saints."

"They're apostles of Christ," said an agent who had yet to speak. He looked at me. "Repeat the missing female victims' names."

I flipped through my notepad until I found the correct page.

"Paige, Olivia, Tayla, Amy, Jordan, and Nicole."

"Are they biblical names, too?" asked Dracula.

I shook my head. "I don't know about the others, but Tayla isn't. It's a modern name, isn't it?"

19

"We'll look it up," said Lawson. "Today, we're hitting the reset button. We will re-interview the victims' family, friends, and co-workers; we will talk to their teachers; we will dig into their social media accounts; and we will retrace their footsteps on the day they disappeared. By the end of the day, I want to know where our victims went on the days they disappeared, I want to know who they talked to, and I want fingerprints and DNA samples from each of their immediate family members.

"Approach this case as if I called you in this morning to work a missing-persons case. Work it from the beginning, but, above all, keep it quiet. Nobody talks to the press. We don't need to spook anyone."

For the next few minutes, Lawson doled out individual assignments. I kept waiting to hear my name, but he never said it. Once he finished speaking, he dismissed everybody and wished us all luck. As the agents filed out of the room, I stood and walked toward him.

"Special Agent Lawson," I said, "I noticed that you didn't mention me."

He glanced up from his paperwork. Then he looked to Delgado.

"You've done good work, Detective, but we're keeping this task force small for the moment."

I tried to smile, but I didn't have a lot of success.

"Paige and Jude were my case. I've already established rapport with their families and their friends, and I'm familiar with the local area. I'm in a better position than anybody on your task force to investigate them."

He considered me for a moment, but then he resumed organizing his papers into a neat stack on the table.

"While I appreciate your position and expertise, this is a federal case with victims in three different states. You don't have the authority to investigate crimes outside Missouri. Not only that, every one of my officers has at least a dozen years' experience investigating complicated murders. It's nothing personal. We'd love to include you in a greater role, but we can't. Since you've got an interest in the case, I'll try to keep you updated."

I lowered my chin. "Are you keeping any locals on this case?"

Lawson looked up from his paperwork and glanced at Delgado. The sheriff walked toward us.

"Sheriff Delgado will act as our community liaison. When we need to contact a local, he'll be our point man. None of our victims came from major cities. We don't want to take resources from communities already stretched thin."

"I see," I said, nodding. "You're kicking us off cases in our communities for our own good."

"Detective," growled Delgado.

"It's all right," said Lawson, glancing at Delgado before focusing on me. "If I put you on my task force, how many detectives would be available in St. Augustine?"

I didn't like my answer, so I said nothing. Lawson looked to Delgado.

"Several officers have retired in the past six months, so we're in the process of securing funding to hire three new detectives," he said.

Lawson looked at me. "As I understand it, you're the only detective on staff right now."

I looked down. "That's right."

"This town needs you more than I do," said Lawson. "I will do what I can to keep you updated. In the meantime, I've got a three-hour drive ahead of me to Hannibal, Illinois."

"Drive safely, Agent Lawson," said Delgado. Lawson thanked him and left the room. I forced a smile to my lips as I looked to my boss.

"What exciting job do you have in store for me today?"

He didn't even hesitate before answering.

"Speed trap."

The speed trap was a spot about a quarter mile outside of town where the speed limit dropped from fifty-five to thirty-five miles an hour. Most people slowed down, but a lot of drivers flew by at sixty or seventy miles an hour. I wouldn't have felt guilty about ticketing them except that someone on the County Council had planted a big bush in front of the sign.

The speed trap had nothing to do with safety. It was all about revenue. In an eight-hour shift, I'd write fifteen to twenty tickets, each of which would earn the town two to three hundred bucks. The County Council funneled some of that money to the police and courthouse, but most of it went into a rainy day fund the council used for pet projects. The system wasn't fair, but it rarely netted locals, and it didn't seem to hurt the tourist trade.

Nobody wanted to work the speed trap. The previous two sheriffs used it as a punishment when officers did something stupid at work. Delgado reserved it for me.

"All right, boss," I said. "Good luck with your case."

"And good luck to you, Detective. Catch them speeders," said Delgado, already turning so he could talk to Agent Lawson. I growled under my breath and left the conference room. The women's locker room was in the basement near the front of the building. I changed into a uniform and met Trisha, our dispatcher, in the lobby. She glanced at me.

"You look nice in a uniform," she said.

"Yeah. I'm living the dream," I said, my voice flat. "Delgado put me on the speed trap."

"I thought he might. Are we still on for tonight?"

"Oh, yeah. They're not keeping me away from this."

"Good. Then I'll see you later tonight. We should have something to work with by then."

"Good luck," I said. "And be careful. If you get caught, more than our jobs will be on the line."

She assured me that everything would be fine, so I walked toward the front door. I didn't always toe the line at work, but I tried to play by the rules. It felt good to break them for once. Unfortunately, I couldn't dwell on that warm feeling. I had speeders to catch.

Chapter 3

I spent the day in a uniform and a car at the speed trap. Most of the people I ticketed took it well and admitted they were driving too fast, but some got snippy with me. Nobody pulled a gun or tried to hit me, but I didn't like being the object of anyone's ire, either.

After nine hours in a squad car by the side of the road, I had written fourteen speeding tickets, three tickets for non-moving violations—lack of current registration once, lack of insurance twice—and one citation for driving with an open container. I also picked up a deadbeat dad who had a bench warrant out for failure to pay eighteen thousand dollars to his ex-wife in child support. We'd hold the deadbeat overnight while an officer from the Kansas City Police Department came to pick him up.

Because of my efforts, the county earned about twenty-five hundred dollars. If a forensic accountant audited the county's books, she'd find graft and corruption on every page.

I loved St. Augustine, but it floated on a lake of dirty money. If we arrested every corrupt politician in town, dozens more would show up to fight for the vacant positions. I'd complain, but that was how modern politics worked. Everything came with a price, and integrity was cheap.

At the end of my shift, I dropped my cruiser off at work, showered in the women's locker room, and then changed into my civilian clothes before heading by the grocery store. There, I picked up seven premade frozen dinners and a bottle of vodka. My shopping list said more about my lifestyle than I wanted, but I didn't care. It was my life; I lived it the way I wanted.

After my brief stop, I drove to my century-old American foursquare. The guy who'd built my house had bought the parts from a Sears & Roebuck catalog. Several generations of a single family had lived in it for most of its life, but when I bought the place, no one had lived in it for years.

When I unlocked the door for the first time six years ago, rust had eaten through the cast iron pipes, the rubber insulation coating the electrical wires had dried out and cracked, and the weatherproofing on the windows had disappeared. Building inspectors in a larger county would have condemned it. It had taken me years, but I was bringing it back from the edge. I didn't even feel embarrassed when people visited anymore. Through hard work and some tears, I had transformed a rotten shell of a house into my home. I loved every inch of it.

I parked in the driveway and went through my front door. Inside, I found three whiteboards on easels in my living room and a white cardboard banker's box full of documents on my coffee table.

I put away the food and vodka in my kitchen before organizing the documents. When I finished, I had ten stacks on my couch, floor, and coffee table. Some held forensic reports, while others held transcriptions of interviews with Paige and Jude's friends, and others held printouts of bank accounts and credit cards. The information probably wouldn't help find our killer—or killers—but it wouldn't hurt.

Once I finished organizing things, I put on a pot of coffee and grabbed a granola bar from my pantry. After that, Trisha and Harry knocked on my door with two more boxes of documents.

"That's a lot of stuff," I said.

"We're just getting started," said Harry. And he was right. As our department's liaison to the task force, George Delgado had access to every scrap of information the FBI produced during their investigation. Delgado wanted a copy of everything, but he refused to copy anything himself. He passed that duty on to Trisha. It wasn't hard for her to make an extra copy of everything for us.

"I made coffee."

"Got any beer?" asked Harry.

"Yeah. Later," I said, nodding to the boxes he and Trisha were carrying. "For now, let's work."

This round of documents came from other police departments about the other missing kids. We read and organized for about an hour in relative silence before Harry ordered a pizza and raided my fridge for beer. After that, we took our first break and ate dinner.

"So, what do we have so far?" I asked.

"Not a lot," said Harry. "Twelve victims, six male and six female, all between sixteen and eighteen years old, and all romantically involved."

I looked around before finding a dry erase marker.

"Give me their names again," I said. As Harry read from his notepad, I wrote the names down on a whiteboard. Beneath the names, I wrote the ages of the corresponding victim. "They're the same age, and the boys are named after apostles. What else do they have in common?"

Trisha shuffled through some papers.

"Olivia King and John Rodgers were sexually active. Amy Hoffman and James Tyler's parents suspected their kids were, too."

"So are Tayla Walker and Matthew Bridges and Nicole Moore and Andrew White," said Harry.

Paige and Jude were, too, so I wrote *sexually active* beneath the names.

"So at least five of the six couples were sleeping with one another," I said. "It's a safe bet the sixth couple was, too. Who would they tell about their sex lives?"

"Their friends," said Trisha. "Possibly siblings."

"A doctor would know," said Harry. "None of these are big towns, but they're all within driving distance of St. Louis. It's possible they all saw the same doctor in St. Louis."

I thought and shook my head.

"The kids from Decatur would have driven to Urbana, and I bet the kids from Mountain View would have driven to Springfield."

"That's where they'd go for a regular appointment," said Trisha. "These kids were sleeping with each other. What if they looked into abortions? They might see somebody in St. Louis for that."

It was a possibility, so I nodded and wrote *abortion?* beneath each couple's name on our whiteboard. "What else?"

For a few minutes, we flipped through papers and read. Most of the police departments had done outstanding work compiling information about their missing teenagers, but a minority took a more lackadaisical approach. Two of the missing boys played football, one wrestled, and three played no sports at all. Three of the girls played volleyball, one played softball, and one was a cheerleader. None of our documents listed clubs in schools.

I wrote the new information down and stepped back from our board. The wrestler was an outstanding athlete who had already won two state championships. He had signed a letter of intent to attend the University of Missouri on a scholarship. The other kids might have been good high school athletes, but none looked like they'd continue playing sports in college.

"How about colleges?" asked Trisha. "They're all high school seniors. What are they doing after high school?"

"According to their parents, Paige and Jude are both looking at the University of Missouri," I said. "As best I can tell, it looks like Olivia King and John Rodgers are both going to Loyola University in Chicago. I don't know about the other kids."

"Tayla Walker and Matthew Bridges are going to Mizzou. Nicole Moore and Andrew White are going to Centre College," said Harry. "That's something we can add. The kids are going to different places, but it looks like they all plan to go to college."

"If that's the only thing these kids have in common, we're in trouble," I said. "Our killer has to know them all somehow."

"He doesn't have to know them the same way, though," said Trisha. "He could have met John and Olivia while driving to see the Mark Twain sites in Hannibal. He could have met Jude and Paige while at the Spring Fair here. For all we know, he's going to a town, eating in the restaurants, or having his car washed, and picking the first kids who meet his criteria."

I sighed and crossed my arms to stare at the whiteboards again. Trisha was right. We had just started this case, but already I could feel the pressure mounting. Our killer picked up Jude and Paige six weeks ago. If he stuck to his schedule, we had two more weeks before he took another couple. Considering the job ahead of us, two weeks didn't seem like a lot of time.

"Do either of you read Angela Pritchard's blog?" I asked.

"I try not to pay any attention to her," said Harry.

Pritchard was a reporter with a television station in St. Louis. I didn't care for her, but someone close to our investigation was feeding her information. Though none of her reports had made it to TV yet, she updated her blog often. It wouldn't take other stations long to pick up her stories.

"We need to pay attention to her," I said. "She's smart, and she knows as much about this case as we do."

"She's calling our killer 'the Apostate,'" said Trisha. "It's a good name. It'll stick."

"I'll check her out later," said Harry, sighing and glancing at his watch before standing. "Other than that, it's getting late. Irene will worry if I don't get home soon."

Trisha pulled out her cell phone and raised her eyebrows. "It is late, and I've got an early morning tomorrow. We'll have more tomorrow evening."

I nodded and stood to walk them out. "We'll meet tomorrow and see what else we can learn. I appreciate you both coming."

Trisha touched my elbow and smiled as she left. She was a hugger. I liked her, but I didn't hug. It wasn't personal, and I sensed she knew that.

"Good night, Joe," said Harry as he passed.

"Night, Harry," I said, shutting the door behind him. I watched them climb into their cars before going to my kitchen and putting ice in a cup and pouring myself a couple shots of vodka. I liked having company over, but I had been waiting for that moment since I came home. The cold liquor danced down my throat and made my entire world feel right.

Now that I was alone, I put on a John Coltrane album and plopped down on the couch to drink and relax. My house normally had one rule: no murder allowed. When Harry and Trisha had proposed that we work this case off the books, I'd agreed without hesitation. Unfortunately, we needed somewhere private in which we could work, and both of their houses had too many people around. I lived alone in the middle of nowhere, so my place was perfect, my one rule aside. With their departure, I could banish death again.

Once I finished my first drink, I poured myself another and sank into the couch. I might have fallen asleep there, but my phone rang at a little before eleven. I recognized the number, but I didn't know why he'd call this late at night.

"Hey, Blatch," I said. "It's late. What's going on?"

Detective Matthias Blatch worked homicide in south St. Louis County. Like me, he was the youngest detective in his squad. Unlike me, most of his colleagues seemed to like him. We had worked a case together not too long ago that put a lot of bad people in prison. He was bright and dedicated to the job, and he laughed easily. I liked him, which I couldn't say about many people.

He paused before speaking.

"Sorry, Joe. I'm working in the basement, so I lost track of the time. You want me to call you at work tomorrow?"

"No," I said, shaking my head and then taking a sip of my vodka. "What can I do for you?"

"This is a courtesy call," he said. "Every two years, my station goes through our cold-case files to make sure they're still unsolvable. I read your name in an old homicide case. Thought you'd like to know."

I took another drink and then shook my head. "I assure you I'm still alive and well."

"You're not listed as the victim. You're the next of kin. The victim was Erin Court."

I hadn't expected to hear her name, so I sat straighter.

"Erin was my biological mother. She died of a drug overdose."

Blatch hesitated. "Who told you she died of a drug overdose?"

"My adoptive mom," I said. "Captain Julia Green of the St. Louis County Police Department. Your file says someone murdered Erin?"

"Yeah," said Blatch, hesitating once more. "This must be a mistake, though. Captain Green wouldn't have gotten this wrong. Sorry I called you."

"Don't hang up, Matthias," I said. "What's your file say?"

"It doesn't matter what the file says. It's a mistake. If Captain Green said she died of a drug overdose, she died of a drug overdose."

"Mom's retired," I said. "She was a taskmaster when she was with the department, but she can't tell you what to do anymore. What does your file say about Erin's cause of death?"

Papers rustled, and Blatch drew in a breath.

"You sure you want to know?" he asked. "You sound upset."

"Just tell me," I said. "And I'm not upset. I'm fine."

He paused. "Someone shot her twice in the chest, once in the shoulder, and twice in the abdomen with a .45-caliber round."

I gave myself a moment to process that.

"Five shots with a .45 is overkill. That's personal."

"That's possible," said Blatch. "Like I said, though, it's a mistake. Don't worry about it. And sorry I called so late. Next time, I'll look at the clock before I dial."

"Sure, thanks," I said. Blatch apologized again and then hung up. I stared at my phone, wondering what that was about. Then I opened the messaging app and sent my mom—Julia—a text message, asking whether she was awake. She didn't respond, so I let myself sink back on my couch to think.

The St. Louis County Police Department kept its records in massive warehouses. They even employed their own li-

THE BOYS IN THE CHURCH

brarians to manage all the data. Blatch was the most meticulous detective I knew. He wouldn't have called me if he had even the slightest doubt about the identity of the woman in his file.

Someone had murdered Erin Court. Julia, my mom, had lied about it to protect me. I wasn't mad, really. Julia's heart was in the right place, but it wasn't necessary. Erin didn't deserve to die, but her death didn't bother me. It was like learning that an annoying neighbor had died. Murder was always awful, but sometimes it was more awful than others.

I downed the rest of my drink and then crunched on the ice before turning out the lights and locking my front door. I had better things to think about than Erin Court. She wasn't worth my time or worry, not when I had my own case to work.

Chapter 4

I slept fitfully, but I woke up sober at a little before seven. Until recently, a massive bullmastiff woke me up almost every morning. Roger had passed away recently, but he had slept at the foot of my bed for so many years that I had forgotten what it was like to sleep alone. I didn't miss his terrible breath or his noxious farts in the middle of the night, but I missed my friend.

I swung my legs off the bed and yawned as I stretched. On a normal morning, I jumped into the shower and grabbed breakfast on my way out the door so I could make it to the morning briefing on time. Today I had other responsibilities.

Around the same time Roger died, I fired my weapon at work while trying to arrest two bad men. I would have taken a week or two off afterward to unwind, relax, and get my head on straight, but with a serial murderer running around, I didn't have that kind of time. Too much was at stake.

Instead, my department had arranged for me to see a therapist during work hours. The appointments wasted everyone's time, but Sheriff Delgado, in his infinite wisdom, told me to go. He liked having me out of the station for a while. So, instead of dressing for work, I put on some yoga pants, a sports bra, and a T-shirt, and I went for a run in the woods behind my house. After half an hour, sweat poured off me, my heart pounded, and bits of dried leaves and dirt clung to my skin and hair.

After cooling off in front of a fan at home, I showered and dressed in work clothing before driving to my therapist's office in downtown St. Augustine. Over the years, I had seen almost a dozen therapists. This was my first meeting with Dr. Taylor, but I doubted she would be different from the others. I appreciated that she wanted to help me, but I didn't need a therapist. I was just fine. After she called me into her office, I sat on a recliner and crossed my legs.

"So," I said, raising my eyebrows. "How are things?"

Dr. Taylor was forty or forty-five. A wooden clip held her straight black hair in a cute bun, and the morning sunlight glinted off her alabaster skin, making her look almost like a doll. She wore a demure green pencil skirt and a white sleeve-less button-down shirt. A simple gold wedding band—the only piece of jewelry on her person—adorned her left hand, while tasteful makeup accentuated her high cheekbones and lips. She probably turned a lot of heads when she walked down the street.

"I'm excellent," she said, smiling and settling into the seat kitty-corner to mine. "Let's talk about you. Sheriff Delgado gave me your service record. It's impressive."

"Thank you," I said, smiling. "I am quite impressive."

She waited for about thirty seconds before speaking again.

"You became a police officer at twenty-two after graduating from college. Then you became a detective at twenty-eight. That's faster than most people progress through the ranks."

I shrugged and nodded.

"Like I said, I'm impressive."

"You have nothing to add?" she asked.

"No. Sounds like you've got all the answers."

She recrossed her legs and then leaned forward. "Okay, then. You've not had an easy life. After your mother's second overdose, the courts ruled that she was unfit to raise you, leaving you to grow up in the foster care system. While in the foster care system, you were raped by one of your foster fathers. Would you like to talk about your mom or your assault?"

"Nope."

She smiled, but it didn't reach past her lips. "What do you want to talk about?"

I shrugged. "You follow baseball?"

She shook her head. "You know why you're here, and it's not to talk about baseball."

I laced my fingers together and shrugged once more. "I've talked to enough therapists to realize I don't need therapy."

"Since the county's already booked the full hour, I'd like to keep talking, all the same. Your department lost an officer lately."

"Two," I said, locking my eyes on hers. "Nicole died, and Preston lost a lung after being shot."

"That makes you angry," said Dr. Taylor, nodding.

I crossed my arms. "Yes."

"You were there when they were shot. Do you feel guilty?"

"No," I said. Dr. Taylor looked at me without blinking. Neither of us said anything for almost thirty seconds. I knew what she was doing because I did the same thing during interrogations. If you sat in a room with someone and stayed quiet long enough, the other person was bound to talk. Nine times out of ten, the technique worked to start a conversation. It didn't always get me what I wanted in an interrogation room, but I imagined it worked well for a therapist. Dr. Taylor didn't realize I liked silence.

I looked out the window and watched as St. Augustine came to life.

"I'm not your enemy, Joe," she said. "You don't mind if I call you Joe, do you?"

"No," I said, smiling at her. "Just don't call me Mary."

"You don't like Mary?"

I shrugged. "I've got nothing against Mary, but it's not my name. It'd be like me calling you Sylvester. Would you like me to call you Sylvester?"

"No," she said, her lips cracking into a gentle smile. "Your mom named you Mary Joe, right? Was it a family name?"

"I wouldn't know. Erin didn't talk about her family much. I never met them."

She nodded. "Do you want to talk about that?"

"No."

"Do you want to talk about Preston and Nicole? I can't imagine how hard it must be to lose colleagues."

I shifted my gaze from the window to the doctor. "They were friends, not just colleagues."

"Do you want to talk about your friends?"

"No," I said, shaking my head.

"Okay," she said, drawing the syllables out. "What do you want to talk about?"

"Since you shot down baseball, I'm fresh out of ideas. You got a favorite TV show?"

She closed her notepad and sat straighter.

"I can't help you if you don't let me."

"I don't need help," I said. "I've seen therapists my whole life, so I understand how this goes. If I say something of substance, you'll poke and prod at it until I feel uncomfortable, and then I'll stand up and leave. I won't get credit for a day of therapy, and the county won't pay you for the session. Nobody wins that way. If we sit here and talk like normal people, though, we'll both get what we need. I'll finish the six therapy sessions my station requires, and you'll get paid for six hours of therapy. Deal?"

"I'm doing this without charge," she said, raising her eyebrows. "My father was a police officer in St. Louis. It wasn't an easy job. Some days, he'd come home so angry he couldn't even talk to us. Other nights, he wanted to hold my sister and me for hours and whisper that he loved us."

I paused and softened my voice. "You seem like a nice person. I can give you a list of names of other people in my station who need your help. I'm fine, but people liked Nicole and Preston. A lot of my colleagues are hurting right now."

She nodded. "I'll take that list, but it won't stop me from asking you questions. If you don't answer them, I'll tell Sheriff Delgado that you're not fit for duty. I'm on your side, but I still have to do my job. I can't do that if you won't even answer basic questions."

My lips pursed as I considered. "So, we can talk about anything?"

"Yeah," she said, nodding. "And remember our conversations are privileged. I can't divulge their contents with anyone—even your boss—except under extraordinary circumstances."

I drew in a slow breath and drummed my fingers on the armrest of my chair, trying to think of something innocuous that would get her attention.

"Somebody murdered my biological mother. You won't find that in your files because I only found out last night."

"Do you want to talk about that?"

"Not especially."

"How'd your mom die?" asked Dr. Taylor.

"My mom lives in Kirkwood. She's fine. Erin gave birth to me, but she wasn't my mom. Someone shot her."

"Do they know who did it?"

I stood and walked to the front window.

"No clue. It's a cold case. It came up in the queue for review, and I know the detective assigned to check it out."

"What happens now?"

I looked out the window at the street below. Most of the buildings in downtown St. Augustine were at least a hundred years old, but their owners maintained them well. The streets were clean, crime was low, and the schools sent a lot of kids to good colleges. It was the perfect small town.

Only, it wasn't.

I could never put my finger on it, but I saw through the beautiful buildings and the neat sidewalks to something underneath. This town had a sickness at its core. I sensed it, just lurking beneath the surface. A cancer, a virus, a poltergeist. As much as I loved St. Augustine, this town was wrong.

I turned back to Dr. Taylor.

"Detective Blatch will check out any new leads. Then, he'll pause the investigation until the next review."

"And are you okay with that?"

I answered honestly. "No. Erin's dead. She didn't deserve that."

The conversation was halting and slow, but we talked about Erin for the next half an hour. Dr. Taylor called that acceptable progress. The topic worked out well. Erin screwed up everything she touched, so she gave me a lot to talk about; plus, she was easy to talk about because I didn't care about her. I might as well have been talking about monetary policy in sub-Saharan Africa for all the impact she had on my life. I should have brought her up in therapy sessions years ago. It would have made my teenage years a lot less annoying.

A few minutes before ten, Dr. Taylor ended the session and told me she'd see me in a few days. I lied and said I looked forward to it. As I left the room, my entire body felt heavy, and my throat ached. Goosebumps formed up and down my arms even as I stepped out into the day's heat. Erin wouldn't leave my mind. That was just like her. Even dead, she ruined my day.

I walked back to my truck and called Trisha to let her know I'd be in late. Since I had fired my weapon while on duty, and since I was seeing a therapist, my employment contract required the department to make reasonable accommodations with my work schedule. A morning off seemed reasonable.

I got inside my car and drove toward St. Louis. My hands turned the steering wheel and flicked on the turn signals without conscious direction from my mind. I was driving toward Dutchtown, an old neighborhood on the south side of town. Where hipsters and young professionals had gentrified many of the surrounding areas, Dutchtown had changed little from when Erin and I lived there.

Erin and I had lived in an apartment two blocks from Grand Boulevard. When my mom told me Erin had died, she said officers had found her body on a vacant lot about a block from that old apartment. She didn't give me an address, but I recognized the lot from her description.

As I approached the location, I slowed and then stopped. Someone had put a white picket fence around the property, but an open gate led to a community garden. Neighborhood gardeners had planted tomatoes, cucumbers, peppers, and other vegetables I couldn't recognize from the street. Daylilies bloomed everywhere. When she was alive, Erin had poisoned everything she touched. It was fittingly ironic that the place of her death had become a garden full of life.

My head felt clearer than it had when I left Dr. Taylor's office, so I took out my phone and called my station.

"Hey, Trisha, it's Joe," I said. "I'm in south St. Louis right now. Tell Delgado I'll be back to work the speed trap in about an hour."

"I'm glad you called because you're not working the speed trap today," she said. "You've got another assignment."

I closed my eyes and groaned.

"What fresh hell is this?"

"A farmer out on County Road 10 called to say he's found tire tracks through one of his fields. Delgado wants you to check it out and make sure nobody's hunting without a license."

"Isn't that the Department of Conservation's turf?"

"Yep," said Trisha.

I paused for a second. "Why are we investigating it?"

"Because the farmer knows Councilman Rogers. The councilman considers this a personal favor. We wouldn't want hunters to tear up the countryside, would we?"

I sighed. "Terrific. He's discovered a whole new way to waste my day."

"It could be worse," said Trisha. "We could have rain."

"Yeah, at least it's not raining," I said. "Okay. Looks like I'll get a walk through the woods."

Chapter 5

The dining hall's roof had collapsed beneath the weight of a fallen walnut tree. Not a single pane of glass remained intact. Before time had ravaged it, Glenn had eaten in that building and sung songs in a small amphitheater not thirty feet away. He and Helen had loved that place, so he hated to see it fall into such disrepair. When he finished his work, he hoped to rebuild it so kids could play in it once more. It seemed like the least he could do.

Today, Helen wore sensible flats and a white cotton dress adorned with black polka dots. A pair of chopsticks from a Chinese place near their house held her hair in a bun. As usual, her tasteful makeup brought out the brown sparkle of her eyes. Time had caught up to Glenn over the years, giving him aches and pains and gray hair, but somehow his sister looked the same as she had when she returned to his life twenty years ago. She had good genes, he supposed. That was how it should have been. She deserved the best in life.

"Do you remember this place?" she asked. "We were so young back then."

"I remember," said Glenn, nodding. "We were happy here."

"I'm glad we found it again," she said, looking toward the storm cellar's door. "Do you hear them in there? They know we're here. They think they're being clever, hiding just inside the door."

Glenn didn't hear anyone, and he doubted Helen did, either, but she knew things. It was one of her gifts.

They had picked up Peter and Mary yesterday from Winfield, a tiny town in Lincoln County, Missouri. He hadn't expected to pick them up so soon, but when the opportunity arose, he and Helen had pounced.

With only fifteen hundred residents, Winfield was a dot on a highway map. Peter and Mary's parents would miss them, but Glenn doubted the local police would worry about two missing high school kids. They'd probably think the kids had eloped and run off. He'd be fine.

Both Peter and Mary were high school seniors, and both ran track. Thin and wiry, neither alone would hurt him, but together they posed a threat. He had the means to protect himself, though.

"How long do you think they'll hold out?" he asked.

Helen bit her lower lip and fluttered her eyelids before answering.

"Not long," she said after thinking. "They don't have stored fat to draw on. We should look for a new couple."

"Already?" asked Glenn.

"Yes," said Helen. "Don't you feel it bubbling up inside you? We need this. It can't wait. We need to go hunting again."

Glenn only knew of two spots to store sinners, and both were currently occupied. Jude and Paige should succumb soon, though. That would create another vacancy. He and Helen could move another couple in soon enough.

"We'll start the search," he said, glancing at his sister. "For now, we need to focus on Peter and Mary. They're new, so they'll be strong still."

"I'll watch the stairs to keep them from running," said Helen.

Glenn nodded. Muscles all over his body tingled with anticipation. He was excited, but he could barely focus.

His shadow had begun whispering to him.

She had been with him as long as his sister had, but she was darker and meaner than Helen. She whispered to him at night when he closed his eyes. Usually, she encouraged him, but other times, she screamed at him until his mind nearly broke. Every other time he had taken a couple, she quieted. She shouldn't have been talking to him now. For now, he could shut her out, but his resolve wouldn't last forever. He swallowed hard and silenced her with his will.

"They always fight the first time," said Glenn, hoping his sister didn't see the strain his shadow had put him under. "I wish they understood what I was trying to do. It's for their own good."

"They've never seen righteousness in their lives," said Helen, shaking her head. "It's not their fault they don't understand. We're their teachers, and we have to have firm hands."

Glenn nodded and reached for the padlock with hands that trembled ever so slightly. The first couple he had brought to this cell—Tayla Walker and Matthew Bridges—had almost killed him. After they spent their first night inside, Glenn had gone to visit them and make sure they hadn't hurt themselves trying to escape. When he pulled open the door, they had rushed toward him, screaming like banshees. He had had to shoot Matthew in the leg and nearly had to run Tayla down with his car to keep them from escaping.

That had taught him a lesson he couldn't forget: The first visit was the most important. If he didn't show the sinners how to behave immediately, they'd fight him for weeks and never learn what they needed to learn.

Glenn pulled off the padlock and tensed his back and shoulders. If Peter and Mary tried to push the door open, he'd stand on it and put the padlock back on. A week of darkness without food would calm them down.

But nobody screamed at him or rushed toward him. The kids had a plan. Every couple had a plan on the first visit.

Glenn reached into the bag at his feet for an Airsoft grenade he had purchased on the internet. SWAT teams used similar devices to simulate flash bangs during training scenarios. They served the purpose well. Before pulling the pin, he grabbed his cattle prod and took a deep breath.

"Do it, honey," said Helen. "Make them hurt."

He looked at his sister and nodded before ripping the ring from his grenade and tossing it into the basement.

"Shit," came a voice from inside. It was Peter. The boy vaulted toward the cellar's steel door, but Glenn had been ready for that. He stood at the top of the steps and kicked hard, hitting the young man in the chin. Peter fell backwards, and Glenn slammed the steel door shut. The two teenagers pounded on the metal with their fists.

Then the grenade exploded.

Outside, it sounded like a shotgun at ten yards. Inside it would have been deafening. The pounding stopped, so Glenn threw open the doors. Mary and Peter huddled in the center of the room.

Where he had installed a fence to separate the prisoners from him in his other cellar, this one was a simple open room. That changed his tactics.

He zapped Mary first with the cattle prod. She flopped to her belly and cried. Then Peter pushed up onto his knees. Glenn kicked him in the ribs and shocked him with the cattle prod until the young man's muscles gave out. For a few moments, he convulsed on the ground like a fish out of water. It almost made Glenn smile.

"Enough, Glenn!" shouted Helen from the steps. "You'll kill him if you don't stop."

Glenn chanced a glance at his sister before releasing the trigger.

"Sorry," he said, drawing in a breath. "I don't know what happened."

Only that was a lie. He knew exactly what had happened. He had kept his finger on the trigger because his shadow wanted him to. She had been whispering to him at night and sharing dreams of beautiful violence with him. Part of him loved her. She gave him power. The other part of him feared her. Now, she spoke to him in her soft, sweet voice.

Ignore her. Helen means well, but she doesn't understand you. Give in to your feelings.

That voice made him want to hold the prod against Mary's neck until she flopped on the ground like her boyfriend. He wanted to hear Peter's anguished cries as his blood mixed with his tears. He wanted to give in, just as his shadow told him to.

But he couldn't yet. It was too early. His sister wouldn't approve, and his captives wouldn't learn their lesson.

"Ask Mary your questions," said Helen. "Make her talk."

Glenn did as his sister asked and stepped toward the girl. Peter reached for his leg, but Glenn stomped on his hand and then shocked him with the cattle prod. The boy gasped and scrambled back, holding his broken fingers. Mary sat in a puddle of her own piss and cried. He knelt in front of her and cupped her cheek.

"Has he hurt you?"

She gave him a questioning look. Glenn smiled.

"Peter," said Glenn, nodding and encouraging her to speak. "Has he hurt you yet?"

Mary's bottom lip trembled, and she shook her head. "I want to go home."

"You are home," he whispered. "You're safe here. I won't hurt you. If you tell me what he's done, I'll protect you."

Big tears trickled down her cheeks.

"I don't understand."

"It's okay," he said. "I was your age once. You can trust me. Did Peter rape you?"

"No," she said, shaking her head, a confused expression on her face. "He loves me."

Glenn nodded and sighed. "He will. It's in his nature. You'll see."

He started to leave when a hand grasped his ankle and squeezed tight. It was Peter. The young man snarled and pulled so hard he almost knocked Glenn from his feet. Glenn whipped the cattle prod around, but Peter rose to his feet and charged before he brought the weapon to bear. The boy's shoulder hit him in the gut and lifted him from the ground. Glenn's breath rushed out of him as his back slammed into the ground. The cattle prod clattered to the concrete.

"Get up!" shouted Helen. "Get up!"

Glenn's lungs wouldn't work. He couldn't breathe or think.

Let me help you. Please.

Glenn opened his mind and relaxed, allowing his shadow to guide his hand. With a gasp, his lungs inflated once more. Peter lay on top of him, scrambling for Glenn's throat. If the kid had been a trained fighter, he would have reared back and punched Glenn in the face. Peter was a boy, though. He didn't know what he was doing.

Glenn did.

The older man wrapped an arm around his captive's neck, enclosing it. He then clasped his hands tight beneath Peter's throat, creating a knot with the knife of his forearm over one carotid artery and his bicep pressing against the other. In a smooth motion, Glenn wrapped his legs around Peter's waist and arched his back, cutting off the supply of blood to the young man's brain.

He counted to thirty before Peter stopped moving. The kid's heart still beat, but he had passed out. Glenn rolled him off before looking for Mary. She had disappeared.

"Where is she?" he called, his voice a snarl that surprised even him.

"Upstairs," said Helen. "I couldn't stop her."

He sprinted up the steps. Mary's dirty-blonde hair fluttered in the wind as she ran toward the car Glenn had driven that day. She was fast and young, but she had nowhere to go. She clawed at the handle of the sedan, but he held the electronic key fob in his pocket. He locked the door before she could open it. Her entire body trembled, and she fell to her knees.

"Please, mister," she said. "I won't tell anybody what happened. Let me go. Please."

He slapped her across the face. She fell against the car crying, so he grabbed a fistful of her hair and yanked her toward the storm cellar.

"You shouldn't have run," he said.

"I'm sorry," she said, stumbling behind him. He jerked hard, breaking some of her roots. When they reached the cellar, he pushed her down the steps. Peter had rolled over onto his back. His eyes were open, and he struggled to sit up.

"I tried to be nice," said Glenn. "You didn't let me."

Mary curled into a ball and cried, while Peter stared with black hate-filled eyes.

Punish them. Teach them. It's the only way.

His shadow wasn't loud, but her power flowed through him.

"Leave them alone, honey," said Helen. "Lock them up and walk away."

"They shouldn't have run," he snarled. Helen hurried to stand between him and the kids.

"Calm down," she said. "You're too worked up."

"I'm fine," he said, gritting his teeth as he stepped past her.

"You've done what you needed to do. They've learned their lesson," said Helen, her voice soothing and calm as she tried to pull him back. He shrugged her off. "You don't need to do this."

"Why didn't you stop her?" he asked, looking over his shoulder at Helen.

Helen hesitated. "I couldn't. She was too fast."

She didn't try. This batch is broken. Finish them.

Glenn ran his hands over his face. His vision flashed red. It did that sometimes.

"She says you didn't try, Helen!" shouted Glenn. "Tell me that's not true."

"Who's Helen?" asked Mary. "Please let us go."

The little bitch's voice became a squawk. When he first saw her, Glenn had been distracted by her raw sexuality, but now he saw her for what she was: a sack of meat. He picked up his cattle prod.

"I told you to shut up."

Her scream didn't even sound human as he shocked her. For the next twenty minutes, he lost himself in the work. They clawed and fought back at first, but that didn't last long. Peter and Mary died, but that was okay. He shouldn't have bothered with them. He saw that now. They were too dull, too simple, too pedestrian. They were common.

As he caught his breath afterwards, he wiped the blood from his cheeks and face with a handkerchief.

"That was unnecessary," said Helen, her lips tight and straight. "Now we have to start over."

"They weren't right," he said. "We didn't watch them enough. Next time, I choose them, and we're going local."

"The closer we pick from home, the more dangerous it is," said Helen. "The police are slow, but they're not stupid."

"Then we have to be smart."

Helen took a step back and shook her head. "You're not yourself right now. I'm going home. You can return when you become yourself again."

She walked away. Somehow, watching her leave him made the heat disappear from his face. The righteous strength that had flowed through him dissipated. He walked up the steps.

"Please don't leave me. I don't like being alone."

Helen turned and drew in a deep breath. She considered him and then raised her eyebrows and put her hands on her hips.

"You were listening to your shadow, weren't you? That's why you killed them. That's why you didn't look like yourself."

He brought a hand to his head and closed his eyes.

"Sometimes her voice is the only thing I can hear. I can't shut her out."

"You're mine," said Helen. "Do you understand that? I won't let her have you."

"I don't think you have a choice."

Helen stepped closer and wrapped her arms around him. Warmth from her embrace flooded through him, banishing his shadow from his mind.

"There's always a choice," whispered Helen. "Make the right one."

For a few minutes, Glenn reveled in his sister's loving touch. Then she touched the tip of his nose and smiled, just as their father had done before he killed himself.

"There you are," she said. "I'm glad you're back."

"Tell me what to do," he whispered. "I'm lost without you."

"We finish our work," she said. "Then the voices will all go dark."

He wanted to believe her, but he couldn't. Still, she held him and made the world feel right.

"All right," he said. "Please make my shadow go away."

"I'll never let her take you," she said, rocking him on her lap as if he were a child. "You're mine."

At that moment, Glenn would have followed his sister into hell itself. As she held him, his eyes closed. Mary and Peter's blood pooled on the concrete and dripped down his chin, ruining his shirt. He didn't care. He felt at peace.

Chapter 6

I drove home and changed into jeans and a T-shirt. Then, I drove to the station, where I dropped off my truck and picked up a marked cruiser. The farmer my department needed me to meet was named Paul Rubin, and he lived in a two-story brick home outside town. I met him at the foot of his gravel driveway and shook his hand. He was about six feet tall, and he had a gray mustache and a craggy, pitted face. His hand was rough and strong.

"Nice to meet you, Mr. Rubin," I said, looking around the property. His front yard was an acre or two of grass ringed by a wooden post-and-rail fence. There were fallow fields to the north and west and woods to the east. A line of trees acted as a windbreak across the road, obstructing my view of a field full of soybeans. The air held a faint chemical odor.

"You must be Detective Court," he said. "I've heard about you."

"Only good things, I'm sure," I said. "Sorry Sheriff Delgado couldn't come out. He's busy with a big case."

Rubin grunted and turned to face the field to the west of his house.

"There's a gate and cattle guard about a quarter mile that way," he said, pointing down the road. "That's where they got in. They followed the fence line for a quarter mile before turning north and parking outside the woods."

"And you think they're hunters?"

He looked at me and furrowed his brow. "Why else would they be here?"

I forced myself to smile. "I don't know. That's why I'm here."

"They're stealing my livelihood," said Rubin. "I'm booked through deer season. My clients won't pay if there ain't any deer left in my woods for them to hunt."

"What have you done to discourage poaching?"

"I called you," he said. "What else am I supposed to do?"

I looked toward the patch of trees that concerned him.

"Are there signs up saying it's private property?"

"There's a fence up," he said. "People don't know what a fence means, that's their problem. Next time somebody drives out there, I'll shoot 'em. I've got a McMillan TAC-338 by my back door. Next person who shows up, I'll put a round right up his ass crack."

I smiled. "Please don't do that."

"What do you suggest, then?"

"Trail cameras would be helpful. If you give us a picture of a license plate, we can make an arrest."

He crossed his arms and spit. It landed about a foot from my shoes.

"You're telling me I've got to pay out of my pocket to do your job for you. That right?"

Again, I forced myself to smile.

"Poaching is hard to prove without cameras. I will look around, but unless I find somebody on the property, there's not a lot I can do. I'm not sure what you and Councilman Rogers expected to happen."

He shut his mouth and looked at the ground.

"Darren Rogers said you were uppity," he said. "You think you're smarter than everyone around you."

I shook my head and raised my eyebrows. "I'm sorry if that's how I come across."

"Sure you are, honey," he said. He drew in a breath and stepped closer. I stepped back. "Do you have any idea how much money I bring to this county every year? My customers are doctors, lawyers, accountants, and dentists. When they come to town, they buy guns and ammunition, they buy camping supplies, they go to our restaurants, and they bring in their wives for the Spring Fair. We're talking hundreds of thousands of dollars in revenue. What do you bring in?"

"Not much. I'm a public servant."

"I'm glad you know your place," he said. "Now get out there and walk around. See what you can find. I would give you a ride, but I've got to go research trail cameras now."

"Have a good day, sir," I said, smiling so I wouldn't call him a schmuck. He glared at me before turning and walking toward his house. I wiped a bead of sweat from my eyebrow and headed out.

Mr. Rubin aside, this wasn't a bad assignment. Delgado could have ordered me to hose vomit out of squad cars or to scrub the floor in the drunk tank, both of which had to be done daily. I liked walking in the sunshine. After three or four minutes, I reached the gate Rubin had mentioned, so I crossed deeper onto the property.

Where waist-high weeds grew in the field, a car had beaten down the brush near the fence line. I followed the car's tracks about a quarter of a mile to a wooded area thick with vines and vegetation. Black walnut trees towered around me. Interestingly, gravel and sand on the ground formed a corridor through the woods. At one time, a driveway had cut through the area.

I searched for tracks or footprints but found nothing. That didn't surprise me. Unless our poacher dropped his wallet, the chances I'd be able to track him down were damn near zero. I was wasting my time.

At least it was a nice day.

I followed the old driveway through the woods. Squirrels raced around me, and birds chattered from the canopy above my head. Insects buzzed everywhere. It was a thriving ecosystem, and it likely had huge numbers of deer. I saw why Mr. Rubin wanted to protect it for his hunters.

About a quarter mile into the woods, the trees thinned around a small wooden church. Dried leaves were piled near its foundation, while the chipped white paint of the clapboard siding almost blended into the surrounding woods as if it were camouflaged. The roof sagged in the building's center. The windows were closed and intact, but a layer of grime had made them opaque to sunlight.

I walked around the building and found the driveway ended here. Someone had cut the padlock that once held the church's back door shut. When the wind died, I smelled gasoline and something foul. The squirrels didn't scurry along the ground, and the birds seemed to avoid the nearby trees.

Something wasn't right here.

Had I merely come across an abandoned church in the woods, I would have ignored it. The broken padlock and the foul odor compelled me to go on, though.

I stepped back and snapped pictures with my cell phone and opened the rear door to the sacristy, the part of the church where the priest would store his vestments and the sacred vessels used in communion and other services. The shelves that once held sacred objects were empty. A nauseating odor wafted toward me.

I covered my mouth and nose with my shirt and stepped through another door into the sanctuary. The moment my feet hit the hardwood of the altar, my breath rushed out of me, and my eyes popped open wide. My heart thudded against my rib cage.

"Shit."

A central aisle ran down the middle of the building. Ten pews sat to its left and right. Black mold covered the walls, while insects had eaten holes through the red carpet. There were bodies on the ground around the altar rail. Someone had burned them until their bones turned black and charred. The sound of angry flies buzzed and throbbed throughout the room as thousands of insects hovered over the corpses.

It was a nightmare. I covered my mouth and stumbled until my back hit a wall. Then I swore again and squeezed my eyes tight. Even with my eyes shut, I couldn't stop hearing the throb of the flies' wings. It was like a hellish ocean wave that wouldn't cease crashing. Every muscle in my body trembled. A fly landed on my cheek, so I swatted it away. The smell was nauseating.

"Do your job, Joe," I whispered, forcing my eyes open.

The scene was still gruesome, but when I opened my eyes again, the shock had worn off. My stomach roiled, making me glad I had eaten little that morning. The victim nearest me had pulled his legs to his chest and balled his hands into fists. His jaw was open as if in a silent, perpetual scream. Tufts of hair remained on the skull, but the fire had burned most of the flesh off. Dr. Sheridan would have to use dental records to ID him.

I hadn't been to church in years, but I made the sign of the cross over my chest as I stepped deeper into the building. My legs trembled, and my head felt light, but I forced myself onward. I was a cop. I had a job to do, and I had to think.

Dr. Sheridan would have to determine the cause of death, but each victim had bones blackened by fire. Whether they were burned before or after they died, I couldn't say. It was horrific, nonetheless.

I needed to photograph the scene as it was upon my arrival in case the first responders had to move something, so I took out my cell phone and snapped pictures.

My fingers trembled. Because of my work, I had seen a lot of terrible crime scenes, but nothing matched the scale of this place. I wanted to run out of there, find somewhere to sit, and close my eyes in the hope that I wouldn't see anything anymore, but I still had work to do.

I took almost a hundred pictures before hurrying out of the church. In the open air of the forest, I drew in deep breaths of fresh air, but the foul odor refused to leave my lungs and nose. My hands shook so much I took three times to dial my boss's number.

"Delgado," he said, answering on the first ring. "What do you need, Detective?"

"Hey," I said, trying to prevent my voice from shaking. I blinked and ran a hand through my hair. "I'm at Paul Rubin's property. He called about some trespassers."

"I know," said Delgado. "I sent you there. What do you need?"

"I found bodies. We'll need a forensic anthropologist, a coroner, a search team, and a lot of body bags. You should call the FBI, too."

Delgado paused. "I'm going to hang up now, Detective. Don't prank me again. I've got a lot of work to do."

He hung up before I could respond. Instead of calling him back, I sent him a picture of charred remains. Within moments, my phone rang.

"I'm on my way. Touch nothing."

"No worries," I said. "After what I saw, I'm never going back inside that building."

Chapter 7

I didn't want to smell the corpses anymore, so I walked about a quarter mile down the road and sat with my back against a walnut tree. For a while, I stayed there, breathing in the fresh air and listening to the sound of birds chirping above me.

After twenty minutes, I fished my cell phone out of my pocket to make sure I hadn't missed a text. Nothing. The momentary reprieve from work gave me a minute to think about what I had seen in the church.

Every victim held his hands in front of his face or across his chest. The bones would have been too brittle after being burned for the killer to move them after burning them, so they had died in those poses. If the killer had burned them inside the church, there would have been scorch marks on the floor and smoke damage to the ceiling. I didn't see any of that, though. The church was his dump site.

That made me pause. Churches were places of rest and reverence. If the killer had wanted to get rid of the bodies, he would have dumped them in the Mississippi River or dug shallow graves out in the woods for them. He displayed them inside that church, though. It was symbolic. This church gave him something.

The victims told another story. Their mouths hung open, their fingers were curled, and they had pulled their legs to their chests in fetal positions. These people died in agony. A forensic anthropologist or coroner would have to confirm it, but it looked like the killer had burned them to death.

It took planning to burn someone. The smell and screams would have drawn attention, so, to pull it off without getting caught, our killer needed access to an isolated location. Even in a rural county like St. Augustine, few places met his criteria. That should help with the search.

As I flipped through the pictures of the church building, I noticed something else interesting. Several crucifixes hung on the wall, but someone had turned every one of them upside down. Everything pointed to a resourceful ritualistic killer—like the one Agent Lawson was tracking. But if the Apostate killed these victims, where did he store the others? Was there another church somewhere with the other kids? And if it wasn't him, what the hell was going on in St. Augustine?

I had far more questions than answers, but that was okay. We had evidence to work with. The killer had touched the door and crosses, and he had walked across an ash-covered floor. Paul Rubin might even know what car the murderer drove. This could break the case.

And now, I needed backup.

I pulled out my phone and called Delgado again, but my call went to voicemail.

"Hey, it's Joe Court again. I'm still out at the scene, and I'm still waiting for you."

I hung up after that brief message and then called Trisha at my station.

"Has Sheriff Delgado called Dr. Sheridan yet?"

She paused.

"I don't know what you're talking about, hon," she said.

I put a hand on my hip and swore under my breath.

"I'm at a crime scene. Did Delgado call anyone yet?"

"No," said Trisha. "What do you have? I'll route officers myself."

"I've got multiple bodies, all burned beyond recognition, in an abandoned country church in the county. Is Agent Lawson there?"

"Jesus," said Trisha.

"Jesus isn't here, Trisha," I said. "I'm alone at one of the nastiest crime scenes I've ever seen, and we need to process this. Is Agent Lawson around? If he is, just patch me to him."

"Lawson and his team drove to Winfield. Our killer took a new couple."

I furrowed my brow and shook my head. "He couldn't have. His pattern is every two months. It's only been six weeks since he took Jude and Paige. Are any FBI agents around?"

Trisha's voice sounded subdued. "Agent Costa is upstairs, but I don't think I'm supposed to disturb him."

I held my breath for a five-count so I wouldn't snap at her.

"Show him the picture I'm about to send you and ask whether he wants to come to the scene."

I ended the call before Trisha could respond and flipped through my photos until I found a wide-angle shot with four bodies in it. I texted that to Trisha's personal phone and got a response within seconds.

Oh, my God.

I texted back and asked her to show the picture to the Bureau. She didn't respond, but I assumed she had gotten my message. For the next few minutes, I alternated between staring at my phone and straining my ears to hear footsteps or sirens around me. Delgado should have arrived by now. If something had tied him up, he should have called the Bureau or the Highway Patrol. We needed all the help we could get.

About twenty-five minutes after I called Trisha, my phone rang again. I didn't bother looking at the caller ID before answering, nor did I bother masking my annoyance.

"Yeah?"

"Detective Court, this is Special Agent Bryan Costa. Your dispatcher showed me the picture you took. I've got a small team at the house of Paul Rubin. Are you still on the property?"

Costa's voice sounded familiar, but I couldn't pair it with a face just yet.

"Yeah," I said. I gave him directions. "I'll see you in a few."

"We're on our way. In the meantime, I'd appreciate if you kept your photographs to yourself and stayed off the radio. Until we know what we've got, I'd like to keep this quiet."

The public deserved to know what had happened in their community, but Costa was right. This would make people panic. Parents would pull their kids from school, but worse than that, people would carry their guns around town instead of stowing them in their cars and homes. Normally, I had no problem with civilians carrying guns. With a serial murderer running around, though, innocent men and women could seem threatening to a panicked parent. Nobody would win if this came out.

"See you in a few."

I hung up, stood, and brushed leaves from my clothes. Three men in suits traipsed through the woods a few minutes later with Dracula, one of the special agents who had questioned me in my station yesterday, in the lead. I nodded to him and smacked a mosquito on my neck.

"Detective," he said, nodding. "I appreciate you calling this in. How did you find this place?"

I told him everything that had led me to finding the church and my conversation with Paul Rubin, the property owner. Dracula dispatched one of his agents to pick Rubin up and drive him to our station for questioning. I doubted Rubin had anything to do with the church or body dump, but we needed to talk to him nonetheless.

"Who have you told about this?" he asked.

"You, Sheriff Delgado, and Trisha Marshall, our dispatcher."

Dracula nodded. "Nobody else?"

I nodded my confirmation.

"Thank you for your discretion," he said. "Walk me through the scene and show me everything you touched."

I followed him, but I didn't like it. Inside the church, the bodies didn't hit me as hard this time, but they still shocked me. Agent Lawson had told me yesterday that every man on his task force had at least a decade of experience working complex homicides, but the scene seemed to chill even them.

"I stayed near the altar and tried not to touch anything," I said, glancing over my shoulder as I heard footsteps approach. Sheriff Delgado stepped through the open door to my right and onto the platform.

"Sheriff," said Dracula, nodding toward him. Delgado looked out over the sanctuary and swore under his breath. "You're our local expert. What is this place?"

Delgado rubbed his chin but said nothing. The agent repeated his question.

"It's just an old church," he said, shrugging. "The county's population has been shrinking ever since St. Louis lost the Chrysler plant ten years ago."

"You guys had that many commuters?"

Delgado shrugged again. "St. Louis didn't just lose Chrysler. A lot of other companies depended on that plant.

A company in St. Augustine made parts for the cars' interiors. When Chrysler closed, the company in St. Augustine closed, too. We lost almost four hundred jobs. People moved away."

Dracula nodded. "Have you heard about this specific church?"

Delgado shook his head. "No, but it looks like a convenient spot to dump a body. It's out in the woods and away from the main road. The county's full of places like this."

Dracula nodded, seemingly agreeing. I had kept quiet so far, but they were wrong.

"It's more than a dump site," I said. "Look around you."

Dracula looked at me with his brow raised. "You got something to add, Detective?"

"Open your eyes, guys. This was a church twenty years ago, but it's not today. Someone's removed the stations of the cross, the priest's vestments, the communion chalice, and the baptismal font. Someone removed God from this building and inverted every cross."

Dracula looked around and nodded. "Okay. What's that get us?"

"Nothing until you look at the victims. Their killer burned them. Not only that, they're in agony. They're being punished. And smell the air. There's gasoline, there's burned skin and hair, but there's something else, too. I didn't recognize it at first, but the building stinks like rotten eggs. That's sulfur, I think."

Delgado looked at me as if I were crazy, but Dracula nodded and shifted his weight from one foot to the other.

"Put this together for me."

"This isn't just a dump site," I said. "Everything in this room is meaningful—the burned, tortured bodies, the inverted crosses, the smell...this is hell. The guy who dumped the bodies is creating hell on Earth."

Nobody said anything for a moment as they took things in, but by the glare Delgado shot me, I'd get a lecture later. I didn't care. I was right. The sheriff broke eye contact with me and looked to Dracula.

"Please excuse Detective Court. She has a flair for the dramatic."

Dracula held my gaze for a moment and then nodded before looking to Delgado.

"The young always do. Let's get out of here before we contaminate the scene further."

I kept my glare to myself. Delgado held his hands toward the door, ushering us outside. I wanted to punch both Delgado and Costa, but that wouldn't have helped anything. Once we were back in the sunshine, Delgado glanced at me and then nodded toward the road that led out of the woods. Agent Costa walked away to make a call.

"Head home for the day, Joe. I'll take over here."

"You need help on this," I said. "Paul Rubin's not the only property owner around here. We need someone to interview them, we need someone to research the history of the property and church, and we need somebody to work traffic. This place will get busy."

"I'm giving you an out," he said, sighing. He furrowed his brow and shook his head. "Recreating hell on Earth? Jesus, Joe. Life isn't like the movies. You've embarrassed yourself and this department enough. They already think we're inbred hicks. Go home before you say anything else that'll make us look stupid."

I balled my hands into fists. "I found this site. It's my case."

"No, it's not," he said. "You're off this one. Now get out of here. I'm tired of asking. If you refuse to leave, I'll escort you from the property and write you up for insubordination."

I clenched my jaw so I wouldn't tell him off. Then I reminded myself that I only needed to put up with him until the next election. St. Augustine would vote someone new in, and Delgado would disappear. And if my fellow residents didn't vote in someone new, they deserved the asshole they got.

I walked toward my truck but stopped as I walked out of the woods. A news van from St. Louis had parked alongside the road, and an attractive woman a few years older than me stood outside, directing a cameraman to set up near the fence. When she saw me, Angela Pritchard's eyes lit up.

"Detective Court," she called. "Can we talk for a minute?"

Even with minimal traffic, St. Louis was a good hour from St. Augustine. That was why Delgado had taken an hour to get to the crime scene and why he hadn't bothered calling in the FBI. He wanted the cameras there when he arrived. It made sense, too. The County Council had appointed him sheriff when the previous sheriff stepped down, but Delgado hadn't run for office in his life. Outside our department, nobody even knew his name. The church would give him exposure he couldn't buy.

"I've got no comment," I said, not bothering to look at her or to slow down my gait.

"Is it true that your team found several charred bodies inside the church?" she asked, hurrying to catch up.

"What church? This is a company barbecue," I said. "I'd get you a hot dog, but I'm not sure how many more people will show up. We may not have enough food. If you want in, call Sheriff Delgado. I'm sure you've got his number."

She turned and walked to her van, where her producer had put a drone with a camera attached to its underside on the ground. I swore under my breath and pulled out my cell phone. Special Agent Costa's number was at the top of my call list. His phone rang twice before he picked up.

"Agent Costa, this is Joe Court," I said. "How thick are the trees above your church?"

"Not very," he said. "Why?"

"Because you've got a camera crew from St. Louis on the road, and they've got a drone."

"Aww, damn."

I couldn't have put it any better myself.

Chapter 8

Even though Delgado had kicked me out of the crime scene, I still needed to write an after-action report. I drove back to town. Since it was the middle of the day, most of my colleagues were out on calls, leaving me my choice of parking spots near the station. That was nice, at least.

Trisha smiled hello as I walked in, but she must have sensed my mood because she didn't press for a conversation. I nodded to her and went to my desk, where I spent the next hour and a half filling out paperwork and cataloging the photographs I had taken of the church.

When I finished that, I would have driven home like Delgado had ordered me to do, but before I could, two men began shouting in the lobby. From that distance, I couldn't hear what they were saying, but if there had been a real problem, Trisha would have flicked a switch beneath her desk to signal an emergency in the station.

I saved my documents before weaving through the maze of desks in the bullpen. The closer I came to the lobby, the clearer the voices became, and I realized why Trisha hadn't triggered the alarm. One speaker was Sheriff Delgado, while the other sounded like Agent Lawson.

I slowed before stepping toward the fray.

"I don't care about her rights as a journalist," said Lawson, his face red. "That crime scene was in the middle of nowhere. She shouldn't have found it."

"She's probably got a police radio," said Delgado. "We don't own the equipment to encrypt our signal."

Lawson may have heard him, but the moment I stepped into the lobby, he looked up at me.

"Get over here, Detective," he said. I hesitated and considered. My paychecks came from St. Augustine County. Agent Lawson's came from the United States federal government. I could have ignored him and walked back to my desk, but I'd never see a piece of evidence in this case again. Paige and Jude were my victims. Agent Lawson was probably a good investigator, but I knew Paige and Jude's families. I knew this community. These were my people. I needed to stay with them through the end.

So I sucked it up and walked.

"Afternoon, Agent Lawson."

The special agent narrowed his gaze at me.

"You found this church and called it in, didn't you?"

I nodded. "Yes, sir."

"Then what?"

Delgado stepped between me and the special agent.

"She's my officer, and she did her job," he said. "She's already talked to Agent Costa. I don't appreciate you speaking to her in that accusatory tone."

It would have been a rare sign of leadership and support from the sheriff but for one simple fact: He wasn't trying to protect me. He was protecting himself. He didn't want me to tell Lawson the truth because that would jeopardize Delgado's access to case material and might even land him in jail for interfering with a federal investigation.

"Sheriff Delgado's correct," I said. "I spoke with Agent Costa at the crime scene and led him through my findings and thoughts. I also took photographs, which I have been cataloging since I returned. I planned to forward my after-action report to the sheriff as soon as I finished."

"I look forward to seeing that," said Lawson, crossing his arms and staring into my eyes without blinking. It was an aggressive, intimidating posture from a man who weighed at least thirty or forty pounds more than me. In an interrogation room, it likely scared people. Out here, it pissed me off. He had no right to lord over me in my station, and I didn't plan to back down.

"Glad to hear," I said, crossing my arms.

We stayed like that for twenty or thirty seconds. Then, he drew in a breath.

"After you found the church, who did you call?"

I blinked but didn't soften my posture or expression.

"Sheriff Delgado. I explained to him the situation and asked him to contact you."

"And what time was that?"

I shrugged. "I'd need to look at my phone."

Lawson waited a moment. He raised his eyebrows when I didn't move.

"Check."

"It's at my desk," I said. "When I heard you two shouting, I thought Trisha might need help, so I hurried here. We rarely get shouting matches between police officers in this station, and when we do, we try to de-escalate the situation."

Lawson nodded toward the bullpen.

"Get your phone and check the time."

"She doesn't need to do that," said Delgado. Lawson glared at him, so I shook my head and sighed, already growing annoyed at the chest thumping.

"It was about two," I said. "If you want an exact time, I'll check my phone. After our first phone call, I texted him a picture I had taken of the scene. He returned my call to tell me not to touch anything."

Lawson nodded. "That was your first phone call. Did you make more?"

I nodded. "I waited for about twenty minutes and called him back when he hadn't shown up. Sheriff Delgado must have been in a dead zone because he didn't respond to my call. I then called Trisha, our dispatcher. She got in touch with Agent Costa on my behalf. Agent Costa arrived at the scene shortly thereafter."

Again, Lawson nodded. "Angela Pritchard showed up at our crime scene at three. It takes an hour to drive from St. Louis, so she likely left her station at around two in the afternoon. According to your statement, Detective Court, only two people knew about this crime scene at two in the afternoon: you and Sheriff Delgado. Did you call Ms. Pritchard?"

I shook my head. "No."

"And you claim you didn't, either," said Lawson, looking to Delgado.

Delgado shifted his weight from one foot to another and shook his head.

"No, I did not, and I resent your question."

"If neither of you called her, how did she show up outside my crime scene an hour after you discovered it?"

Delgado said nothing. I had nothing to say. Lawson raised his eyebrows.

"You think she showed up by chance?"

Again, neither of us said anything.

"Fine," said Lawson. "Show me your phones."

I stepped back and almost chuckled. Delgado shook his head.

"I've indulged this for long enough," said Delgado. "You and your people are guests in my station. I don't appreciate you accusing me or my detective of a crime."

"Okay," said Lawson, looking to me. "The sheriff won't show me his phone. You want to show me yours? I'd consider it a personal favor. Agent Costa spoke highly of your work at the church. You can't stay in St. Augustine forever. My recommendation would open a lot of doors for you in law enforcement in St. Louis and Kansas City."

I opened my mouth, but I was too surprised to say anything. Then Delgado and Lawson started arguing again. The politics in my department were venal, and every politician in the county held his hand out and his wallet open twenty-four hours a day. Still, St. Augustine was my home. I had never thought about leaving, but with Lawson's recommendation, maybe I could.

Showing him my phone wouldn't have been unethical. At this point, it was a piece of evidence, nothing more. Besides, Delgado would have thrown me in a burning dumpster if it helped his career. He didn't deserve my protection.

I started toward my desk, but the sheriff called out before I took more than a step.

"Stop right there, Detective," he said. I looked to Agent Lawson and then Delgado. Delgado focused on the special agent. "Detective Court's phone is the property of the St. Augustine County Sheriff's Department. She can't turn it over to you without my permission any more than she could turn over one of our cruisers. That's not her call. If you want to see her phone, you need a warrant. I'll talk to the county attorney and see how to proceed from there."

Lawson appraised the sheriff.

"Think about what you're doing," said Lawson, raising his eyebrows.

Delgado turned his chin up. "I already have."

"All right, then. I'll contact the US Attorney's Office and get the ball rolling."

"You do what you've got to do," said Delgado.

Lawson hesitated before taking the stairs to the second floor. Delgado and I watched him go. Once Lawson left, the sheriff turned.

"He approaches you like that again, tell me. I'll handle it."

I held his gaze before looking to the ground. Trisha was typing at her desk, avoiding looking at us.

"You're a moron," I said.

When I looked up, Delgado had put his hands on his hips and stared at me with a dumbfounded expression on his face.

"Excuse me, Detective?"

"Your head's so far up your ass you don't even understand what you've done or why Lawson's pissed," I said. "We're trying to find a serial murderer. We found where he dumps his victims. This place was important to him. We could have put cameras up, and we could have stationed a surveillance team nearby. Even if he didn't visit for weeks, he would have come eventually. We would have arrested him.

"But you called Angela Pritchard because you hoped to get your face on TV. The Apostate knows we found it. He won't come back now."

Delgado blinked and shook his head. "We don't know this was the Apostate's church."

I lowered my chin. "If this isn't the Apostate's church, then we've got another killer out there. He's murdering people and dumping their bodies in a church. Either way, you told the world about his hideout before we could catch him. That was self-serving and stupid."

The sheriff considered.

"Go home, Detective," he said, his voice soft. "And remember, this case is confidential. Don't talk to anybody about this."

"Sure," I said. "See you tomorrow."

He grunted before walking toward the stairs that led to his second-floor office. His movements were slow, and he kept his head down. For a split second, I felt sorry for him, but then I thought of Jude Lewis and Paige Maxwell, of Olivia King and John Rogers, of Tayla Walker and Matthew Bridges. With the two new victims Agent Lawson was investigating, the Apostate had abducted fourteen children. If not for Delgado and Angela Pritchard, an FBI surveillance team could have waited and arrested him. Nobody else would have had to die.

My sympathy for Delgado died right there. He didn't deserve it. He had screwed up, and innocent people would pay the price.

Chapter 9

I drove home at a little before five in the evening. My job didn't have many perks, but it kept me busy for ten or twelve hours a day. I liked that. I liked even more that my work mattered and helped people. To top it off, it made my life easier. My caseload gave me little time to consider my life. Now, as I drove back to an empty house with the sun up and the birds chirping from my trees, a dull melancholy spread through me.

I missed my old dog most on days like this. Roger always made my day brighter, but more than that, he had forced me to talk to people on his daily walk. I hadn't realized how much I'd gotten out of Roger's walks until I stopped doing them.

Rather than dwell on things I couldn't change, I parked in my driveway, grabbed two frozen dinners from my freezer, and walked to my neighbor's house. I didn't know how old Susanne was, but she had retired over twenty years ago from the St. Augustine County school system. She was kind and good. I couldn't have asked for a better friend.

I knocked on her door, and when she saw me, her face lit up. I held up the boxed rice bowls.

"I can't cook, but I brought dinner," I said.

She looked at my rice bowls and then to me with a bemused smile on her face.

"I have half a potpie in the fridge," she said. "It's left over from my bridge club. How about I warm us up real food?"

I looked at my rice bowls. "This is real food. It's organic."

She patted me on the elbow and turned to walk toward her kitchen. "We'll get you fattened up, sweetie. Don't worry."

I stayed with Susanne about two hours. We talked about our days and about Roger. He used to come to her house every morning and spend the day with her while I was at work. We both missed him. I'd get a new dog in time, but for now, my memories kept me company.

Susanne gave me a big hug after dinner, and I left her house feeling much better than I had when I arrived. It was nice to have a friend.

When I got home, my house didn't seem as lonely as it had, but it was still empty. Harry, Trisha, and I had cleaned up yesterday, but we had left piles of papers stacked on the floor. Whiteboards filled with notes about the Apostate blocked the windows.

The church had held a lot of bodies. I wondered who they were. Was this a new dump site? An old one? Were there other bodies out there somewhere? Were his other victims still alive?

I couldn't answer those questions, but I would—hopefully before he killed anyone else.

It was a little after seven in the evening, so I plopped down on my couch and called Harry's cell phone to update him on the case.

"Harry, it's Joe. I'm not interrupting anything, am I?"

"Just doing the dishes with Irene."

I nodded. "When you're done, call me. I wanted to talk about the Apostate."

Harry hesitated. "Hold on just a second."

He asked his wife whether she minded finishing the dishes alone while we spoke. Irene agreed if he put things away once they dried. I had only met Irene a handful of times, but I liked her. She was intelligent, and she wasn't afraid to stand up for herself. Police work was hard and time intensive. A lot of marriages buckled under the strain, but Harry and Irene listened to each other and sacrificed for each other's needs. They seemed happy, and I was happy for them.

Eventually, Harry got back on the phone.

"I saw the news at six. You're famous once more."

I grunted. "What did I do for my newfound fame?"

"Angela Pritchard implied you were feeding her information about the case. She said you were close to finding the killer."

I rubbed my eyes and sighed. "Delgado's the source, and we're nowhere near finding the killer."

"I figured," said Harry. "Trisha texted me to tell me we wouldn't be getting anything new today. I expected George to piss off the feds, but I had hoped he'd last more than two days."

"It is what it is," I said. "We'll pick up bits and pieces where we can, but for now, we've still got a lot to work with. You've lived in the county for a while. Have you ever heard of that church?"

Harry paused. "No, but I've never been much of a churchgoer."

"Then find someone who is," I said. "The scene in the church was ugly. Someone burned these kids to death. The Apostate isn't just killing them; he's punishing them. Someone hurt this guy, and he's getting revenge. Learn what you can about that church. Maybe something happened there."

Harry paused and then sighed.

"If you're right, and he's punishing these boys and girls, he's doing this for a reason," he said. "We pull too many layers back on this, we might find something we don't want to see."

"If our killer was abused as a child, I'll arrest him and the people who hurt him," I said. "That's my job."

Harry drew in a breath. "All right. I'll see what I can find out about the church."

Harry and I talked for another few minutes, but we didn't figure anything out. After hanging up, I poured myself a drink from the bottle of vodka in my freezer and sat back down in the living room.

For a few minutes, I watched an old episode of *Game of Thrones* on my DVR. Today, Cersei, a main character, gave a speech about all the things she'd do to protect her children. The conversation reminded me of Erin, my biological mother, and everything she'd failed at in my childhood. That took the fun out of my evening's entertainment.

I downed my first drink in a gulp and returned to the kitchen for a refill. There, I stopped and looked at my phone and the laptop beside it on the counter. I didn't think about Erin often, mostly because I didn't care about her. Knowing someone had murdered her didn't change that, but I still wondered. Did she know her killer was coming? Did she deserve it? Did she think about me toward the end? Did she even care about the daughter she lost?

My eyes were a little glassy, and a heavy feeling welled in my gut as I opened my laptop. I didn't remember many of Erin's friends, but one could probably answer my questions. Lacey Rayner. Like my mother, she had worked outcall as a prostitute. Unlike my mother, she was smart enough to use birth control, so she didn't have kids. Growing up, I used to call her Aunt Lacey. Every time she came by, she brought me a piece of candy.

When Erin's clients asked her to stay overnight, I'd sleep at Aunt Lacey's apartment. She'd braid my hair, and we'd watch movies together. She smelled nice. Erin smoked cheap menthol cigarettes, and the stink permeated my clothes, the car, and my bed. Until I entered a foster home, the smell was inescapable. At Aunt Lacey's apartment, though, I took bubble baths that left me smelling like perfume. She treated me like a princess, but more than that, she had made me feel wanted and loved.

I lost touch with her when I entered the foster care system, but I had loved Aunt Lacey. She was always kind. I considered for a few minutes and then accessed the license bureau's database from my laptop. It was an abuse of my position, but I looked her up.

Aunt Lacey was the only Lacey Rayner in the system, and she lived in Creve Coeur, an upscale suburb in west St. Louis County. It was an area for doctors and lawyers, and she looked good in her license photo. Life had gone well for her. She deserved it.

Before I could stop myself, I tapped her number into my cell phone. Aunt Lacey's phone rang four times before going to voicemail. I considered leaving a message, but I didn't know what to tell her. I hung up. That was for the best. After all these years, I doubted Lacey would remember the little girl whose hair she used to braid.

After that, I closed my laptop and finished my show in the living room, but my mind didn't stray far from Erin. At about ten, I locked the doors and then turned down the lights. As I closed my eyes to sleep, I found my mind drifting.

My childhood hadn't been all bad. Christmas was always nice. Most of Erin's clients had families, so they didn't want to spend the holidays screwing a hooker in a cheap motel. That meant I had Erin all to myself, and without regular dates, she didn't have the money to buy booze or drugs. For a time, Erin was sober. She was like a real mom. One year, she even hung stockings on the windowsill. Santa brought me six pairs of colorful socks and a big box of Milk Duds. It was the best Christmas I ever had.

Erin Court wasn't evil or mean, but she had been a terrible mother. Still, I had loved her, and, in those quiet moments when I was honest with myself, I missed her. As my eyes closed, and my conscious mind shifted to dreams, I smelled the flowery notes of her perfume and the herbaceous mint of her menthol cigarettes, and I felt content.

That was how it had always gone, though. Erin had never disappointed me in my dreams. The disappointment always came when I woke up.

Chapter 10

Glenn's heart pounded, sending blood rushing through his system with every compression. His thumb paused over the play button on the remote. His right foot bounced on the ground, while the heel of his left rested on his right thigh. A song kept playing repeatedly in his head, and he couldn't help but hum along with it.

"You like her, don't you?" asked Helen.

Glenn glanced over at his sister. They sat together in the living room of his home. The house wasn't much, but it was his—purchased in cash, the way his father had taught him. The front porch sagged, and the roof leaked into the attic, but he had plans to fix those. Aside from its minor imperfections, the home had a lot to love. Its oak hardwood floors were original, as were the baseboards and crown molding. Everything in that house spoke to its history. At times, it felt almost alive.

Helen sat on the other end of the sofa with a bemused smile on her face. The reflected light of the television danced off canvas curtains he had made himself from painters' tarps purchased at a local hardware store. They looked surprisingly professional, and almost four hundred people had pinned pictures of them when he posted them to Pinterest.

"I don't even know her," he said. Helen smiled. The two of them had already burned the blood-soaked clothes they had worn to the storm cellar, so now Helen wore thick flannel pajamas. A tie held her hair in a loose ponytail behind her. He wore jeans and a white T-shirt.

"You can't hide it, honey," she said, leaning toward him and winking. "Mary Joe is a pretty girl. Millions and millions of years of evolution have programmed you to like girls like her. There's nothing wrong with that."

He flicked his eyes to his sister before shaking his head.

"I don't want to talk about this."

"Okay," she said. "If you don't want to talk about your feelings, let's talk about your girlfriend."

Glenn followed his sister's eyes to the television. While he had punished Mary and Peter in his dungeon, the police had found his church. He had expected them to find it eventually, but it still left him horrified. Glenn had stopped going to Mass after his father died, but he had never stopped believing. That church was sacred to him. He had made it into a symbol of justice and righteousness. Watching the police traipse all over it as if it were some kind of public toilet tore into him and made him sick.

Angela Pritchard first announced the find on her Twitter feed, but then every news outlet in the region had picked it up. Pritchard would push her grandmother off a cliff to get a story. That drive combined with her highly placed sources in law enforcement made her worth following. She called him the Apostate. The nickname didn't fit, but it looked as if it was catching on with the media. An apostate renounced his religion. Glenn renounced nothing. He lived his faith and exalted in righteousness. Pritchard didn't understand him, but that didn't matter.

Even as ignorant as she was, Glenn had considered taking Pritchard at one point. Helen had convinced him she wasn't worth the risk. She was beautiful, true, but she wasn't for him. She didn't matter the way his true targets did, so Glenn bided his time and did his work in secret and in solitude.

Until now.

His finger trembled as he hit the play button. Pritchard claimed the police were close to an arrest, that he was insane and deviant, that he molested his "victims" before killing them as part of some sick ritual. She was wrong, but Glenn didn't blame her. The news had become entertainment, and Angela Pritchard was entertaining—especially when she wore something with a plunging neckline.

He paused the video as Detective Mary Joe Court stepped into the frame. She was perfect. He had met her once about three years ago, but he hadn't realized how special she was. Now he saw the calm intelligence in her eyes and the strength of her character. Her thick blonde hair bounced with every step of her graceful walk, and though she frowned on camera, Glenn knew her smile could light up an entire room. She was beautiful and ripe, verdant and untamed, like a field of meadow grass and wildflowers.

"She certainly does have a presence about her," said Helen. "I can see why you like her."

"I think she's the one."

Helen considered the television for a moment and then shook her head.

"I don't think so, sweetheart," she said, her voice a whisper. "Look at her. She's talking to that reporter. She's telling her lies about you."

But she wasn't whispering lies. He had watched the video with Detective Court dozens of times already, and he had memorized every frame.

"She's protecting me," said Glenn. "When she talks to Angela, her posture stiffens, her skin flushes, and she balls her hands into fists. She's angry. Angela Pritchard is the interloper. Mary Joe is protecting my church. She knows its significance. She understands me."

Helen sighed and tried to touch his hand. Glenn scooted away.

"Honey, I'm the only one who understands you. Come here. I can see you're upset. Let me hold you."

Glenn looked at his sister. He had found comfort in those arms for more nights than he could count. Not tonight, though.

"My shadow knows me, too," he said.

"No, she doesn't," said Helen, her voice full of contempt. "She's a fool, and you're a fool if you listen to her."

Helen's wrong. I can bring you to life.

His shadow whispered in the back of his mind. It was a lover's caress, and it sent a shiver down his spine.

"She's talking to you now, isn't she?" asked Helen. "Don't listen to her."

I can give you Mary Joe. She's destined to be with you.

Glenn's entire body shuddered.

"Shut her out," said Helen, her voice strong. "Remember what she made you do this afternoon. You can't control her. I love you. I'm your family. Trust me."

Helen was right, but it took an effort to ignore his shadow's seductive voice. He looked at his sister and then down to his hands.

"I'm tired of this," he whispered. "I'm tired of fighting every day."

"You don't have to fight her alone," she said. "I'm here with you, and I'm not going anywhere."

For a few minutes, they stayed there on the couch, and Glenn drank from his sister's calm stillness. His shadow's voice, once more, went silent. His throat loosened, and the knot in his belly unraveled. Still, his mind refused to focus. Something clawed at his consciousness. It was a need and itch he needed to scratch.

"I want her," he whispered. Helen looked at him. Her eyes held kindness and sympathy. "Mary Joe. I need someone in my life. I need her."

"If Mary Joe is the one, then you'll have her," she whispered.

He nodded and silently thanked her. Helen didn't lie. With her assistance, Mary Joe would become his. It would take time and coaxing, but he'd have her eventually. For now, though, he needed another way to scratch his itch.

"The cellar is empty," he said.

Helen considered for a moment and then drew in a slow, deep breath.

"And you want to fill it. Are you sure you're ready after what you did to Peter and Mary?"

"I've learned from that mistake," he said, nodding.

Helen pursed her lips.

"You have people in mind?"

He nodded. "They're local. They won't be easy, but they're here. We can get them tonight."

A smile cracked Helen's lips.

"If they're local, Mary Joe will be the investigating officer. Is that your plan?"

"Would that be such a bad thing? I can watch her work."

"Okay," she said, drawing in a breath as she thought. "We'll watch her together. She deserves a chance."

"Thank you," he said, feeling a wave of peace and calm crash over him. Helen straightened.

"Go get ready, Romeo," she said, nodding toward the staircase that led to his second floor. "Get dressed. You can't punish the wicked in your pajamas."

Chapter 11

My phone rang at one in the morning. For a moment, I thought I felt Roger at the foot of my bed, but it was just a blanket I had kicked down. I didn't know what happened to dogs after they died, but wherever he was, I hoped he had beef jerky. Little in the world had made him quite so happy.

My cell rang again as I stretched and yawned. Since I was the only detective in St. Augustine County, I got late-night phone calls reasonably often. I reached for the pillow beside me and held it over my ears, but that didn't even muffle the ringtone. I sighed and rolled over to grab my phone.

"Yeah?" I said, my voice hoarse as I answered.

"Joe, sorry I'm calling," said Officer Jason Zuckerburg. Zuckerburg was our night dispatcher. He had been a police officer for longer than I had been alive and could have retired whenever he wanted. That was a common theme around my station. "I've got a double homicide with your name on it."

My muscles relaxed, and my head sank into my pillow.

"I'm on limited duty until my therapist clears me. You know the story."

"Yeah, I know, but Delgado's still on the Apostate murders, and you're the only other person in the department who's ever worn a detective's badge," he said. "I can call the Highway Patrol and ask them to take over, but until they assign somebody, we need a detective at the scene. You're up."

I groaned. "Damn you and your sound judgment."

"My wife says it's my worst trait."

I rubbed the sleep from my eyes, hoping the world would look better. It didn't, but I told him I'd be at the scene as quickly as I could, anyway. The address he gave me put the home on the outskirts of the west side of the town of St. Augustine. Developers hadn't touched that area, so most of the homes had large plots of land with lots of trees and wildlife. The victims could have been wealthy, middle class, or dirt poor. I wouldn't know until I got there, so I didn't know what kind of case I'd be digging into.

Crime—even violent crime—transcended social class, but I liked knowing what kind of world I was about to walk into. Wealthy people responded better to a detective in a blazer and slacks than one in a polo shirt and jeans, while a detective in a suit might intimidate less affluent people. I planned my outfits by the response they elicited at a crime scene. Today, I compromised by putting on a white button-down shirt, a brown blazer, and dark jeans. The blazer hid my firearm and looked reasonably nice. Plus, I could take it off if necessary.

I put the homeowner's address into my GPS and headed out. The drive took about fifteen minutes on dark roads. As I crested a hill, I saw blue and white police lights flashing in the distance. There was a mobile-home park to my right and a small, single-story home to my left. The victim's house was about a quarter mile away at the bottom of the hill.

I pulled to a stop on the side of the road near the home and hung my badge from a lanyard around my neck. Emily Hayes, one of our uniformed officers, approached me with a flashlight in her hand as I stepped out of my car. She flashed the light over me, and I held a hand to my eyes.

"Joe?" she asked, lowering the light to the home's long, sloping driveway. "That you?"

"Yeah," I said, blinking so my eyes would adjust to the dark once more. I walked toward her. "What have we got?"

"Sorry about the light," said Emily, tucking her flashlight between her arm and side. She read from a notepad she took from her utility belt. "Original call came in at twenty after midnight. The caller was a twelve-year-old female named Mackenzie Foster. She said a man had come into the house and shot both of her parents while she hid beneath her bed. The male victim is Mark Foster. The female victim is his wife, Lilly Foster."

I let out a slow breath. "Jeez. The kid okay?"

Emily tilted her head to the side. "Physically, yeah. I called the Department of Children's Services, and they're sending a social worker down for her. She and Tracy Carruthers are in my car, but the poor girl is so upset I thought EMTs might have to sedate her for her own safety."

"I can imagine," I said, nodding. At twelve years old, Mackenzie was old enough that her memories would be vivid and reliable enough to help guide my investigation. If I could get her to talk, she'd be a good source of information and could help me put the people who murdered her parents in prison. Of course, that cut multiple ways. At twelve, she'd remember every awful detail of this night for the rest of her life. As much as I would appreciate her assistance, the tradeoff wasn't worth it.

I walked toward the house and then looked to Emily. "Make sure Mackenzie's available. I'd like to talk to her this evening before she goes to sleep."

Emily hesitated and then nodded as she followed me toward the house. "I'll do what I can."

The home's front door was still open. The deadbolt had ripped through the wooden sill, and a dirt footprint was clearly visible on a door panel. I stopped and snapped pictures of both with my cell phone. Our crime-scene technicians would do the same thing, but I liked having pictures for my own files.

"Where was Mackenzie when the shooter kicked in the front door?"

Emily flipped through her notes.

"In bed."

"Did she share a room with anybody?"

"Her room has a single bed, so I don't think so. When I arrived, I found the door broken, so I announced myself and cleared the house room by room. Mackenzie came out from hiding as I finished my search. She was crying, and she had blood on her feet, so I picked her up and carried her to the car. I took some pictures of her feet with my cell phone to document what they looked like upon my arrival."

I glanced at Emily and then the front yard. There were three St. Augustine police cars in front of the house, but I couldn't see any of our other officers. Hopefully, no one had touched anything after Emily cleared the house.

"Okay," I said. "Where's everybody else?"

"Gary Faulk and Shane Fox are knocking on doors now to see whether the neighbors saw anything. I'm the only officer who's been inside."

"And you're sure the house is empty?" I asked, lowering my chin. Emily thought but then nodded.

"I checked every closet and in every cabinet big enough to hold someone. I also checked under the beds. You should be alone."

"I appreciate it," I said, looking toward the house. "I'll walk through and take pictures. See whether you can get in touch with Darlene McEvoy with the county crime lab. She's not on call, but we need somebody competent to collect forensic evidence. After that, call Dr. Sheridan. We'll need a coroner to collect the bodies. Unless there's a problem we can't overcome, I plan to keep this case in-house."

Emily wrote that down but then nodded. "You want me to start a logbook?"

"If you haven't already. You'll be the first entry, and I'll be the second."

"Got it," she said. She paused and held my gaze before tilting her head to the side. "I've never been the first responder to a homicide."

"You handled it like a vet," I said. She smiled, so I winked. "If there's a murderer hiding in the basement, though, I'll change my assessment."

The smile left her face, and her posture straightened. "I checked the basement."

"I know," I said, smiling just a little and hoping she'd smile. "It was a joke."

"Oh," she said, forcing a smile to her lips but keeping her posture straight and formal. "I don't think I've heard you make a joke before."

"Sadly, I think you have," I said. "I'll check out the house and refrain from telling more jokes. You did good work tonight."

"Thank you, ma'am," she said.

I smiled again, hoping that would help her relax. She kept her shoulders back and her head high, like a soldier greeting his or her commanding officer. As I focused on the house again, I took pictures of the entryway with my phone.

Aside from the broken door, little stood out. The entry led to a living room on the right and a kitchen straight ahead. A flush-mounted ceiling light cast a dull yellow luminescence over the tile floor and beige walls.

After snapping a few pictures, I put my hands in my pockets and stepped forward, paying careful attention to the floor beneath me so I wouldn't step on blood or other evidence. I found the first victim in the kitchen. He was a middle-aged, heavyset male, and he lay facedown on the ground. No bullet wounds marred his back, but a puddle of blood had pooled around his belly and chest. He wore boxers but no shirt or shoes. Very likely he had run from his bedroom when he heard the noise.

I snapped pictures of the kitchen before walking to the dining room and then the living room. There, I found three pairs of bloody footprints on the ground. One set was small and showed the outline of someone's toes. That belonged to Mackenzie. Another set was larger than Mackenzie's, but it had few details. If I had to guess, that set belonged to someone who wore socks. The third set was larger still, and it had the outline of a shoe. If I had to guess, it came from an adult male. He had a much longer stride than I did, which probably put him at six feet tall or more. Mark Foster hadn't been wearing shoes, so those footprints probably came from our killer.

I took a couple more pictures and then continued down the hallway. The first bedroom on my left had pink walls and light pink carpet. There was an unmade single bed in the corner. A comforter decorated with hearts lay on the ground.

I couldn't see any blood. The next bedroom I passed—this one was on the right—also had pink walls, but the chic decorations belonged to an older girl. The desk held a picture of a tall, muscular young man and a very pretty young woman. Both wore evening attire, and both stood arm in arm in front of a brick home. It looked like a prom picture.

I took my own pictures and then walked to the master bedroom at the end of the hall. A middle-aged female with brunette hair lay on top of the covers in bed. Her killer had shot her three times in the chest. I hadn't seen shell casings on the ground in the kitchen, but there were several here. We'd have plenty of evidence to go on, at least.

I left the house and found Emily on the front lawn. She nodded when she saw me.

"Anyone inside?" she asked.

"No," I said. "You did well. When you talked to Mackenzie, did she mention her older sister?"

Emily took her notepad from her utility belt and flipped through pages.

"Mackenzie thought she was at her boyfriend's house for the night. She snuck out and did that sometimes."

"And what's her name?"

Emily went quiet and read through her notes. "Her name is Trinity Foster. Her boyfriend is Thad Stevens."

I held my breath, expecting her to correct herself, but she looked at me with uncomprehending eyes.

CHRIS CULVER

"Repeat the boyfriend's name again," I said. Emily looked at her notes and raised an eyebrow.

"Thad Stevens," she said. "I've got his address if you want it."

"Yeah, I want it," I said, taking out my phone to call Jason. He answered before his phone finished ringing once. "I need you to send a car to the home of a young man named Thad Stevens."

I held the phone to Emily as she read the address aloud. Jason typed for a few moments and then placed a call on another line. I waited and grew more impatient every moment. After about three minutes, Jason got back on the line.

"Okay," said Jason. "I've got Bob Reitz on his way to the house. He's seven minutes out. Any idea what he's expecting?"

"No, so Reitz needs backup," I said. "I'm at the scene of a double homicide. We've got a young woman named Trinity Foster who's missing. She's Thad Stevens's girlfriend."

Jason typed for a few moments. "I've rerouted two more cars, but I'm not sure what you're getting at."

"The kid's name is Thad. I'm guessing it's short for Thaddeus," I said. I waited a moment, but Jason didn't respond. "History knows Thaddeus as St. Jude Thaddeus or Jude the Apostle. The Apostate is targeting young men named after apostles and their girlfriends. We've got a missing girlfriend and two dead parents. If we've got a missing apostle, we've got a problem."

106

"Oh," said Jason. He paused. "That's bad."

"Good. Now you understand," I said. "Call Officer Reitz and tell him what he's walking into. And make coffee. Our station's going to get busy."

Chapter 12

J ason returned my call ten minutes after I called him.

"Thad's gone, but his parents are alive," he said. "It looks like he snuck out and took his car. How do you want to proceed?"

"Even if Thad and Trinity are safe, we need to find them. Call the Highway Patrol and tell them we need every officer in the state looking for Thad's car. After that call, have the officers at Thad's house get his cell number from his parents. If it's on, we can track his phone. I'll call Agent Costa with the Bureau and bring him in."

"You want me to call the sheriff and tell him what's going on?"

Even before Jason finished speaking, my head throbbed. Delgado had been a competent detective, but he was a terrible boss. If I called him, I might as well go home because he wouldn't let me do anything. Still, the County Council had named him sheriff, which meant he called the shots. I swore under my breath.

"Yeah," I said, grimacing even as the words left my lips. "Call him but downplay the situation. Tell him there are signs the victims committed suicide."

Jason paused. "Are there signs they committed suicide?"

"The evidence is inconclusive," I said. Jason hesitated.

"If that's how you want to play this, that's how we'll play this."

"Good. Thank you," I said. I called Agent Costa next because I didn't have his boss's personal phone number. Costa answered on the second ring and listened as I explained the situation.

"It's thin," he said. "Aside from Thad's name, do you have anything else connecting your case to the Apostate?"

"No, but it's still early," I said. "Thad and Trinity even might be shagging in his car with no clue that Mark and Lilly are dead."

He sighed. "I'll get a team."

I thanked him and pocketed my phone before snapping my eyes toward Officer Hayes. She stood in the front lawn inside the pool of light cast by the lights in the home's entryway.

"Emily, I need to talk to Mackenzie. Is she still in your car with Tracy?"

Emily nodded and pointed to the cruiser closest to my truck. It was dark, so I couldn't see anybody inside, but I nodded anyway before walking toward the vehicle. As I approached, Officer Tracy Carruthers opened the front passenger door and stepped out.

"Hey, Joe," she said.

"Hey, Tracy," I said. "Mackenzie okay?"

Tracy tilted her head to the side and shrugged. "She saw her mom and stepdad gunned down."

"Stupid question," I said. "You think she'll talk?"

Tracy looked to the car. "It won't hurt to try. Good luck."

I thanked her and sat in the front seat. The vinyl felt warm from Tracy's back, and the air was stuffy. Mackenzie had brunette hair like her mom, freckles, pointed ears, and thin, sunken cheeks. I smiled at her when she looked up at me. Tiny red blood vessels striated the whites of her eyes, and her bottom lip quivered. I wanted to give her a hug and tell her that things would be okay, but I couldn't. Things weren't okay and probably never would be. Instead, I smiled.

"Can I get you anything? Water? A soda? Something to eat?"

She shook her head.

"No."

"Okay," I said, still smiling. "I'm Detective Joe Court. You can call me Joe. I'm here to find out what happened tonight. First, though, how are you doing? Are you scared?"

Again, she shook her head, but she wouldn't meet my gaze.

"Okay," I said, forcing my voice to be soft. "Take your time and tell me what happened tonight."

Mackenzie's voice was slow and uncertain at first, but it grew to a normal cadence. She wasn't forthcoming with details, so I had to ask a lot of questions. I had expected that, though. She said she was in bed when she heard a loud crash. It scared her, so she came to her door. There, she saw her stepfather, Mark Foster, running down the hallway. He told her to go back in her room and hide, so she went back inside and slid beneath her bed.

As she did that, she heard shouting. Her mom screamed. Then there were three gunshots. She didn't know who they belonged to, but she saw a pair of tennis shoes run by her door toward her parents' room. She then ran into the hallway. Her stepfather was on the floor in the kitchen. She ran to see whether he was okay, but there was blood everywhere. He was dead when she got there. She then ran through the kitchen and back to her bedroom as the shooter and her mother shouted at each other. Then she heard more gunshots.

The story explained how Mark and Lilly had died and how Mackenzie had gotten blood on her feet, but it was a lie, nonetheless. I kept my voice soft as I smiled at her when she finished.

"You did nothing wrong tonight," I said. "You didn't shoot your parents. If you had, I'd smell the gunpowder on you. If I'm going to arrest the person who shot your mother and stepfather, though, I need the truth. Can you tell me the truth?"

Her lower lip quivered, but she swallowed hard. "I didn't lie."

I kept my smile on my face even as the muscles of my shoulders and back tensed.

"There were three sets of footprints in the house. One set belongs to you. The other set belongs to the man who shot your mom and stepfather. Who does the third set belong to?"

She shrugged but said nothing.

"Are they your sister's footprints?"

Mackenzie shook her head. A pit grew in my stomach.

"Where is she now?"

She crossed her arms but said nothing.

"Was your sister home when the man came in?"

She shook her head. "No."

"Have you seen her tonight?"

"No," she said again, shaking her head but not meeting my gaze. I stayed silent until she glanced up at me.

"I'm here to keep you and your sister safe. You can help me do that by telling me the truth. Your mom didn't have blood on her feet, so she didn't make that third set of footprints. I think the tracks are Trinity's. She walked through your stepfather's blood, and then she walked down the hall. I think she checked on you. Where is she now?"

"She wasn't there," said Mackenzie, tears now streaming down her cheeks. "I swear. I haven't seen her all night."

"Are you sure?"

She nodded, so I straightened.

"Okay," I said. "I'll keep working on this. You'll stay in the car with Officer Carruthers. If you change your mind about anything you've told me, I'm more than happy to listen."

"I won't change my mind," she said.

"Okay," I said, already opening my door. "I'll be right outside."

I fought the urge to slam the door. The kid's story made little sense, but I couldn't force her to tell me the truth. The harder I pushed now, the more likely she was to shut down. My best option was to give her some space. We had every officer in the county looking for Trinity and Thad. I had to trust they'd be enough.

For the next hour, I stayed on the front lawn and coordinated with the rest of the team. Delgado stayed home, but Special Agents Costa and Lawson came out. They even brought an FBI forensics team with them, which I appreciated. Darlene McEvoy, the woman who ran our forensics lab, was a terrific lab scientist, but she didn't have the resources of the FBI.

As the Bureau's technicians searched, I talked to Officers Gary Faulk and Shane Fox, both of whom had spent the preceding hour talking to the neighbors. Two people reported hearing gunfire, but neither had called the police. Half an hour after the Bureau arrived, Agent Lawson joined me on the lawn with a sigh.

"Your witness...she mention how her family makes a living?"

I shook my head and furrowed my brow. "We didn't get that far. Why?"

He pursed his lips and looked at the ground.

"What'd you find?"

"A little over seven hundred grams of cocaine," he said. "It was in the toilet tank in the master bedroom."

I brought a hand to my forehead as a dull ache spread through my gut. Like every law enforcement agency in the world, we made drug arrests every day. I couldn't remember the last time we found that much cocaine in one house, though. At the street level, that'd be worth about a hundred thousand dollars. If the homeowners sold primarily to dealers, it'd probably be worth half that.

"You find any money or guns?" I asked.

"Nope," he said. "This might have been a robbery."

I swore under my breath. Even if they provided drugs to every dealer in the county, the family maintained a low profile. The home had never come up in our daily briefing, and I had never even heard rumors about a major dealer who lived with his wife and kids outside town. A guy capable of hiding in plain sight that well might have had enemies, but he would have had plans to deal with them.

He might not have had plans to deal with a teenage daughter and her boyfriend, though.

"Mackenzie lied about her sister being here tonight."

"Oh, yeah?" asked Lawson, crossing his arms.

"If this is a robbery, it might be an inside job."

Lawson tilted his head to the side, considering.

"So your theory is that Trinity and Thad killed Mark and Lilly for drug money. That would mean the footprints belong to Trinity, Mackenzie, and Thad."

I nodded. "Yeah."

He nodded to himself. "It's worth considering. My techs got pictures of the prints. I'll make sure those are available to your team. You might have closed your case already."

"First, I've got to find the kids," I said, already trying to think of my next steps. I'd start by finding out what I could about their cell phones. If we could track those down, we'd have them before the sun came up. If they were smart and turned them off, we'd have a tougher job, but we still had options. They were kids, so they couldn't disappear forever. I hoped we got them before they hurt themselves or anyone else.

I hated cases like this. Even if we made an arrest, nobody would win.

As I pieced things together, I glanced over to find Agent Lawson still standing beside me. He wasn't looking at me. Instead, he focused on the house.

"Sorry," I said. "Was there something else?"

He hesitated. "You didn't call Angela Pritchard."

I raised my eyebrows and considered him, unsure what he was getting at. "So I've told you."

"I'm pretty sure Delgado did. He was nervous about me looking at your phones."

"Being nervous about having the FBI look at your phone doesn't make you guilty of anything. Maybe he was trying to protect me."

Lawson snickered. "He doesn't need to protect you. You're smart enough to use a burner when committing a crime. He's not."

I allowed a smile to creep onto my lips. "The best compliments are backhanded."

We watched the house for another moment before he turned.

"You heading home?" I asked.

"To the hotel," he said, nodding. He paused. "Can I give you some advice?"

"Feel free," I said.

"You're a better detective than your boss, and he knows that. People like Sheriff Delgado don't take well to playing second fiddle to someone better at their job than they are."

I nodded. "I've noticed that."

"If he goes down, he will take you with him," said Lawson. "Take that how you will."

I thanked him, so he nodded and left. It wasn't new information, but it reminded me of my place in this department. I'd worry about it later. I had a double homicide to investigate and two kids on the run. My career could wait.

Chapter 13

I stayed at the house for another half hour. The FBI forensic technicians had bagged the evidence, but they hadn't touched a pair of laptops found in the master bedroom. With both homeowners dead, I didn't have to worry about invading someone's privacy, so I put them on the tailgate of my pickup and fired them up.

One looked like a standard family computer. The internet history showed visits to Netflix, Amazon, and Instagram, but nothing nefarious. The other laptop was password protected. St. Augustine didn't have the resources to hire a dedicated computer crimes expert, so we'd have to either hire a consultant or ask the Highway Patrol's computer forensics people to examine it when they could.

In addition to the laptops, Agent Lawson had left me a spiral-bound notebook his team had found beneath the master bedroom mattress. It had columns of figures and dates and cryptic notes. That notebook would probably form the cornerstone of a major drug investigation. I hated getting it the way we had, though.

CHRIS CULVER

I left Darlene McEvoy in charge of the house. Dr. Sheridan, our coroner, hadn't arrived yet, but his assistant told me he was on his way. Someone from the Department of Children's Services had already taken Mackenzie into custody. She'd need therapy after watching her mom and stepfather be gunned down, but at least she'd have a chance.

I drove to Thad Stevens's house and found a St. Augustine police cruiser waiting for me in the driveway. The front door was ajar, but Officer Bob Reitz came out the moment I knocked. Reitz was in his early forties and had long since lost most of his hair. He shaved the rest, making him look a little like Mr. Clean. His demeanor was quiet, but he could get loud when needed. I liked working with him. He was a good officer, and he took care of his family, which I respected a great deal.

"Evening, Joe," he said, nodding.

"Hey, Bob," I said. "Are Thad's parents inside?"

He nodded. "Yeah, but they're not in good moods."

With their son missing and two dead people at his girlfriend's house, I figured as much.

"You mind sticking around? I'm not here to deliver good news."

He lowered his voice and craned his neck toward me.

"Is the kid alive?"

"I think so," I said. "There's a chance he's my murderer, though."

Bob put his hands on his hips and sighed. "That won't go over well."

"It rarely does."

Bob grunted. "Let me introduce you to the family. They're inside."

Officer Reitz and I walked inside. The front room had oversized couches and a stylish coffee table. I followed the sound of whispered voices to the kitchen, where I found a middle-aged couple sitting around a round table with chairs for four. Both had thin faces and eyes clouded by exhaustion.

Mr. Stevens stood when we entered. Mrs. Stevens stayed seated.

"Did you find my boy?" asked Mr. Stevens.

"No, but we're looking for him," I said. "I'm Detective Joe Court with the St. Augustine County Sheriff's Department. If you don't mind, I'd like to ask you some questions."

Mr. Stevens cocked his head at me and narrowed his gaze. "What questions?"

"Background questions so we can find your son," I said. "Let's sit and talk."

Mr. Stevens looked to his wife before sitting. The two resumed holding hands. Both had furrowed brows and watery eyes. I sat across from them and started by introducing myself and asking for their names and occupations.

Mr. Stevens's first name was Jerry, and his wife was Jamie. Both taught in the St. Augustine County school system, and they had lived in the county most of their lives. They also described Thad. He seemed like a good kid. He was on the high school baseball team and planned to go to the University of Missouri. Trinity and Thad had dated for over a year, and they complemented each other well. Thad was a dreamer, but Trinity kept him grounded. Jerry and Jamie seemed happy that they were together. I listened and took notes before diving into my own questions.

"Okay," I said. "We're still very early in this investigation, so my questions might seem strange, but they all have a purpose. Do you have any of Thad's shoes?"

Jerry looked to his wife before focusing on me again.

"Why do you need his shoes?"

"In case we find footprints or other identifying marks. It'd be helpful if we could get his toothbrush and a comb as well so we have a DNA sample."

Jamie hesitated but then nodded. "I'll get what I can."

I looked to Bob. "Can you get evidence bags for me? Two paper bags for the shoes and two plastic bags for the comb and the toothbrush."

Bob agreed and then left. I focused on Jerry again.

"We're early in the investigation, so we're still gathering information. Did you know Trinity's parents?"

Jerry brought a hand to his brow before shrugging.

"I've met her stepdad at one of Thad's baseball games. I never met her mom."

I flipped through pages of my notepad for a clean page.

"Did you like the stepdad?"

Jerry raised his eyebrows and then tilted his head to the side. "He seemed fine. It seemed a little strange that he'd go to a high school baseball game when he didn't have a kid on the team, but he said he played ball in high school."

"Okay," I said, nodding. "Did the other parents react to him like they knew him?"

"No," said Jerry. "Why?"

"Like I said, we're early in our investigation. We're trying to put together a picture of everyone, so every observation here helps," I said. "Did your son know him?"

Jerry crossed his arms. "He's been dating the man's step-daughter for a year."

I interpreted his response as a yes, so I nodded.

"Did he like him?"

Jerry's lips flattened into a straight line, and his eyes went cold.

"Ask him when you find him."

I nodded and forced a smile to my lips. "Do you have any guns in the house, Mr. Stevens?"

"Why does that matter?"

"It's a standard question," I said, still smiling. "Do you keep firearms in the house?"

"Why are you asking that?"

His eyes bore into mine, and he leaned forward. Neither of us said anything until Officer Reitz walked back into the room with the evidence bags.

"I've got the bags you requested," he said. "Everything all right, Detective?"

I didn't respond, but I was glad Bob was in the room. He hadn't shown any aggression toward me, but Jerry had fifty pounds on me and a substantial reach advantage. In the close confines of his dining room, he could hurt me before I could get my firearm out.

"Do you think my son murdered his girlfriends' parents?" asked Jerry.

"I'm investigating a case," I said. "Your son and Trinity are missing. Trinity's parents are dead. If I don't ask these questions now, a defense attorney will ask why I didn't investigate alternative suspects when I take the actual murderer to court. I'm doing my job. If you had died, I'd be asking the same questions of your friends and family. So please answer my questions. Do you keep firearms in the house?"

Jerry's nostrils flared as he breathed. I counted to thirty before he opened his mouth.

"Yes, there are firearms in the house. My son and I hunt. Is that a problem?"

"Not at all," I said. "How about pistols?"

He hesitated before answering. "I owned a .45, but somebody broke into the house three weeks ago and stole it. They also stole two rifles and a shotgun."

"Were they secured in any way?"

He uncrossed his arms and paced on the other side of the table.

"Yes. They were in my gun safe."

"Who has access to your gun safe?"

He paused and looked at me. "Do you even know what kind of weapon shot the Fosters?"

"Not yet," I said, shaking my head. "But we'll find out. Who could access your safe?"

"A few people," he said.

I had interrogated enough people to know if I pushed Jerry much harder, he'd kick me out of the house.

"I'm sorry to hear someone broke in, but I can get all the details I need from the police report."

He resumed pacing and shook his head.

"There was no police report."

Missouri law didn't require Jerry to report that someone had stolen firearms from him, but most people did so they'd have a report to file with their insurance company. Even if someone stole his guns, this didn't look good for him.

"I understand," I said, nodding. "If you'd like, Officer Reitz and I can file a report for you right now. Your insurance company might owe you some money."

"No, thank you," he said, shaking his head. "It's time for you to leave."

"So you don't want to help us in this investigation?"

Jerry looked from me to Officer Reitz and then back to me.

"Your officer told me my son and his girlfriend were missing and that her parents were dead. I'm not stupid, and I watch the news. I know who's out there. You led me to believe the Apostate had abducted my son, but now you're coming to my house like he's a killer. I don't appreciate that one bit."

He fumed, but I kept my calm.

"I wish I could tell you what's going on, but I can't. Your son's missing. Like you said, he's got the name of an apostle. His girlfriend is named Trinity, another religious name. The Apostate might have taken him. The FBI is considering that possibility. I'm a local detective, though. I have to consider other theories, and I'm sorry to say this, they'll cut close to home. Did you know what Trinity's stepfather and mother did for a living?"

He shook his head. "No."

"Would it surprise you to hear they dealt drugs?"

Jerry blinked as he thought through the question.

"I don't know the first thing about that."

"Did your son ever mention it to you?" I asked. "In my experience, when the parents are involved in an illegal enterprise, their teenage kids know. In this case, if Trinity knew, Thad likely did as well."

He rubbed his chin and then shook his head.

"You two need to leave."

"We need to find your son," I said. "You can help us keep him safe. If he killed Mark and Lilly Foster, we need Thad to come in on his own. Even if he did something, he's young, and he's got a lot of life ahead of him. He's seventeen, so he's still a minor. The courts can expunge his record. He can go to college and have the life he deserves if he turns himself in."

I was laying it on thick, but Jerry considered it anyway. Then he swallowed hard and nodded toward the front of the home.

"Please get out of my house," he said, his voice so soft I could barely hear him.

I waited for a moment to see whether he'd say anything else, but he didn't.

"We need his shoes and his toothbrush," I said.

"Then get a warrant."

It was almost a snarl. I stood and brought my hand down to hover near my firearm.

"Okay, Mr. Stevens," I said, nodding and speaking in a calm, deliberative voice. "We're leaving now."

"Get out."

Officer Reitz and I backed up without taking our eyes from Mr. Stevens. Upon reaching the entryway, we turned and walked outside. Jerry slammed the door shut behind us and then threw the deadbolt. Reitz let out a relieved sigh and then glanced at me.

"For a moment there, I thought he might hit you."

"Me, too," I said, nodding. "You got anything pressing going on tonight?"

"Just the usual," he said.

"Good," I said. "Then get in your car and park in front of the house. If anybody leaves, call it in and follow. If they get rid of evidence, I want you to document it with your phone. I'll talk to the prosecutor and see whether we can get a search warrant."

Bob started toward his cruiser but paused before getting in.

"You think the kid did it?" he asked.

"I hope not, but I'm following the evidence."

He shook his head and whistled.

"You are the ice queen, aren't you?" he asked, smiling as if he had just given me a compliment. I had heard the nickname whispered behind my back, but I had pretended they weren't talking about me. My lips flattened. Part of me wanted to tell him he shouldn't mistake professionalism for a lack of feeling, but that wasn't a conversation to have in public. So I nodded toward his cruiser.

"You've got a job to do, Officer Reitz. Get to it."

The smile slipped off his face.

"Yes, ma'am."

He got in his car and then parked on the street kitty-corner to the house so he could see if somebody ran out the back. I walked to my truck, where I squeezed my hands into tight balls. Ice queen. That was how my colleagues saw me. Cold, impersonal, unfeeling. They didn't know me at all, but that didn't matter. Thad and Trinity were out there, and I needed to find them before they hurt themselves or someone else.

Chapter 14

After leaving Thad's house, I called the county prosecutor. He didn't appreciate a call in the middle of the night, but worse than that, he said we didn't have enough probable cause to get a search warrant for Thad's bedroom. He was right, too. We had no physical evidence connecting them to the shooting, and no witnesses had put them anywhere near the scene at the time of the shooting.

My conversation with the prosecutor lasted about ten minutes. Once I learned we wouldn't get back into Thad's house soon, I told Officer Reitz to return to his regular assignment. I, meanwhile, spent the next six hours at Trinity Foster's house. We bagged every piece of evidence we found, we photographed every single footprint half a dozen times or more, and I re-interviewed every neighbor before they went to work.

Despite a thorough search, we found no money, guns, or drug paraphernalia. I wondered whether they had another facility they worked out of.

After the search, I drove to my office, where I researched my victims. Fortunately, that didn't take long because neither Mark nor Lilly Foster had ever been arrested, and no suspect had ever mentioned them in an interrogation. Drug dealers rarely impressed me, but I had to hand it to these guys: They were good.

That left me in a place I didn't like being. Thad and Trinity were my only suspects. I hoped it wasn't them. After striking out at every turn, I spent the next two hours typing up my interview notes, drinking coffee, cataloging photos, and writing reports.

On television and in books, detectives dressed well and sped through town in unmarked cars. They got to solve crimes and go home without spending a single moment in their station.

In reality, paperwork was the lifeblood of the criminal justice system. A criminal defense lawyer could read my paperwork and see who collected every piece of evidence we found at a scene, she could learn how and where we had stored it, and she'd learn why we had collected it. Everything was transparent. I knew what I did for a living, and it had nothing to do with justice. I put bad men and women in jail so they wouldn't hurt other people, and my reports were a vital step in that process.

At a little after eight in the morning, Delgado held the roll-call meeting in the first-floor conference room. I skipped because I didn't want to answer questions yet, especially if Delgado would leak those answers to the media. Instead, I drove to St. Augustine's high school. The school had about four hundred students total from St. Augustine County and a few neighboring areas. It was a good school, and it helped attract a lot of wealthy people from St. Louis who didn't mind a commute.

The high school sprawled across the rural landscape. It wasn't attractive, but it didn't need to look pretty to be effective. I parked in the lot and walked to the front entrance. Kids were out for the summer, but the office staff still locked the front doors to keep strangers from wandering around the campus. I hit the button for the intercom and waited for someone in the office to answer.

"Yes?"

The voice came from a speaker beside the door. I held my badge toward the camera suspended from the ceiling and smiled.

"Morning. I'm Detective Joe Court with the Sheriff's Department," I said. "Is the principal in?"

"Is your visit personal or business?"

"Business," I said, looking around. Across the street, a cornfield extended to the horizon, and the air held a whiff of an insecticide or fertilizer. The parking lot held few cars. I turned back around as the door buzzed, allowing me inside.

I had gone to the school three times since becoming a police officer. The first had involved a young woman who killed herself under suspicious circumstances. I wasn't a detective then, but the detective assigned to the case had taken me because he thought it would be helpful to have a young woman around when he interviewed the students. My second visit had been about Paige and Jude. Now, I came to talk about Trinity and Thad. It didn't seem fair to have this many tragedies in one place.

The principal, Mr. Berry, stepped out of an office as I walked into the building. He held his hand out to shake.

"Morning, Detective," he said. "What brings you by?"

"Ill tidings," I said. "A pair of your students are missing. Thaddeus Stevens and Trinity Foster."

Berry winced and then closed his eyes.

"Why is the Apostate targeting my kids?"

"I don't think the Apostate is involved."

He furrowed his brow and cocked his head to the side. "Then what's going on?"

"I can't share details yet," I said, looking down the hallway. "Is your guidance counselor around? I'd like to talk to him, too."

Berry nodded and then blew out a long breath before leading me down the hallway to a suite of offices separate from those of the school's administration. There, we walked through the door of a man who wore jeans and a yellow polo shirt. He was in his mid-fifties. His curly black hair clashed with his deeply inset blue eyes. He wasn't a big man, but he looked fit. When he saw the two of us standing in his doorframe, he stood from his desk.

"Morning," he said. The nameplate on his desk said he was Mr. Saunders. I leaned forward to shake his hand.

"Mr. Saunders, I'm Detective Joe Court from the St. Augustine County Sheriff's Department. I'm here to talk to you and Mr. Berry about two of your students."

Saunders smiled.

"It's nice to see you, Detective, although I'm sorry for the circumstances," he said. "We've met before. You came after Bethany McGuire killed herself."

"I remember," I said, nodding and forcing a smile to my lips. "Bethany's death was a tragedy. Unfortunately, I'm here for another one."

"Then have a seat," said Saunders. "If you'd like, I can make coffee."

"I would love coffee," I said. "I've been up all night."

Saunders nodded and got to work on a drip-style coffee maker in the corner of his office. A few minutes later, I held a Styrofoam cup of steaming, black coffee. It tasted unpleasantly astringent, but the caffeine woke me up. That was all I needed. I thanked him before putting my cup on his desk and reaching for my notepad. Saunders sat behind his desk, while Berry and I sat on upholstered chairs in front.

"Okay, so I'm here because someone murdered Trinity Foster's mother and stepfather last night. Trinity and Thad Stevens might be involved. I'm hoping you two can shed light on the kids that would explain this."

Both men sat straighter.

"Oh, my," said Mr. Berry. "When you said they were missing, I assumed someone had abducted them."

"That's still a possibility, but we're exploring alternatives," I said. "I got off on the wrong foot with Thad's family, so I don't have a clear picture of either kid yet. Did they ever have disciplinary problems or problems with drugs?"

Mr. Berry looked at Mr. Saunders. Both men looked perplexed.

"No," said Mr. Saunders. He leaned forward and then typed at his computer. Then he read something and nodded. "Neither even received a demerit in their time here."

"They were smart, too," said Mr. Berry. "Both took honors classes. Thad was a good baseball player. These kids weren't saints, but they wouldn't kill Trinity's parents."

I wrote notes and then looked up.

"Nothing would please me more than to learn these two are hiding in some love shack," I said, nodding. "Until we find them, though, I need you to bear with me. Did Trinity ever flash a lot of cash around?"

Berry looked to Saunders. The counselor leaned forward and shook his head.

"No," he said. "Teenagers are professionals at hiding things, though."

I nodded and locked my eyes on him. "Did you know her well?"

He shook his head. "She was one of four hundred students. I talked to her about applying for financial aid for college, but beyond that, she's a name in a computer. There are only so many hours in the day, and I'm the only counselor on staff. I have to prioritize those students who are struggling."

I nodded and wrote a couple of notes and glanced up to find Mr. Saunders's eyes on me. Mr. Berry was looking at me, too, but not like Mr. Saunders. The counselor appraised me the way a wolf might have studied a rabbit. It wasn't sexual; it was something else, and it made chills travel down my spine.

I brought my elbows into my sides and adjusted my position, allowing me to close my jacket over my chest. Saunders cleared his throat and leaned back.

"Okay," I said, looking to the counselor. "Even though you try to focus on those students with problems, do you know who Trinity and Thad hung out with?"

"I can put together a list of boys on the baseball team and a list of the boys and girls in the art club. Trinity was an active member, if I recall. Those kids will be able to point you to Trinity and Thad's friends."

"I'd appreciate that," I said, closing my notepad and putting my pen back in my purse. I stood to leave when Saunders cleared his throat.

"You're not from around here, are you?" asked Mr. Saunders.

I looked at him and raised my eyebrows. "Excuse me?"

"You didn't go to school here," he said. "That's what I meant. I would have remembered you."

I forced a smile to my face and shook my head. "No. I went to high school in St. Louis."

"Oh, which high school?"

I pretended I hadn't heard him. He may have been trying to be polite, but he was giving me the creeps. Thankfully, he took the hint and shut up.

"Are you sure the Apostate didn't kill Lilly and Mark before abducting the kids?" asked Mr. Berry.

I paused and raised my eyebrows.

"It's possible, but the facts of the case have led me to look elsewhere. Either way, every uniformed officer in the state has seen their pictures by now. We want to bring them in unharmed."

That placated the two educators, so I started toward the door, but Mr. Berry cleared his throat, calling for my attention. I turned and raised my eyebrows.

"Something else?"

"You probably don't know yet, Detective, but has anybody said anything about funeral arrangements? I went to high school with Lilly, and I've known Mark for a lot of years."

I looked at him up and down. "How well did you know them?"

"Pretty well," he said. "They were friends."

"I see," I said, nodding. "Just FYI, we found well over half a kilo of cocaine in their master bedroom toilet tank. In your position, you should be careful when you make friends."

Mr. Saunders opened his eyes wide, shocked. Mr. Berry shook his head.

"I don't believe that. I've known Mark for too long."

"Believe whatever you want. I'm being honest," I said. "They were dealing."

I turned to leave when I heard Mr. Saunders say something.

"I'm glad they're dead," he said. "Drugs have no place in modern society, especially around children."

I stopped and considered him. The guidance counselor's face was red, and his eyes looked angry.

"This is an open murder investigation. I understand the sentiment, but you should be careful about your word choice."

"Of course," he said. "And I'll get a list of Trinity and Thad's classmates."

He smiled once more, but the anger didn't leave his eyes. I didn't know what to make of him, but I didn't like him. I gave them both my business card with my contact information and left the building within half an hour of arriving. As I got in my car, I called the front desk at my station.

"Trisha, it's Joe," I said. "Is Special Agent Lawson in?"

"He's upstairs," she said. "Something wrong?"

"No, but there's more to Trinity and Thad than we know. Let Lawson know I'll be in to talk to him. I've got a bad feeling about my case."

Chapter 15

G lenn Saunders watched the detective sashay out of his office. He had known Mary Joe was special, but after seeing her in person again, he realized she was so much more than he expected. Everyone in St. Augustine knew her story. She grew up in the foster care system, but instead of protecting her, that foster care system failed her. Her foster father drugged and raped her. When she grew up, her foster father left prison and came after her once more. She shot him and proved herself stronger than anyone could have imagined. It was hard not to admire her.

If anyone could understand his mission, it would be her. That she was beautiful proved God wanted them to be together.

After she left, Glenn took the rest of the day off. Excitement and energy coursed through him in equal measures. Detective Mary Joe Court. Detective Mary Joe *Saunders*. He whispered her name, enjoying the way it rolled off his tongue. She may not have understood their connection, but she'd be his soon.

He locked his door and drove home, where he found his sister in the living room eating ice cream. How she ate ice cream and junk food all day and maintained her figure, he didn't know, but somehow Helen managed it. She smiled at him when he came in.

"You look happy."

"I am," he said. "Detective Court came to my office. I'm going to take her soon."

Helen smiled.

"I'm glad you found someone who makes you happy."

"She does," said Glenn. "But first, we need to clear out a cell. We'll take care of Paige and Jude today. I'm too excited to stay home."

"I'm glad, sweetie," said Helen, picking up her container of ice cream and taking it into the kitchen. She came out a moment later after stepping into a pair of strappy black flats. "Let's go get them."

Before leaving, Glenn made a peanut butter and jelly sandwich and put it in a Ziploc bag. Inside the car, Glenn checked his cattle prod's charge. Then, he and Helen drove out to his car lot, where he picked up another vehicle before driving to the dungeon. He thought about visiting Thad and Trinity first, but they needed more time in the dark before he could do anything with them. Paige and Jude would be ripe and ready.

Several days had passed since he had last visited, but little had changed from the dungeon's exterior. The big progress would come inside. Glenn opened the padlock that secured the door and pulled the heavy piece of steel aside. The interior was dark, and a damp odor wafted outside.

"Hello?" he called.

No one responded, so he looked back at Helen.

"Think they're still alive?"

She shrugged. "We'd smell them if they were dead."

She was right, so he slipped on his doctor's mask and reached into his pocket for his cell phone, which he used as a torch to light his way until he reached the bottom of the steps. There, he flicked on the overhead light. Paige and Jude were on the bed, holding one another. Both were breathing, but they looked emaciated and sick.

The actual act of starving was painless, but the secondary effects ravaged the body. Paige and Jude had entered his dungeon strong and healthy. Now, their muscles had atrophied and weakened so they no longer even sensed their own thirst. That led to dehydration that robbed their skin of moisture, leaving it dry and cracked. Every movement would have hurt.

"Jude," said Glenn, approaching the gate that separated him from his prisoners.

Jude raised his head. His eyes were almost glassy.

"I've got something for you," said Glenn, reaching into his pocket for his Ziploc bag. He took out a quarter of the peanut butter and jelly sandwich. The last time he had done this, Jude had been gallant and offered his girlfriend half a sandwich. He suspected this time would be different.

Jude swung his legs off the bed and approached the chain-link fence with his hand outstretched. He swayed almost drunkenly on his feet. Paige looked up and watched but didn't move.

"Go ahead," said Glenn, passing the quarter of a sandwich through the chain-link fence. Jude's hands trembled as his fingers touched the white bread. Jude stared at the sandwich as if he didn't know what it was. Then, he shoved it in his mouth without even looking at Paige. Glenn's shoulders relaxed, and he exhaled a relieved sigh.

"He's ready," said Helen. Glenn looked over his shoulder to see his sister. She forced a pained smile to her lips. Then she nodded. With Glenn's gentle push, Jude would soon give in to his nature and become an animal. He and Helen both hated this part, but it was necessary.

Glenn turned his attention to the young man.

"Are you still hungry?"

"I hurt," said Jude.

"I'll get you some medicine," said Glenn. "It'll make you feel better."

"Please help us," he said.

"Blessed are those who hunger and thirst for righteousness," said Glenn, reciting a favorite piece of scripture. "I can give you everything you need, but you have to earn it."

After eating even a quarter of a sandwich, Jude looked stronger and fitter than he had a moment earlier. He'd need that strength now.

"What do I need to do?" asked Jude.

"Do you admit that you're a sinner?"

"Yes," said Jude, nodding. He seemed sincere, but he didn't understand the depths of his own depravity yet.

"I wish I believed you," said Glenn, his voice almost a whisper. "Prove it. Go to Paige and take her."

Jude blinked, unsure of what he asked.

"I don't understand," he said.

"Yes, you do," said Glenn. "Give in to your nature. I can see it in your eyes. You want her. Take off her clothes and lay with her as a man does with his wife."

Jude looked to his girlfriend, shaking his head.

"She doesn't want to. Maybe if you give her some food. We'll do whatever you want."

"Food is for the strong," said Glenn. "If you want to eat, prove that you're a man. Rape your girlfriend."

"No," said Jude.

"Okay," said Glenn, smiling. The others had resisted at first, too. They all gave in soon enough. "Once you change your mind, you can have the rest of the sandwich. You can even share it with her. If you don't, you will both die here in more pain than you can ever imagine. Think about that. I'll be outside. Start when you're ready. I don't plan to watch."

Glenn didn't wait for a response. Instead, he put the sandwich on the ground outside the fence. Then, he walked to Helen and helped her up. The two intertwined their fingers and climbed the steps, just as they had done many times before. Helen cried, but she understood what they were doing.

They stopped at the top of the stairs and waited for almost ten minutes before Paige cried out.

"Please, don't."

She was louder than he had expected. The others had barely been able to whisper by this point. Everything about this couple had surprised him, though. He should have expected this as well.

"I don't want this."

Paige's voice was equally strong this time. Glenn squeezed his sister's hand.

"This had to happen," he said. "It won't be long now."

Helen nodded. For a few more moments, Glenn listened to the struggle downstairs. The bile rose in his throat as he heard Paige fight, cry, and fail to protect herself from her boyfriend's advances. As the teenagers coupled in the dungeon, Glenn removed a five-gallon bucket he had purchased at a home center from his trunk. He then walked down an overgrown path to a lakeshore that had once been alive with the sounds of laughing children. Now, it was silent.

Glenn filled his bucket to the brim and carried it to his dungeon. Helen sobbed at the top of the stairs, while no noise at all came from the bottom. Jude must have finished.

"Go," whispered Helen. "He did what he had to do. Now it's your turn. Finish this. Please."

Glenn nodded and carried his bucket downstairs. Paige lay on the cot. Her eyes were closed, and a threadbare blanket covered her to her chin. Jude sat on the ground beside her. Neither cried, which was unusual. From the start, though, Paige and Jude had exhibited an unusually strong bond for people this age. They had leaned on each other. It allowed them to last weeks longer than anyone else. Now that Jude had shattered that bond, this should go easier.

"It's time to go home," said Glenn, looking at Jude. "Your family will know what you did, but I'm sure they'll forgive you in time."

"What about Paige?"

Glenn drew in a breath through clenched teeth and shook his head.

"Paige has to stay. She has other appointments."

"What appointments?"

Glenn looked down and paced in front of the chain-link fence.

"It doesn't matter," he said. "After the betrayal you put her through, anything I can do would seem like a lover's kiss."

"I didn't want to hurt her," he said.

"And yet you did," said Glenn, turning to face him. "That's who you are. You need to accept that."

Jude stood and shook his head.

"I won't let you hurt her."

"I'm not going to touch her," said Glenn. "When her appointments arrive, I'll tell them to be gentle with her."

"Will you let her go afterwards?"

Glenn shook his head and knelt to look in Jude's eyes. Kids were so easy to manipulate.

"She's never leaving this place. She'll die here, but you get to choose how that happens," he said. "Option one, I take you home right now. You'll grow up and live a happy life, but you'll leave someone you love down here. Men will line up to have her just as you did. Option two, I give you a bucket with water, and you end her suffering. You become a hero and save her the pain of what comes ahead. It's your choice."

"I won't hurt her again," said Jude. "Please don't make me."

"You won't be hurting her," said Glenn. "You'll be saving her. As exhausted as she is, she won't fight. She'll welcome the release. Help her die. Drown her. You're the only one who can do it."

"And then I'll go free?" he asked.

"Sure," said Glenn. "Then I'll set you free."

Had Jude been healthy, he could have overpowered Glenn, but in his present state, he couldn't overpower a child. Paige didn't have the strength of a child, though. It wouldn't be long now. Glenn unlocked the padlock that held the gate shut but didn't open the door.

"Walk to the far wall and put your hands flat against the stone."

Jude did as Glenn asked and scurried away, allowing Glenn to step into the cell unmolested. He put the bucket beside Paige's bed. She didn't react. Once Glenn had the bucket in place, he stepped out and walked upstairs, where his sister waited for him.

"It's always surprising when they break," said Helen, leaning her head against her brother's shoulder once he sat down. "When we first tried this, I didn't know it would work."

"If you hurt someone enough, he'll do anything to make it stop," said Glenn.

"I suppose that's right," she said, squeezing his arm. Together, they sat and listened as the wind rustled the leaves of nearby trees, as insects buzzed, and as Paige thrashed her face inside the bucket as her boyfriend drowned her. With every moment Paige struggled, Helen squeezed tighter until Glenn thought her fingers would break through his skin.

And then there was silence.

"I did it," Jude called a moment later. "Now come down and let me go."

Glenn rubbed his sister's back.

"It's okay, sweetheart," he whispered. "No one will ever hurt you again. I'll take care of you this time."

She nodded and closed her eyes. "Do what you have to do."

He walked down the steps, knowing his task with this couple was drawing to a close. When he reached the bottom of the steps, he paused. The light was off. He thought he had left that on, though. It didn't matter at this point. If the light bulb had burned out, it had burned out. He'd get a new one for the next couple.

As he stepped forward, the gloom surrounded him. He couldn't see Paige's body, but water had spilled onto the floor.

"Jude?" he called. He paused and waited.

"Do it!"

Paige screamed. Glenn's breath caught in his throat, but before his eyes could adjust to the darkness, water hit him in the face. A shadow flashed to his left as something sharp and barbed pressed into his neck.

Then, pain exploded all over his body as electricity coursed through his system.

Chapter 16

I drove to my station and walked to the conference room the FBI had borrowed for their Apostate task force. The room was quiet, but a few agents sat in front of laptops around the conference table. Delgado was gone, but Agent Lawson closed a laptop at the head of the table and stood before walking toward me with a crooked smile on his face.

"Morning, Detective," he said, nodding. "Your dispatcher told me to expect you."

"Thank you for not going into hiding," I said. Lawson's lips curled into a smile, but it disappeared behind his professional countenance. "I'd like to talk to you again about Trinity and Thad, my missing teenagers. I'm still early in my investigation, but this looks like the Apostate."

"Walk with me," said Lawson, already heading toward the door. I followed along a step behind him as we left the room. "We can talk outside."

"Okay, I guess," I said. "But like I said, I visited—"

"It's a nice morning, isn't it?" asked Lawson, interrupting me as we approached the stairwell that led to the lobby.

"It's all sunshine all the time here in St. Augustine. Can't complain about that, huh?"

I hesitated as we walked down the stairs.

"Yeah, the weather's been nice lately—"

"It's too hot in the summer for me, though," he said, once more interrupting me before I could talk. "I'm four years from retirement, but my wife and I are looking for places. We like Irvine, California. The Pacific regulates the temperatures pretty well, so it doesn't get too hot in the summer, and it never gets too cold in the winter. Sounds just right for me."

Once more, I hesitated before speaking. We had reached the lobby. Trisha smiled from the front desk but said nothing. I smiled at her but focused on Agent Lawson. Evidently he wanted to make small talk. I could play along for a while.

"What would you do in California? You're not old enough to retire."

We crossed the lobby, and he held open the front door for me.

"I'll get something in private security for a while," he said. "Then, maybe, I'll take up golf."

"If I were in California, I think I'd learn to sail. It looks fun."

Lawson grunted as we passed through the door and onto the street. Once the door shut, Lawson glanced at me.

"Sorry about that. Your station has ears," he said. We walked a few feet down the sidewalk before he stopped and cocked his head at me. "You really want to learn how to sail?"

"Yeah," I said, smiling and imagining it. "Can you imagine drinking coffee in a boat in the middle of the ocean with nothing around and no sound but the waves beating against the sides? It sounds peaceful."

"It sounds lonely," he said.

"I'd be alone, but that wouldn't mean I'd be lonely."

"I'll take your word for it," said Lawson. He drew in a breath as we walked down the sidewalk. "I got an email this morning from Sheriff Delgado. After an exhaustive search, he determined that someone used his cell phone to contact Angela Pritchard and leak the information about the Apostate's church."

"I'm truly shocked," I said, my voice flat.

"He claimed someone stole the cell phone from his desk a week ago, but he promised to do his best to find it."

I glanced at Lawson but didn't break stride. "I hope you don't believe that."

"I do not," he said. "He's a weasel, but he's a weasel with authority. He gave me a stolen-property report dated six days ago alleging that someone took his cell phone from his locker in the men's room of your station."

"Okay," I said, nodding and putting that together. "He called Angela Pritchard and made a false police report to cover his ass."

"That's pretty much how I see it," said Lawson. "And that's the problem. If we're right and Delgado has that phone now, he's got evidence of a crime committed in his station, and he's covered by paperwork. I shouldn't have reacted the way I did to you two. I should have kept my concerns quiet and nailed him before he had the chance to point the finger elsewhere. I'm sorry."

I tilted my head to the side. "No harm, no foul, I guess. Where are we walking, anyway?"

"Coffee shop up the street," he said. "And there is harm. That phone is a weapon. He won't have enough to charge anyone with a crime, but if he hides that phone in your desk or in the desk of someone else he dislikes, he'll have every justification he needs to fire people."

The muscles in my back stiffened.

"Well, damn," I said. "I didn't consider that."

We walked for another few minutes.

"You want to talk about your missing kids now?" asked Agent Lawson.

"I'd rather run my boss over with a truck."

"Me, too," said Lawson. "Barring that, tell me what you found out about Trinity and Thad."

I scowled but then drew in a breath and nodded.

"They're still missing. I talked to the principal at their school, and he said they had a lot in common with Jude and Paige. They were the same age, they played sports, and they came from similar households. If the Apostate has a type, they're it."

Lawson nodded. "Except for drug dealer parents. None of the other kids had that kind of history."

"And nobody knew Trinity and Mackenzie did, either. Maybe the Apostate didn't know."

"That's possible," said Lawson. "It raises an issue, though. These kids are healthy athletes. We assumed the Apostate knew his victims well. We were thinking he might have been some kind of church official. If he doesn't even know his victims, though, how is he getting them to do what he wants? Thad weighs about two hundred pounds. He would have put up a fight if someone threatened his girlfriend."

It was a good question, one I couldn't answer. We walked for half a block and stopped at a street corner, where I saw a pair of girls crossing toward us. There was an older girl on a cell phone a few steps behind them. The older girl looked annoyed, which made me think she was babysitting her younger sisters. It reminded me of something.

"Mackenzie Foster lied about what happened to her and her sister," I said. "I thought she was covering for her sister and Thad, but what if she was covering for the Apostate?"

Lawson raised an eyebrow and then tilted his head down. "Like she's working with him?"

"No," I said. "More like he told her he'd kill her and her sister if she told anyone the truth. She's just a kid. If a crazy man with a gun threatened someone she loved, she might do what he said."

Lawson considered.

"Let's assume you're right. Let's assume the Apostate took Thad and Trinity, killed Trinity's parents, and threatened Mackenzie. He's escalated his behavior and become a lot bolder. He's taking risks he hasn't taken before. Why?"

"He knows we're on to him, and he's scared," I said. "He's worried he won't be able to finish his work before we catch him."

"And that work is?" asked Lawson.

I considered what I had seen so far and shook my head. "I don't know."

"At least our ignorance puts us all on the same page."

Agent Lawson and I walked the remaining half block to Rise and Grind, where he held the door open for me. I ordered a chai latte, and he got a black coffee and pecan roll at my suggestion. Our food and drinks came out within just a few minutes, and we took a table by the front window. An elderly couple sat at a table nearby, and three teenage girls sat near the front door. Otherwise, the dining room was empty.

Lawson almost said something, but I held up a hand to stop him once I noticed the teenage girls casting sidelong glances in our direction. I smiled at them. One of them stood from her table and walked toward us.

"Are you Detective Court? I saw you on TV," she said. I nodded and smiled again. "I'm Emma."

"Hi, Emma," I said. "What can I do for you?"

"We knew Paige," said Emma, looking over her shoulder at the other girls. "She was older than us, so we weren't friends, but she was nice."

I nodded again. Lawson looked annoyed at having our conversation interrupted, but I kept a smile on my face, encouraging her to keep speaking.

"Everybody says she was nice," I said.

Emma looked down.

"Is she dead?" she asked. "Nobody will tell us anything, and our parents won't even talk to us about it. There's all this stuff online, and we don't know whether it's true or whether it's made up or what."

"What kind of stuff are you seeing online?" asked Lawson.

"Just rumors," said Emma. "Nobody knows what's going on. We're scared."

Lawson started to say something, but I spoke before he could. I had been a young girl once, so I knew how to speak to one.

"It's okay to be scared. You may not see us, but we've got a lot of officers out on the streets. Until this blows over, it's best if you stay in groups and keep your phones handy. If someone creepy approaches you in the street, tell him to leave. If he doesn't, call 911. Nobody will judge you or think you're overreacting. At home, don't answer the door unless you know the person behind it and are expecting them. Most of all, use your head. If a situation seems wrong, call the police. If you use your eyes and your head, you'll be okay."

She didn't seem convinced, but she nodded.

"What about the Apostate? They say he's, like, some kind of devil worshiper."

"We're searching for him," I said. "If you want to help, call the police if you see something creepy. We'll take care of the Apostate."

"Okay," she said, turning. "Thanks, Detective. I saw Angela Pritchard's news story about you. I'm sorry."

"Thank you, but it was a long time ago."

Emma nodded and went back to her group. Lawson sipped his coffee and lowered his voice.

"Do people ask you about cases often?"

I shrugged. "More than usual since Jude and Paige disappeared. The Apostate scares people. It's natural."

He nodded and drew in a breath before reaching into his jacket for a notepad and flipping through pages.

"Our coroner identified the bodies at the church through dental records. Victims are John Rodgers, Matthew Bridges, James Tyler, Simon Fisher, and Andrew White."

I recognized the names from my initial research into the Apostate.

"Where does he dump the girls?"

"Not a clue," said Lawson. "Approximate times of death range from one year to two months. On two of the victims, our coroner found soot in the trachea below the vocal cords.

They had breathed in smoke, which means the Apostate burned them alive. You told Bryan Costa the Apostate had turned that church into hell. It was an astute observation."

My tea had cooled enough to drink.

"I don't like being right about that."

He put his cup down and glanced up at me with a crooked half smile on his face. "I rarely say nice things to people. You should accept the compliment."

"Thank you," I said, returning his smile with a tight one of my own. "What do we do next?"

"Keep working the double homicide. The Apostate didn't kill your victims or abduct Trinity and Thad. I'm sorry."

I put my drink down and furrowed my brow.

"Is that conjecture, or do you know something I don't?"

"We've ID'd the Apostate from a fingerprint found in the church," he said. "He's an art history professor who sits on the admissions committee at Waterford College—which every victim applied to. He's a loner, he's white, he's intelligent, and he had access to every victim's admissions application. He fits our profile, and he's got a flair for the dramatic. Two years ago, he curated an exhibit at the St. Louis Art Museum called *Expositions from Hell*. It was a series of paintings by Hieronymus Bosch."

I stayed silent as that set in.

"Does he have a record?" I asked.

"No, which is why it took us a while to find him," said Lawson. "We found a set of prints at the church but didn't

THE BOYS IN THE CHURCH

have anything to match them with until a couple of hours ago when a member of the college's custodial staff gave us a cup from his office."

I looked down at my drink and nodded.

"Why would an art history professor murder his potential students?" I asked.

Lawson sipped his coffee and then took a bite of his pecan roll while tilting his head to the side and raising his eyebrows.

"If you want answers, you're in the wrong business. In law enforcement, we make arrests. If we're lucky, we prevent tragedy. We don't give answers. I thought you'd be excited to hear we're close to arresting a serial murderer who's already killed a lot of people."

That broke me out of my stupor. I drew in a breath and nodded.

"I am glad, but it's bittersweet," I said. "If you're right, Trinity and Thad are once again my primary suspects in the murder of Mark and Lilly Foster. For a while, it was nice to think they were innocent kids."

"Don't focus on innocent or guilty. Focus on alive and dead. Trinity and Thad may have killed Mark and Lilly Foster, but they're alive. They'll spend a few years in prison, but they'll get out when they're still young enough to rebuild their lives. You can give them a chance to start over. Before you can do that, though, you've got to catch them."

He was right. He was also inspiring. Without wishing it, I found the corners of my mouth turning upward.

CHRIS CULVER

"That was helpful," I said. "You're much better at giving speeches than my actual boss."

Lawson smiled.

"Thank you," he said before drinking his coffee. "Like you said, I'm not your boss, so you don't have to listen to me. But can I give you some advice on your case?"

"Sure," I said, resting my elbows on the table.

"You've been up all night after working the entire day previous. Go home and sleep."

I scoffed and picked up my tea. "That's your big advice? I was expecting something wise and uplifting."

"You're no good to anybody if you're exhausted. You've got a good team, and they're working. They need a leader who can keep up with them, not somebody so tired she struggles to put her thoughts in order."

I raised an eyebrow. "Do I sound as if I'm struggling to order my thoughts?"

"Not yet, but it's not even noon, and you've got a lot of work ahead of you," said Lawson. "Trust your team. Go home, sleep, and then get an update."

"No one has ever ordered me to take a nap before."

"It wasn't an order," said Lawson. "It was a suggestion."

I focused on my paper cup of tea and felt my limbs grow just a little heavy. I stood as a dull, constant pain traveled up my legs and into my spine.

"Looks like I'm going home to take a nap," I said. The moment the words left my lips, I yawned. "If I didn't know

156

you were an FBI agent, I'd suspect you put something in my drink."

Lawson stood up. "Go home, Detective. You've earned a few hours off."

"Yes, sir," I said, picking up my tea. Lawson and I walked back to the station in relative silence. Once we reached the building, he went inside, while I got in my truck. As I drove home, I wondered what it would be like to work for a boss like that. Sheriff Delgado was a horrible human being, but the two sheriffs before him had been good at their jobs. I had learned a lot working with them, but none of them had ever reminded me of my reasons for becoming a police officer. They had never made me feel as if the work mattered. Agent Lawson did. That was a rare gift. I hoped his employees appreciated that.

Once I got home, I locked up, changed into some pajamas, and crashed onto the bed for one of the best naps of my life.

Chapter 17

I slept for a few hours and woke up when the hinges of my front door squealed open. The sun still beat against the curtains in my bedroom, and my lips were chapped, but my body felt relaxed and strong. I swung my legs off the bed.

"Hey, Joe, you around?"

The voice belonged to Harry Grainger, St. Augustine's former sheriff and one of the very few persons who had a key to my house.

"In my room," I called. "Give me a minute."

I threw on a pair of jeans and a clean white T-shirt before leaving my bedroom. Harry was in the living room, looking through the piles of paper on my coffee table. He had a white file box at his feet and a coy smile on his face.

"The county's only full-time detective sleeping through the heart of the day," he said. "Oh, how the standards have fallen since my retirement."

"Shove it, boss," I said. "I picked up a double homicide late last night and didn't get much sleep. What's going on?"

"Just delivering the day's gossip," he said, motioning toward his file box. "It's thinner than usual."

I nodded. "Yeah, Agent Lawson is boxing Sheriff Delgado out of the Apostate case. I'm surprised we can access anything. Trisha still at work?"

Harry nodded and sat down to pop the top off the box.

"Most of what we've got are phone dumps from the victims," he said, pulling out two thick manila envelopes. "The boys and girls who were dating spoke to each other often, but none of the couples contacted the other couples. So that's a dead end."

I yawned and stretched.

"The Bureau's got a suspect," I said. "They matched fingerprints at the church to a man who fits their profile. They've got their guy."

Harry paused and cocked his head at me. "Why haven't they made an arrest?"

I shrugged. "I don't know. Maybe they're trying to shore up their case against him. Maybe they're hoping he'll lead them to his other victims if they watch him long enough. Either way, they've got him under surveillance twenty-four hours a day. He didn't kill my victims last night."

Harry leaned back and crossed his arms. "Is that a bad thing?"

"Yeah. My case is ugly. I don't want to talk about it."

He nodded. "Who's the Bureau's suspect?"

"An art history professor on the admissions committee at Waterford College. The kids all applied to the same school, so he had all their contact information. That was the connection. He fits the profile, but even if their profile is off, it's hard to argue against fingerprints."

Harry ran a hand across his brow and then looked at the stacks of paper on the ground and the whiteboards scattered throughout the room.

"So it's over. I hate to admit it, but I'll miss this," he said. "I was useful again."

"Oh, even if you're not working a case, you're still useful," I said. "Just look at all the stuff you carried into my living room. I mean, you've got at least a few more years until your back and legs give out. You can start a moving service. You can call it 'Old Man and a Truck.'"

"Ha," he said, his voice and face flat and devoid of emotion. I smiled.

"You're a friend who's there when I need him, too, so you've got that going for you."

Harry's expression softened a little, and he nodded.

"At least I've got that," he said. "Because I care about you, I'll leave all the heavy file boxes in your living room. I know how hard it is to find time to exercise when you're on the job. This way, you dovetail two activities into one."

"You're a real pal," I said, standing.

Harry stood and nodded. "Since this is over, I'm going fishing. If you need anything, call me."

"Will do, old man," I said. I walked him to the front door and waved as he drove off. I felt better than I had when I first got home, but I didn't feel energized. Still, I had work to do. I pulled out my cell phone to call Darlene McEvoy with my forensics lab, but I stopped and groaned when I saw a reminder on the screen. I had a meeting scheduled with my therapist at five. Terrific.

I took a shower and then made a turkey and cheese sandwich for a late afternoon snack before hopping in my truck. It didn't take long to drive downtown, so, before going to my session, I stopped by Rise and Grind for the second time that day and purchased a bottle of water along with a cheese danish. The danish tasted good, and the water was wet. I couldn't complain.

Afterward, I went to Dr. Taylor's office and did my best to avoid saying anything personal for an hour. It took work to stay evasive that long with a persistent therapist, but eventually Dr. Taylor's frustration overcame her professional demeanor.

"This will be our last meeting," she said near the end of our session. "I can give you the names of other therapists, but you obviously don't value my time or expertise."

"It's not personal," I said. "You're a good therapist, but I don't need therapy."

She smiled, but it didn't reach her eyes.

"Do you have nightmares?" she asked.

"Everybody has nightmares."

"Do you have them every night?"

I looked out the window.

"If you lived my life, you'd have nightmares, too."

"I know I would," she said, nodding. "And I'd see a therapist."

I smiled to humor her and then tilted my head to the side.

"The nightmares are a symptom, doc. I've had them my whole life, and I can deal with them. The things I have a hard time dealing with are my memories. Can you do anything about those?"

She blinked and then folded her hands together.

"I can help you process the things that have happened to you to help you overcome the tragedies of your past. That's my job."

"I've already processed my memories. I know who I am. My mother was a drug-addicted prostitute who couldn't get her life together to take care of her kid. I'm a woman whose foster father raped her before she even had a driver's license. I'm the adopted daughter of a family that loves and supports me. And I'm the woman who fired her weapon in the line of duty while trying to protect two of her colleagues—one of whom died and the other of whom was permanently injured.

"I also drink too much, I have few friends, and I push away everybody in my life because I don't want anyone to hurt me. Some days I feel sad. Other days I feel lonely. I still wake up every morning and put on my badge and go to work because that's my job. If you can help me do my job better, great. If you can't, thanks for trying. I appreciate what you're doing, but I'm fine."

Dr. Taylor blinked and smiled, her expression soft.

"Leaning on other people doesn't make you weak," she said. "You understand that?"

I tilted my head to the side. "Intellectually."

Dr. Taylor closed her notepad. "Do you have someone you can talk to? A friend? A boyfriend?"

"I'm well-loved," I said.

She lowered her chin. "Please answer my question. Do you have someone you can talk to?"

Trisha at my station would sit and talk if I needed her. Harry would, too. As much as I cared about them, though, I couldn't open up to them. Only one person came to mind.

"My mom. She was a police officer."

Dr. Taylor considered me and then stood and walked to her desk.

"I'm signing your return-to-duty form," she said. "If you're willing to talk like this, I wouldn't mind seeing you again. Maybe once a month."

"Is that necessary?"

She looked up at me. "It would help you, but it's just a recommendation. Think about it. In your job, it's nice to have someone objective to talk to."

"Sure," I said. "I'll think about it."

"That's all I can ask for," she said, smiling.

I left the doctor's office a few minutes later and drove to the grocery store, where I picked up a frozen pizza and ingredients for a salad. It was a lot of food for one person, but it'd get me through two or three days. When I reached the house, I turned on my oven and checked my phone. While in Dr. Taylor's office, I had missed one call from my station and two others from the same unknown number.

As a detective, I passed out a lot of business cards to potential witnesses and sources, so it wasn't uncommon for complete strangers to call at crazy hours to tell me things. Most of those calls wasted my time, but now and then somebody offered information I never would have gotten otherwise.

The caller could have been a witness on a case. Or it could have been a lonely person who thought I had a nice ass. I got those calls, too. Whoever it was, I needed to return it. I dialed the number and sat down at my breakfast table in the kitchen. The phone rang three times before a small, female voice answered. My entire world stopped at once because, with one word, I knew who had called me.

"Aunt Lacey?" I asked.

"Joey?"

I had loved Aunt Lacey, but I hadn't expected to feel my throat tighten or my skin to tingle when I heard her voice again.

"Yeah," I said. "It's Joe. I called you the other day. I hope I didn't bother you."

"No, honey," she said, her voice still as sweet as I remembered. "You're not bothering me. How are you? I've seen you on TV."

I didn't know which news appearance she was referencing, but cops didn't make the news for good things. My appearances had been for reasons worse than most lately.

"I'm good," I said. "I'm happy."

"I'm glad to hear it," she said. We lapsed into an uneasy silence for a few seconds. Then I cleared my throat.

"I called because I was hoping to talk to you about Erin," I said.

"Your mom," said Lacey. I shook my head even though she couldn't see me.

"I came out of Erin, but she wasn't my mom," I said. "It's important you understand that."

Lacey drew in a pained, low breath. "Erin tried her best. She loved you."

If Erin had loved me, she would have gotten her life together for me. Lacey didn't want to hear my vitriol, though, and I hadn't called to start a fight. Besides, as much as I wanted to hate Erin, I couldn't. Years ago, I had made a conscious decision to cut her out of my life. I gave up feeling anything at all toward her. Even still, my skin grew hot, my throat tightened, and my heart pounded.

"I understand she thought so," I said, trying to keep my voice level and controlled. "I didn't call you to hear excuses for her."

Lacey paused.

"I'm sorry if that's what you think I was doing," she said, her voice soft. "I'm glad you called, Joey. I've missed hearing your voice."

It wasn't a rebuke, but it stung like one. I drew in a deep breath and ran a hand across my face. My arms and legs felt heavy. Lacey was fifty or sixty miles away from me, but I wanted to get behind my furniture and hide.

"I'm sorry I lost touch. Life got hard after Erin overdosed. I was bouncing around from one foster home to another."

"It was hard for me, too. I lost my friend, and I lost my niece."

Growing up, I didn't have a grandma or a big sister to hold me at night and tell me I'd be okay. I had a mom who shot heroin and turned tricks in cheap hotels. Aunt Lacey was the closest thing I had to family. She hugged me when I cried and loved me even when I misbehaved. She hadn't wanted anything from me, either. At the time, I didn't understand how rare that kind of love was. I did now. For a few seconds, my lips moved, but no words came out. Finally, I drew in a breath.

"I'm sorry," I said, blinking hard as my eyes grew moist. "This is harder than I thought. I need to go."

"Don't hang up yet," said Lacey. "You and your mom had differences, but she left you some things when she died. You need to call her lawyer. She's a nice lady. Her name is Brenda Collins. She works in Clayton."

"Erin gave me enough memories and scars as is," I said. "Whatever this lawyer has, tell her I don't want it. If it's valuable, she can donate it to the Salvation Army."

"Honey, you need to call—"

"I've got to go," I said. "I'm sorry. I'll talk to you later."

I hung up before she said anything else. Then I stared at my phone, half-wishing for her to call me back and half-dreading to hear it ring and to see her number on the screen. I had so many emotions running through me that I didn't have names for most of them. My skin felt both hot and cold, my heart raced, my eyes burned with tears, and every muscle in my body twitched.

Above all that anger and pain, though, I felt guilty. Aunt Lacey had loved me, and I had loved her. She may not have been a blood relative, but she had cared for me when Erin couldn't. She deserved better than to be pushed out of my life and forgotten.

I didn't want to feel all that anymore, so I put my phone on the breakfast table and grabbed a glass from the cupboard beside my sink. Pizza and salad could wait. Now, I needed a drink. I poured myself two shots of vodka from the bottle in my freezer and felt the ice-cold liquid slide down my throat.

More than friends, more than family, more than anything, I needed relief. That was why therapy didn't work for me. As long as I could remember my past, I'd grieve for it. Liquor made me forget. It was as simple as that.

I poured myself another shot and carried my glass to the living room, where I sat down on my sofa—just as I had sat hundreds of times before—and drank until the world stopped hurting.

Chapter 18

My alarm woke me up at a little before seven the next morning. My mouth felt as if it were stuffed full of cotton balls, and my head pounded with every beat of my heart. At least I wasn't nauseated. Those were the worst hangovers. Headaches and dry mouth I could deal with.

I swung my legs off the bed and walked to the kitchen, where I choked down two big glasses of water and two ibuprofen. The pills and water would take time to work through my system, but both ought to help me feel better. After that, I took a shower, got dressed, ate a cup of oatmeal, and then headed out.

My station was buzzing as I arrived. The morning shift was heading home, and the day shift was just coming into work. I grabbed a cup of coffee from the break room and joined the rest of the staff in the conference room for that morning's briefing. Delgado seemed even more cantankerous than usual and expressed his disappointment in the amount of gas our patrol officers had wasted answering calls and the relative dearth of tickets written by our officers manning the speed traps the night before.

I was tempted to remind him that serial murderers kept the tourists and speeders away, but I kept my mouth shut through the ten-minute briefing. Delgado didn't ask about my homicide case, which was just as well because I had nothing new to report. At ten after eight, the sheriff dismissed us all, and I tried to walk to my desk. Before I could even leave the conference room, though, he put a hand on my elbow.

"You hold on a sec, Detective," he said. "I want to talk to you."

I turned and forced a smile to my lips. "Sure."

The two of us watched and waited while our colleagues left. Once we were alone, Delgado focused on me with his arms crossed.

"Didn't see too much of you yesterday," he said. "Care to share what you were doing?"

"In the morning, I was working a homicide. In the afternoon, I was sleeping after having been awake the previous twenty-four hours."

He nodded and glowered. "I suppose you ladies need your beauty sleep."

Delgado's idiotic jabs had long since stopped making me angry. Now they annoyed me.

"Anything else?" I asked, raising my eyebrows and forcing a smile to my face.

"You had coffee with Agent Lawson."

"I did," I said, nodding.

"What did you talk about?" he asked, stepping up on his toes so he could look down his nose at me.

"My private conversations are my own. I had coffee with a colleague during a break. If that's a problem, you can take it up with my union rep."

He blinked a few times and shifted his weight back to his heels.

"You've never liked me, have you?"

"That's not true," I said. "Before we worked together, I was completely indifferent toward you."

Delgado held his eyes on me for a moment before sighing and walking toward the conference room's table and pacing along the far side of the room.

"We've got a problem in this station," he said. "Somebody's been leaking confidential information to the press."

"So I've heard," I said, raising my eyebrows. I lowered my voice as if we were conspiring. "I hear they had the audacity to steal the sheriff's cell phone and use that themselves to make it look like the call came from him."

He stopped pacing and turned toward me with his arms crossed.

"What did you hear about that?"

I scoffed. "Oh, come on, George. You called Angela Pritchard and told her about the church."

"Why would I do that?"

I scoffed again and shook my head before seeing he was serious.

"Okay, sure," I said. "If you want to play a game, I'll play along. You called her because it was a big break in a huge case. It got air time across the Midwest. The County Council appointed you to your position, but to stay in the job, you'll need to win an election. That's hard to do when nobody knows you, but if you become the guy who broke the Apostate case, the campaign slogans will write themselves."

He narrowed his gaze. "You have a devious mind, Detective."

"No, I don't," I said, shaking my head. "I'm leaving now. I've got better things to do than to waste my time talking to you."

He said something else, but I left before he could finish. As long as Delgado was the sheriff, my future in the department was questionable, but as long as I had a job, I'd do it the best I could. That meant ignoring my boss and getting to work.

I walked downstairs to our small forensics lab. The stainless-steel door was locked, but light spilled through its frosted-glass panel. Nobody answered my knock, but somebody was around. I leaned against the wall for about five minutes, waiting. When Darlene came down the stairs with a cup of coffee in her hand, her eyes opened wide.

"Oh, hey, Joe," she said, smiling. "I was getting coffee upstairs when I got caught by Jason Zuckerburg on his way out the door. He's a talker."

I smiled and nodded. "I've heard that."

Darlene stepped past me and used a key from her purse to unlock the lab.

"Coming from you, I don't imagine this is a social visit," she said, opening the door. I hesitated.

"What makes you think this isn't a social call?"

Darlene stopped in her tracks and cocked her head at me.

"I assumed," she said. "You're not the talkative sort. Emily Hayes said you made a joke the other day."

"I remember," I said. "She didn't think it was funny."

Darlene smiled before turning toward her office. "You'll get better. What can I do for you, Detective?"

I looked around. Our forensics lab had a thousand clean and well-appointed square feet. Darlene walked toward a desk built into the far wall. White evidence boxes stacked four high surrounded her like a child's fort.

"I was hoping to see where you were on the Lilly and Mark Foster murders."

"Sure," she said, raising her eyebrows. "Your killer shot his victims with a nine-millimeter pistol. Dr. Sheridan extracted five bullets, which I've examined. By the twist and the lands and grooves, they were fired by a Glock 19. If you find a firearm, we should be able to test for a match.

"Based on the quantity of drugs found in the house, I requested assistance from the State Highway Patrol. They're going to try to break into the victims' cell phones to see what they can find."

"Did you request a dump of their texts and phone calls?"

She nodded. "I did. Their cell provider hasn't responded to my request."

I nodded and put my hands on my hips. "Thanks for your work on this. I appreciate it."

"My pleasure," said Darlene. I gave her a half smile before turning to leave. She called out before I could even take a step. "Hey, Joe. I shouldn't ask this, but do you think the Apostate killed Lilly and Mark?"

I turned toward her and shook my head. "No. Part of me wishes he had, but my strongest suspects are a couple of teenagers."

A smile formed on Darlene's lips.

"Cases like this make me glad I don't have children."

"You and me both," I said, turning. "Let me know if anything turns up."

Darlene said she would, so I walked upstairs. For the next fifteen minutes, I wrote notes at my desk and checked my email before stretching and giving myself a moment to think. With the Apostate out, Trinity and Thad were my prime suspects in the murders of Lilly and Mark Foster. By now, every police officer in the state would have seen their pictures, and every trooper with the Missouri Highway Patrol was looking for their car. If they were in Missouri—or any of the surrounding states that exchanged information with us—we'd find them. I hoped they came in before anyone else got hurt.

As I started writing an email to the Highway Patrol's liaison to thank him for his help on the Lilly and Mark Foster cases, I noticed Agent Lawson walking toward my desk. He looked at me and gestured with his head toward the lobby.

"Time to get moving, Detective," he said. "We've got a busy morning, and we're late for a briefing upstairs."

"Oh, yeah?" I asked, straightening.

"Yeah. It's a big meeting, and you want to be in on it."

I allowed a polite smile to form on my lips. "I usually make that decision for myself."

Lawson's lips were straight, and his demeanor was professional, if a little stern.

"Do you trust me, Detective?"

I tilted my head to the side. "I don't trust anyone around here."

"Probably smart. Give me your phone and come upstairs anyway."

"My phone?"

"Yep," he said. "That's the price of admission, and it's non-negotiable."

Lawson hadn't led me astray or lied to me so far. I didn't think he'd lie now, but giving him my phone felt strange. Still, I reached into my purse.

"Do I get a receipt or anything?"

He scoffed, but his lips curled upward. "Come on. Just give me the phone. I'll keep it with me until we're done."

I handed him my cell, which he powered off and put in an inside pocket in his jacket.

"So what did I earn by giving you my phone?"

"A seat at the table," he said. "We're arresting the Apostate this morning."

I shot to my feet.

"Did you tell Delgado?"

"No, but he found out anyway. He's upstairs, but my people are watching him. Let's go."

I nodded and followed the FBI agent upstairs to the second-floor conference room. About a dozen FBI agents stood around in tactical vests. The room held a nervous, almost frantic energy. These men and women understood what lay ahead for them.

As Lawson walked through the room, the crowd quieted. Sheriff Delgado stood by himself at the foot of the conference room's table. Lawson walked to the head and smiled to his team.

"Morning, everybody. You know why we're here and what we're doing. Our suspect lives on a half-acre plot in a developed residential area. Our plan is to drive to the suspect's neighborhood in civilian vehicles and park in the locations I have already given you. At my signal, Mike's team will infiltrate the suspect's home through his front door, while Stacy's team surrounds the house from the rear. Everyone else will stay in their cars in case the suspect evades our other teams. A helicopter will be overhead in case he bolts."

Lawson opened a folder on the table in front of him and sorted through some documents before holding up a picture.

"Our suspect is Gallen Marshall."

The instant I saw the picture, I gasped before I could stop myself. Lawson looked at me, his brow furrowed, before focusing on his team again.

"Mr. Marshall is a forty-seven-year-old Caucasian male. We consider him armed and extremely dangerous. He lives alone, although female students frequently visit and stay the night. You all know your jobs, and most of you have seen this information already. Let's get to it."

Three agents clapped, but most of them left the room, preparing for the job ahead. Lawson and Sheriff Delgado crossed the room toward me.

"Something you want to tell me, Detective?" asked Lawson.

"I know your suspect," I said, glancing at Delgado and then at Lawson. "He didn't do this."

Chapter 19

Delgado glowered at me and crossed his arms.

"How do you know he's not the Apostate?"

I glanced at Delgado and then at Agent Lawson. "We should talk in private."

"Anything you say to him, say to me," said Delgado. "I'm your superior officer."

I looked at Delgado. "You're my boss, but 'superior' is a stretch."

"Excuse me?" he asked, cocking his head to the side and raising his eyebrows. Lawson cleared his throat before I responded.

"How do you know Gallen Marshall?" he asked.

Once more, I glanced at Delgado before looking toward the FBI agent.

"I'd rather have this conversation in private."

"Were you sleeping with him?" asked Delgado. I scowled at him.

"No, and please don't ask about my private life again," I said. "It's inappropriate. You should know that."

Agent Lawson crossed his arms and blinked, his eyes hard. "How do you know him, Detective?"

I exhaled a long breath, considering my options. Another request for privacy would simply add fuel to Delgado's innuendo-filled speculations. Even though I knew Marshall, I hadn't done anything wrong. I had nothing to be ashamed of.

"My mom persuaded me to go to an Alcoholics Anonymous meeting. She wanted me to see what it was like," I said, looking at Delgado. "I'm not a drunk, okay? Put that on the record. I went because my mom asked me to go, not because I needed to go."

Delgado scoffed and rolled his eyes, but Lawson's expression didn't change.

"How does Gallen Marshall fit into this?"

I tilted my head to the side. "I'm not supposed to talk about what goes on in the group, but he was there."

Lawson nodded and looked to Sheriff Delgado.

"Can you excuse us for a minute, George?" he asked.

"This is my station," he said, pointing toward the ground. "You don't get to kick me out."

"Okay," said Lawson, putting a hand on my elbow. "Detective Court and I are going for a walk."

Delgado sputtered something, but Lawson hustled me out of the building. Two minutes later, we climbed into the front seats of a black SUV in the parking lot, and he drew in a deep breath.

"Okay," he said, nodding. "You've got my attention. Tell me about Marshall."

I shook my head and closed my eyes. "I shouldn't have even told you I saw him at a meeting. It's called Alcoholics *Anonymous* for a reason."

Lawson drew in a slow breath.

"Based on what you know of him, does he pose a threat to the arresting team or himself?"

My shoulders slumped.

"Yeah," I said, my voice low. "He's depressed. Four years ago, his wife died of metastatic breast cancer. That's when he started drinking. A year later, he tried to kill himself by driving into a tree. He hit his head on the windshield, but he didn't die. Since then, he's been trying to stay sober, but he has a hard time. He's angry at God for allowing his wife to die, and he's mad at himself for becoming a drunk. He doesn't think he's got a lot to live for. If your team shows up with weapons drawn, there's a good chance he'll turn it into a fight."

Lawson nodded and drummed his fingers on the steering wheel before drawing in a breath.

"Okay. I'll update my team. Thanks for this."

He opened his door, but I put a hand on his arm, stopping him.

"I'm not sure this is your guy," I said. "How sure are you about this?"

Lawson stopped moving and looked back at me.

"Very. Aside from the fingerprint at the church, he fits our profile. He led a movement at Waterford College to remove all religious iconography from the campus and to remove all references to religion from the school's fight song and motto. He's got a problem with religion and religious people.

"Not only that, his position on the admissions committee at Waterford gave him access to the personal information of every one of our victims. Some of them even mentioned they were dating another applicant in their personal essays. Those kids who didn't mention their partners in their essays probably mentioned them online somewhere. It's standard practice for admissions committees to look up applicants on social media nowadays.

"Bottom line, Marshall knew these kids, he understands religious symbolism, and we found his fingerprints on two different pews at the church. We can tie him to the site of a body dump."

The evidence was compelling. I looked out my window and sighed.

"I guess I don't want to believe I met a serial murderer and failed to see him for what he was."

"It wasn't just you," said Lawson. "It was his colleagues, his friends, and his surviving family. You met him at a meeting. His neighbors talked to him every day and had no clue."

That was true, but I wasn't the average person. I was a police officer, and I should have seen something. It didn't even register that Marshall was anything but what he appeared to be. He may have murdered those kids, but I didn't stop him when I should have. That was on me.

"Let's pick him up."

Lawson and I returned to the station. Delgado said nothing, but his glare told me he planned to chew me out when he had the chance. As much as I liked St. Augustine, and as much as I enjoyed being a detective, my tenure in this station was running out. When the County Council appointed Delgado as the sheriff, it tacitly gave me an ultimatum: do as Delgado says—even when your professional instincts say he's wrong—or look for a new job. Every day brought me closer to leaving.

Lawson addressed his officers upstairs again while I grabbed my tactical vest from my locker. Then we headed out. Lawson and I took his SUV while Delgado elected to drive by himself in his personal pickup. Gallen Marshall's neighborhood was about two blocks from the main entrance of Waterford College, making it popular with the school's staff and faculty. The homes were nice and modern while the lots were large enough that kids had ample room to play. There were basketball hoops in a lot of driveways.

"It's crowded here," I said. "The neighbors would have heard if he kept teenagers prisoner here."

"Agreed," said Lawson. "We've been watching him for four days, but we're not sure where his kill room is yet. One of my agents has compiled a list of abandoned churches in Missouri and the surrounding states. We'll find it."

I stared out my window, wishing I shared his confidence. Churches didn't pop up in the middle of nowhere. Their congregations built them to serve the local community. If he had dumped bodies at another church, somebody would have found it by now.

As we turned a corner, the car slowed.

"Son of a bitch," said Lawson. I followed the special agent's gaze toward a news van on the side of the road. Angela Pritchard, a cameraman, and a third man in jeans and a button-down shirt stood outside, preparing to film. "How did she get here before we did? Delgado didn't even know what was going on until about fifteen minutes ago."

"She must have been staying in town," I said. Lawson swore again and stopped the SUV as his cell phone rang. Lawson answered his phone and glared at the reporter. She looked at us, but she didn't come near us. Lawson swore again as the antenna on the news van lifted for a live broadcast. After about thirty seconds on the phone, Lawson hung up and reached down to the armrest on his door to unlock the vehicle.

"Marshall just left Waterford. He's driving a gray Acura SUV. You know Pritchard, so talk to her and persuade her to move. If Marshall sees her, we've got a problem."

Though I had told Angela Pritchard I had nothing to say to her several times in the past few weeks, I wouldn't have said I knew her. We didn't have time to squabble over semantics, though, so I nodded and stepped out. Lawson backed up the SUV and disappeared down a side road. I waved toward the news van as Ms. Pritchard walked toward me.

"Detective," she said, smiling that fake news-anchor's grin. "We're about to go live, so it's good you're here. You can fill my audience in on what's happening in the Apostate investigation."

"We need you to turn the camera off, get in your car, and drive out of the neighborhood," I said. "This is a dangerous situation, and we can't guarantee your safety."

Pritchard tilted her head to the side and sighed. "You've got a suspect in the Apostate case, and you're about to make an arrest. If you think I'm leaving now, you're nuts. We have every right to broadcast from a public street."

I looked around. From my current vantage, I had clear sightlines to the road outside the neighborhood, the neighborhood's entrance, and to two different intersections. As soon as Marshall turned onto the street, he'd see the news van. And that was a problem.

Families lived in this neighborhood. There was a kid's bicycle in the driveway of the home nearest Pritchard's van and a tricycle beside the front door of the home next door. Our quick strike and arrest would turn ugly unless we made Pritchard disappear right now. We didn't have time to argue.

"Fine," I said. "What do you want? You want an exclusive with the FBI agent in charge of the investigation? I can get you that. I can't guarantee he'll answer your questions, but I can get you in the room with him. Just leave now."

She thought for a few moments. "Agent Lawson has a certain presence about him, and his FBI badge is sexy, but you're a ratings gold mine, Joe. People love you. That background piece I produced about you six weeks ago got so many views it almost took our web server down. We got calls for weeks about that piece. People like you. They want to understand you better."

"Fine," I said, nodding. "I'll give you an interview. Take your antenna down and get out."

She shook her head. "While I'd appreciate an interview, that's not what I had in mind. I want a feature story. Life behind the scenes in a real, working police station with a real, working police officer. I want to know about your struggles, your triumphs, your regrets, your successes...I want everything, and I want it on camera. We'll show the world your life—the good and the bad. How does that sound?"

I wanted to tell her it sounded like the worst idea I had ever heard of, but I held my breath when I noticed movement out of the corner of my eye from the entrance. It was a gray SUV.

"Get out of here right now."

That drew the cameraman's attention. Pritchard turned her attention to her producer.

"Did you get that, Jack?"

He nodded, took a step back, and pointed toward the news van again. Muscles all over my body twitched.

"Get in your van and leave. Please. If you don't do as I ask, people will get hurt."

"Why would they get hurt?" asked Pritchard.

The gray SUV turned down the street. The world seemed to slow. I tried not to look at Marshall's SUV as he passed, but even from a distance, I recognized him in the driver's seat. His eyes passed over me and Angela Pritchard. Then he sped up.

"Get out of here right now," I said, waving the news crew toward their van. "This area isn't safe."

The SUV's tires shrieked as the heavy vehicle came to a stop in the driveway of a brick home half a block away. Marshall vaulted out and sprinted toward his house. As he did that, a red sports sedan careened through the neighborhood's entrance while a black SUV hurtled toward the house from the other direction. The news crew practically fell over each other jumping out of the road as the little red car sped toward Marshall's house. Agents in tactical vests jumped out of both cars and sprinted toward the home and then through its open front door.

I brought my hands to my head, my heart pounding. The men inside the home were screaming. The sound was more animal than human.

"Gun! Gun!"

I almost dove to the grass as multiple gunshots rang out. Men inside the home screamed, but I couldn't understand what they said. Then, there was silence. I didn't know what was going on, but we needed medical assistance. I pulled out my phone and called Trisha to request an ambulance. As I did that, Pritchard started speaking.

"We're broadcasting live at the home address of Gallen Marshall," she said, leaning close to the camera and whispering. "My sources within the FBI and the St. Augustine County Sheriff's Department have told me that law enforcement has identified him as the Apostate killer. There's been a shooting inside the home. We don't know who's alive and who's not, but we'll be staying on the scene as long as we're safe."

I wanted to punch her, but that wouldn't have looked good on live TV, so I stayed off camera while Pritchard and her crew filmed the house. Trisha routed paramedics to our location. When Agent Lawson's black SUV pulled up to the home, Pritchard pointed him out by name and rank. He ran into the house where he stayed for five minutes before leaving once more and walking toward us. Sirens blared in the distance as the paramedics drove over.

Pritchard stood straighter and walked. Then she motioned for her camera crew to follow.

"Agent Lawson, I'm Angela Pritchard with KSTL news. Can you tell us what just happened?"

Agent Lawson's eyes were cold and angry. He looked at the camera.

"Yeah. I can tell you what happened. My team and I executed a high-risk arrest warrant on a dangerous suspect.

When we arrived at the scene, we found a camera crew had beaten us here. Our suspect saw that camera crew and ran inside for a weapon. The moment my officers announced themselves, the suspect opened fire, hitting two of my men."

Lawson looked to Pritchard.

"Congratulations, Ms. Pritchard. You turned a routine but high-risk arrest into a dangerous situation in which two men—two fathers and husbands—were shot."

Even as Lawson spoke, Pritchard turned to her cameraman and ran her hand across her neck, telling him to kill the feed. As Lawson walked away, she sighed.

"How much of that made the air?"

"Up to 'congratulations,'" said the producer.

She looked thoughtful for a moment, but then she smiled. "We'll edit that scene out when we rebroadcast."

I walked away, but Pritchard hurried to catch up with me.

"My offer still stands, Detective," she said. "I'm a fan. I'd make you look good."

I stopped walking and looked into her eyes. She smiled that big, fake newscaster grin.

"Piss off."

Chapter 20

Glenn's eyes fluttered open. His entire body felt stiff and weak, and his neck burned. At first, he didn't recognize his surroundings, but then his eyes adjusted to the dark. He shivered as he sat up. Water slid down his back and into the puddle in which he sat. He slipped off his mask and tossed it to the ground.

"Helen?"

His voice shook as his eyes passed over the dark room.

"Oh, Glenn," said Helen, running down the stairs. "What happened?"

He looked around again. The cell was empty. Paige and Jude had disappeared.

"I don't know," he said, reaching to his neck and grimacing. They had burned him somehow, but in his addled state, he couldn't figure out what they had used. Then he saw the broken light bulb hanging from a chain on the ceiling. He rubbed his eyes. "How long have I been out?"

"I don't know," she said, putting a hand on his shoulder to help him up. He waved her away.

"Did they hurt you?"

"They knocked me down," she said. "I hit my head on a rock."

Glenn stood, but a wave of dizziness threatened to overtake him. He fell back against the wall. Then he closed his eyes and took deep breaths until the world stopped spinning. He had his wallet in his back pocket and his cell phone in his left pocket. They had taken his keys, though.

He looked at Helen.

"Did they take the car?"

"I don't know," she said. "I passed out. I didn't see."

He nodded and walked up the steps. His car was gone. He covered his face with his hands. The police weren't here yet, which meant he still had time to escape. Glenn took his cell phone from his pocket and checked Uber. The nearest car was in the town of St. Augustine, which meant it would take twenty minutes to get there.

He requested a ride and provided his destination, a used-car lot of sorts. As he waited in the sun, his clothes dried, and his temper simmered.

"My phone says I've been out for almost twenty-four hours. Paige and Jude should have gone to the police by now. Where are they?"

"Maybe they're dead," said Helen. "Maybe they got into a car accident."

"This proves it. I need a partner," he said, walking toward the road.

"I'm your partner," said Helen, hurrying to walk beside him. "We do everything together. Who else could you want?"

He glanced at her and sighed. "I know you've done your best, but I need someone to carry the load. We need to move up the timeline. I need to pick up Mary Joe. The sooner we pick her up, the sooner we can break her and the sooner she can help me."

Helen stopped walking and crossed her arms. "Do you have any idea how dangerous it will be to abduct a police officer?"

Glenn stopped and looked at her. "They could have killed me."

"But they didn't," she said.

"I got lucky," he said, continuing to walk toward the stretch of highway where his Uber driver would pick him up. "I need someone who understands what I'm doing and who can help me. Frankly, I need someone who can stop the sinners from running away before I'm done with them. That's not you."

Helen still didn't move, but even from ten feet away, he could almost hear her teeth grinding.

"You don't even know her."

"I will, though," he said. "We don't have time to argue. Paige and Jude have escaped. Mary Joe will work their case. That means her house will be empty. We'll search it and find out what we can about her."

Helen shook her head and sighed. "This is stupid."

Their Uber driver arrived about ten minutes later. She seemed hesitant about dropping him off in the middle of nowhere, but he explained he had a cabin in the woods and that he'd be just fine. Then he gave her a generous tip. She thanked him and drove off without saying another word.

Every couple Glenn and Helen had cleansed brought with them a vehicle. The police had already found Paige Maxwell's car, and he had just lost Simon Fisher's Ford Focus, so he picked up a green Buick that had, at one time, been owned by a young man from Decatur, Illinois. Then he drove.

Mary Joe Court lived in a lovely historic home on a nice piece of property outside town. Glenn had driven by it four times in the past couple of days and seen no one. They'd be just fine today.

"This is a bad idea," said Helen, refusing to even glance at him as he parked their car on the side of the road about a quarter mile from Mary Joe's house.

"I wouldn't need her if you'd get off your ass and help out more often," said Glenn. "Did you even fight back when Jude and Paige escaped?"

Helen said nothing as he opened his door. They walked toward the home in silence. Once they reached the yard, Helen opened her mouth to speak.

"What do you hope to learn here?"

Glenn glanced at her and then took a pair of medical-grade nitrile gloves from his pocket. He snapped them onto his hands.

"First, we need to learn whether she has a boyfriend. If she does, it might take her longer to break. I will need to prepare for that. Second, I want to find out what kind of things she likes to eat. I want her to feel comfortable. Third, I need to see what size clothes she wears. I want her to look nice while she's in my company."

Helen smirked. "Aren't we Mr. Romance? Making her comfortable, buying her clothes."

"I'm tired of your voice, Helen," he said. "Unless you have something constructive to say, shut up."

She brought her fingers to her lips and drew them across as if she were zipping her mouth shut. Glenn wanted to smack her, but he didn't think it was appropriate to hit women unless absolutely necessary. Together, the two of them climbed onto the porch, where they found two rocking chairs and a terra-cotta pot full of tennis balls.

Helen rolled her eyes as he tried the front door and found it locked.

"She's a cop, Glenn," she said. "Did you expect her to leave her front door unlocked?"

"Did I say you could talk?"

She smirked and said nothing. In the backyard, he found a well-used trail that meandered through the woods. A gravestone marked the edge of the property. An empty—but very large—doghouse occupied a prime spot beneath an old tree near the home. A low cedar fence surrounded it.

"Tell me if you hear barking," he said, checking to see whether she had locked the back door. She had.

"Her dog is dead," said Helen. "That's its grave at the edge of the woods."

Glenn glanced in the direction his sister pointed before reaching into his wallet for a lock-pick set.

"That's unfortunate," said Glenn, kneeling on her back steps so her deadbolt was at eye height. His father had taught him how to pick locks when he was a boy. Edward Saunders, Glenn's father, had owned a custom furniture and mill-work shop. Sometimes they restored old cabinets, trunks, and doors. Knowing how to pick the locks themselves kept them from having to call a locksmith every time a customer brought in something they couldn't open.

Mary Joe had a nice deadbolt, but he had plenty of time and all the privacy he could want. Getting her door open took about ten minutes, but it wasn't a problem. He and Helen walked into her kitchen. The room's white walls and tile floor reminded him of an old diner. Helen stood beside a small round table and made a show of looking around.

"This is illuminating," she said, nodding. "I've learned a lot about Mary Joe from this."

"Shut up," he said, opening cabinets. She had a lot of dishes and glasses, but little food.

"Hey," said Helen upon seeing the third cabinet. "She likes Frosted Flakes. Learning that was more than worth risking our lives over."

Glenn glared at her but said nothing as he finished searching the remaining cabinets. He found more cereal, a few cans of vegetables—green beans mostly—and half a loaf of multigrain bread. Unlike every other cabinet in her kitchen, her liquor cabinet overflowed with an abundance of choices. She had three kinds of bourbon, two kinds of rum, a bottle of tequila, and four different liqueurs he had never heard of.

Helen smiled but remained silent as he opened her refrigerator door. Inside, she had three apples, half a gallon of orange juice, two containers of Chinese takeout, and two cases of beer from a microbrewery in St. Louis. Her freezer held frozen meals, two bottles of vodka, and a bottle of gin. When he closed it, Helen couldn't take it anymore. She giggled.

"Seems your little girlfriend drinks most of her calories," she said. "You want to take her home or to a rehab facility?"

Glenn told her to shut up, but she wasn't wrong to worry. Mary Joe had an awful lot of alcohol for one person. They'd have to work on that.

Once he finished searching the kitchen, Glenn walked into her living room. It was a mess. Whiteboards on mobile easels blocked most of the sunlight from reaching the interior, while stacks of documents covered the coffee table and floor. Glenn's eyes drew everything in.

"You're not the only one doing opposition research," said Helen, walking to one of the whiteboards. Someone had written the word *Profile* on it and then written various characteristics beneath it—most of which fit Glenn well. Helen looked toward him and smiled as she pointed toward the board. "She thinks you're intelligent. That's funny."

"Shut up, Helen," he said, taking his cell phone from his pocket to snap pictures of everything she had written. He didn't want to stay in the house longer than he had to, but it wouldn't hurt to know what the police thought of him. Once he had photographed every board, Helen cleared her throat.

"Are we done now?" she asked. "Or do you want to stay for a while in case Mary Joe comes home? We can get drunk together. It seems to be the closest thing she has to a hobby. That and hunting you."

He rolled his eyes and turned toward the kitchen, where he had seen a small hallway. It led to a bedroom with an en suite bathroom. An unmade king-sized bed rested against the far wall between two windows. There was a dresser against the wall on the right and a chest of drawers to the left. Curiously, a set of wooden steps led to the bed.

Helen walked to the bed, patted a pillow, and then shook her head.

"Your girlfriend is a slob," she said. "She doesn't even make her bed."

"I'm sure you'll teach her to be a better housekeeper," he said. Mary Joe kept an end table on either side of the bed. He didn't know which side of the bed she slept on, so he started by checking out the end table on the right. As soon as he opened the drawer, a bottle rolled inside. Glenn felt his shoulders sink, but Helen laughed.

"The more I see of this girl, the more I like her," said Helen. "I'm thinking she might have an alcohol problem, though."

"I'll help her," he said, crossing the room to check out her other end table. This one held paperbacks. She liked science fiction. He hadn't known that going in. Details like that could make her experience with him easier. He picked up a copy of *The Moon Is a Harsh Mistress* by Robert Heinlein and showed it to Helen. "She likes reading. That'll help."

"We'll get her some books," said Helen. "Now let's go."

"In a minute," said Glenn, walking to her chest of drawers. Her end table hadn't held condoms or other birth control methods, so she probably didn't have a boyfriend. He'd be the only man in her life.

He opened her top drawer and found simple cotton underwear. It was nice, but a beautiful woman like her deserved something more sensual. He took a pair so he'd know her size and then closed the drawer. In her second drawer down, she had bras and socks. Socks were easy enough to size, so he ignored those. He took a bra, though. It looked simple, but it must have done its job. He'd get her something pretty.

He searched her chest and dresser drawer by drawer until he had taken a complete outfit for her. Then he went to her bed and grabbed one of the eight pillows on her bed. She'd appreciate that once he took her.

When he finished, he closed everything up the way it had been when he arrived. Helen was in the kitchen, waiting for him.

"We can't just take her, you know," she said.

Glenn nodded. "I know. She's a cop. We need to study her movements and plan this one."

"That's not what I mean," said Helen, shaking her head. "You need to deal with Trinity and Thad. They're nowhere near ready, but once you have Mary Joe, you'll forget all about them. They'll rot, and then I'll have to deal with them."

Glenn forced a cold smile to his face. "What do you want, Helen?"

"Get rid of them," she said. "If you don't plan to feed your goldfish, you might as well dump them down the toilet right away."

"Fine," he said. "Anything else you want me to do, your highness?"

"You can curb the attitude for starters," she said. "I can make your life hell if I want to. Don't forget that."

"You'll never let me forget anything," he said.

She rolled her eyes and walked through the open rear door. He grabbed the pillow and clothes he had taken and left. The day had started poorly, but it had improved greatly. He had lost Jude and Paige, but neither had seen him without his mask. They couldn't identify him.

He'd watch Mary Joe for a while, and then he'd take her. He'd show her the world and make her happier than she could ever be on her own. Together, they'd right the sins of his past and make the world a better place.

But first, he'd have to break her.

That was a worry for tomorrow, though. For now, he held her pillow and her clothes and imagined better days ahead.

Chapter 21

A gent Lawson and I walked toward the house. Four special agents had erected a perimeter around the yard, which Angela Pritchard was smart enough to avoid crossing. Still, I lowered my voice.

"I called my dispatcher and asked her to send paramedics," I said. "I think we can get a helicopter if needed. It might be quicker."

Lawson shook his head and swore under his breath again.

"Thank you, but I think we'll be okay. My guys were wearing vests. The rounds didn't go through them. We used a Taser to subdue Mr. Marshall, but he'll be okay."

My shoulders relaxed, and I breathed easier.

"That's good," I said, nodding. Lawson grunted but didn't otherwise respond. I stayed on the front lawn while he walked inside the house. After five or six minutes, Sheriff Delgado came from a side street and stood beside me.

"I hear we got him," he said.

"After he shot two FBI agents," I said.

Delgado sighed and looked down. "Are they dead?"

"No. They were wearing bullet-resistant vests," I said. "This shouldn't have happened. Angela Pritchard screwed everything up."

Delgado shook his head. "We couldn't have done anything differently. Woman's got instincts and sources we can't stop."

"If that's the story you want to stick with, go for it," I said. "Good luck."

Delgado said nothing until Agent Lawson came out of the house and walked toward us.

"Detective Court tells me Marshall shot two of your men," said the sheriff. "They doing okay?"

"They're fine," said Lawson. "So is Mr. Marshall. We got lucky. We could have lost someone today."

"Good to get lucky sometimes," said Delgado. "You can use my station for your interrogation. I bet Marshall's got a cabin somewhere around here. You find that, you'll find his other victims."

"I appreciate the offer," said Lawson. "You better be thanking your lucky stars nobody died today."

Delgado said nothing. Then he stepped back and put his hands on his hips.

"For the record, I didn't know Pritchard was in town. I didn't call her. You can check my phone."

Lawson snorted and looked away. "Then congratulations, Sheriff Delgado. You picked up a burner cell phone."

"I don't like your implication, sir."

"I don't care," said Lawson, glancing at the sheriff for the first time. "Gallen Marshall shot two of my officers today because of you. He saw Pritchard and reached for a gun. Without her, he wouldn't have seen us coming."

"I'm not the only person who could have called her," said Delgado. "Your team knew what was going down. Joe knew what was going down. Anybody could have called her, so don't put this on me."

"I confiscated their phones before I told them what was going on. You refused to give yours up. You're no longer welcome at my crime scene. Please step away."

Delgado held up his hands and started backing up. "I'm leaving, but you can't blame me for your team's screwups."

"Get out of here, George," I said. "I don't want to fill out the paperwork if Agent Lawson beats you up."

Delgado rubbed his hands together as if he were wiping them clean. Then he walked away. Agent Lawson glowered at him for a while before focusing on me.

"Thank you, Detective," he said. He paused. "How's your double-homicide investigation going?"

I tilted my head to the side. "It's going. The Highway Patrol is looking for Thad Stevens's car, and their technicians are going through a computer found at the crime scene. We've got a lot of potential suspects, but Trinity and Thad are the strongest at the moment. Unfortunately, they're still gone, and none of their friends know where they are."

Lawson nodded but said nothing.

"Unless you need me, I'll head out," I said. "Do you have my cell phone?"

Lawson shook his head. "I left it in the conference room at your station. Sorry. Let me talk to my team. I'll give you a ride back."

"I'd appreciate that."

He nodded, but his eyes were a little distant. After a moment, we walked to his SUV. Neither of us said a word until we reached my station.

"Thank you for your professionalism, Detective. I've enjoyed working with you, but with Mr. Marshall in custody, we'll pull back to St. Louis to sort out any remaining loose ends."

I hadn't worked with Lawson much, but it was bittersweet to see him leave. Having an FBI agent around had kept Delgado on his toes. I had liked that.

"Good luck in St. Louis," I said.

He nodded. "We'll be in touch."

It was a clear dismissal, so I got out of the car and went to my desk inside the station. There, I spent the next hour writing a statement describing that morning's events.

After that, I dove back into the Mark and Lilly Foster murder investigation. Trinity Foster and her boyfriend were still missing, but they weren't my only suspects. Mark and Lilly had a lot of cocaine in their house, which meant they bought and sold drugs. If I could find who they bought from and who they sold to, I'd have new suspects.

So I spent the rest of the day talking to narcotics detectives in St. Louis, Kansas City, and Memphis. I also drove around and talked to every drug dealer I knew in St. Augustine County. I learned a lot about the drug trade in the mid-south, but I learned nothing about Mark and Lilly. At a little after six, I drove back to my station to fill out paperwork and document my day.

The shift had changed over about an hour ago, so I had the bullpen to myself. I typed my notes, checked my email to see whether Darlene from the forensics lab had sent me an update, and then called the liaison from the Missouri Highway Patrol to see whether anyone had spotted Thad's car or whether they had anything new on the computer taken from the Fosters' home. The news was negative on all counts.

I hadn't solved my case, but Agent Lawson had arrested the Apostate with only minor casualties, Sheriff Delgado had made a fool out of himself once more, and I had vodka and gin in my freezer waiting for me at home. I planned to celebrate. After shutting down my computer for the day, I stretched and yawned, ready to go home.

"Joe! I need you in here now."

It was Jason Zuckerburg's voice, and it sent a hard shiver down my spine.

I didn't know what he wanted, but I ran toward the receptionist's desk with my hand over my pistol's grip. Six people stood near the station's big oak front doors. My feet slowed, but my heart continued to race. At first, I wasn't sure what

I was seeing, and then their features came into focus. Both Paige and Jude had lost considerable amounts of weight, but they stood in front of me.

I counted to ten and blinked, expecting them to disappear in some kind of dreamy haze. They didn't, though. This was them. I blinked and covered my mouth.

"You're alive," I said, my voice a whisper. "How are you alive?"

Paige stepped forward. She had sunken cheeks, and it looked as if some of her hair had fallen out. Her clothes and skin, however, looked clean.

"We killed him," she said. "He's dead. We killed him and stole his car."

I nodded and took an uncertain step forward, not comprehending what she'd said. My legs felt shaky. Before I could stop myself, I laughed. Behind me, Zuckerburg did, too.

"You're alive," I said again. Now that the initial shock was wearing off, I smiled and felt it with my entire body. As a police officer, I had seen humanity at its worst. I had seen people hurt each other for no reason at all, I had seen married men and women abuse each other in the worst ways, and I had seen people I cared about die. As bad as those days were, they were balanced by the good days when I got to help people and make my community safer. Sometimes, I even got to save someone's life. I couldn't remember the last time I'd felt like this at work, though.

An overwhelming sense of lightness spread through me. I had spent weeks looking for Paige and Jude. I had trudged through the woods, talked to their friends and parents, searched their rooms at home. Then, after finding nothing, I had written them off as dead. I had accepted that my missing-persons case had become a homicide.

I had been wrong, though. I could have cried. Or danced.

"You're alive."

I couldn't stop whispering it. Zuckerburg walked around the desk and leaned toward me, breaking me from my delighted reverie.

"If these guys killed the Apostate, we need to call Agent Lawson," he whispered. "They arrested the wrong guy this morning."

He was right, so I nodded and looked to Paige and Jude and their parents and smiled.

"We have a lot to talk about," I said. "Officer Zuckerburg will take you to the conference room in the back. You can relax for a few minutes. I've got to make calls."

Chapter 22

While I called Agent Lawson, Jason called St. John's Hospital. The doctors at St. John's rarely made house calls, but they made an exception for this case.

Things moved fast after that. An ER physician and two nurses came in an ambulance and checked Paige and Jude out. They were dehydrated and malnourished, but neither showed signs of infection or serious illness. The nurses started IVs on both kids. It would take time, but they'd recover physically. A registered dietitian from St. John's even agreed to create a diet plan for them to speed things along.

Unfortunately, the soul was a lot harder to heal than the body, and both already exhibited signs of severe PTSD. They had each other, though. I didn't put a lot of stock in teenage relationships, but they'd survived hell for each other. Maybe they could learn to live for each other, too.

Once we figured out the kids were okay for the moment, we dove into the investigation. Agent Lawson interviewed Paige in the second-floor conference room while Agent Costa interviewed Jude in the first-floor conference room.

The Apostate abducted Paige from the library, where she had volunteered. She had stepped out the back door to smoke a cigarette, but before she could even light up, someone stepped out of the tall shrubs near the building. She never even saw her assailant's face. He pressed a sweet-smelling rag to her mouth. She tried to scream, but in doing so, she breathed in fumes that knocked her out.

Jude's story was similar. He got a message on Snapchat, supposedly from Paige, asking her to meet him at the library because her car needed a jump-start. He waited for her at the same break area from which the Apostate had abducted his girlfriend. Then, somebody came out from the bushes. His assailant pressed a sweet-smelling rag to his mouth, which knocked him out. When Jude regained consciousness, he was on the ground in a concrete dungeon with a chain-link fence. Paige lay beside him on a cot.

They stayed in that room for weeks, but their captor always wore a mask. He came to them often and gave them water but never food. That was why they were malnourished. They were scared and thought they would die. Early on, their captor said he'd release them if they gave him the PINs to their bank accounts. Obviously, that was a lie.

They escaped because their captor made a mistake. He left the chain-link fence open and gave the kids a bucket of water. The room's only light came from a bare bulb that hung on a long chain from the ceiling. Jude broke the light against the chain-link fence's post and then waited. When their captor came down the steps, Jude threw the bucket of water on him. Paige then grabbed the light's chain and tugged as hard as she could. She pressed it against their captor's neck, shocking him. Then, they took his car keys and ran. They assumed he was dead.

Instead of going to the police station right away, they drove to Paige's house, where they sat and held each other on the couch, waiting for her parents to come home. Unfortunately, they didn't know her parents had moved out of the house a few weeks after she disappeared. They fell asleep and only woke up the next day when Paige's mom came home, having heard from a neighbor that someone was in the house. They had slept for almost twenty-four hours. After their ordeal, I couldn't blame them.

The story was horrifying, but it explained a few things. It also gave us a lead. Jude, Agent Lawson, Sheriff Delgado, and Jude's mom and dad crammed into Sheriff Delgado's SUV to see whether they could figure out where the Apostate had held them. Paige, Agent Costa, and Paige's mom stayed in the conference room to go over her statement again.

I didn't have an assignment, but I didn't want to go home. So I stayed and drank terrible coffee and watched Agent Costa, Paige, and her mother write a formal report. At about eight, my phone buzzed with an incoming text message.

Hello, Mary Joe.

I didn't recognize the number, so I ignored it and slipped my phone back in my pocket. It buzzed again. And then again.

Are you at work? What are you wearing?

I needed my phone, so I couldn't just turn it off. Half of St. Augustine County knew my phone number, but most people had enough common sense to avoid harassing a police officer. I excused myself and walked to the bullpen, where I flicked my thumb across the screen and opened the settings on my phone to block the number. Before I could, I got another text message.

Are Paige and Jude with you?

It felt as if something very cold had gripped my belly. I typed a response.

Who is this?

The response came almost in seconds.

A friend. An admirer. A potential lover. You know who I am.

In other circumstances, I would have rolled my eyes. Here, the entire world seemed to disappear except the screen of my phone. My heart thudded in my chest. No one should have known about Paige and Jude. I used voice-to-text to enter my response.

A name would be nice.

The sound of the station's front door opening carried through the lobby and to the bullpen in which I stood. I ignored it.

The newspaper calls me the Apostate.

For a moment, my throat tightened. I should have called out for somebody, but the bullpen was empty.

I don't believe you.

My phone went silent for a full minute before it beeped once more.

Ask Jude how he liked the peanut butter and jelly sandwich.

Jude wasn't in the building, but I walked back to the conference room anyway. Agent Costa sat to Paige's left, while her mom was to the right. All of them had their backs to me.

"Hey, Paige," I called. The three turned around. Agent Costa furrowed his brow, but I ignored him for the moment. "Does Jude like peanut butter and jelly sandwiches?"

The color drained from Paige's face. She gasped and covered her mouth, and I knew the man texting me wasn't lying. It was him. My stomach felt as if I had just plummeted a hundred stories straight down.

"Agent Costa, I need to talk to you in private right now," I said.

He nodded. We hurried outside and shut the door while Paige hugged her mother. Costa crossed his arms.

"Tell me about this sandwich."

"I can't," I said, holding up my phone so he could see the screen. "Someone texted me and said he was the Apostate. I told him I didn't believe him, and he told me to ask Jude about a peanut butter and jelly sandwich. I didn't know what that meant. Paige does, though. She's holding back on us."

Costa blinked as he took that in. Then he covered his mouth and nodded.

"Keep him talking," he said. "And give me the number he's contacting you from. We'll worry about Paige and Jude later."

I read him the number, and he dialed his phone and stepped away from me. I focused on my phone again.

What's your real name?

I knew he wouldn't tell me anything, but I needed to keep him talking.

We're not there yet.

I then asked him what I should call him. He didn't respond for at least a full minute.

Doctor.

"He wants me to call him doctor," I said, glancing at Agent Costa. "Didn't you guys think he could have been a doctor at one time?"

Costa considered but then looked away.

"Paige and Jude both said he wore a gold mask that covered his eyes. They said it had a beak. It may be a plague doctor's mask."

I furrowed my brow. Costa straightened.

"It was a mask worn by physicians in the seventeenth century," he said. "Doctors would stuff the beak with herbs and breathe through it because they thought that would prevent them from getting the bubonic plague from their patients. It's in a video game called *Assassin's Creed*. My kid plays it late at night when he thinks I'm in bed."

"Kudos for video games," I said, focusing on the phone again and typing.

Plague doctor?

The Apostate responded almost instantly.

Very good, detective. You have spoken to Paige and Jude.

I looked to Agent Costa. "Tell me you've got a location on this guy's phone."

"We're working on it," he said. "He's connected to a cell tower in St. Augustine County. I'm already mobilizing a team."

To catch him, we'd need to know more than the cell tower he had connected to, but I nodded anyway.

"Good. I'll try to keep him talking."

Costa grunted, and I thumbed in a message.

I want to understand you.

He didn't respond immediately. My muscles felt twitchy, and my fingers trembled. I couldn't stand still, so I paced beside my desk.

You will. First, it's my turn. Why do you have stairs beside your bed?

At once, it felt as if someone had covered my feet in cement. I couldn't move. I could barely breathe. Costa must have seen my reaction because he walked to me and looked over my shoulder. I sucked in a quick breath and typed a response.

They're for my dog. How do you know about them?

"Don't engage him again," said Costa. "He's making this personal. You don't want a serial murderer in your head."

My phone buzzed, and I swore under my breath as I read the message.

I'll enjoy breaking you, Mary Joe.

I clenched my jaw and showed my phone to Costa. He covered his mouth but said nothing.

"It's too late to avoid making this personal," I said. "He's been in my house."

Chapter 23

I went by my locker in the basement and grabbed my department-issued bullet-resistant vest. Agent Costa was in the lobby waiting for me as I climbed the steps. He was on the phone, so I turned to Jason Zuckerburg.

"Who's on duty tonight near my house?"

He drew in a breath and focused on his computer for a moment. "DeAndre Simpson and JD Phillips are about a mile away. They're looking for drunks, but fishing is light tonight."

"Unless they're occupied, send them to my house but tell them to hang back until I arrive. I've had a break-in."

Zuckerburg typed and then looked at me.

"They're on the way. You need anybody else?"

I looked to Agent Costa. He had finished his phone call and walked to us.

"Bruce Lawson and Sheriff Delgado will meet us at your place," he said, looking to me before focusing on Zuckerburg. "Jude Lewis and his parents will be coming in. Make sure they're comfortable in the conference room. We'll need to talk to them again soon."

Zuckerburg nodded and said he'd look for them. Then Costa and I left. We took separate cars to my house, but we both parked in the driveway. Within moments, two St. Augustine County police cruisers joined us. I met the small team in front of my car.

"My house has a door in the front and a second in the back. Agent Costa and I will clear the house room by room to make sure we're alone. DeAndre, I want you in the front. JD, you're in the back. Just watch the doors. If you hear us shout for help, please come in and help us. I don't anticipate finding anyone in the home, but it's possible. Questions?"

The team had none, so DeAndre and JD got in position by the front and back doors, and Agent Costa and I searched the house room by room. It felt almost surreal leading a man I barely knew through my house, like it was some kind of bad dream. It wasn't a dream, though. I felt sick.

My place wasn't big, so it only took a few minutes to clear it. Once we finished, we left and stood on the front lawn. Delgado and Lawson arrived a few minutes later. The two FBI agents then went to Lawson's SUV to talk in private, leaving me alone with Delgado.

"Jude couldn't find the Apostate's hideout," said Delgado. "He tried his best, but it's dark. He got pretty upset, so we didn't want to push him."

"They're holding back on us," I said. "The Apostate contacted me and told me to ask about a peanut butter and jelly sandwich. When I did, Paige clammed up."

Delgado narrowed his eyes. "You don't think they're working together, do you?"

I screwed up my face and shook my head. "You've seen them. He starved these kids. If Paige and Jude are doing the Apostate's bidding, they're not doing it willingly. I think they're just scared."

"How'd he get your phone number?"

I shrugged. "Maybe from the station's website, maybe from one of my business cards."

Neither of us said anything more until Lawson and Costa walked toward us.

"I have twelve FBI agents in St. Augustine County trying to track down the Apostate," said Lawson. "Unfortunately, he turned off his phone after talking to Detective Court. We'll keep looking, but I'm not optimistic we'll find him without more information. In the meantime, I'd like Detective Court to walk through her house by herself and look for anything out of place. What's he moved, what's he touched, and what's he taken? While you're inside, I also want you to pack a bag. You'll be staying elsewhere tonight. That sound okay to you?"

I nodded, so Lawson wished me luck. Inside the house, my kitchen, living room, and first-floor powder room looked as they always did. If the Apostate had touched anything, he'd put it back. Then I walked to my bedroom and grabbed a gym bag from my closet. I threw in two T-shirts and a pair of pants, but when I opened my underwear and sock drawer, I stopped and felt my stomach flutter.

I hated laundry day because it always felt like a wasted afternoon in which I could have been doing something productive. Because of that, I kept track of my clothes. If I had three pairs of clean underwear left, that meant I had two days before laundry day. This morning, I had two pairs left. Now, I had one.

I opened the drawer with my bras inside and swore under my breath. My appearance mattered, but I had never spent a lot of money on my clothes. My one exception was a bra I had bought at a Bloomingdale's on Michigan Avenue in Chicago. Audrey, my sister, had talked me into it when I last visited her. It cost me a hundred bucks, which meant it cost more than most of my outfits, but Audrey said I looked great in it. She didn't say that often, but when she said it, she meant it. Now that bra was gone.

I stepped back and looked at my bed next. I loved the feel of clean sheets, but I hated making my bed almost as much as I hated doing laundry. When I left for work that morning, my bed had been a disheveled mess. Now, somehow, it looked even worse. I was also missing a pillow.

It took that moment for my feelings to catch up. My stomach roiled, and bile rose in the back of my throat. The muscles of my legs twitched. I sucked in two deep breaths, hoping to dispel my growing sense of nausea, but nothing I did could stop my hands from trembling. I felt violated.

I stayed in the room for a few minutes, but it didn't make me feel better. Sheriff Delgado, Agents Costa and Lawson, and several St. Augustine police officers waited on my front lawn. I walked toward my boss and the FBI agents and nodded.

"He was here," I said. "He went through my clothes and stole a pair of underwear and at least one of my bras. He also stole a pillow from my bed."

Delgado didn't seem to know what to say, but Lawson nodded.

"Dirty or clean?" he asked.

"What?" I asked.

"Your bra and underwear," said Lawson. "They speak to different pathologies."

"Clean," I said, raising my eyebrows and feeling a fresh wave of revulsion wash over me. "Jeez. I didn't even check my dirty laundry hamper yet. That's just gross."

"Yeah, it is," said Lawson, nodding and stepping onto the porch with his hands in his pockets. I held the door open for him as he stepped inside. When he saw my living room and the files and whiteboards inside, his eyes widened. Delgado walked in a moment after us and had a similar reaction.

"You've been busy," said Lawson, walking to the whiteboard on which I had scribbled notes. "Did you put the profile together yourself?"

Delgado walked to my coffee table and picked up a stack of documents. "You didn't have access to these, Detective. How do you have them?"

Warmth spread to my face and across my body. Though I tried to keep the panic from my expression, I swore over and over in my head. I had lived with the whiteboards and file boxes in my living room for so long I barely remembered I had them. Now, my gut flip-flopped, and my throat tightened. I almost swore, but I kept my mouth shut as I tried to think through my options.

"This isn't what you think," I said, hoping to buy myself another moment.

"What is it, Detective?" he asked, stepping forward. His voice held more than a hint of malice. "Because, from my vantage, it looks like you broke just about every regulation we've got on the books."

In fact, there were entire sections of Missouri's criminal code and St. Augustine's own manual of regulations and rules I hadn't violated, but I didn't think reminding him of that would get me anywhere. Instead, I drew in a breath to tell him I was just doing my job, but Agent Lawson cleared his throat before I could.

"I gave her the papers."

Both of us looked at him with our brows raised.

"You?" asked Delgado.

"Yeah," said Lawson, flicking his hard, green eyes toward me before fixing them on Delgado again. "When working a case like this, I find it helpful to have outside perspectives now and again. Detective Court is an intelligent officer, and I was glad to hear her opinion."

Even though Lawson spoke well of me, his eyes were flinty and hard, and he leaned forward and positioned his feet outside his shoulders. He looked like an animal getting ready to pounce. It was almost unnerving.

"If you wanted a fresh perspective, you could have asked me," said Delgado. "I'm on the task force. That's my job."

"The Apostate abducted young women. I wanted a young woman's perspective on the case. If you were thirty years old and female, I would have asked you," said Lawson. "Since you're not, I approached Detective Court and asked her to look over things in her free time. She was never derelict in her duty or assignment. She did nothing wrong."

Delgado shifted his weight over his heels and then looked at me and then to Lawson. "You two are thick as thieves, aren't you?"

"I appreciate your candor and help, Sheriff," said Lawson, "but I can handle this from here. Why don't you step out-side?"

Delgado bristled and narrowed his eyes at me.

"Next time another law enforcement agency asks you for a favor, I expect you to clear it with me before you start."

I nodded, and Delgado huffed and left the room. Once my front door shut, I held up my hands toward Lawson.

"Before you say anything, I'm sorry. This was my case before you came along, and I didn't want to give it up. I copied the files at work and brought them here to study on my own."

Lawson crossed his arms and nodded, his face implacable. "Who else has seen them?"

I considered lying to him, but I had never been a great liar.

"Trisha Marshall. She's our dispatcher, but she's a sworn officer. Harry Grainger saw them, too. He's the former sheriff."

Lawson's expression softened as he nodded.

"At least they're law enforcement," he said. "The Apostate saw them, too. He's been in your house."

"I made a mistake, but I thought it was a risk worth taking. Sorry."

"Stop talking," said Lawson. "It was a mistake. You made it. Own up to it. Don't make excuses and don't apologize. Just tell me you won't do it again."

I straightened and looked him in the eye. "I won't do it again."

"Good," he said, reaching into his pocket for a key chain. He slipped a thumb drive from the ring and handed it to me. "Get in your truck and drive to your station. This thumb drive has copies of everything we've found. The Apostate is still alive. I want you to go through our profile and papers and tell us what we missed. Start with the victims. We thought he picked them by looking through their applications to Waterford College. Find out how he's actually doing it."

I looked at the key chain. "That's a tall order."

"You wanted to be part of the case," he said. "Now get going. My team will search your house and see what they can find here."

Even before the words left his lips, my stomach contorted, and my breath became shallow. This building was more than four walls and a roof; it was my home. I grew up in the foster care system, so I rarely got hugs at night, and when I did, they almost always came with strings attached. If I did the laundry and cleaned the kitchen and bathrooms, I'd have a warm bed. If I did the dishes, I could have dinner. For most of my childhood, love was transactional, and hugs were the signature on a contract.

As a child, that was okay. When I hit puberty, though, things changed. My foster fathers watched me in a way they hadn't before. Even then, they had made my skin crawl. My foster mothers were often even worse. When I was thirteen, one foster mother called me a slut because she caught her husband taking pictures of me bending over to pick up my backpack while I wore a skirt. I had never even kissed a boy, and in this woman's eyes, I was a slut because her husband liked looking at thirteen-year-old girls.

My life taught me to shut out the world. If I kept my head down, if I hid in plain sight, people almost forgot I was there. They couldn't hurt me if they forgot I was around.

I mattered in my house, though. I could be myself in those walls without worry. The Apostate creeped me out, but he was crazy. He might have tried to attack me, but he'd never be able to see the real me.

Agent Lawson, though, profiled people for a living. He'd see a hallway devoid of family pictures, he'd see a freezer that held only frozen meals and vodka, he'd see a dog bed without a dog, and he'd see guest bedrooms without beds. He'd see how alone in the world I was. He'd see through the facade I put on every morning over the person I was. Every muscle in my body trembled at the thought.

I swallowed all that down and embraced the cold frigidity to become the person my colleagues thought I always had been. I became the ice queen. My heart slowed, and a still calmness spread from my chest and then to my extremities. I was fine. I didn't need others in my life. They just got in the way.

Lawson surveyed the room. I hesitated before clearing my throat to get his attention. He raised his eyebrows and cocked his head to the side.

"Make sure you lock up when you're done," I said. "If you break anything, I'll send you a bill."

Lawson locked his gaze on mine. For a split second, I thought I saw some kind of recognition flicker in his eyes, but then it disappeared as a tight smile spread to his lips.

"Good luck, Detective."

"You, too, Agent Lawson," I said. I hesitated before leaving. "What do you want to do about Paige, Jude, and their families?"

"I'll send them home and have an officer sit in their driveways in case the Apostate tries to finish the job. We can interview them again tomorrow after they've slept."

I nodded before turning and heading toward the front door. Sheriff Delgado stood on the front lawn as I walked out, but I ignored him. I ignored the FBI's forensic van, too. Everybody was just doing a job. It didn't matter that they were going through my house. I had nothing to hide or feel ashamed of.

When I got to my station, there were a pair of drunks shackled to chairs in the lobby. One snored, but the other was wide-eyed. He had a bruise on a cheek and a few drops of blood on his shirt. When he saw me, he smiled a crooked grin.

I looked to Jason, our night dispatcher.

"Somebody taking care of these two gentlemen?"

"For the moment, I am," he said, "but when she gets back, these are Alisa Maycock's guests. They'll be staying the night."

I nodded. "If she needs help, let me know."

Jason nodded and began to say something, but then one of the desk phones rang with an emergency call. I let Jason work and walked to my desk in the bullpen. Though I had seen most of the documents on Agent Lawson's thumb drive, it had been a few days since I sat down with the paperwork.

I spent the next several hours reading through reports. The FBI agents were meticulous, neat, and thorough. At a little after one in the morning, I stretched, grabbed some papers I had printed, and then waved goodbye to Jason on my way out the door. St. Augustine didn't have too many clothing stores, but we had a Walmart that was open twenty-four hours a day. I bought some new underwear, pajamas, and a new top, and then drove to the Wayfair Motel, a cheap motel by the interstate, where I rented a room for the evening.

The moment I took off my pants, I fell into bed without bothering to put on the new pajamas. It was the first night in three or four days I had gone to bed sober, but I was so exhausted that it didn't matter. My eyes closed as soon as my head hit the pillow. As I drifted to sleep, I prayed I'd forget my nightmares before I woke.

Chapter 24

My cell phone woke me up at a little before nine the next morning. Muscles all over my body ached, but my head felt clear, and my stomach felt calm. It was nice to wake up without a hangover.

I blinked and cleared my throat as my phone rang a third time.

"Okay, okay," I said, rolling over in bed. Before answering, I stretched my arms above my head and glanced at the caller ID. The caller had a St. Louis number, but I didn't recognize it.

"Yeah? This is Detective Joe Court," I said, rubbing the sleep out of my eyes. "What can I do for you?"

"Ms. Court, thank you for answering. My name is Brenda Collins with Watkins, Marsh, and Willis. Lacey Rayner gave me your name and said I should call. Is this an okay time to talk?"

I sighed and closed my eyes. "If Aunt Lacey gave you my name, that means you represent Erin Court."

"I represent her estate and the trust she created," said the attorney. "Is this an okay time to talk?"

I looked around me, hoping something in the room would inspire a believable excuse. The sun beat against the curtains over my room's only window. People outside giggled. That could have been kids, or it could have been prostitutes coming home for the evening.

The Wayfair Motel was a critical component of Vic Conroy's golden triangle of businesses. The Sheriff's Department didn't know everything Conroy owned, but he ran the strip club across the street, the truck stop beside it, and the motel. Girls started by working the parking lot of the truck stop when they were fifteen or sixteen. An industrious girl could pull in five hundred or a thousand bucks a night servicing the long-haul truckers who came by to fill up.

When those girls got old enough, they'd dance at the strip club and perform outcall services at the motel across the street. By the time the dancers turned thirty or thirty-five—too old to continue selling their bodies at the club or the motel—they could have earned Conroy a couple hundred thousand dollars each. At that point, they moved on or became maids at his motel.

I hated patronizing a motel owned by a man who exploited young women for profit, but it was cheap and clean, and it had been open when I needed a room. One day, we'd arrest Conroy but not until we had enough to imprison him for life. I had bigger concerns at the moment.

"I'm sorry, but I'm busy with a case at the moment," I said. "Thank you for calling."

I pulled the phone from my ear.

"When are you free? I can drive to your house and meet you in St. Augustine, or you can come to my office."

Evidently, she wasn't going away. I groaned before answering.

"I appreciate that Erin hired you, but I want nothing to do with my birth mother. She was a cancer. If you've got a box of personal mementos sitting in storage somewhere, just throw them away. If something has value, donate it to the Salvation Army."

"I've already taken care of her personal items," said Ms. Collins. "At the time of her death, your mother rented an apartment on Kingshighway Boulevard. At Erin's request, we donated her clothes to a shelter for battered women years ago. We sold her furniture, kitchen appliances, and various household items at auction for nine hundred and forty-four dollars."

I nodded and forced a smile to my face, hoping it would come through my voice.

"That's great. I'm glad. Donate that money to the same women's shelter you took her clothes to. I'm sure they can use it."

The attorney paused. "I can do that, but we need to talk about your mother's other financial assets."

"My mother was a prostitute and a drug addict. When she had money, she spent it on drugs."

Again, Ms. Collins paused. "Before dying, your mother created a living, irrevocable trust, of which you're a beneficiary. At the time of her death, that trust had two hundred and forty thousand dollars. Over the past eleven years, that trust fund has earned an average annual return of just over nine percent in a low-cost mutual fund. With interest, it is now worth well over six hundred thousand dollars. It's your money. I can't donate it without violating the rules of the trust."

My breath caught in my throat.

"Are you still there, Detective?" asked Ms. Collins after a pause.

I nodded but then realized she couldn't see me. Then I cleared my throat.

"Yeah, I'm here," I said. I hesitated. "Erin couldn't even get her life together long enough to visit me after my foster father raped me. How did she have that kind of money?"

"I don't know, but it's a sizeable inheritance. I'd suggest you talk to a wealth advisor to help you invest and manage it. If you'd like, I can make a few recommendations."

I shook my head and then drew in another breath. All my life, I had fought for, scrimped, and saved every dollar I had. Erin had never given me a thing. Even when I was a kid, she had brought me from restaurant to restaurant at closing time to beg the managers for food they would otherwise throw out. That was how Erin did her grocery shopping. How the hell did she get a quarter of a million dollars?

Part of me wanted to drive to that lawyer's office and interrogate her until she told me everything I wanted to know. Another part of me, though—a big part of me—didn't care.

"What happens if I don't want the money?"

The lawyer paused. "Nothing. If you don't want the money, you don't have to take it. I—or someone from my firm—will continue to act as trustee until your death. Then, the trust will be dissolved, and the trustee will donate the remaining funds to the St. Louis County food bank. It's the charity your mother designated."

"She wasn't my mother," I said.

"It's the charity Erin designated," said Ms. Collins. "You don't have to decide now, but I can't dissolve the trust and give the assets away. The trust exists until your death."

Six hundred thousand dollars was more money than I had ever seen in my life. That would let me fix up my house, buy a new truck, and fund my entire retirement without worry. I could stop living paycheck to paycheck. But I didn't want it. Erin didn't get that money legally. If I took it, I'd be as bad as her.

"Did Erin leave a note or anything to explain this?"

"No," said Ms. Collins. "Sorry."

I raised my eyebrows and shook my head.

"Okay," I said. "Thanks for your call. I'm working a murder, so I don't have time to deal with this. For now, can you sit on it?"

"I will," she said. "The money is in a low-fee index fund. It will be fine there."

I thanked her and hung up but didn't get out of bed. It had been almost ten years since Erin died and at least fourteen years since I last saw her. Our last visit had been in St. Louis University Hospital. She had overdosed on heroin, and the attending physicians wanted to keep her for a few days to make sure she didn't overdose again. Even then, she had been a beautiful woman. Unfortunately, the ugliness of her addiction had shown through everything she did.

Once the doctors left, she had begged me to go to her dealer and buy dope for her. When I told her no, she slapped me and told me to leave. I cried big, ugly tears in my social worker's car. I never forgot that moment because that was the moment I realized I'd be alone for the rest of my life.

Erin didn't deserve to die for the things she had done, but it didn't surprise me that someone had murdered her. That she had a quarter million dollars shocked me. Erin may have given me birth, but I didn't know her at all. What's more, I no longer wanted to know her.

I stayed in bed for another few moments, thinking. That didn't get me anywhere, so I threw the covers down and rolled over so I could grab my pants from the ground. I showered and dressed in the clothes I had purchased at Walmart the day before. Then I sat on the edge of my bed and called Detective Blatch.

"Matthias," I said. "It's Joe Court. Are you still working the murder of Erin Court?"

"Officially, no. I've closed it again. Why?"

"I just found out she left me almost a quarter million dollars when she died. It's in a trust fund managed by an attorney named Brenda Collins."

He paused. "Do you remember Erin ever having that kind of money?"

"Nope," I said. "Which is why I'm calling you."

He paused again. "That's interesting. I'll call the lawyer and see what I can find. Do you want me to call you if anything pops up?"

"Nope," I said again. "I've got enough on my plate already."

"I gotcha," he said. He paused. "Everything okay? You sound tired."

Normally I didn't like it when people asked me questions like that. It usually felt patronizing, but for some reason, I didn't mind that Blatch was concerned about me. I almost smiled.

"I'm good, but thank you. You slept since I last talked to you?"

He laughed just a little. "Barely, but that's life when you're the low man on the totem pole."

"I hear you," I said, tucking a stray hair behind my ear. "Good luck getting more sleep, and thanks."

"And good luck on your case."

I hung up a second later and got my stuff together before heading out.

I didn't bother going by my house that morning. Even if the FBI had finished processing the scene, they would have put a seal over my door to prevent anyone else from going inside and to maintain the chain of custody on evidence they might not have known to collect. That's what I would have done, at least, and Agent Lawson was at least as smart as I was.

Instead, I drove straight to work. As usual, Trisha sat at the front desk, but she stood and leafed through some papers the moment she saw me.

"Hey, Joe," she said. "You're still looking for Trinity Foster and Thad Stevens, aren't you?"

"Yeah. No luck so far, though."

"A driver found Thad's car this morning at the bottom of a hill way out in the country," she said. "Looks like they went too fast around a curve, slid, and then rolled down an embankment. Both kids were inside and DOA. It doesn't look like they were wearing seatbelts."

"Well, damn," I said, sighing. I scratched the back of my head, giving me time to think. "Where are they?"

"Out on County Road 10. Middle of nowhere. Highway Patrol is out there now. Because two people died, they'll investigate, but it looks like an accident."

I knew County Road 10 very well, unfortunately. A hunter had found Paige Maxwell's car deep in the woods about half a mile off the road. Then, while we searched for evidence, a tornado ripped through the area. It flattened a cabinet shop nearby and killed a couple of civilians. It nearly killed me and the coroner's assistant, too.

"Thanks for the update. Is Agent Lawson upstairs?"

Trisha nodded. "Conference room. The sheriff's out and about, so you won't run into him."

"Thank the Lord for small favors," I said. Trisha smiled and wished me luck. I thanked her once more and bounded upstairs to the conference room, where I found Agent Lawson talking to somebody on the phone while two other members of his team read through documents. Lawson nodded when he saw me and pointed to a chair. I sat down to wait. Once he finished his call, he walked toward me.

"Morning, Detective," he said. "You find somewhere to stay last night?"

"The Wayfair Motel. It's by the interstate."

"I'm familiar," said Lawson, nodding. "My team and I stayed there for a night before the proprietor kicked us out. He said we were bad for business."

"He is a pimp," I said, tilting my head to the side.

Lawson smiled for a moment, but then his lips straightened once more.

"We searched through your house and found four sets of prints. One was yours, another belonged to your mother, a third belonged to Harry Grainger, and the fourth belonged to your neighbor, Susanne Pennington. She's a nice lady. She made us coffee and asked me to make sure you were eating well."

"Susanne is a friend," I said, smiling. "When can I get back in?"

"Give us another day," said Lawson. "I talked to Paige and Jude this morning. They've amended their statements."

"Oh?" I asked, raising an eyebrow.

"This time, Agent Costa and I spoke to them without their parents in the room. They didn't want to worry their mothers, so they had held back a few details."

"Okay," I said, crossing my arms. "What kind of details?"

"The Apostate starved them so he could control them," said Lawson. "Paige lost almost thirty-five pounds. Jude lost almost fifty."

"Jeez," I said, shaking my head as that sunk in. "It makes sense in a really sick way, I guess. It would make them weaker."

Lawson closed his eyes and nodded. "Weakness may have been part of it, but he tried to use food to get them to do what he wanted. He offered Jude a peanut butter and jelly sandwich if he'd rape Paige. The Apostate didn't want to watch. He just wanted Jude to do it. He called Jude a sinner."

I screwed up my face. "That's awful."

"It gets worse," said Lawson. "After Jude pretended to rape Paige, the Apostate offered to let him go on the condition that Paige stay in the basement so other men could assault her. If he didn't want other men to rape her, he had to drown her in a bucket."

I leaned against the table, closed my eyes, and shook my head.

"Why is he doing this?" I asked. "It doesn't make sense. What could he possibly get out of it?"

Lawson smiled a little, but it didn't quite reach his eyes.

"If you could answer that, I'd question your mental health. In this business, we don't answer the why questions. We just put the crazies in jail."

I nodded and took a deep breath.

"What do you need from me?"

"At the moment, we've got this handled," said Lawson. "The best thing for you is to focus on your own duties. Sheriff Delgado will be glad to have you."

I thought about the car accident Trisha had mentioned and nodded.

"Delgado won't be glad to have me, but I have work to do. Call me if you need me."

"Will do, Detective," he said. "Oh, and hey, before you go, we released Gallen Marshall this morning. He resisted arrest and shot two of my men, but he was innocent of the crime we were arresting him for. It'd get really ugly if we charged him. He also agreed not to sue us for tasing him."

"Did you ever figure out how you found his prints in the Apostate's church?"

Lawson sighed and looked to the ground. "He was a pho-tographer, and he liked to take pictures of abandoned build-ings, including churches. He's published two coffee-table books full of his pictures. One is called *Abandoned Missouri*. The church was on the cover. We should have found that before we went to his house."

"Are the men he shot okay?"

"Yeah. One of them's already back at work. The other guy took a week off," said Lawson, nodding. He lowered his voice. "Good luck out there, Detective."

"You, too."

I didn't know what to think about the Apostate. It took a truly sick person to starve another person, let alone to coerce a young man into hurting someone he loved. The world would be a better place without him in it. I couldn't focus on the Apostate, though. That case was in good hands. I had a car accident to investigate.

Chapter 25

G lenn didn't know how his sister stayed so composed in this heat. While sweat poured down his back and face, Helen looked content sitting on a barstool in the garage. An oscillating fan blew her dress in the breeze and provided welcome relief from the stifling heat and humidity, but it didn't improve her foul mood one bit.

"What'd you do with Detective Court's underwear?"

Glenn set his pliers down and gripped the edge of his worktable to steady himself. Then he met his sister's glare with one of his own. His head pounded, and the world spun around him as if he had just stepped off a roller coaster. Worse than that, things weren't where his eyes told him they were. He had tried to slap Helen earlier, and his hand had just passed right through her as if she were nothing at all.

"I threw them away," he said. "She won't miss them. I've ordered her a dozen pairs that are more to my taste."

"If you really think she'll wear those clothes you ordered and parade herself around for you, you're a moron," said Helen, shaking her head. "We're wasting our time here."

They had been arguing since they left Mary Joe's house. Helen couldn't handle the thought of sharing him with another woman. To punish him, she had kicked him or shouted at him every time he had closed his eyes. She hadn't let him sleep since they had lost Jude and Paige. She was such a jealous bitch.

"Her wishes don't matter," said Glenn, shaking his head and positioning his rifle in his gun vise. "She'll learn how the world works. If she doesn't, I'll punish her."

Worse than merely keeping him awake, Helen had taken every chance she had to remind him that Mary Joe had called the FBI when she found out he had been in her home. She *invited* Agent Lawson inside. Glenn saw it on the news. Ostensibly, he was there to collect evidence and investigate, but Glenn knew Agent Lawson's true purposes. The FBI agent saw a beautiful woman and decided to take her for himself—never mind that she already belonged to him.

Agent Lawson was a snake. Glenn would protect her, but first Mary Joe had to learn a lesson. She had to learn he was the only man in her life worth having. Good girls didn't invite strange men into their houses. Good girls said no when men knocked on their doors. And if Mary Joe couldn't keep Agent Lawson out of her house, she should have burned it down around him while he was inside. That was how you took care of snakes. You smoked them out and cut off their heads.

Helen thought he was a pervert for ordering Mary Joe new, comfortable underwear, but Agent Lawson probably took entire duffel bags full of her clothes. Lawson didn't care about Mary Joe, but he wanted her all the same. Men like him couldn't understand women. Thrusting, grinding, sweating, screwing. That was all they knew. They didn't know what it meant to love or protect someone.

Glenn hated his sister, but at the moment, he hated Mary Joe even more. He saw the way she looked at that FBI agent. She liked him. Realizing that had been like a dagger to his heart. She shouldn't have let Agent Lawson in. She shouldn't have smiled at him. Those smiles were for him alone. Good girls didn't smile for strange men.

He needed to teach Mary Joe to be a good girl. He needed to hear her scream for what she did. No one escaped punishment for their sins, not even her.

Glenn focused on his rifle. The weapon had a fiberglass stock coated in gray non-slip rubber and a heavy twenty-inch barrel with a muzzle threaded for a suppressor. After he'd added a good optics package, it had become his favorite weapon in the world to shoot.

"She's already hunting you," said Helen. "She'll kill us if she finds us."

Glenn glanced up at her but said nothing as he reached into the trigger guard assembly to press the release button. The bolt slid out with little resistance.

"I don't want to have this conversation with you," he said, taking the bolt to his vise so he could disassemble and clean it.

"You need to have this conversation with me," she said. Glenn slid the underlug on the bolt's cocking piece into his vise, allowing him to separate the bolt's body from the striker assembly. "We started this to put the world right and to punish the wicked. What are we doing now? Trying to pick up some stupid girl?"

Glenn continued disassembling the bolt action on his rifle until he had everything inside the bolt on a clean white towel on his bench. From there, he removed the trigger guard and barrel action from the stock.

"Do you think Dad would want you doing this?" asked Helen.

Glenn's hands trembled, but he didn't look up at her.

"Look at me, honey," said Helen, her voice soft. "You knew our father better than I did. Would he want you doing this?"

"Dad taught me how to do this," said Glenn.

"No, he didn't," said Helen, reaching to his face and tilting his chin upward so he'd look her in the eyes. "Our father may have taught you to hunt, but he didn't teach you to do this."

Only he did. Glenn's father, Edward, had been a Marine sniper and fought in Korea during the Chosin Reservoir campaign. The Marines credited him with fifty-three confirmed kills during his military career. Glenn's father hadn't spoken about the war often, but he had never left it.

"You didn't know our father," said Glenn. "You left too early. If you had known him, you'd know this was the only thing he'd want me to do."

Helen paused and cocked her head at him.

"Do you talk to Dad?"

He looked down at his weapon and removed the magazine spring and follower.

"Dad's gone. He left me like you did."

Helen reached for his chin again to lift his head, but she yelped as he slapped her hand away.

"Sorry," he muttered as he disassembled the trigger assembly.

"That's okay," said Helen, rubbing her hand. She took a deep breath and leaned forward. "Did Dad come back like I did?"

"Drop it, Helen," he said, glancing at her. "After you disappeared, it was just the two of us."

"Do you talk to him now?" she asked.

Once he had the trigger assembly taken apart, Glenn moved to his barrel vise.

"Did Dad come back?" asked Helen, her voice growing lower and more insistent. "Tell me, Glenn."

Glenn glanced up at his sister.

"No. Jesus, Helen. Are you seriously asking whether I see the ghost of our dead father? I'm not crazy. Our father died. You've seen his grave."

Helen nodded and breathed through her nose.

"Good. Then what are you doing?"

For just a split second, he clenched his jaw as a sharp, piercing pain radiated out from the front of his head. Then he took two breaths before securing his rifle's receiver to the top half of his action wrench. Once he finished, he clamped the barrel between a pair of oak bushings in the vise and used the action wrench to separate the barrel from the action. The process took strength and several specialized tools, but within ten minutes of sitting down at his workbench, he had his entire rifle disassembled and ready for a thorough cleaning.

"I can't keep my eyes open, Helen. If I answer your question, will you shut up and let me sleep?"

She considered. "Depends on your answer."

"Fine," he said, glaring at her. "I'm preparing."

"What are you preparing for?"

Glenn felt his lips press into a tight line as he glanced up.

"You think you're smarter than everyone," he said.

"I've never thought I was smarter than you," she said.

"Good," he said. "Because you're not. You didn't even have a plan, did you?"

"What are you saying?"

"There's no end game to this," he said, allowing his anger to enter his voice. "I listened to you. I did everything you told me to do. You told me we would right the wrongs done to you, but all you've done is hold me back. You're a liar, and you ran away when I needed you most. Mom died, and then you left me and Dad alone."

"I never wanted to leave you," she said, leaning across the workbench to cover his hands with her own. "It wasn't my choice. You're my little brother. I love you, and I'm here to protect you. What's gotten into you? This doesn't even sound like you."

He pulled his hands back and then stood. "Maybe I learned who I should put my faith in."

Helen blinked and then straightened. "And who is that?"

"You know," he said. "She's been here all along."

"Her," said Helen, her voice sharp. "Your shadow."

"Yes," he said, nodding and feeling his skin grow warm with self-righteousness. "She told me the truth. You don't know what you're doing. You're just trying to control me."

A tear slid down his sister's cheek and then to the ground. "How can you say that?"

"How can you deny it?" he asked. "You're weak. You left when I needed you. You left when Dad needed you. You mean nothing to me, and you meant nothing to him."

"I've kept you alive."

"You've kept me in the dark."

Helen covered her mouth as red spread across her forehead and into her cheeks, marring her beautiful face.

"Do you want me to leave? I'll walk out right now. You'll never see me again. Is that what you want?"

Let her go. You're stronger without her.

Though his shadow's voice sounded soft, she was powerful. She had been coming to him at night, whispering to him, telling him the truth. She wasn't family, though. He didn't know what she was, but she wasn't kin. Helen was all he had left.

"I don't know what I want. You've got me so screwed up, I don't even know what I'm doing anymore."

"Then stick to the plan," said Helen, once more covering his hands with her own and squeezing. This time, he didn't pull away. "This can still work."

No plan can work without a goal. What are you going to accomplish?

Glenn put his hands flat on his workbench and stared at his rifle. He wasn't a military-trained sniper, but with that rifle and the Schmidt Bender PMII optics he had installed, he could hit targets with a .300 Winchester round at nine hundred yards. At that distance, his opponents wouldn't even hear the shot before they died.

"Suppose we take another couple," he said, keeping his voice slow and composed. "What will we accomplish?"

"We save other girls from a predator. You know what happened to me. Only you can put that right. That was enough at one time."

It was never enough. You can change the world.

Glenn blinked and shook his head before standing and walking to the cabinet where he kept his gun-cleaning supplies. When he returned to his bench with solvent and clean rags, he looked to his sister.

"The police are too close. There won't be an arrest; the FBI will kill me."

"If that's how you feel, we can run," said Helen. "You've got the money. We can start over. We can be a family."

If we run today, we'll run every day of our lives.

He listened to his shadow and knew she spoke the truth. She understood the world.

"We can't run. We have to make a stand."

"I don't like this," said Helen, shaking her head. "This isn't you."

"But it is," said Glenn. "All this time, you've told me I was doing something right. You told me we were bringing you justice, but we weren't. You were getting revenge."

Helen's face went hard.

"Revenge is justice, Glenn."

"If that's true, you were looking at the wrong people."

Glenn held his sister's glare until her face softened.

"What are you saying?"

"While you've been bitching about Mary Joe, I've been planning," said Glenn. "We're broadening our target list. They need to hurt for what they did to us."

"Who's going to hurt? What are you even talking about?"

He smiled at her. "Everybody. If you want to hurt the shepherd, slaughter his lambs. Now shut up and let me work."

Helen didn't look convinced, but she nodded anyway and shut her mouth. For that, at least, Glenn felt grateful. He hadn't wanted to kill her, too.

Chapter 26

I signed out a marked cruiser and drove to County Road 10, where I found two white Highway Patrol cruisers and a black Highway Patrol SUV off the side of the road. Forested hills dotted the landscape, as they did all over this part of Missouri, and the road swooped and curved back on itself, hugging the hillsides. We worked on a lot of car accidents in areas like this. Few, thankfully, resulted in fatalities.

I parked behind the SUV and stepped out of my vehicle. The air carried a hint of pine resin and dirt on a warm breeze. Ahead of me, the road curved to the left. To the right of the pavement, the ground sloped to a tree line about fifty feet away. There was a white car at the base of the slope with several uniformed officers arrayed around it. Judging by the damage to the sod and to the vehicle's roof, it had rolled at least a few times on the way down.

A woman in her midthirties stepped out of the SUV as I approached. She wore a navy blazer, jeans, and a blue and white striped shirt. It was a nice, professional outfit, the kind I would have liked to have been wearing. Instead, I wore the same blazer I had worn the day before and a top I had purchased at Walmart. I flashed my badge at her and then looked down at the accident.

"I'm Detective Joe Court," I said. "My dispatcher told me you found Thad Stevens and Trinity Foster."

"Detective Jill Turley," she said, holding out a hand, which I shook. She nodded toward the car. "We found them. What's your interest?"

"They were potentially my suspects in a double homicide. I had hoped to talk to them and eliminate them."

Turley put her hands on her hips and looked toward the crashed vehicle.

"Does your homicide involve a nine-millimeter, by chance?"

I nodded. "Yeah. Coroner pulled five nine-millimeter bullets from the bodies. Our forensic technician thought they came from a Glock 19."

Turley turned toward me, her eyebrows raised.

"You may have solved your homicide, then. We recovered a Glock 19 from the vehicle."

I sighed and put my hands on my hips.

"Not how I hoped this would end, but I'll take it. My forensics team will need the pistol."

"I'll make it available to you," she said, taking a step back. "There's something else you should see. Come on."

I followed her toward the spot where Thad's car had slipped off the road. A sports car might whip around that corner at fifty miles an hour on a dry day, but any rain or snow would prevent the tires from getting traction. A small miscalculation could make a driver slide right off the hill—just as Thad's car apparently had.

"Tell me what you see," said Turley.

I glanced at her and furrowed my brow. She raised her eyebrows, imploring me to continue, so I looked straight ahead again.

"The scene of an accident," I said. "Thad and Trinity were driving and misjudged their speed. Maybe it was dark, maybe their car slipped on debris, or maybe they were drunk. However it happened, they didn't make the turn, and their car rolled off the hill."

"That's what it looks like," said Turley. "But where are the skid marks? Where are the indications the car slid? Where's the debris on the road the driver had to swerve to avoid? It's summer, so they didn't have to worry about snow or ice. The road's in good shape, too, so they didn't slide on gravel. If they were drunk, we would have smelled booze on the corpses. We didn't. This was no accident."

"You think somebody set them up?" I asked, furrowing my brow.

"I think somebody pushed the car off the hill," said Turley. "Once we found a firearm in the trunk, we dusted the trunk lid for prints. Someone had wiped it clean. The steering wheel, interior door handles, and gear selector have also been wiped clean. If Thad drove this car off the hill, he did so without touching a single thing inside."

"That's a problem," I said, nodding and thinking. "We found a car not too far from here that belonged to Paige Maxwell. The Apostate abducted her and her boyfriend. They escaped before he killed them."

Detective Turley lowered her chin and furrowed her brow. "You think the Apostate did this?"

I tilted my head to the side. "It's possible, but if he did, he stepped way out of his routine. What do you need me to do?"

Turley considered. "You offering to assist on this case?"

"For now," I said. "My boss will have me cleaning toilets by the end of the day, but I'll do what I can until he tells me otherwise."

"Sorry about the toilets," she said. "If you want to help, I need information. Who comes out here, who are the nearest neighbors, and who owns the property? It's background information, but it could point me toward potential witnesses."

I nodded, more to myself than to her.

"Sure. I can find the property owner in county records, and a guy at my station can tell me about the neighbors."

"That's why I like working with locals," she said, reaching into the inside pocket of her blazer for a business card. I did the same, and we exchanged cards. She looked at mine. "Call me if you find anything good. In the meantime, if I need you, I'll call."

"Sounds good," I said, turning toward my cruiser. While Detective Turley got back to work, I sat in my car to think.

I had driven all over St. Augustine County, but even I rarely got out to that stretch of County Road 10. Trinity and Thad's killer not only knew where it was, he also knew where the guardrail had a break, he knew where a car could roll off, and he knew when to come so that employees from the chicken processing plant—the nearest business—wouldn't be around. Our killer was a local.

Once I got back in my car, I drove to the county court-house, but I pulled out my phone along the way and called Dave Skelton, a uniformed officer in my department. Dave had grown up in St. Augustine and knew the county well. He was a good cop now, but he had raised hell as a teenager. From the stories I had heard, he slept with just about every woman his age in the county, and he had smoked marijuana on every hilltop, valley, glade, and meadow within a hundred-mile radius. He also knew every moonshiner, survival-ist, and backwoods guide in the area. If anybody could tell me about that stretch of Highway 10, it'd be him.

His phone went to voicemail, so I left him a message. Detective Turley would have to wait. After that, I parked beside the courthouse and looked up property records. That stretch of property had last been owned by Pennington Ho-tels, Inc. It was part of a twenty-four-acre parcel that had in-cluded a gravel driveway and a twelve-hundred-square-foot cinder-block building. The company had stopped paying property taxes almost twenty years ago, which made me wonder how helpful this would be.

I thanked the clerk and walked back to my car. A twelve-hundred-square-foot building was too small for a hotel, and cinder block was too cheap for a villa or cabin for wealthy customers. If I had to guess, it was a garage or a maintenance shed. Someone who worked at the shop might know where cars were likely to slide off the hill. A mechanic or maintenance worker might have even known how to rig a car to drive over an embankment.

I drummed my fingers on the steering wheel. After twenty years, this was so tenuous it didn't even feel like a lead, but I used my cruiser's laptop to open the license bureau's database. St. Augustine County had three residents with the last name Pennington. Two of them were in their late twenties, which meant they would have been in elementary school twenty years ago when the company was still active. The third resident, though, looked right.

I checked my messages to see whether Dave Skelton had called me back, and then I put my car in gear and drove toward my house. Instead of pulling into my driveway, I drove past it and turned left at a mailbox with the name *Pennington* written on the side.

Susanne must have seen me pull in because she came outside with a smile on her face. I hugged her on the front porch. I didn't usually like hugging people because it felt too intimate. Susanne hugged without ulterior motives, though.

She wanted nothing except to be my friend. Seeing her usually made my whole day brighter.

"Have you had lunch, honey?" she asked, pulling back a moment later. "I've got good turkey in the fridge."

"No, but this isn't a social call," I said. "I'm here because I'm working a case. Have you ever heard of Pennington Hotels?"

The smile slid from her face. She blinked a few times and then drew in a breath before smiling once more.

"That was my husband's company."

"We found a pair of bodies on property your husband once owned," I said. "You mind talking about the company and your former employees?"

Her smile dipped once more, and she considered me before nodding.

"I expected this to catch up to me."

The remark surprised me, but I tried to keep my face neutral.

"You expected what to catch up to you?"

She put a hand on my elbow.

"Come on inside, sweetheart," she said. "We've got a lot to talk about."

Chapter 27

T hough we lived a quarter of a mile from one another, Susanne and I had identical houses. The family that had built her home saw my house during construction and liked it so much they put up one of their own. Unlike my house, though, hers had never gone vacant, and it had all the original architectural details. I was more than a little jealous.

We walked through her living room to the kitchen at the home's rear. There, she made coffee, while I sat and waited. When the coffee finished brewing, she sat across from me at her small breakfast table and handed me a mug. For a moment, we sat and sipped. Then I cleared my throat.

"You don't talk about your husband often," I said.

"He was a bastard," said Susanne.

She didn't elaborate, but she didn't need to. She didn't speak poorly of people without reason.

"What happened to his hotel?"

She cocked her head to the side. "You've never heard of Pennington Hotels?"

I shook my head. She smiled.

"Pennington Hotels, my husband's company, operated forty-three locations across Missouri, Tennessee, Iowa, Arkansas, Kentucky, and Kansas. We even owned a spa in Hot Springs, Arkansas. We were high-society folk."

"What happened?"

Susanne sipped her drink and shrugged. "When Stanley died, he left debts to pay. I sold the company to pay them."

I nodded, though her stiff mannerisms told me there was more to the story than she had let on. That didn't change what I needed to know, but it made me think.

"As I told you earlier, I'm working multiple murders," I said. "The most recent involved a young man and woman who died on property once owned by your husband's company."

"Stanley and I owned a lot of property back then."

"I understand," I said. "Thad and Trinity aren't the only crimes tied to that area, though. About seven weeks ago, we found a car belonging to a young woman named Paige Maxwell on property bordering your husband's property. She and her boyfriend were abducted and held in some kind of dungeon. They escaped, but the man who abducted them nearly killed them."

"I saw the story on the news. It's awful."

"It is. Here's where we're at with the investigation: We have a serial murderer who dumped a car near your husband's property. Someone—possibly the same person—murdered two more young people in the same area.

This second murder required knowledge only a local would have."

"And you think this local worked for Stanley," said Susanne, drawing everything together before I could say anything.

I nodded. "It's a long shot, but it's a possibility."

"No one's worked for Pennington Hotels in a long time. Where were your bodies found?"

"Just off County Road 10. According to our records, it once had a twelve-hundred-square-foot cinder-block building and a gravel driveway. Does that sound familiar?"

A tight smile formed on Susanne's lips.

"That does, actually. I went there several times after commissioning pieces for our house. It was Pennington Hotels' woodworking shop. Back then, it made sense to have someone in-house to repair cabinets and tables and other furniture. A man named Edward worked there. I don't remember his last name, but he built the table we're sitting at and the coffee table in my living room. He was a nice man."

If he worked on the property for any length of time, he'd have the local knowledge needed to kill Thad and Trinity. I nodded.

"Is he still around, you think?"

"Maybe," she said, shrugging, "but if he's alive, he's older than I am."

That put a damper on things. Susanne was a capable woman, but I doubted anyone her age could do what the Apostate did.

"That's helpful," I said, trying to keep the disappointment out of my voice. "While I'm here, can I ask you another question?"

"You can ask me any question you want, sweetheart," she said.

"Serial murderers often try to recreate traumatic events from their pasts. The Apostate goes after young couples. So far, they've all been juniors or seniors in high school. He forces the boys to rape and murder the girls. Then, we think, he burns the boys alive..."

Even as I spoke, I knew I shouldn't have opened my mouth. Susanne squeezed my forearm as she brought her other hand to her mouth.

"I'm sorry," I said, lowering my voice. "That was too much, wasn't it?"

Susanne held up her hand to stop me from saying anything else.

"I love you, but I hate the ugly world you live in. I've asked you before not to bring your work here. Please don't make me ask again."

Part of me wanted to tell her she lived in that same world and that by ignoring the world's ugliness, she let it fester and grow unchecked. She didn't need to hear that from me, though. She had seen the world's ugliness firsthand. I couldn't blame her for running from it. That was her choice. I softened my voice.

"Most days, I'm not a fan of the world I live in, either. I shouldn't have brought it up. Sorry."

She looked at our hands. Neither of us said anything. With other people, silence felt awkward, but with Susanne, it was comforting. I didn't have many people in my life who made me feel like that, and I appreciated it.

"I'm sorry, but I can't help you," she said. "I wish I could. If you're looking at the history of crime in St. Augustine, I'm not the person you should ask."

She was right, so I nodded. More than merely being right, though, she made me think. I stayed for another few minutes but then drove back to my station. Doug Patricia, one of our uniformed officers, sat behind the front desk, typing while he spoke on the phone and routed officers somewhere. I nodded hello and walked to the basement.

Where a larger department might have had an entire division dedicated to the preservation and storage of evidence and old files, we had a locked storage vault and Mark Bozwell, an ornery, sixty-year-old asshole who couldn't keep his eyes above my neckline.

I walked through the basement to the evidence room's heavy steel door. Inside, welded wire cages and steel shelves holding boxes of evidence stretched forty or fifty feet ahead of me and maybe thirty feet to my left and right. The front desk was empty.

"Hey, Mark?" I called. "It's Detective Joe Court. I'm here to search the file cabinets."

A cage clanged shut. Then, keys jangled as the evidence clerk walked toward me. Mark had buzzed white hair and shoulders so wide he had to turn sideways in some doors. If he had been a little taller, he would have been big enough to play football in college or maybe even the NFL, but given his short height, he looked more like a wrestler than anything else.

When he turned down the aisle and saw me, he slowed. I could almost feel his eyes on my chest and legs, so I crossed my arms to limit my exposure.

"What can I do for you, Detective?" he asked once he reached his desk, smiling and pretending he hadn't been checking me out.

"I need to go through the file cabinets," I said. "The Apostate kills his victims in a unique way. I want to find any cases with similar circumstances."

Mark narrowed his eyes and nodded.

"How do you plan on doing that? Our modern records are digital, but our case records from before 1995 are paper."

I forced a smile to my lips.

"I guess I'll be doing a lot of reading," I said. He narrowed his eyes at me incredulously, so I sighed and tilted my head to the side. "St. Augustine only gets ten to fifteen murders a year. Even if I search through fifty years of files, we'll only have a couple hundred murders. Of those, a handful will involve drownings. I'll pull out the files I need and put everything back after I'm done."

Mark drew in a deep breath and crossed his arms.

"It's doable, I guess," he said. "Sheriff Delgado has asked me to clear any unusual requests with him, though."

I allowed the smile to leave my lips as a headache formed at my temples.

"You've done this job for a long time, Mark. Is it unusual for a detective to request access to old case files?"

The evidence clerk took a step back and held up his hands as if I had attacked him.

"I'm following the procedures the sheriff has outlined for me, Joe. If you want access to the filing cabinets, I've got to log the request and cross-reference it to your active caseload. I'm only allowed to give out information if it relates to a detective's assigned duties."

I closed my eyes and let out a long breath.

"Fine. I'm working a double homicide involving a young man named Thad Stevens and a young woman named Trinity Foster. It's possible they were murdered by the Apostate."

Mark considered me before stooping to pull open the middle drawer of his desk. He pulled out a spiral-bound notebook and flipped through pages. I shifted my weight from one foot to the other as I squeezed my jaw tight.

"My notes from the roll-call meeting this morning say you're working the cases of Mark and Lilly Foster. The sheriff didn't mention Trinity Foster or Thad Stevens."

"I'm working a case. Give me the keys and get out of my way, Mark. I understand that you're trying to do your job, but so am I."

He considered before shaking his head. "I'm sorry, Detective, but the sheriff's made it clear I'm only supposed to give out information if it relates to a detective's assigned duties."

"Fine," I said, taking a step back. "I'll call the sheriff."

As I took my phone from my purse, Mark shook his head. "You won't get a signal down here."

He was right because I didn't have a single bar. I left the evidence vault and walked until I had a connection. By then, I was halfway up the stairs to the lobby, so I figured I might as well go straight upstairs to Delgado's office and confront him face to face.

Before I made it, my phone beeped with three incoming text messages. All came from a number I didn't recognize. The first message said *Mary Joe?*, the second message asked how Paige and Jude were, and the third message asked whether I had asked Jude about the peanut butter and jelly sandwich.

It didn't happen often, but crazy people sometimes liked to insert themselves into investigations to which they had no connection. Maybe it made them feel important, or maybe they were bored and needed something to do. I didn't know why they did it, but they did. This wasn't a random crazy person, though. We hadn't released any information about the peanut butter and jelly sandwich. This was him. Again.

I walked to the lobby and texted back.

What do you want?

His response was almost immediate.

You.

I shuddered.

"You all right, Detective?"

I looked up to see Doug Patricia looking at me from the front desk. I forced myself to nod.

"Fine, thank you," I said. "Call Sheriff Delgado and tell him to come in. I've got the Apostate on the phone again."

Doug furrowed his brow but didn't move, so I lowered my phone.

"Just do it, Doug!"

Doug nodded and ripped the phone from the cradle as I ran upstairs. The door to the conference room was closed, but I threw it open without knocking and nearly hit Special Agent Bryan Costa.

"Easy, Detective," he said, furrowing his brow and stepping away from the doorway. "I was going to get coffee."

I looked around. Costa and I were alone.

"Where's Lawson?" I asked.

"On a smoke break. Why?"

"Because the Apostate just sent me another text message."

Chapter 28

"**Y**ou sure it's him?" asked Costa.

"He asked me about the peanut butter and jelly sandwich," I said. "We haven't released that information."

Agent Costa nodded and considered for a moment. I looked around the room. Someone had stacked file boxes against the walls, wiped the whiteboards clean, and taken the laptops from the conference table. It looked like a storage room once more. No one else was around.

"Where's the rest of your team?" I asked.

"Gone," said Costa. "We're pulling back to St. Louis. After finding the evidence boxes at your house, Sheriff Delgado told us we're no longer welcome in his station."

I swore under my breath and nodded as I tried to figure out what to do.

"We need to find Agent Lawson and tell him I've got the Apostate on the phone."

"I'll take care of that," said Costa. "Keep the Apostate talking as long as you can."

I nodded and pulled a chair from the table to sit down. For almost thirty seconds, I could only stare at my phone. Then, the door swung open, and Agent Lawson burst into the conference room. He wore a gray suit, white shirt, and red tie. Even from my seat, I could smell cigarette smoke. Costa put his phone into his pocket.

"What's he said?" asked Lawson.

"Not much yet," I said. "I asked him what he wants. He said he wanted me."

Lawson looked at Agent Costa. "Call Jamal and tell him we need this guy's phone tracked. I'll call Major Henderson with the Highway Patrol and see whether he can spare troopers. Joe, you keep talking to him. We can't lose him this time."

"I'm on it," said Costa, already thumbing through entries on his phone.

None of them looked at me, so I typed a response without their input.

I want to help you.

I waited almost a minute for his reply.

No, you don't. But you will once I break you.

Agent Lawson paced on the other side of the table and cast occasional sidelong glances at me as he spoke on the phone. I caught his eye, and he walked to stand beside me and read the messages the Apostate had sent me.

"What do you think?" I asked.

Lawson blinked and considered. "He's confident, and he's got a plan. Ask him about it."

It was a good thought, so I nodded and typed in a message.

Why are you interested in me?

He didn't respond right away. I drew in a breath and waited. Finally, my phone buzzed.

Because you know why I have to do this. You'll help me.

Lawson read it over my shoulder.

"That make any sense to you?" he asked.

"No, but it makes sense to him," I said, shaking my head. "That means we should be able to figure it out if we think about things from his point of view. He abducts young people—a boy and a girl. He starves them over the course of several weeks to make them cooperative and then gives the boy food if he assaults the girl. He then tells the boy that other men will assault the girl unless he kills her. That's the story Jude and Paige gave us, right?"

Lawson nodded. "Yeah. Does it make sense to you?"

I shook my head. "Not really, but there's another step Jude and Paige never got to. After the boy kills the girl, the Apostate burns the boy alive. We learned that from his church. That's the critical step. He punishes the boy. He sends him to hell. That's why he thinks I would understand him."

Lawson furrowed his brow. "You lost me on the last part."

"When I was a teenager, my foster father raped me. When he got out of prison, he came after me again, and I killed him.

I punished him. That's why the Apostate is interested in me. He thinks we're alike in some way."

Lawson looked at Agent Costa. Costa shrugged and continued his conversation.

"Then say that," said Lawson, straightening. I nodded and typed.

Some people deserve punishment.

I sent it and held my breath. Within moments, my phone beeped with an incoming text message.

Is that why you became a cop?

I typed before either of the FBI agents could say anything.

Yes. I punish those who deserve it.

"Space your messages out. Keep him talking as long as you can," said Lawson, looking up to Agent Costa. "Where are we with the trace?"

"Jamal and his team are triangulating the Apostate's position now," said Costa. "He's local."

Lawson relayed that information to the Highway Patrol. After a few moments, Lawson looked at me.

"Highway Patrol has sent a dozen troopers our way," he said, covering his phone once more. He looked at me. "The Apostate has contacted you twice now. Why?"

"Probably the same reason he broke into my house and took my underwear," I said. "I think he likes me. He wants a friend."

Lawson nodded, his eyes distant as he thought. Then he resumed his conversation with the Highway Patrol. My phone beeped again, but I ignored it for the moment and focused on Agent Costa.

"How many agents do you have in the county?" I asked.

"Just me and Bruce," he said. "Everybody else is at the office in St. Louis or out in the field."

"Go downstairs and talk to Doug Patricia. He's our dispatcher. It'll take time for the Highway Patrol to get here, but our department has officers on the ground right now. As soon as your technical people find the Apostate, we can send a team to pick him up."

Costa looked at his boss. Lawson nodded.

"Do it."

Agent Costa hurried toward the door. I looked at the message on my phone.

"Are you religious?" I asked, reading aloud.

"Come again?" asked Lawson.

"It's the message the Apostate sent," I said, typing my response. "I'm telling him I believe in God."

Lawson told the Highway Patrol officer he'd call him back. Then he crossed the room and sat beside me and stared at my phone. Within moments, it beeped again with an incoming text.

That's not an answer.

Lawson read it and nodded.

"Keep him talking. Elaborate, but be vague."

I typed in a message.

God and I have a complicated relationship.

Lawson read the text and nodded, so I sent it.

"That's good," he said. "Ask him how he feels about religion next. Tell him you saw his church and that it intrigued you. Ask him whether he ever attended services there."

I waited for a response from the Apostate, but none came for almost thirty seconds, giving me time to stand and think.

"That's too aggressive," I said. "If we push him too hard, he'll pull away. He's still feeling me out. We need to keep the chase going."

My phone beeped with another incoming text message. Lawson picked it up and read aloud.

"Don't go to church today," he said. He paused and blinked before looking at me. "Do a lot of churches hold Saturday services here?"

I shrugged. "I don't know. I'm not a big churchgoer."

Lawson nodded, his eyes distant. "That was a warning. The Apostate cares about you. He doesn't want you hurt. He's going to attack a church today and doesn't want you there."

"Sounds reasonable," I said. "I guess."

Lawson reached into his pocket and pulled out his phone.

"You don't seem convinced."

"An attack on a church doesn't fit his profile," I said. "Everything he's done so far has been targeted."

"No profile is ever complete or a hundred percent accurate," said Lawson. He dialed a number. "Stacey. It's Bruce.

Get on the phone and send the entire team back to St. Augustine. Tell them lights and sirens. I need them here now."

As Agent Lawson spoke, Costa came back in the room.

"The Apostate's phone is off," he said. "We think he was on the interstate between here and St. Louis."

Lawson nodded and looked at me.

"We need to start calling churches. If they have something going on tonight, we need to persuade them to cancel and allow my agents to search their facilities. If the Apostate hid an explosive in a church, we need to find it before people get hurt."

"That request might sound better coming from the sheriff," said Agent Costa.

"Then get him," said Lawson, looking to me once more. "The Apostate knows your cell number, your address, and your life story. I need a list of everybody you've met while working this case."

"I can get you the list, but I don't know how much it will help. Angela Pritchard shared my story with the entire world, my cell number is on the Sheriff's Department website, and my address is on the county assessor's website. My job makes me a public person."

Lawson sighed before nodding.

"I understand," said Lawson. "Work with Sheriff Delgado and start calling churches. We need to put together a list of potential targets, and then we need to shut them down before he takes out anybody else."#

Chapter 29

The wind held steady from the west, but even halfway up the water tower, it didn't bother him. St. Augustine had built the tower in the early eighties when Glenn had been in college. It was a hundred and seventy feet high and held well over a million gallons of fresh water. In a power outage or disaster, the town would open the valves, and the tower would provide a day's worth of water to the mains at almost a hundred pounds per square inch of pressure, more than enough to run showers, toilets, and major appliances across the county.

Today, that tower would serve a different purpose.

The rifle case strapped to Glenn's back impeded his movements but not as much as the rope and harness slung over his shoulder. Helen, just beneath him on the ladder, wore a breezy top and black fingerless climbing gloves. Her expression was unconcerned, even relaxed.

"Enjoying the climb?" he asked, resting for a few seconds and looking down.

"I don't think it's so bad," she said, smiling. "Nice breeze, pretty day. Are you not having fun?"

Kick her. Break her fingers.

Glenn could almost close his eyes and imagine himself giving in to his shadow's demands. He would have enjoyed watching Helen plunge to her death, but he still needed her. She was his compass. Without her, he lacked direction. That gave her power over him. As if reading his thoughts, Helen smiled even broader.

"I dare you to try to knock me off," she said. "You'll fall and break your stupid little neck."

"I don't want to talk to you," he said, looking up and resuming his climb.

"Then shut up and listen," she said. "We have a good thing together, and you're going to ruin it for nothing."

"I'm doing this for you," he said. "Everything I've done is for you."

"You're doing this because your shadow wants you to. You're weak, Glenn. You've always been weak," said Helen. "You're like Dad. Mom had balls, but you killed her before she passed them on to you."

He said nothing and climbed the remaining seventy feet to the scaffolding at the top of the tower. The height gave him clear sightlines to Waterford College, to downtown St. Augustine, and to every building, parking lot, and park in between. The breeze was stronger that high, but he knew how to compensate for it.

"I didn't mean to kill Mom," said Glenn, once his sister finished climbing the ladder. "At least you got to meet her. I don't even remember her voice."

Helen considered him before pulling herself onto the scaffolding and sitting with her feet dangling over the edge and her chest pressed against the guardrail. Though she was five years older than him, she almost looked childish.

"I'm sorry I said that," she said.

"No, you're not. She died in childbirth. You never forgave me," said Glenn, stepping into his climbing harness and then securing the long rope around the guardrail near his sister. As tall as the water tower was, it would take him four and a half minutes to climb down the ladder once he did his job. He had timed it twice already. That was four minutes too long.

As soon as he pulled the trigger, the sinners would look for him. If it took almost five minutes to get down, they'd easily find him suspended a hundred feet in the air on a ladder. A controlled drop from a rappelling rope shortened his descent to under thirty seconds. He'd disappear by the time the police even thought to look for him.

"I don't understand why we're doing this," said Helen. "This is an unnecessary risk."

With his harness secure, Glenn unzipped the bag in which he carried his rifle, a task made more difficult by his climbing gloves. Unlike his sister's gloves, his had fingers. He'd leave smudges behind, but no prints.

"Your way wasn't working," he said, setting up the carbon-fiber tripod system that would hold his rifle steady. "I'm tired of talking to you. Let me work."

Kill her. Throw her off the side.

Glenn didn't know how much Helen weighed, but he doubted it was much. He could toss her over the side as his shadow suggested, and she'd careen to her doom in seconds. She wouldn't have time to scream. His world would go quiet once more.

Only, that would simply trade one master for another. Helen watched over him. She loved him. Her embraces and sweet words had helped him through more rough patches than he remembered. His shadow was a black hole that sucked in the light. She didn't love him. She didn't even care about him. His shadow only wanted to be fed. Helen kept her at bay. She protected him.

He hated this. His fate had never been his own. It never would be, either.

"I hate you, Helen."

"But you love and need me, too," she said. "And I love and need you."

He nodded. A weight far greater than gravity pressed down on him, threatening to buckle his knees.

"Mary Joe was never mine," he said. "I thought she was the one for me, but she wasn't."

Helen took her gaze from the town and reached out a hand. He squeezed her hand between his own.

"No, she wasn't, but I'm yours. I've always been yours, and you've always been mine," she said, smiling her sweet, beautiful smile. Almost at once, the weight left his shoulders, his hands steadied, and his muscles relaxed. His shadow's voice quieted. "You're stubborn, Glenn, just like Dad was. I'm here to guide you and help you."

"Can you tell me about Mom?" he asked.

She moved his hands toward his rifle. "Tonight, sweetheart. Now, I want you to prove how much you love me. Since we're up here, we'll use the platform. Kill Detective Court. As long as she lives, she's a threat."

Glenn nodded. Helen was right. He would die soon—even he understood that—but he had work to finish. Mary Joe could ruin everything. She needed to die.

Slowly, he nodded.

"I'll take care of her."

Helen patted him gently and lovingly. "Good. Let's get to work."

Within five minutes of the Apostate's last message, we had six uniformed officers making calls to churches in St. Augustine and a dozen troopers with the Highway Patrol searching the interstate and surrounding roads for anyone who matched the little we knew about him. The Highway Patrol had good officers, but nobody knew what to look for. They were wasting their time.

I walked to my desk. About half the foster families with whom I had grown up went to church, so I had attended services at just about every kind of Christian church in existence. Some churches had hundreds or even thousands of members. They had softball leagues, gymnasiums, and professional coordinators who planned events. Other churches were single rooms in a strip mall. They were lucky to have a pastor.

Even if Lawson spoke to a representative from every church in the county, he'd miss events. Modern churches played so many roles in the community that few would have a single point of contact who knew everything that occurred inside their buildings.

We needed to be smarter.

Once I reached my desk, I pulled out my phone and called Rise and Grind. A young man answered, but he gave the phone to Sheryl, the owner, when I asked.

"Hey, Joe," she said. "What can I do for you?"

"Sheryl, hey," I said. "I need your help. You've got people going through your shop all the time, and you hear them talk. Has anyone mentioned church events today?"

She drew in a breath.

"No. Well, not really," she said. "Father Mike came by this morning and picked up a gallon of coffee. His church is sponsoring a Habitat for Humanity house on Hickory Boulevard. Does that count?"

I nodded and wrote it down.

"Yeah. That's great. Anything else going on?"

"I don't know," she said. "Hold on just a second."

She must have muffled the phone because her voice quieted as she spoke to someone else.

"Jeremy says there's a club at his high school called the Fellowship of Christian Athletes, and they're holding a picnic in Magnolia Park."

I nodded and wrote it down. "Does Jeremy know anybody involved?"

After some back and forth, she gave me the faculty sponsor's name and other details. I thanked her and hung up. Both the Habitat for Humanity build and the club picnic would involve dozens of people congregated in a small area. They'd be enticing targets.

I called the Catholic church first. It took about half a dozen phone calls to track him down, but I talked to Father Mike, who happened to be at the Habitat build site. Once I told him there was a potential threat, he agreed to shut everything down and send everybody home.

The faculty advisor for the Fellowship of Christian Athletes was a little more difficult. She told me the high school had received six threats in the previous year alone, none of which had amounted to anything, but all of which had disrupted the lives of her students. Absent a specific threat to her event, she wasn't going to cancel it.

After wasting twenty minutes with Mrs. Busby, I hung up and walked upstairs to the conference room. Agents Lawson and Costa, Sheriff Delgado, and two uniformed Highway

Patrol troopers sat around the table talking. Lawson waved me in as I opened the door.

"So far, we've found six churches with events today. We've convinced four to postpone. We're putting teams together to search all six, and we'll post officers outside of each during their services. Has the Apostate contacted you again?"

I shook my head. "No, but I've got another gathering to add to the list. It's a picnic in Magnolia Park sponsored by the Fellowship of Christian Athletes, a club at the high school. The picnic starts in about an hour. I couldn't persuade them to cancel."

Lawson considered for a moment.

"An hour?" he asked, raising his eyebrows. I nodded, and he looked to the sheriff. "How quickly can you get a team together?"

"We'll find out," said Delgado, standing. "Detective Court, you're with me. Let's go."

I hesitated and then followed the sheriff out of the room, wondering what he wanted me for.

"Agent Lawson thinks the Apostate's working alone," said Delgado, talking while we walked toward the lobby. "He's got twenty-four FBI agents with tactical training en route, and the Highway Patrol has another forty troopers in the county. I've called in the night shift, so we have forty-four of our own people around town. If the Apostate shoots up one of our churches, he'll regret it."

"We'll get him," I said, hoping my voice sounded more confident than I felt.

"Hell yes, we will," said Delgado. "You don't get to kill kids in Missouri and get away with it, not while we're on duty."

When we reached the front desk, Officer Doug Patricia nodded toward us both.

"Sheriff Delgado, Detective Court," he said. "What's up?"

"I need eight officers to meet Detective Court at Magnolia Park. The Apostate might be coming to hurt kids there. We need to make sure he fails."

"Okay," said Patricia, focusing on his screen. "You want anybody in particular?"

Delgado looked at me.

"Whoever's on duty," I said. "We need a show of force. If eight marked cruisers surround the park, the Apostate should think twice before going there. We'll stop him before he hurts anybody."

Delgado held up a hand.

"That's not how we'll handle this," he said. "I appreciate your gusto, but we've got to consider the opportunity in front of us. The Apostate's coming after us somewhere. If we do this right, we can get him off the streets permanently. I want your team out there, but I want them in civilian clothes, and I don't want to hear of a police presence anywhere near the park."

I gave Delgado a sidelong glance.

"Using kids as bait is a bad idea," I said. "A lot can go wrong."

"That's why you're out there," said Delgado. "I need my best people on this."

My back stiffened as the realization hit. If we caught the Apostate, Delgado would go down as the small-town sheriff who took down the most dangerous serial murderer in Missouri's history. If the Apostate shot a kid or one of my officers, though, the blame would fall on me. Either way, Delgado got something he wanted. I didn't even realize we were playing a game, and he had already won.

Doug Patricia made calls to put the team together, and I leaned toward the sheriff and lowered my voice so only the two of us could hear.

"If someone dies today, I'll make sure it comes back on you."

"I'm sure you'll try your best, Detective," he said, patting me on the shoulder. "Good luck."

Delgado turned and left. Every muscle in my body tightened, and the blood flowed through my veins so quickly it sounded like a waterfall behind my ears. Arguing or fighting wouldn't have helped anything. I had a job to do and kids to keep safe, and that started with thinking my way through the problem.

Magnolia Park had a creek to the south, Waterford College to the west, a road to the north, and a residential neighborhood to the east. The Apostate could come from almost any direction, but there'd be enough big trees for cover and ample room for his intended victims to run. Not only that, we'd have eight officers plus me on the grounds and fifty or a hundred more officers who could arrive within minutes. If he was stupid enough to show up, we'd be ready for him.

That was why I couldn't shake the feeling we were running into a trap.

Chapter 30

After getting a team together, I grabbed my bulletproof vest from the women's locker room and then went back upstairs. Agent Lawson stood beside the front desk, signing a piece of paper. He glanced at me and then slid his paper to Officer Patricia.

"Sheriff Delgado wanted my request for additional manpower in writing so he can bill the federal government for services rendered."

"That sounds like something he'd do," I said. My team was assembling at the park, but I hesitated before leaving. Lawson noticed and nodded toward me.

"You ready?" he asked.

I blinked and thought before answering.

"The Apostate's not an idiot."

"I agree," said Lawson. "He has goals, and he's capable of enacting rational plans to attain them."

I hadn't put it in those words, but I nodded anyway.

"Why did he contact me?" I asked.

Lawson straightened and drew in a breath. "He's got an interest in you, so it's possible he wants to keep you safe."

I nodded. "It's also possible he's setting us up. This could be a game to him."

"Even if that's true, it changes nothing," said Lawson. "He made a threat, so we'll follow up."

"Have you seen Magnolia Park?"

"I've driven by it," said Lawson.

I looked to Officer Patricia and asked for a pen and a piece of paper. He handed me both, and I drew a rectangular shape on the paper.

"The park is about two hundred acres. It has six tennis courts, a softball field, a pavilion, a playground, and trails through the woods. Waterford College is to the west, there's a creek to the south, a road to the north, and a residential neighborhood to the east. The main entrance and parking lot are on the north side, but there are pedestrian entrances from the college and neighborhood."

I updated my drawing with the locations I had mentioned. Lawson nodded.

"It's bigger than I thought."

"Yeah, it's a nice park," I said, looking at my crude map. "A bomb wouldn't work here. People are too spread out. I'm not too worried about a truck, either," I said. "Even if the Apostate stole a semi and tried to run people down, there are plenty of trees to hide behind and plenty of open space to escape to. If he comes, he's most likely going to have a gun."

Lawson nodded.

"I agree," he said. "What do you plan to do?"

I looked at my map. "Three teams with three officers each. One will set up near the road. I'll assign a second team to the neighborhood entrance and a third team to the entrance near Waterford."

Lawson pointed to the south end of the map.

"What about this creek?"

"This time of year, the creek is twenty feet wide and six feet deep. The water moves quickly, too. I doubt he'd come in from that direction."

Lawson straightened and nodded. "It's a fine plan. If he comes, you'll stop him."

"Which he knows," I said. "That's the problem. He wouldn't have told me to stay away from church if he planned to hit a church or a church event. I'm not buying this. We need to rethink what we're doing."

Agent Lawson's lips curled into a tight smile. It reached his eyes, and then it disappeared.

"Suppose we keep your team members downtown instead. What will happen if he shows up at the park with a tactical rifle?"

I leaned against the counter and sighed. "He'd shoot a couple dozen people before we got there."

"And that's why you're going to the park," said Lawson. "There are no right answers. We'll bring the resources we have to as many locations around town as we can. We'll do our best."

I sighed. "Damned if we do, damned if we don't. Is that about right?"

Lawson shrugged. "Not necessarily. This may be his idea of a joke. Or maybe he'll show up somewhere, and we'll make an arrest."

I raised my eyebrows and nodded. "I guess that's possible."

"It's more than possible. Everything's going to be fine," he said. "Good luck, Detective."

I sighed and checked to ensure I had an extra magazine for my firearm and that the straps of my tactical vest were tight before nodding.

"You, too, Agent Lawson," I said. "Looks like I'll be spending the day in the park."

Agent Lawson nodded, and I started toward the front door. Despite his reassurances, I suspected we were making a mistake. Something would happen today. The Apostate had something planned, and nobody would escape unscathed.

***

Glenn held up the anemometer and watched as the fan turned. Then he looked to Helen, who sat with her back to the water tower and her knees to her chest. She held a pencil in her right hand and a notepad in her left. Glenn didn't need her calculations, though. At this range, he could do everything in his head.

"Temperature is eighty-four degrees; wind speed is four and a half miles an hour from the east. Distance to target is approximately nine hundred meters."

She nodded and wrote down the information.

"Near threats?" she asked.

Glenn focused first on the base of the tower and then on the surrounding buildings.

"None within five hundred meters. Multiple within a thousand."

Helen nodded again. "Reference points from left to right."

Glenn swung his rifle to the left and looked downfield through his scope. Then he swung it to the right as he called out landmarks.

"Left side intersection, a thousand yards. Gray brick structure, eight hundred yards. Red bed and breakfast, nine hundred yards. Mississippi River, seven hundred yards."

He looked up to see Helen writing the information down.

"We have three sections," she said. "Section one is from the intersection to the gray brick structure. Section two is from the gray brick structure to the bed and breakfast. Section three is from the bed and breakfast to the Mississippi River."

"Subdivide them by Fourteenth Street," said Glenn. "Near targets alpha, far targets bravo."

"Understood," said Helen, nodding and writing. "With the subdivision, we have six sections. One, two, and three

Alpha, and one, two, and three Bravo. Shooter, lock and load."

Glenn didn't know where his sister had learned to call targets, but she did it well. He inserted a magazine into the weapon.

"Got it," said Glenn, focusing downfield. "I've got movement in section two-bravo. Female, fifteen to sixteen years old. She's one of my students. She's walking her dog."

"Confirmed," said Helen. "Check parallax."

Glenn adjusted the parallax compensation knob on his scope to sharpen his view.

"We're good."

"Shooter, hold over two point four," said Helen.

Glenn relaxed his muscles and slowed his breath as he squeezed the trigger. His target was named Madison, and she was fifteen. She had enrolled in pre-algebra her freshman year, although Glenn thought she could have handled a more advanced class. Her father and mother were both alcoholics.

"Ready," he said.

Glenn's lungs were empty, and his heart slowed. He would squeeze the trigger between beats. Madison was smart, but she had a devious mind. Two weeks before summer break, she had come to his office with tears in her eyes and a sob story on her lips. She said her English teacher threatened to flunk her if she didn't give him a blow job in the bathroom.

Unknown to Madison, Mr. Janikowski's urologist had recently diagnosed him with testicular cancer. He was on so many painkillers he wouldn't have been able to get it up even if he'd wanted to. He hadn't propositioned her. Madison was mad at him because he wrote her a demerit for showing up late to class. That demerit gave her ten for the year, which resulted in an automatic two-day suspension. Glenn would lose no sleep over taking her out.

"Relax, shooter," said Helen.

Glenn drew in a breath and took his finger from the trigger. He almost felt disappointed, but shooting her wouldn't have accomplished anything. His real targets were still unavailable.

"We're dialed in," he said, looking at his sister.

Helen nodded. "Now we wait for the guests of honor to arrive. This will be fun."

Glenn doubted it would be fun, but he had a job to do. Soon, a lot of people in St. Augustine would die.

***

Magnolia Park wasn't far from my station, so it only took four or five minutes to drive there. The parking lot had spots for twenty cars. All were occupied. Several young people carried coolers and lawn chairs toward the pavilion, while others stood in small groups and talked to one another. My team of eight officers stood on the grass beneath a big silver maple at the edge of the lot.

I parked about a block away on the side of the road and jogged to meet them. I split them into three teams, one led by me and the other two by officers with sergeant stripes. Delgado had wanted them to wear civilian clothes, but they had all been on patrol when Doug called them. All of them wore uniforms and tactical vests, but none carried long guns. I would have liked each fire team to have a rifle, but we'd work with what we had.

Before we split up, I took questions.

"Do we have any idea what this guy looks like?" asked Sergeant DeAndre Simpson.

"White guy, probably twenty-five to fifty-five. He's likely physically fit," I said. "And if he's here, he'll be shooting at you. You should be able to recognize him."

Two officers laughed, but it was a serious warning. Nobody else had questions, so I looked at each of them in the eye.

"Okay, everybody, you know your assignment. We're here to keep people safe. The Apostate's probably not coming here, but if you see someone aiming a weapon at you or the civilians, put him down. This guy is smart, armed, and ruthless. Watch each other's backs. We'll pull out as soon as the picnic is over."

The team nodded and split apart, but we stayed in radio contact. Officers Emily Hayes, Gary Faulk, and I took the entrance near Waterford College, while the other teams took up positions on the north and east. For about an hour, my team and I sat and watched the kids play volleyball and set up their picnic. Then Emily and Gary's radios emitted an ear-splitting emergency siren. All three of us stopped moving at once and listened. I held my breath.

"All available units, we have reports of multiple shots fired at the chapel at Waterford College." Trisha's voice was calm, but I could sense the undercurrent of fear. "I repeat, all available units, we have an active shooter at Waterford College."

Multiple officers reported they were moving toward the college. I looked at both Gary and Emily.

"Did you guys hear gunshots?"

"No," said Gary. Emily shook her head.

"I didn't, either," she said.

This wasn't right. I dialed the station's back line, but it was busy. Then I called Trisha Marshall's personal cell phone. She didn't answer, either, so I called Sheriff Delgado. His phone rang twice before he picked up.

"We can't talk, so—"

"Shut up and listen, George," I said, interrupting him. "My team and I are at Magnolia Park. We're right on the edge of Waterford's campus. We didn't hear any shots."

Delgado paused for a split second.

"I don't care what you heard. Three people reported a shooter at the chapel. Get your ass and your team over there now."

He hung up, and I pulled the phone from my ear and looked around. We were about a hundred yards from the pavilion at which the high school kids were having their picnic. They laughed in small groups and played volleyball as if they didn't have a care in the world. Smoke and the smell of grilling meat wafted on the breeze.

"What do we do?" asked Emily.

The college had its own police force, but they only had two or three officers on duty at one time. I didn't even know if they carried guns. None of us had heard gunshots, but Delgado had given me a direct order.

"Emily, you stay here and call our other teams and tell them to hold their positions in the park. I know Waterford's layout, so Gary and I will run to the chapel. I don't know what's going on yet, but Sheriff Delgado says there's an active shooter. If our shooter comes this way, take him down. We'll have a lot of officers in the area soon, so you won't be alone long."

Emily nodded, so I looked to Gary.

"Let's go," I said, already running toward the path that led to the college. We made it about a hundred yards before we heard the first gunshot.

It didn't come from the college.

#

Chapter 31

G lenn blew the air out of his lungs and held it. His finger hovered over the trigger.

"Shooter, target in section one-bravo," said Helen.

Glenn swung the barrel to the left until he saw the section.

"Contact," said Glenn. "I've got a middle-aged man. Gray suit, white shirt, red tie. He's coming down the stairs."

"Confirmed target," said Helen. "Wind speed is five miles an hour. Engage when ready."

Glenn tracked the FBI agent with his rifle. At this distance, it would be too hard to hit a target on the run. He had to be patient.

"Multiple targets exiting the police station," said Helen. "Engage at will. I don't have a rappelling rope, so I'm getting out of here."

Glenn didn't take his eye from the scope. "I'll see you later, Helen."

She disappeared down the ladder with silent footsteps. The agent stopped at the foot of the steps and looked over his shoulder. Glenn saw his chance and pulled the slack out of the trigger.

Then he fired.

The sound reverberated against the metal structure behind him. Nine hundred yards away, the FBI agent fell down. It was a good shot, but Glenn didn't have time to savor it. He slid the bolt back on his rifle and chambered a second round before finding a second target. It was a woman in a light blue Highway Patrol officer's uniform. He centered the reticle on her chest and squeezed the trigger. She, too, fell down.

Five times he pulled the trigger, and five times someone fell. When his magazine ran dry, Glenn breathed again. His heart raced. He hooked himself to his rappelling rope and backed up to the ladder and touched off. The descent was fast but controlled. His feet hit the ground thirty seconds after his last shot. Faintly he heard screaming but none of it near him.

When he reached the bottom of the tower, he unhooked himself. Helen was on the ground.

"Come on," she whispered. "We've got to go. You did beautifully."

"I didn't get her," he said, already running toward his car. On any other day, he would have looked suspicious running downtown while wearing climbing gear, but with people screaming at the police station, no one noticed him today. When they reached his car, he opened the door. Helen dove across the driver's seat to the passenger side. He sat down and closed his door.

"You did everything you could," she said, beaming at him. "I'm proud of you for trying. We'll go to her house and kill her. Don't worry."

He nodded, turned the keys in the ignition, and pulled away from the curb. Then he looked at Helen. She was radiant as she patted his shoulder.

"This was more fun than I thought it'd be," she said. "Let's do this again."

I stopped running midstep. The shot came from the downtown area, so I whirled around. Gary slowed and stopped beside me. Emily wasn't far away, so she ran toward us.

Then another shot rang out. A kid at the volleyball court dove into the sand, but it didn't look as if he were hurt. The other kids froze. My breath caught in my throat.

Then another shot rang out. I didn't know what the hell was going on, but I pointed toward the kids at the volleyball court.

"Everybody, get on your bellies now. Make yourselves small."

The kids dove. Then another shot rang out. Emily, Gary, and I crouched low.

"Where are these shots coming from?" I asked.

Gary pointed toward town and grimaced as the gunman fired for the fifth time. Emily pulled her radio from her utility belt and turned up the volume. It was silent, which I appreciated. Our officers knew enough to stay off the radio during an emergency. We had little cover in the park, but the shots sounded at least half a mile away.

After the fifth shot, we waited, expecting more. The kids looked up at us. Gary looked around before focusing on me.

"What do we do?"

"We stay and wait for an update," I said. The moment I spoke, the breeze shifted, allowing me to hear helicopter blades cutting through the air. The Highway Patrol's blue and gray helicopter streaked through the air maybe two hundred feet above the tree line seconds later. It was close enough that Emily covered her ears.

"They were in a hurry," she said.

"They must be looking for our shooter," I said, feeling a worried pit grow in my stomach. I looked at Emily. "Are you sure your radio's on?"

She looked at it and nodded. "Yeah."

I licked my lips and tried to slow my breathing. If she had an update, Trisha would have radioed us already.

"What do we do?" asked Gary.

"We hold our positions," I said. "We've got forty or fifty kids here. We need to keep them safe."

So we waited. Five or six minutes later, a single-engine plane flew overhead at a low speed. I watched as it banked over the town and turned around. It was a search pattern. Shortly thereafter, a blue medical helicopter streaked overhead.

"What the hell is going on?" I asked.

Gary shook his head but didn't stop looking around. Emily shrugged. A moment later, sirens shrieked in the distance.

"Can I have your radio?" I asked, looking to Emily. She nodded and handed it to me. I hit a button to talk. "Dispatcher, we need an update."

I held the radio and listened to the static.

"All officers, hold position," said a male voice I didn't recognize. "We have a sniper in an elevated position. There are multiple fatalities. Stay under cover until further notice. And stay off the radio."

I swallowed hard and handed Emily her radio back.

"You heard the man," I said. "Keep your eyes open. We need to move the civilians to the pavilion and ride it out until we get help."

Emily looked toward the kids. "What do we tell them?"

I considered and raised my eyebrows. "The truth. They'll be more cooperative that way."

My team agreed, and for the next three hours, we huddled beneath the pavilion and pretended its stone veneer walls and asphalt shingles would provide cover against a sniper. Thankfully, no one else fired a gun. Late in the afternoon, the same male voice who had answered my radio call earlier notified us that the scene was clear. We let the kids go home, and I drove downtown.

Three armored vehicles had parked on the street in front of my station, shielding it from the rest of the neighborhood. There were press vans nearby, but uniformed officers had kept the reporters well away. Forensic technicians in navy FBI windbreakers collected evidence and photographed the scene with grim expressions on their faces. Though someone had removed the bodies, blood spatter covered the sidewalk.

George Delgado and Special Agent Bryan Costa sat on the hood of a St. Augustine cruiser across the street from our station. Their heads were down as if they were praying, but neither said a word. Delgado nodded as I approached, but he didn't meet my gaze. His eyes held little emotion. I walked slowly toward him, dreading each footfall but knowing I couldn't stop.

I had seen the blood. I saw the damage. We had lost people today. My arms and legs grew heavier with every step. I reached my boss and Agent Costa.

"I'm glad you're okay, Joe," said Delgado without looking up from his hands.

"Who'd we lose?" I asked.

Neither man said anything, so I repeated the question.

"Bruce Lawson is dead," said Costa. "Round hit him in the heart."

It hit me like a physical blow. I stumbled back until I hit the rear of a Highway Patrol cruiser. The car dipped as I transferred my weight to it.

"Who else?"

"Special Agent Linda Parish," said Costa. "You didn't know her. She worked in St. Louis. Your colleagues were already deployed, so they weren't here. He shot two Highway

Patrol officers, too. One of them died on the scene. The other one died in the air ambulance on the way to St. Louis."

I swallowed. "I'm sorry."

"A girl named Madison died, too," said Delgado, his voice low. "She was walking her dog and happened to be nearby. I guess he thought she looked like a good target. He didn't give them a chance. He shot 'em as they walked out of the building."

I ran a hand across my face. This was why the Apostate had warned me to avoid church. He knew I'd tell my colleagues and that FBI agents from across the state would come. They had been his targets all along.

"Agent Lawson was a good man," I said. "I'm sorry."

Costa nodded but said nothing.

"Who called and said there was an active shooter at Waterford College?" I asked.

Delgado grunted. "Kids. They hatched this idea online to protest Gallen Marshall's arrest. They knew we'd respond in force if multiple students called and said there was a shooter on campus. When we got there, they planned to march and wave signs at us. The whole thing was streaming live on the internet. We're still searching for the guy who set it up."

"What do you need me to do?"

Delgado looked up and shrugged.

"Go home and call your mom. Tell her you're okay."

I straightened as some of my strength returned.

"What about this case?" I asked.

"The bureau will handle it," said Agent Costa. "We've got a team of specialists and tactical officers flying out from DC right now."

"What should I do?"

"Like your boss said, go home," said Costa, standing. "If you'll excuse me, I've got work to do before my superiors get here."

Agent Costa left, and I looked at Delgado. He held up his hands before I could say anything.

"Get out of here. Nobody needs you here."

"What happened to the girl's dog?" I asked. "Madison. You said she was walking a dog."

Delgado raised his eyes. "Why would I know what happened to the goddamn dog? Five people are dead, Joe. Who cares about a stupid dog?"

"I do," I said. "Enough bad things have happened today."

Delgado narrowed his eyes. "If I see him, I'll tell him you're looking for him."

I didn't bother responding. I just walked away. The FBI had locked down the area around our station, but my badge let me get into most places. They didn't know who the shooter was, but they tracked him down to the water tower. He had left his rifle. Hopefully that'd give us some clues.

I spent half an hour walking and looking for an unattended dog, but I didn't find one. Finally, one of St. Augustine's uniformed officers told me the Humane Society had found him near the river. They would hold him until Madison's parents could claim him. At least that was something.

Even after a short walk, I knew Delgado was right: They didn't need me. The FBI had brought a mobile command center and dozens of special agents. If I stayed, I'd merely get in the way.

On my way back to my truck, I passed by Rise and Grind. Agent Lawson and I had gone there for a cup of coffee not too long ago. He had said he planned to move to California with his wife when he retired. Now, his wife would never see him again. I climbed into my truck and sank deep into the seat. Delgado had told me to leave, but I didn't want to go home. I needed a drink.

Chapter 32

St. Augustine had half a dozen bars within walking distance of my truck, but the shooting and police barricades had closed those. I drove to The Barking Spider, a working-class bar on the edge of town, and parked in the lot. The sun would set soon. Drinkers were stopping by after work.

I took my phone from my purse and called my parents' house. Dad answered right away and gave a relieved sigh when he heard my voice.

"I've been watching the news. I'm glad you called."

"Me, too," I said. "Have they identified the victims yet?"

"No," said Dad, "but your mom called a colleague with the Highway Patrol. He said they lost two troopers, and the Bureau lost two agents. He also said a civilian got shot."

"Yeah," I said, my voice low. "The civilian was a fifteen-year-old kid out walking her dog. Why would anyone do that? What could he have gotten from that?"

Dad paused.

"I don't know, hon," he said. "I'm sorry. Why don't I come down and pick you up? You can stay with us."

I wiped away a tear that threatened to fall from my eye.

"No, but thanks," I said. "I need to stick around here. Work will need me after this."

"Then your mom and I will drive to you. We can bring an air mattress and sleep in your living room."

I almost smiled, but I shook my head.

"That's sweet, but you don't need to," I said. Jake—the bouncer at The Barking Spider—propped open the front door with a chair and lit a cigarette. "Besides, if you come here, Dylan will throw a huge party while you're gone. You'll be lucky if he doesn't burn the house down. I couldn't do that to you."

Dad grunted. "I love your brother, but he is a shit sometimes."

"We can't all be the favorite," I said, my voice flat. I loved joking with my dad, but I couldn't put any enthusiasm into it.

Dad paused. "Your mom just got in. You want to talk to her?"

My throat tightened. Dad was an optimist. Before he retired, he had been a fireman. He was a genuine hero who rushed into burning buildings to save people. Mom had been a detective who specialized in sex crimes. She had spent her entire career talking to men and women who tried to hide how much they hurt. Where Dad believed me when I lied and said I was fine, Mom would see right through me. She'd recognize I was anything but fine.

"I should get going," I said. "I've got some—"

The phone bobbled as Dad handed it off. Mom's voice came on next. It was soft and understanding. My throat tightened even further.

"Hey, honey," she said.

"Mom," I said. I counted to ten, expecting her to say something. Then my mouth opened before I could stop myself. "I'm having a bad day."

"Your dad and I saw the news," she said. My eyes fluttered as a tear fell.

"A friend of mine died today." I paused and looked at the dashboard. "I shouldn't say he was a friend. Agent Lawson was a co-worker. He was a good co-worker, though. He worked for the FBI. I hadn't met the other people who died, but I knew him."

"It's hard when that happens."

I swallowed the lump in my throat. "I don't want to keep doing this."

"What do you want to do, then?"

"I don't know. I just don't want to do this."

Mom said nothing for a few seconds. Then, she cleared her throat.

"After what you've been through, I think it'd be a mistake to decide today," she said. "Whatever you do, though, your dad and I will support you. If you want to quit, we can help you out. We don't have a lot of money, but we can help support you while you find a new job."

I thought back to my conversation with Brenda Collins, the attorney who'd called me about my biological mother's will.

"You wouldn't need to give me anything. I've got more money than I can spend."

Mom chuckled softly. "St. Augustine must pay their officers better than St. Louis. When I was your age, your father and I struggled to pay the rent with two salaries."

"Erin left me some money when she died," I said. I paused. "I also know someone murdered her."

Mom paused for almost a minute. "Are you upset?"

"That someone murdered Erin?"

"That I lied to you about it," she said.

Mom was seventy miles north, but I shook my head as if we were in the car together.

"You were trying to protect me. I was fragile back then. I wouldn't have reacted well."

She sighed. "I should have told you. I'm sorry."

"It wouldn't have mattered. You were my mom when I needed you most. Erin gave up on me."

We settled into silence for a moment. Then Mom cleared her throat.

"It's none of my business, but can I ask how much Erin left you?"

"It's a trust fund, and I didn't ask about the details," I said. "Her lawyer said the fund started with two hundred and forty thousand dollars, but it's been in the stock market for the past eleven years. Now it's worth over six hundred thousand dollars."

"Whoa," Mom said.

"Yeah. It's a lot of money, but it doesn't feel like mine."

Mom paused. "Where did Erin get that much money?"

"I don't want to know."

"The detectives working Erin's murder need to know about it. Erin was penniless her whole life. How did she die with a quarter million dollars?"

I closed my eyes. "I already told Matthias Blatch. He was working her case."

"You keep in touch with Detective Blatch?"

"Some."

"Good. He's nice."

She didn't seem to have anything else to say, so I cleared my throat. Before I could tell her I needed to go, she started speaking again.

"I'm going to pack a bag and come down."

I shook my head.

"I've got too much to do," I said, glancing at the bar. "Even with the shooting, we've got a case to solve. We need to get this guy before he hurts anyone else."

"Promise me you won't drink too much tonight."

My back stiffened. "I'm not a drunk."

Mom paused. "I know."

The bouncer looked to my truck and gave me a friendly wave. Jake was in his early forties, but his wife was at least ten years younger than him. She had been a stripper at Club Serenity, but I didn't know whether she had performed out-call services like many other girls in the club, or whether she had worked her way up the truck stop parking lot. Though I had never met his wife, Jake was a nice man. We talked when the bar wasn't busy.

I gave him a tight smile and focused on my phone call.

"Sorry to cut you off, but I need to go."

Mom, once more, hesitated. "I love you, honey. I want what's best for you."

My chest felt tight. "I know. And I love you, too."

"Will you call me tomorrow?"

"I will," I said. A moment later, I hung up and leaned my head back. Somehow, I knew anything I drank that night would taste like ashes, and I knew I'd still drink until I passed out. It wouldn't be fun, and I'd hate myself in the morning, but at least for a while, I could forget my day. Dr. Taylor, my therapist, had given me her home number for days like this when I needed someone to talk to. As much as I appreciated that, I didn't want to talk to her. I needed a friend.

I nodded once more to Jake before turning on my car and driving out of the lot. As I sat in the drive-through of a fried chicken place near the interstate, my phone buzzed, signaling an incoming message. It was from Trisha, and she wanted to talk about our investigation into the Apostate. As much as I needed to talk to a friend, I didn't want to talk about the case.

The line crept forward as the driver in front of me picked up her order.

My fingers dialed the number of the only person in St. Augustine I wanted to see.

"Susanne," I said, once she picked up. "It's Joe. Is this a good time?"

"It's always a good time for you, dear."

"I'm picking up some fried chicken. Do you have dinner plans?"

When Susanne spoke, her tone told me she was smiling.

"I do not, and I would love to have dinner with a friend if you're available."

"Thank you. I've had a long day. I didn't want to eat alone."

"A young woman with fried chicken will never eat alone if she doesn't want to."

I nodded and smiled. "I'll see you soon."

She said she looked forward to it and then hung up. When I got to the window, I ordered enough fried food, sides, and cherry pie for a family of five, but I didn't care about the calories or the expense. I had dinner plans with someone who cared about me, and already, I felt better than I had in hours. I was lucky to have the friends I did.

Chapter 33

The FBI had cleared my house, so I drove home after dinner with Susanne. I drank a few drinks, but I didn't let myself get drunk before going to bed.

My doorbell rang at a little before six the next morning. I rolled over and covered my face with a pillow but didn't get out of bed. Then the doorbell rang again, and my phone buzzed on the end table. I threw my pillow down and groaned. I had gone to bed wearing an old T-shirt and little else, but still my sheets were damp from perspiration. The air was humid and warm. That was life without central air-conditioning in central Missouri in the summer.

I swung my legs off the bed and grabbed my cell phone. The text had come from Trisha.

I'm at your door. We need to talk.

I groaned again before texting her back to tell her I'd be there in a minute. When Roger had slept at the foot of my bed, I'd enjoyed a consistent morning routine. He'd yawn, fart, or roll over, waking me up as the sun rose, and then we'd go out for a run in the woods. Toward the end of his life, Roger had stopped going for the run with me, but he

had always waited for me at the porch and looked excited to
see me when I came back. I missed that routine. I missed my
friend.

Rather than dwell on such maudlin thoughts, I dressed
and walked to the front door. Trisha was alone outside.

"Morning," I said, forcing a smile on my face. It was early,
but I was sober. That didn't happen often. "What's going
on?"

"I texted you yesterday," she said, stepping past me to go
inside. "We need to talk."

"Make yourself at home," I said, stepping back. I cared
about Trisha, but the intrusion into my quiet morning annoyed me. "You want coffee while you're here?"

"Yeah, sure. You alone?"

I furrowed my brow and shut the front door. Trisha
shot her eyes around the room as if she were expecting the
boogeyman to jump at her.

"I'm alone," I said. "What's going on?"

"Are you sure you're alone?"

I raised my eyebrows. "How could I be confused about
whether I'm alone?"

She swallowed and nodded before looking at the ground.

"The FBI arrested Harry early this morning."

My eyes popped open. "You're kidding."

"I wish I were. They kicked down his door at three in
the morning. Irene and Carrie came to my house in tears. I

called George Delgado, but he couldn't do anything. I had nowhere else to go."

"Okay," I said, nodding as my mind tried to process what she had just told me. "I'll put on coffee. You tell me what happened."

Trisha followed me to the kitchen, where I put on a pot of coffee and toasted two pieces of bread. I didn't have butter, so I ate them plain while the coffee brewed. Trisha sat at the breakfast table and fidgeted like a kid who needed to use the bathroom.

"Walk me through this," I said. "What's going on?"

"The Bureau's new team came in last night, and they put a mobile command center in the parking lot. They're not even using the conference room."

"I figured they'd do that."

Trisha nodded and paused as if she were considering what she wanted to say.

"Agent Lawson was a good investigator," she said, speaking slowly. "He talked to potential witnesses, families, police officers...everybody who could give him information. The woman replacing him doesn't know what she's doing."

"How so?" I asked.

Trisha wrapped her hands around the coffee mug but didn't pick it up.

"You saw Lawson's profile of the Apostate. Based on what he saw, he thought the Apostate was a forty-five to sixty-year-old, fit white male. He believed he had a high standing in society, which enabled him to interact with his victims and persuade them to go with him. He said the Apostate was intelligent and that he had access to large tracts of property, which would allow him to kill his victims without alerting the neighbors. Lawson also thought the killer was a local. He was looking for someone who grew up in St. Augustine County and who knew you."

I nodded and raised my eyebrows. "That could be hundreds of people."

"Yeah, but the Bureau's technical team tracked the trajectory of the shots fired yesterday to the water tower. There, they found a Remington 700 SPS tactical rifle and rappelling rope."

I nodded and walked to the coffee maker. "What do they know about the rifle?"

"The original owner purchased it from a shop called Outdoor Renaissance in Indianapolis. The Bureau picked up the original owner, but he said he sold it for cash at a gun show."

I poured two mugs of coffee and carried them to the table. "How did you learn all this?"

"Irene showed me Harry's arrest warrant. It listed the probable cause," she said. "Before becoming a police officer, Harry spent six years in the 101st Airborne Division in the Army. He's an expert marksman with experience rappelling from fixed platforms. He knows you, he grew up in St. Augustine, and he's the right age and sex. Also, the range master at the rifle range out by the old Reid Chemical plant said he's seen Harry with a Remington 700. A search this morning found .308 Winchester rounds in his house but no rifle chambered for that round on the property."

I swore under my breath and sat up straighter. To have that much information, the Bureau must have investigated him days ago. It made me wonder whether Agent Lawson's attempts to get close to me were a genuine interest in my abilities or an attempt to get inside information on a suspect. I guessed it didn't matter. Lawson was dead, and Harry was in custody.

"Where was he yesterday during the shooting?"

"Fishing."

I wanted to roll my eyes, but I held back given the situation.

"And knowing Harry, he was fishing in some no-name lake in the middle of nowhere."

"Yeah, so he has no alibi. And he knew everything we knew about the Apostate investigation. Without him, it might have taken us years to put together the pattern."

"Which they'll use against him," I said, rubbing my eyes and feeling my shoulders sag. "I assume he has a lawyer."

"Even if he does, Harry's in federal custody for multiple murders. He's tough, but he's still an old man. The government thinks he killed multiple federal agents. They won't be gentle with him."

"I'll talk to Agent Costa and tell him they've made a mistake. This is insane."

She looked at the table. "George Delgado already tried. Costa didn't even take his call. They're closing ranks on this one."

"Then we need to find the real shooter," I said.

Trisha flashed me a desperate smile. "Any idea how we do that?"

"Does the front desk still have a key to the evidence vault?"

"Yeah, but Mark Bozwell's finicky about that place. We try not to go down there except in emergencies."

"This is an emergency," I said. "Give me a minute. I'm going to get dressed."

She nodded and sipped her coffee while I walked to my bathroom to brush my teeth and get ready for the day. It gave me a few minutes to plan. Ten minutes after I left Trisha in the kitchen, I emerged from my room wearing a navy blazer, white button-down shirt, and jeans. Trisha looked up at me.

"You ready?" she asked.

"Yeah. Let's go."

We drove separate cars to the station and got there at half past six. The FBI had cordoned off the front door and taken over most of the parking lot, so we parked on the street and entered the building through a side door that served as an emergency exit most days. The building felt somber. Few people were around.

"What do we do?" asked Trisha, as we walked to the bullpen.

"The Apostate starves his victims until the boys are so hungry they're willing to rape and drown their partners for food. Then he burns the boys alive."

Trisha nodded as we weaved through the desks. "That's what Jude and Paige said."

"If he did it to them, he did it to every couple," I said. "The ritual matters for this guy. Something happened to him that makes this a meaningful act. We need to find out what."

"And how do we do that?"

"We read," I said. We reached my desk a moment later, and I pulled out my chair. Where my station's digital archive only went back to 1995, the Missouri Secretary of State's website had death certificates going all the way back to 1910. Those death certificates didn't provide much information, but they listed the causes of death of everyone who had died in St. Augustine for the past hundred years.

Trisha took over a desk beside mine, and the two of us searched the database for the next hour, looking for men and women whose deaths the coroner had determined were caused by drowning, asphyxiation, smoke inhalation, or acute burns. The search wouldn't cover everyone, but it gave us a lot of names to work with. We then narrowed the search by looking at those whose deaths the county considered homicides. That left us with six names from the past fifty years.

Once we finished, I looked at Trisha. "What time does Mark Bozwell open the evidence vault?"

"8:30."

I looked at my watch. "So we've got an hour. Get the key from the front desk. I'll meet you outside the vault."

Chapter 34

H elen and Glenn stared in disbelief at the woman sitting across from them at the kitchen table. It was like magic. One moment, he and Helen had been alone. Then, she had appeared. If Glenn hadn't witnessed it, he wouldn't have believed it. First, he had seen thin wisps of black smoke, and then that smoke had thickened and coalesced into her, smile and all. It was like something from a dream.

By Helen's face, it was a nightmare.

"Hello, Glenn," said Detective Court, pushing back from the table and crossing her legs. Until now, he had only seen Mary Joe wearing jeans, but today she wore a cream-colored skirt and an off-the-shoulder top. The outfit showed off her muscular legs and toned arms. Her blonde hair fell against her shoulders and possessed just enough of a wave to curl around her ears. Glenn had always found her attractive, but, with some minor changes, she had become the gorgeous woman he had dreamed of.

"Get out," said Helen. "You don't belong here."

"He's asked me here, though," said Mary Joe, looking to Glenn and smiling. "He needs me. Isn't that right, sweetheart?"

Glenn's lips moved, but he couldn't force sound to pass through them. Mary Joe leaned across the table to put her hands over his. Her touch was electric. He gasped but didn't dare pull his hands back. Mary Joe bit her lower lip and looked at him with eyes that shone with internal fire. Everything about her was alive with strength. He almost wilted in front of her.

"We don't need you," said Helen. She put a hand flat on Glenn's back. Cold passed through him, quenching Mary Joe's fire. "We're strong together. Isn't that right, brother?"

Glenn tried to listen to Helen, but he couldn't take his eyes from the exquisite creature in front of him.

"Who are you?" he asked, his voice so soft he couldn't hear himself above the sound of the air conditioner.

She lowered her chin. "You know who I am, sweetie."

"You're his shadow," said Helen, her voice flat.

"I didn't think you were real," said Glenn. Mary Joe traced a finger along his knuckles and nodded.

"I'm real, and I'm here because you need me," she said, looking into his eyes once more. "You called me."

"No, he didn't," said Helen, standing and pulling Glenn's arm. He stayed seated. She sighed and looked at Mary Joe. "We're packing because we're leaving town. We don't need you."

"How'd it go at the water tower?" asked Mary Joe.

"I killed them," said Glenn. "Four cops and one little bitch named Madison."

Mary Joe giggled and brought a hand to her mouth, and Glenn smiled. Mary Joe's laughter brought light to the world in a way nothing else did. Glenn had watched Mary Joe on TV, but he had never seen her smile like that, and he had never heard her giggle. It was the most wonderful sound he had ever heard.

"You should smile more often," he said. "You're beautiful when you smile."

"If you want me to smile, I will," she said.

"She's not real, Glenn," said Helen. "You understand that, don't you? She's a figment of your mind."

Mary Joe rolled her eyes and then sighed before reaching her hand across the table once more and placing it on the meat of his forearm.

"Can you feel my hands on yours?" she asked, leaning forward so close he could hear her whisper. "Can you feel the heat of my breath on your face? Can you smell the mint of my toothpaste? Who gets to decide what's real and what isn't?"

Glenn's heart seemed to stop. Every muscle of his body grew tight.

"I don't know," he said.

"I'm as real as you are," she said, leaning back and relaxing. "And I'm here for you."

Glenn wanted to reach across the table and touch her, but he didn't know whether he should yet. He had dreamed of this moment, though. He had wanted Mary Joe from the moment he saw her. And now, she sat across from him and gazed into his eyes.

"You're so beautiful," he said.

"You make me feel beautiful," she said.

Helen scoffed and then sat beside her brother. "She'll just slow us down, Glenn."

"Slow you down from what?" she asked. "Your statement implies that you have a plan, but I've watched you for a long time, Helen. You're not a planner."

"I plan everything," said Helen, her eyes narrowing. Mary Joe smiled.

"What are you doing, then?" she asked. "Are you going to pick up two new kids to add to your pointless collection?"

"It wasn't pointless," said Glenn. "My work with Helen was important. Don't speak ill of what you don't understand."

Mary Joe took her hands from Glenn's and leaned back.

"I shouldn't have said that. I'm sorry. You punished men who deserved it. There are few nobler things anyone can do," she said, nodding and batting her eyes. "Those boys you punished, though, aren't the only ones who deserve to die. An infection flows through this town's veins. You and I are the cure. Together, we'll bring the disease to light."

"We need to get out of here," said Helen. "If you want to bring her with us, brother, that's fine, but you need to pack."

"What do you think we should do?" he asked.

Mary Joe considered him and then leaned forward to trace her finger over his knuckles. Her light touch sent electric charges up and down his spine, and he gasped. She smiled and bit her lower lip once more.

"Why did you kill Madison?"

Glenn considered before speaking. He had told Helen he killed her because he wanted an easy target to settle his nerves. That wasn't the complete truth, though. He had dozens of easy targets. Doubtlessly, many of them deserved a round in the heart, but so had Madison.

"She was a liar," he said, allowing a snarl to enter his voice. Helen looked at him askance, but he didn't take his eyes from Mary Joe's. She understood. He could see it in her eyes. "She said Eryk Janikowski had threatened to fail her in English if she didn't give him a blow job in the bathroom. Eryk has testicular cancer. Blow jobs in the bathroom are the least of his concerns at the moment. She tried to ruin a good man's life."

"So you killed her," said Mary Joe, her eyes shining. "It's not murder if it prevents future suffering."

"That's right," he said, nodding. "That's why I pulled the trigger. It's why Helen and I did what we did."

"And it's why we don't need you now," said Helen, her voice hard. "We get along just fine. Now please stop confusing my brother. If you care about him, tell him to pack his bag. We need to leave. We would have left yesterday if the police hadn't been watching the roads out of town."

Mary Joe nodded and looked into Glenn's eyes.

"I love you," she said. "I've always loved you, and I know you love me, too."

"I do," he said, nodding.

"Then you know I wouldn't lie to you," she said, her voice low. "Helen has helped you, but this is the end. Even if you run, they'll find you. Helen can't help you anymore. You need me. Together, we can make your last moment meaningful. You can matter."

"Don't listen to her," said Helen. Where righteous anger had once tinged her voice, now it wavered. "Please don't leave me."

"I'll never leave you, Helen. You're mine, and I'm yours," said Glenn, looking at Mary Joe's hands on the table. "But Mary Joe is right. I killed police officers. This is the end."

"Please don't say that," said Helen. "She doesn't even have a plan. I can get you out. If we disappear now, nobody will look for us for weeks."

"Maybe they won't look for you right away, but they will look for you," said Mary Joe. "They aren't stupid. Glenn can't escape his death forever. We need to consider how to shape his legacy. That's why he needs me."

"Tell me what to do," said Glenn.

Mary Joe squeezed his hand. "Do you remember Donna Lockwood?"

Even the thought of Donna Lockwood brought a smile to his lips.

"It's hard to forget Donna—or those swimsuits she used to wear. My friends and I would spend hours at the pool watching her twirl that whistle on the lifeguard stand. She was my first love, I think."

"Stop," said Mary Joe, winking. "You're making me jealous."

"She married her high school boyfriend after he knocked her up forty years ago," he said, smiling. "You've got nothing to worry about. She's got grandkids. I see her in the grocery store sometimes."

"St. Augustine's a small world," said Mary Joe, nodding. She paused. "Do you remember how crowded the pool was? Even in the middle of the week, there'd be so many kids packed on the pool deck, you couldn't find space to put down your towel. And the fence kept you from lying on the grass. You had nowhere to go."

He envisioned the scene and held Mary Joe's gaze. Her breath was almost shallow.

"I remember," he said.

"This town is sick," said Mary Joe. "It'll be hot today. People love the pool on a hot day."

"Yeah," said Glenn, nodding. "Might be two hundred people there."

"And that fence will pen them in like dogs in a kennel. You still have that big gun with the extended magazine?"

She meant his Hechler and Koch MR556. It was a tactical rifle capable of shooting nine hundred rounds a minute at almost three thousand feet per second. It was accurate and reliable. Credible rumors floated around the gun world that SEAL Team Six had carried HK 416s—the military version of the 556—when they took out Osama bin Laden. Though Glenn's civilian version lacked the automatic firing capability of the military rifle, he still enjoyed taking it to the range. Not only that, his extended magazine would give him sixty shots before he needed to reload. He could do a lot of damage with sixty shots.

"Yeah, I've got it," he said, thinking. "During the week, the pool will be full of families and kids."

Mary Joe nodded. "Yes. And they won't have guns, either. They'll be in bathing suits. There won't be anyone to stop you. This town is rotten, and that rot infects everyone within its borders. There are no innocents in St. Augustine. You know better than anyone."

She was right about everything. Helen had been his helper in life. Mary Joe would become the friend who guided him to his death.

"Don't listen to her," said Helen. "Go into your room and pack your bag, Glenn. We'll get out of here. We can go to Canada or Mexico. By this time next week, we could be on the beach somewhere. We can start over. Please just give me a chance."

"I can't do that," said Glenn. "They'll never stop searching for me. Even if I escaped, we'd have to run for the rest of my life. I can't live like that. Mary Joe is right. We have to kill their children. It's the only way for them to see the wrong they've done."

Glenn stood. So did Mary Joe. Helen reached for his hand. Tears fell from her cheeks.

"Please tell me you don't plan to give in to her. If you do, I die."

Mary Joe left the kitchen and walked toward the hallway that led to his bedroom. Glenn focused on Helen.

"I love you, Helen. I'll never forget you."

She covered her eyes and sobbed. Glenn looked to Mary Joe for support. She stood with her back to him, but she brought her hands to her waist and pulled her top up, exposing her flawless, soft skin. The fabric hit the ground a moment later, and she looked over her shoulder.

"Come on, sweetheart," she whispered. "I know you love Helen, but I have so much more to give you."

"I'm sorry, Helen," he said without turning his head. "I've got to go."

Glenn took Mary Joe's hand and followed her to his bedroom. The moment he had seen her, he knew Mary Joe Court was the woman of his dreams. She was the love of his life. He wished he had more time to show her everything she meant to him. They only had the morning, though. This was the right choice. He'd make love to Mary Joe, and then they'd fulfill their final mission.

Today, God would have mercy on no one.

Chapter 35

T risha and I spent twenty minutes in the vault. Her key got us through the front door while my lockpick made short work of the filing cabinet's locks. We pulled out six files. Two of them were thin, but the other four ranged from a single inch-thick manila envelope to five two-inch-thick binders. It would take time to read through every interview note, search warrant affidavit, and report, but we didn't need to read everything. We only needed to find similarities.

Even that was a tall order.

After grabbing what we needed, we closed the file cabinets and locked the door. Since both Trisha and I were police officers, we hadn't broken the law, but we could both kiss our jobs goodbye if Delgado caught us. Given everything I had seen in the past few weeks, that wouldn't be the worst thing that could happen.

At my desk, we split the files up and got to work. I took notes, but little stood out until I got to my third file. It only had a dozen pages in it. One was a report from the dispatcher, saying a counselor at a summer camp had found a body.

A second page was a log sheet from the crime scene. The file contained no reports, photographs, or anything else to indicate the investigating officers had done anything.

"You got anything promising?" I asked.

Trisha blinked and then shook her head.

"Not really. I've got a man who died in a house fire set by his spouse. She wanted to burn the place for the insurance money and didn't realize her husband had come home from the bar. He had passed out drunk in the garage. The wife got life in prison. There's no mention of a rape. I've also got a file about a little girl who drowned in her backyard swimming pool. The prosecutors declined to charge her parents. That's sad."

I leaned back. "The drowned girl have any siblings?"

"A younger brother, and I know him," she said. "He became a priest when he grew up. I didn't know he had a sister."

I raised my eyebrows and tilted my head to the side. "Hard secret to grow up with."

She nodded. "The third file involves a young man who hanged himself. There's no rape. You have anything interesting?"

"No," I said, shaking my head. "I've got a woman trapped in a car after an accident. The car caught fire, and she died inside. The other driver was drunk, so the prosecutor charged him with vehicular manslaughter. He got fifteen years in prison. I've also got a man who got drunk and drowned while fishing. His fishing buddy was also drunk. Detectives on the case thought the fishing buddy might have drowned his friend, but the evidence was inconclusive."

Trisha crossed her arms. "What about your third file?"

I pushed myself back from my desk. "Victim's name was Helen Saunders, but somebody cleaned out the file. We've got a report of the original call to 911 and a log sheet of the original crime scene, but nothing that could help us."

"Helen Saunders, Helen Saunders, Helen Saunders..." Trisha repeated the name over and over under her breath. "She's familiar, but I don't know why."

I flipped through the notes I had taken from our death certificate search. "She was thirteen when she died. The coroner found water in her lungs. That ring any bells?"

"No," she said, shaking her head. "When was it?"

"1971," I said, looking at my notes again. "Long time ago."

"Almost fifty years," said Trisha. "If she was thirteen in 1971, she'd be sixty-one years old today."

I did the math in my head and then nodded.

"That sounds right."

"Sixty-one isn't old," said Trisha. "You stay here for a moment."

I nodded and checked my email while she jogged to the front desk. A few minutes later, Trisha returned with Jason Zuckerburg, our night dispatcher. His uniform was a little tight over his belly, and his wrinkled face had deep furrows in the brow, but he always had a smile on his lips. That was rare among the men and women who had spent their lives in law enforcement.

"Trisha said you needed help."

"How old are you, Jason?"

He raised an eyebrow. "Old enough to know it's impolite to ask."

"So pretty old," I said. He hesitated before tilting his head to the side and nodding.

"Why?"

I leaned forward just a little and raised my eyebrows. "Is the name Helen Saunders familiar?"

He crossed his arms and took a step back. "Tell me you're not trying to set me up with some old lady whose husband just died. I'm married."

"No," I said, shaking my head. "We're looking into a murder that happened in 1971. The victim would have been your age. Her name was Helen Saunders. Did you know her?"

"In 1971, I lived in Dogtown in St. Louis. I didn't move here until '82 after the Army discharged me."

I rubbed my eyes and sighed.

"It was worth a shot," I said, looking at Trisha. Then, I shifted my gaze to Jason and smiled. "Thanks, Jason. We might need you later, but you should get back to the desk."

"If your murder happened in '71, we should have plenty of information," said Jason. "Just ask Mark Bozwell when he gets in. He'll get you the file."

"We've got the file. It's incomplete."

"Let me look at it, anyway. I know people from back then."

I cocked my head to the side and slid the manila folder across my desk toward him.

"If you want to kill time," I said, "knock yourself out."

He pulled out a chair from a desk beside mine and sat down to read. Trisha went to get coffee while I spun around in my chair and tried to think of what other leads we had. After a few minutes, Jason looked up and slid a paper toward me.

"Lead detective on your murder was Alexander Carney. He retired in '93 and died about ten years later."

"Think his widow would have kept his old case file?"

"I don't know," said Jason, "but the number two officer on the case was Keith Fox."

I didn't recognize the name, but Trisha smiled and looked at me.

"Keith is Harry Grainger's uncle," she said. "He's still alive, isn't he?"

"Last I heard," said Jason. "I think he lives at Sunrise Manor out by the river."

It was an assisted living facility a few blocks from our station. We got called there three or four times a year when family members accused the facility's staff of mistreating their relatives. Three years ago, we arrested a nurse for stealing an elderly man's Rolex, but we had never seen evidence of physical abuse or neglect. The facility was clean, well-managed, and appropriately staffed. They did a tough job and charged top dollar for it. If Detective Fox lived there, life had turned out okay for him. Hopefully he'd talk to us.

I thanked Jason for his help, and then Trisha and I piled into my car. The drive didn't take long, so we parked outside the building at half after eight. Already, several residents sat on rocking chairs on the porch to read, talk, and watch the world go by. A couple at the far end of the building played chess. It looked peaceful.

People smiled at us and returned to their previous activities as Trisha and I walked inside. A young woman wearing navy blue scrubs smiled at us from the front desk.

"Hi, we're here to see Keith Fox if he's available," said Trisha.

"Are you family or friends?" she asked.

"We're co-workers," I said. "We need to see Detective Fox."

The nurse looked at my badge and furrowed her brow.

"Everything okay?" she asked.

"We need to ask him about a case he worked," I said. "It was a long time ago."

She nodded before picking up a radio from her desk.

"Mr. Fox exercises in the morning, but I'll have someone check if he's up for visitors."

"Thank you," I said, stepping away from the counter. Trisha and I walked to a seating area near a television. An older woman told us she had reserved every seat and that we should eat shit. An aide must have overheard because she came over to talk to her, but we took the hint and continued standing.

About ten minutes after we arrived, a young man—also wearing scrubs—came out of a hallway to show us to Detective Fox. Though the detective had his own room, he was sitting on a rocking chair on the back porch, watching a coal barge float down the Mississippi. Age had wrinkled his pale skin, but it had left him with lively blue eyes. A trimmed white beard covered his chin and cheeks, while the laugh lines at the corners of his eyes grew pronounced as he smiled at us.

"Officers," he said, standing and gesturing to the teak rocking chairs beside him. "Have a seat. Harry's the only cop who visits me anymore. You ladies are a treat in comparison."

I smiled. "We're here to talk about Harry, actually."

"Oh?" he asked, blinking. "Don't tell me he got hurt yesterday. We heard the gunshots, but the news didn't name the victims."

"Harry's fine," said Trisha. "Physically, at least. The FBI has arrested him. They think he's the Apostate killer."

Detective Fox snickered at first, but then the smile left his face.

"You messing with an old man?"

"I wish," I said. "The FBI picked him up. We need to talk about one of your old cases. It might have a connection to the Apostate, but we're not sure. It was the death of a young woman named Helen Saunders."

The light in Detective Fox's eyes dimmed, and his shoulders became stooped. In an instant, he had aged ten years. Then he blinked and looked toward the river.

"I wish you hadn't said that name," he said. Trisha and I let him gather himself. "I assume you've looked at the file."

"What's left," I said. "Someone took out the interesting parts."

"I thought they might do that," he said, nodding. He sighed. "Get comfortable. If you want to know about Helen, this'll take a while."

Chapter 36

G lenn and Mary Joe made love for almost two hours. He didn't know where Helen was, but he couldn't find her anywhere in the house afterwards. Somehow, he knew he'd never see her again. She had been his companion for years, always lurking in the shadows. Whenever he had needed encouragement, she had been there with a kind word and a hug. He missed her already, but he had Mary Joe now. She'd be with him until the end. Still, he wished she had said goodbye.

After searching his house for his sister, he walked back to his bedroom, where Mary Joe still lay in the bed. She had pulled the sheets over her chest, but she bit her lower lip and blinked.

"Back for more?" she asked, raising her eyebrows.

He smiled. "I wish. Have you seen Helen?"

The good-humored grin left Mary Joe's face, and she looked down at the sheets.

"Why do you want to see her?"

"She's my sister. I wanted to tell her goodbye."

Mary Joe smiled again, but there was a hint of sadness to it.

"She had to go. She understood that her time with you was over."

Glenn swallowed. "I see."

Mary Joe held out her arms. "Come here, honey."

Glenn let her hold him for a few minutes, but it didn't comfort him the way Helen had. That was okay. He and Mary Joe had a different relationship. It was better in some ways.

After a few moments, their intimate, tender embrace shifted as her lips found his. They kissed and made love once more—their final time, Glenn surmised. He would die today. He and Mary Joe both knew it. Spending his last day with Mary Joe, one of the few persons in the world who could understand him, seemed fitting.

Afterwards, as Mary Joe nestled against his chest, Glenn sighed and thought to the job ahead of them.

"We should prepare," he said. "The pool will open soon. We should scout it out."

Mary Joe kissed his neck before drawing away.

"Get your gear together while I shower. We'll go together."

He nodded, and she climbed out of bed and went to the en suite bathroom while he dressed and walked to the gun safe in the basement. His HK MR556 fired 5.56 NATO rounds, which he purchased in bulk online. Glenn's father had ingrained in him how important it was to maintain a firearm. A dirty firearm was like a dull scalpel. Just as no self-respecting surgeon would expect to do his job with a dull scalpel, no decent soldier should put away a firearm while it was dirty.

He carried the weapon to the workbench in his garage, where he checked to make sure it functioned properly. As he worked, he looked up and noticed the stool Helen used to sit on. She hadn't wanted him to shoot at the police from the water tower, but it had worked out fine. He had killed people who deserved it, and he had gotten away.

He'd get away this time, too. Mary Joe would see him through.

Once he finished checking the weapon, he loaded his high-capacity drum magazine, a tedious and time-consuming job. When he completed that task, he found Mary Joe in his kitchen. She must have used Helen's makeup and hair supplies because she once more looked perfect. Her skirt and top were even wrinkle-free—surprising, considering they had been on the floor. She smiled at him from across the room, and his heart felt light just to see her. He couldn't believe someone that wonderful would look at him with those eyes.

"Is everything okay?" she asked.

"Yeah," he said. "My rifle is ready to go. I'll bring a pair of pistols, too, in case I run out of ammunition before I run out of targets. Are you ready?"

She nodded, so he grabbed his keys, and they got in his car. Traffic was light, but he passed a dozen police cars—Highway Patrol officers and locals—in the fifteen-minute drive to the community pool. The cops would make things hard. His rifle could belt out hundreds of rounds a minute, so the shooting wouldn't be a problem. He needed a plan to get away. He wished Helen were in the car with him.

"Penny for your thoughts?" asked Mary Joe as they approached the park.

He glanced at her and smiled despite the situation.

"This'll be harder than I thought," he said. "There are so many cops. They'll be there as soon as I fire."

She put a hand on his shoulder.

"You'll only need a few seconds."

"But how do I get away?"

Mary Joe said nothing for a moment. Then, she slipped her hand down to his knee, which she squeezed before crossing her arms.

"Life's a one-way trip, honey," she said, her voice soft. "It hasn't been fair for you or Helen. I know you want to do your job and escape, but I don't think it's going to happen today. I'm sorry."

He swallowed.

"Maybe Helen was right," he said, glancing at her. "If I run now, we can spend more time together before they find me. We'd be like Bonnie and Clyde. We could make our way down south, shooting up convenience stores as we go."

Mary Joe shook her head. "We're not in a movie. If we run, they'll find us. You only get one shot, Glenn. You've got to take it and make it matter."

"I don't want to die," he said, his voice low.

"Me, either," she said. She paused. "Let's check out the pool. We'll put together a plan."

"Okay," he said. They drove a few more silent moments before pulling into Sycamore Park. St. Augustine County, for all its problems, had wonderful parks. Sycamore Park was the smallest in the county's park system, but it had batting cages, a softball field, a playground built to resemble an old wooden fort, and the public pool. Ancient sycamore, silver maple, and gum trees shaded everything but the pool deck, making it comfortable even on warm summer days.

The parking lot near the pool was full, so Glenn parked on the street behind a Volkswagen and stepped out. A breeze rustled the tree leaves around him, and he could hear boys and girls shouting from the pool and nearby playground. Mary Joe joined him at the side of his car and hooked her elbow around his. Then she rested her head on his shoulder. Glenn had at least twenty years on Mary Joe, so they probably looked like a father and daughter out for a stroll. He didn't care. People could think what they wanted.

They walked outside the playground's chain-link fence. A dozen or more kids climbed on and ran around the wooden structure. Mary Joe smiled and waved at a little boy who ran near the fence, but he must not have seen her because he didn't react. Glenn breathed in the sweet, clean air.

"Dad took me here when I was little," he said. "It was fun."

"It's a nice park," said Mary Joe. "If I had kids, I'd take them here."

"If we had kids," said Glenn, nudging her. She laughed.

"Of course," she whispered. "I'm yours."

They walked in silence for another few moments. Though much of St. Augustine County had rolling hills, Sycamore Park had a gentle slope. Glenn preferred to have a perch from which to shoot, but he could shoot from the ground just as easily.

The pool didn't look impressive from a distance. Fifty years ago, it might have looked like a resort, but now the mint green concrete buildings and cracked pool deck looked dated and worn, and the overgrown faux-tropical landscaping looked unkempt and wild. A tall chain-link fence surrounded the property, reminding him of a prison.

Glenn and Mary Joe followed a well-worn path alongside the fence. Children and a few parents lined up not ten feet away to jump from the diving board. If Glenn had brought a gun, he could have shot them all in a second.

"This is good," said Mary Joe. "They'll fall all over each other trying to escape. It'll be easy."

Glenn nodded. "We can start at the snack bar. If we go at noon, we can shoot people as they wait in line for lunch. They'll have nowhere to go. If I come from the locker rooms at the south end, the people at the diving board will run to the north once they hear the first shot. They'll back themselves into a corner. When they climb the fence, I'll pick them off. Then I can hit the sunbathers."

Mary Joe nodded and continued walking but said nothing.

"You don't like the plan?"

She sighed. "It's fine if it's what you want to do."

Glenn stopped walking at the northeast corner of the complex. The nearest sunbather was at least twenty feet inside the pool deck, giving them some privacy.

"What would you do?"

Mary Joe turned toward the pool and gestured.

"Go through the locker room, but instead of shooting up the snack bar, hit the kiddie pool first. Every parent in the complex will run over to save the kids. You'll mow them all down."

Glenn brought a hand to his face. His legs trembled, so he leaned on the fence.

"I don't want to hurt children."

"I don't care what you want," said Mary Joe, her voice hard. "You asked for me to come. Have the strength to follow through. Our job is to make this town bleed. You won't do that by holding back."

Glenn swallowed hard. "There has to be another way."

Mary Joe crossed her arms and looked across the pool deck.

CHRIS CULVER

"The county built this pool in 1974. You remember? Your dad took you to the opening. He got drunk and cried in the backyard afterwards."

Glenn cocked his head to the side. "How do you know that?"

"I know everything, sweetheart," said Mary Joe, her voice now cold. "How do you think St. Augustine—a broke, podunk county—paid for this pool?"

"I don't know," he said, shaking his head.

"Yeah, you do. Your dad knew, too," said Mary Joe. "Your sister paid for it. The town got a bargain because your dad was weak. You're not. Give your sister's death meaning. Show this town what she bought them."

"Where is Helen?" asked Glenn.

"You know where she is," said Mary Joe. "She's with Olivia, Tayla, Jordan, Trinity, Mary, and Nicole. You couldn't save those girls, but you punished the men who hurt them. Now punish the men and women who hurt Helen. Please. If you love her, show it. Kill the kids. All of them. Show this town and county what it means to bleed."

Tears fell down Glenn's face as he nodded. Mary Joe was right about everything. This was his final mission. St. Augustine had a cancer inside it. Helen and Mary Joe had given him a knife to excise the disease. This was his moment. He'd fulfill his destiny.

And he'd burn this town to ashes around him.

342

Chapter 37

Detective Fox hunched his shoulders and leaned forward, looking every bit the elderly man his age said he was. Neither Trisha nor I said anything. Detective Fox's hand trembled as he reached for his mug. After taking a drink, he drew in a breath and sighed.

"Helen Saunders was a beautiful little girl," he said. He looked up at me. "St. Augustine was smaller back then. We knew everybody. Her mom had died giving birth to her little brother, so it was just Glenn, Helen, and their daddy. Helen looked just like her mom. I told Edward that he needed to teach her how to shoot just to keep the boys away."

I smiled and reached into my jacket for a notepad in case he said something we could use.

"She was sweet, too," he said, looking toward the river again. "The police and fire departments used to have a bake sale before the holidays. Our wives made cakes and pies, and we sold them from our stations. We pretended it was a competition, but the money all went to the same place. Every year, Helen made us brownies. They weren't from a box, either. She made them from scratch. She didn't have to do that."

Detective Fox lapsed into silence after that. I cleared my throat.

"What happened to her?" I asked.

He drew in a pained breath and blinked.

"This was the summer of '71. It was real hot that year. I remember because the sheriff made us carry canteens everywhere we went in case people needed water."

Once more, he paused.

"Tell me about Helen," I said. He glanced at me and nodded.

"Have you heard of Pennington Hotels?"

"I'm familiar with it," I said.

"They were a big deal back then," said Fox. "Stanley Pennington ran this county from his kitchen table. His company was the biggest employer in town, and you couldn't get elected without his say-so."

I nodded.

"What does Helen have to do with Stanley Pennington?"

"I'll get to that. Back then the town of St. Augustine had two districts. We had the poor part of town—it's where my family lived—and we had the rich part of town with people like the Penningtons. Every summer, the rich kids went to Water's Edge. It was a summer camp run by some church people. The cabins were named Matthew, Mark, Luke, John,

Thomas, Jude...you know, apostles. They thought it was clever. I bet they skipped Judas."

He smiled, but I couldn't appreciate the joke, so he cleared his throat and continued.

"The kids would go canoeing and hiking, they'd do crafts, sing songs, go to church—you know, church camp stuff. Poor kids stuck around town and got in trouble."

"Go on," I said, nodding. Fox gave me a sour look, clearly annoyed at the interruption.

"Like I said, Stanley ran this town back then," he said, beginning once more. "He saw these poor kids doing stupid stuff, so he came up with an idea. If a kid could stay out of trouble all year and if they kept their grades up, he'd give them a scholarship so they could go to camp for free. Everybody won. It didn't change the world, but it gave kids something to look forward to."

Trisha and I both nodded. The story was taking time, but I didn't want to interrupt again and miss an important detail.

"Did Helen win one of these scholarships?" I asked.

He nodded. "She and her brother, Glenn, sure did."

"Helen's death certificate says she drowned in suspicious circumstances," I said. "You were the secondary detective on her death investigation. What happened?"

He blinked a few times and refused to look at me.

"It wasn't just a drowning."

"Okay," I said, nodding. "What was it?"

He rocked back and forth on his chair, but he still wouldn't look at me.

"Our dispatcher called Detective Carney and me to the camp real early one morning. The counselors had found a body."

He paused and drew in a breath.

"When we got there, we found Helen. She was on the beach about a mile from camp. Her pants were beside her, and her shirt was bunched up around her neck. She was facedown in the water."

He swallowed. Trisha and I both held our breath.

"The coroner got out there and turned her over and found that her attacker had stuffed her underwear and bra into her mouth. The doc thought it was to keep her from screaming. Her attacker hurt her real bad and then dumped her there like garbage."

Detective Fox blinked.

"I spent a year in Vietnam, so I've seen a lot of things nobody should have to see. I never forgot the look on that little girl's face, though. She was crying when he killed her. It's been almost fifty years, and I still get sick when I think about what happened to her. What do you think it says about me?"

I raised my eyebrows. "It says you're human. Tell me about the investigation."

Detective Fox cleared his throat and then reached for his coffee. His hand didn't tremble as much as it had earlier.

"Yeah, we investigated. We talked to her friends and family. Helen was a kid. She never even had a boyfriend. Men are men, though, and they notice girls like her. She kept a diary and talked about this handsome counselor who flirted with her. His name was Antonio Mancini, and he was a freshman at St. Louis University. He came to St. Augustine for the summer to be a camp counselor.

"We picked him up and interviewed him. He told us he was with some other counselors drinking the night Helen died. We checked with them, and they told us they had asked him to come, but he declined because he had a date."

Detective Fox went silent. My gut twisted.

"Was his date with Helen?" I asked.

"Not according to Antonio. Once we debunked his first alibi, he said he was gay and that he was out with another counselor named David. So we talked to David. David denied being gay and said he had felt sick that night, so he went to bed early. Antonio said David was lying and that they were really out in a hotel in south St. Louis County having sex. Antonio didn't know the hotel's name, and none of the hotels we visited remembered either man."

Trisha furrowed her brow and shifted her weight forward so she could rest her elbows on her knees.

"You remember a lot about this case."

"This one stuck with me," said Fox.

"Did you have physical evidence tying Antonio to Helen?" I asked.

"No, but it didn't matter. Like I said earlier, Stanley Pennington ran this town back then. He and the sheriff got drunk and paid Antonio a visit. They damn near beat him to death. By the time they finished, his face was pulp. He had broken ribs, broken fingers, a broken nose...you name it, they broke it. They said Antonio had attacked them, and that they had defended themselves, but everybody knew what happened. They beat the stuffing out of him because Helen's daddy couldn't."

It wouldn't have been the first time a police officer had allowed someone to exact personal revenge on a murderer. It also explained why someone had removed most of the investigative file.

"What happened to Antonio?" I asked.

"He took his beating and ran," said Fox. "Back then, we didn't have DNA testing, and we didn't have anything tying Antonio to the crime scene. We couldn't prosecute him. Some days, I wished I had joined Stanley and Walt that night. I would have liked to get a few shots in."

I nodded. The story made sense on a superficial level, but it didn't sit right with me.

"Helen's little brother was named Glenn?" I asked.

"Yeah. We talked to him, but he was just a little boy," said Fox. "Helen was five years older than him. Their real mom had died giving birth to Glenn, so Helen was the closest thing he had to a mom. Losing her broke his heart. I never knew what happened to him."

I looked up from my notepad. "He became a teacher at the local high school. Now he's the guidance counselor."

Detective Fox nodded and used his chair's arms to push himself to his feet. His legs seemed unsteady, but he didn't fall.

"I'm glad to hear Glenn turned out okay. Edward, Glenn's daddy, killed himself. I don't think he could take losing his daughter. I don't blame him," he said, his eyes just a little glassy. "If you ladies will excuse me, I have matters to attend to inside."

"Sure," I said, looking to Trisha. We watched him go inside. Then Trisha turned.

"What do you think?"

"It was a church camp, and the cabins were named after Apostles. We need to find Glenn Saunders," I said, taking out my phone and calling the front desk at my station. Jason Zuckerburg answered. "Jason, it's Joe Court. I need you to put together a team and pick up Glenn Saunders. He's the guidance counselor at the high school. He's likely armed and very dangerous."

Jason paused and typed for a few moments before saying anything.

"I can do that," he said. "Looks like he lives in town. Who is he?"

"I think he's the Apostate."

Jason said nothing for a full minute.

"How sure are you about that?"

"Pretty damn sure," I said. "We'll know more as soon as you pick him up."

"Okay. I'll tell the team to expect you."

"No," I said, shaking my head. "If Glenn Saunders is the Apostate, he's got to have a kill room somewhere. Everything he's done has been meaningful to him. His choice of kill room would be meaningful, too. I'm going to the Water's Edge summer camp. It's where this whole thing started. God willing, it's where it'll end."

Chapter 38

I t took longer to find Camp Water's Edge than I expected, mostly because the camp had ceased to exist almost fifty years ago. It was off Highway 62 in the middle of nowhere, and the turnoff was little more than a break in the tree line. I drove right past it twice before I saw it.

"You think the Apostate's doing this for his sister," said Trisha.

"Yeah," I said, flicking on my turn signal as I pushed the brake pedal. My old truck shuddered under the hard deceleration. "He's recreating her death and then punishing her rapist over and over. This guy's been battered his whole life. His mom died in childbirth, someone raped and murdered his sister, and then his dad committed suicide. By recreating Helen's death and punishing the wrongdoer, he gives himself a feeling of control over something uncontrollable."

"This is messed up," said Trisha.

"Yeah," I said, turning onto a rutted dirt road. The surrounding woods were thick at first, but they opened into a clearing alive with native grasses and wildflowers. Someone had driven here recently and often to keep the ruts clear of vegetation. In the distance, the rusted metal remains of a soccer goal protruded from the earth like a monument to the summer camp this place had once been.

I kept my eyes open, but nothing stood out. After a few moments, we passed a second tree line and found cabins lining the road on the other side. Many had collapsed porches and roofs, while time had ground others down to the foundation.

"If anything moves, tell me," I said, glancing at Trisha. She nodded.

"Will do."

I continued to follow the trail until it ended after a long line of cabins. There, I parked in the tall grass. Before getting out of my car, I chambered a round in my firearm and looked to Trisha.

"Are you armed?"

She shook her head, so I used my truck's keys to unlock the glove box and handed her the Glock 26 subcompact I kept inside.

"It's a nine-millimeter, and it's got ten rounds in the magazine and one in the chamber. Make your shots count."

She sighted down the barrel. Trisha may have sat behind a desk most of the day, but she was a sworn police officer. She'd do just fine.

Outside, the air was hot and thick with humidity. Bees buzzed from wildflower to wildflower in the fields around us. A single line trampled through the grass straight ahead to a large wooden building. A heavy, thick tree trunk had crushed the roof, collapsing the walls.

"You see anything?" I asked. Trisha never stopped looking around even as she shook her head.

"No. I think we're clear."

I nodded and followed the path through the grass. The weeds were waist high. A man could have lain hidden in the grass, but I'd see him the moment he popped up. I kept my pistol low and crept forward. Trees ringed the field. When the wind blew, I smelled something both familiar and vile.

Trisha and I followed the path toward the broken building. The building was larger than the cabins we had passed, so it must have been an administrative building—or maybe the mess hall. Trisha and I walked around until we found a storm cellar on the eastern side. One door was open.

I looked at Trisha before stepping toward it. Even from a few feet away, the fetid air made me wrinkle my nose.

"Anybody in there?" I called. Nobody answered, so I called again. Again, nobody answered, so I looked at Trisha. "Watch my back, please."

She nodded, so I stepped into the black. Sunlight penetrated to the bottom of the steps but little further. The air was heavy with urine and feces. I wanted to cover my mouth, but I reached into my pocket for my cell phone instead and pulled it out to use as a torch. The room was approximately twenty feet by thirty feet. A chain-link fence bisected it at the center but allowed movement throughout the room with a gate. A padlock lay on the ground, and a chain hung in the center of the room. It had a broken light bulb in a socket. Beyond the fence, a bucket and cot rested against the far wall.

My heart pounded, and beads of sweat slipped down my forehead and into my eyes. This was the place Paige and Jude had described. Trisha and I needed help, so I left the cellar and found her standing at the top of the steps.

"What'd you find?"

"A cage," I said, looking at my cell phone. My connection had one bar, so I dialed the back line at my station. Jason Zuckerburg answered quickly.

"Jason, it's Joe. Tell me our team picked up Glenn Saunders."

Jason paused.

"That's a negative. Marcus Washington walked around, but the house was secure, and Saunders's car wasn't in the driveway. One of his neighbors said she saw him drive away this morning."

I swore under my breath.

"He's our guy," I said. "Everything fits. The camp, Helen, the church. I need you to call the FBI and send them my way."

"Where are you?"

"Camp Water's Edge. It's off Highway 62. It's in the middle of nowhere. I'll meet the team by the entrance in my truck."

"I'll call Delgado and have him call the Bureau. We'll see what they say."

"Tell them I found his kill room. And tell them to get off their asses and move. This guy's already killed a lot of people. We need to get him before he kills anybody else."

"I'll tell them."

"Good. We'll be waiting." As I hung up, I looked to Trisha and held out my car keys. "It's out of our hands now. Let's hope the brain trust knows what they're doing. You take my truck and park by the entrance for the FBI. I'll wait here."

Glenn slowed and then stopped as he turned onto his street. Two marked police cars had parked along the curb in front of his house. Mary Joe touched his shoulder.

"Don't stop in the road. Turn around in somebody's driveway. We need to go by your dad's old shop."

"Why?" he asked, furrowing his brow.

"Because we need a new car, and you've got four there you took from people you punished," she said. "We can take John Rodgers's Kia and swap the plates with Nicole Moore's car. The police won't be looking for a Kia with plates from Illinois."

"But if they look up the plates, they'll know I switched them."

Mary Joe paused. "If they run the plates, they'll find the discrepancy and pull you over, but it will be a traffic stop. It'll be one officer. She'll walk toward your car to find out what's going on. You'll roll down your window, and she'll lean down to talk to you. As soon as she does, point a pistol at her forehead and squeeze the trigger. We'll be fine."

Glenn nodded as a shudder passed through him. His stomach was tight, but there was something else, too. His senses had become hyper-aware of the world around him. It was like God had reached down and turned up the dials. Even though she sat in the passenger seat, he caught the subtle sweetness of Mary Joe's breath, the musk of her sweat, and the herbaceous notes of her perfume. He never wanted to leave her side.

Glenn nodded and drove.

"My long guns are all at the house," he said. "I've only got a pistol in the car."

Mary Joe glanced at him. "How many rounds do you have?"

"Eight in the magazine and one in the chamber," he said, already knowing it wasn't enough. "We'll drive to St. Louis. There are gun shops there that won't ask questions. We can still hit the pool before it closes."

Mary Joe shook her head.

"We'd need at least a thousand dollars, and you don't have that kind of cash. If the police are at your house, they're probably monitoring your credit cards," she said. "As soon as you pay, they'll get you. We need to go to the school."

Glenn raised an eyebrow. "The school doesn't have guns."

"No, but Finley Berry does."

Glenn shook his head.

"Finley doesn't like me. There's no way he'll let me borrow a gun."

"That's why you'll kill him and steal the keys to his gun safe at home."

Glenn considered the plan and then nodded. He didn't look forward to shooting up the pool, but he understood its necessity. Shooting Finley would be personal, though. This, he would enjoy.

"Let's go to work, then."

Chapter 39

M y old truck came bouncing over the landscape about fifteen minutes after Trisha left. A caravan of SUVs, minivans, and police cruisers followed. I flagged them down and directed them to park in a field so they wouldn't disturb the scene. Agent Costa and a woman in dark gray slacks, a matching gray blazer, and a white button-down shirt stepped out of the lead SUV. Half a dozen agents and Trisha followed from the other vehicles.

"Agent Costa," I said, nodding to the special agent as he walked toward me. He returned the nod and looked to the woman beside him.

"This is Deputy Director Alexis Koch," he said. "Director Koch, this is Detective Joe Court with the St. Augustine County Sheriff's Department. She worked the case with Bruce."

Director Koch's green eyes bore into mine as I shook her hand. A tight smile came to her lips, allowing wrinkles to form around her eyes and mouth. She was in her early fifties, if I had to guess, and she looked fit. As best I could tell, she didn't carry a weapon.

"Ma'am," I said.

"Detective," she answered before shooting her eyes around the scene. "Bruce Lawson was a friend of mine, and he spoke highly of you. Tell me what you've got."

I walked her through everything Trisha and I had done that morning. Koch nodded and asked questions but kept her reactions neutral throughout the conversation. When I finished speaking, she brought a hand to her face and considered me.

"Do you have any physical evidence tying Glenn Saunders to these killings?"

"Not yet, but we have a strong circumstantial case. From the start, we wondered how the Apostate was meeting his victims. Saunders knew four of them. He could have met the others at a college fair. He also knew how to talk to teenagers and make them trust him. Saunders ticks off boxes we didn't even know to look for."

Koch drew in a breath and screwed up her face.

"And you guys never suspected him until now," she said.

"We didn't have a reason to," I said. "He gave me the creeps when I interviewed him, but I didn't think he was a murderer."

Koch's eyes went distant as she watched two special agents approach the cellar.

"Does he have family or friends around the area?"

"His mother, father, and sister are dead," I said. "He may have distant family around, but I don't know."

She glanced at me out of the corner of her eye.

"Bruce said you were smart," she said. "How do you plan to find him?"

I hadn't expected her to ask that, so I thought for a moment.

"Position officers on every interstate on-ramp and have them stop everybody who looks like Saunders. You should also put out an APB on his car and try to track him via his cell phone. You should monitor his credit cards, too."

"That's a good start," she said, turning. "What else would you do? How would you track down his friends?"

"Start at work. I interviewed him there not too long ago. He seemed chummy with the principal."

"Good. Go there," said Koch. She looked to Agent Costa. "And you go with her."

Costa hesitated but then nodded and looked to me. "Where's your car, Detective?"

I turned and pointed.

"I've got my truck. Let's go."

Trisha tossed me my keys, and Costa and I hurried to my truck. Once I reached the highway, I floored the accelerator. In one of my department's marked cruisers, the acceleration would have pushed me against my seat and rocketed the car forward. My old truck got loud, but it didn't move much faster.

Once I got up to a reasonable speed, I let my foot off the gas. The noise decreased to a tolerable level. Costa cleared his throat.

"I'm glad your friend Harry isn't our killer."

"Me, too," I said, shooting him a glance. "What made you guys look at him, anyway?"

Costa tilted his head to the side and shrugged as he watched the passing countryside out the window.

"We looked at everybody. Harry fit our profile better than most."

I nodded and drummed my fingers on the steering wheel.

"Did you guys look at me?" I asked.

He glanced at me. "Female serial murderers are rare. We didn't discount you offhand, but you didn't make the final list."

I drove for another minute in silence before I looked to Costa again.

"Did Delgado?" I asked.

Costa humored me with a smile. "Does it matter?"

I shrugged. "Well, not really, I guess. It's just that St. Augustine County elects its sheriff. I thought it'd be amusing if, during his election campaign, the local paper learned the FBI had once suspected Delgado was a serial murderer."

Costa looked out his window again.

"It's the policy of the Federal Bureau of Investigation to stay out of politics wherever possible."

I tilted my head to the side. "So, is that a yes?"

"That's a no comment, Detective."

We said nothing until we reached the high school. The parking lot was nearly empty, just as it had been on my previous visit. I parked in the fire lane in front of the building and stepped out of my truck.

"Was it this empty when you were here before?" asked Costa, who had stepped out of the passenger seat.

"Yeah," I said, walking toward the building. "The students and teachers don't come back until August."

Costa followed me toward the building and stopped the same moment I did. The school had eight commercial glass and steel front doors. The doors wouldn't have come cheap, but the thick tempered glass provided a good compromise between visibility and security. Someone had broken the glass on the far left door. A hammer lay on the ground.

I reached to my waist and took my firearm from my holster. Costa did likewise.

"You want to call this in?" I asked.

"Yeah, but after we find out what we've got. I'd rather not pull officers away from the summer camp just because some kid broke into his high school."

I nodded and walked forward. Glass crunched under the soles of my shoes. A warm breeze blew from the field across from the school, carrying with it the sweet scent of cut grass. Before opening the door, I pressed the button on the intercom and waited and watched through the glass. Nothing and no one moved inside.

I reached for the door handle but stopped as the faint sounds of a siren carried toward me. Within seconds, a pair of marked police cruisers appeared on the road. Both Costa and I holstered our firearms. I held up my badge as the cruisers parked behind my truck in the fire lane. Officers Shane Fox and Destiny Rogers hurried out of their vehicles. Both gave me quizzical looks.

"Detective Court?" asked Destiny. "You get the call, too?"

"No," I said, looking to Costa. "This is Special Agent Bryan Costa with the FBI. We're here to talk to the principal and anyone else inside. Why are you here?"

"Somebody tripped the alarm twelve minutes ago," said Shane. "Jason called the office, but nobody answered. We're here to check it out. Is there a problem?"

"There could be," I said, raising my eyebrows. "Keep your eyes open, and get your firearms out. Watch each other's backs."

Shane lowered his chin.

"What are we walking into here?"

"Probably nothing, but be ready anyway," I said. "Costa and I will follow you in."

The uniformed officers checked their firearms and then pulled the front door open. Gray and white terrazzo marble floors flowed from the front doors, through the cavernous entryway, and then to classrooms on the left and right. The sound of our footsteps echoed off the floor and metal lockers, but nothing moved. The heavy silence felt eerie.

"Costa and I will go right," I said. "You two go left."

Both Fox and Rogers nodded and did as I asked. Costa and I passed half a dozen dark classrooms before coming to the administration's suite of offices. The fluorescent lights buzzed as they lit the rooms. The door was open, but we found no one inside the reception area.

"You hear anything?" I whispered. He shook his head but nodded toward a hallway inside the office suite.

"There were two cars outside. There should be two people here."

"Yeah," I said, adjusting the grip on my firearm. Costa nodded, and we crept toward the office suite's interior hallway, being careful to avoid stepping on any blood on the ground. The hallway was wide enough for us to walk beside one another. The vice principal's door was locked, but Principal Finley Berry's door was open. My stomach dropped as I stepped into the doorway.

Principal Berry lay facedown on the floor in front of his desk in a puddle of blood. The back of his skull had been blown clean off. Judging from the blood around his torso, he had been shot in the chest several times. This was overkill. This was personal.

"Shooter's gone," said Costa. "Back up so we don't disturb the scene. We'll clear the rest of the building and call in a forensics team."

I nodded my agreement and walked out. Costa and I checked every room on our side of the building and found no one—dead or alive. Officers Rogers and Fox, though, found a middle-aged woman who had locked herself in a storage closet. She was hyperventilating, but she kept saying over and over that it was Glenn Saunders. We had figured as much.

With the building secured, I walked to the front doors and called Sheriff Delgado to tell him what we had found. He said he was on his way. With the calls made, I bent to look at the hammer our killer had used to break the door.

Return to G. Saunders if borrowed.

It was written on a notecard and taped to the handle. If I had neighbors who borrowed tools, I would have done the same thing. I pointed it out to Agent Costa, who covered his mouth and stepped back.

"There was no ritual here," he said. "Saunders had a process for the young people he killed. He was controlled and meticulous. This is all rage."

I nodded. "Yeah. The game's changed. This guy won't stop on his own. We need to find him."

Costa glanced up at me. "How?"

"No clue."

Chapter 40

Delgado beat even our uniformed officers to the crime scene. I briefed him, and then he walked inside to check out Finley Berry's body firsthand. Agent Costa paced on the sidewalk and made phone calls, while Officers Shane Fox and Destiny Rogers sat with the woman they had found—Janice Crawford—in Shane's cruiser.

About ten minutes after Delgado arrived, almost a dozen FBI agents—including Deputy Director Koch—pulled to a stop beside my truck. Costa hung up, and then the two senior FBI agents conferred before Koch walked to me. Agent Costa and the other FBI agents walked inside.

"You were right, and I was wrong," she said. "Saunders is our killer. Your friend Harry Grainger is innocent. I already requested that we release him from custody."

I blinked, unaccustomed to honesty at work.

"Thank you. I appreciate it," I said. I gave myself a moment to think. "Has anyone briefed you?"

"Agent Costa called and filled me in. Where's Sheriff Delgado, and where's this woman you found?"

As if on cue, the sheriff emerged from the school and walked toward us.

"Director Koch," he said, nodding to the FBI agent before looking to me. "The witness is with one of my sergeants. Did you ID the body, Joe?"

"He's Finley Berry," I said. "He's the principal."

Delgado nodded and looked at Director Koch.

"I've got a forensics team inbound," he said. "The school has cameras in the hallways, cafeteria, gym, and entrance-ways, but I'm not sure whether they were on. If Saunders came from town, he passed two gas stations with cameras pointed toward their pumps. Either one might have caught video of his car. The hammer outside is compelling evidence. We've got enough to make an arrest."

Koch nodded. "I'll make agents available in an advisory capacity, but it sounds as if you've got this under control."

"We do," said Delgado, looking to me. "I need you to start a logbook, Detective Court. We need a detailed account of everyone who goes into the building."

Director Koch stepped away. I cleared my throat and forced a smile to my face.

"Are you trying to insult me by telling me to sit on the corner and fill out paperwork?" I asked.

He stepped closer.

"We need to document and secure the scene, Detective. This is part of the job. We don't always get the glamorous assignments. Now start a logbook. I won't ask again."

For my entire career, I had tried to be a good officer. Four years ago, when Delgado and his partner had asked me to search through the dumpster behind the Pizza Palace for a suspect's bloody clothes, I did it. It was disgusting, but that was my job. I had been the youngest person in my department, which put me on the lowest rung of our department's ladder. That was how things worked. Three years ago, I routinely hosed out the drunk tank on Sunday mornings. It was an awful job, but it was my responsibility as the lowest-ranking member of our department.

Now, I carried a detective's badge. On a normal day, I wouldn't have minded sitting outside to fill out paperwork. But today wasn't a normal day.

Today, we had an armed serial murderer running through town. We didn't know where he was or what he planned, but unless we stopped him, he'd hurt people. My research had led to Glenn Saunders's identification. My identification had led me to his kill room, and my conversations with Agent Costa had led me to the high school. Without my work, neither Delgado nor the FBI had a thing.

I lowered my voice.

"No."

Delgado furrowed his brow. "Excuse me?"

"Fill out your own logbook, George. This is my case. I've met our killer. You haven't. I won't sit on the sidelines now."

Delgado crossed his arms and raised his eyebrows.

"Are you refusing an order, Detective?"

"A stupid one, yes," I said, stepping forward. Delgado walked backward, maintaining the distance between us. "It's not your first stupid order, either. You told Mark Bozwell to deny me access to any files in the evidence vault without a direct connection to my caseload. Do you remember that?"

Delgado said nothing for five or six seconds. Then he sighed.

"We're not here to talk about Mark Bozwell."

I spoke slowly so he'd understand me.

"Because you barred me from the evidence vault when I needed to search it, you prevented me from identifying Glenn Saunders as a suspect. If you had let me do my job, I could have stopped some of this. Mr. Berry is dead because of you, and that's a problem. You're not just incompetent, you're stupid. You can try to fire me for insubordination, but I'll make sure everyone in the state knows what a royal screw up you are. If you push me, I swear to God, I will push back twice as hard."

Delgado's face grew red, but he said nothing before turning and walking away. I looked to Director Koch. She considered me for a moment before speaking.

"That was quite a speech."

"I've been holding it in for a while," I said. I paused and tilted my head to the side. "You think that will make it into my employee evaluation at the end of the year?"

"You think you'll make it to the end of the year after saying that to your boss?"

"Fair point," I said, raising my eyebrows and nodding. "So what's your next move?"

She considered me. "You tell me. You've worked this case. Where would Saunders go?"

"Wherever he can hurt the most people," I said.

She crossed her arms and narrowed her eyes. "You don't think he'd go after a specific target?"

"I have no idea anymore."

She nodded and then looked over her shoulder to Sheriff Delgado. He glared at me but walked over.

"How many officers do you have?"

"Forty-four," said Delgado. He looked at me before locking eyes with Director Koch. "You know what happened the last time Detective Court suggested we put officers in the field, right? Saunders might be setting us up again. Has anybody thought of that?"

Koch looked at me. "Has he contacted you?"

"No," I said, shaking my head. "He's not setting us up."

"I still don't like it," said Delgado.

"Too bad, George," I said. "We're police officers. It's our job to protect people who can't protect themselves."

"Okay," said Delgado. "Since you're so sure of yourself, where should we send them? We have no idea where this guy will attack. If he's even planning an attack. If it were me, I'd be getting out of town now."

"We'll keep officers near the interstates," said Koch. "We also need to send officers to any locations where large numbers of people gather. I'm talking shopping malls, schools, offices, anywhere with a large number of targets in a small area."

"This is St. Augustine. We don't have shopping malls or big office buildings," said Delgado. "The schools are closed, too. He could be anywhere."

"Who are your major employers?" asked Koch.

"There will be a couple hundred people working at the plant at Ross Kelly Farms, but they can lock that down quickly," I said. "Reid Chemical is closed, so we don't have to worry about them. The local school system is out for the summer, but Waterford College is open. We should call its Office of Public Safety. Its officers will know how to protect their property better than us."

"Good," said Koch. "Where else?"

"Club Serenity has a lot of foot traffic," I said. Koch furrowed her brow. "It's a strip club near the interstate. There's a truck stop next door, so it does a good business. We should have a team downtown, too."

Koch nodded. "This is good. Can you think of anywhere else we should deploy, Sheriff Delgado?"

Delgado exhaled a slow breath before tilting his head to the side. "There's an event at the Boy Scout camp off Highway 62. Dave Skelton's there now with his boys."

That got our attention.

"How many people are there?" asked Koch.

Delgado blew out a long breath and shrugged. "Couple hundred. Boys from all over the state have come in."

"That's our priority," said Koch. "Get in touch with your officer in the field, and tell him what's going on. We'll send men down there. I'll work with your dispatcher and my own teams to get officers elsewhere around town."

Delgado nodded and walked to his cruiser. I watched him and then looked to Director Koch.

"What do you want me to do?"

She looked toward the school.

"Do you have tactical training, Detective?"

I blinked and then slowly shook my head. "No more than most officers."

"Then you and Agent Costa are working a double homicide," she said. "You're more valuable here than you would be in the field."

My shoulders slumped, but I forced my expression to stay neutral. Homicides were among the toughest, most important investigations a detective could undertake. I should have been proud that Director Koch would ask me to work one alongside one of her own investigators. It was among the highest compliments she could give me, but it still made me feel like a kid whose basketball coach had ordered her to come off the court and ride the bench.

"I'm on it," I said, smiling. "Agent Costa and I won't let you down."

The corners of her lips curled into a tight smile.

"I know you won't, Detective," she said. She paused. "You look like I punched you in the face. Buck up."

I stood straighter. "I'll do my best, ma'am."

She and most of the other agents left a few minutes later, leaving me alone with Agent Costa. The FBI forensics team was busy at Camp Water's Edge—where they had found a second kill room in a second cellar—so Darlene McEvoy and two uniformed officers with forensics training came from our station to work the scene. Darlene was an excellent lab scientist, so we were in good hands.

While Costa supervised them, I walked around the exterior of the building to check the other doors and windows. I also noted the security cameras near the roof. Assuming those cameras were recording at the time of the shooting, we'd have video of Saunders pulling into the lot, breaking into the front door, and walking to the administrative offices. We wouldn't have footage of the murder itself, but with the hammer found by the front door and the fingerprints we were likely to find inside, we'd have ample evidence for a conviction.

After circumnavigating the building twice, I joined Agent Costa inside. Dr. Sheridan and Sam, his assistant, were wheeling Berry's body out. I nodded hello to them both before looking to Costa.

"Every door and window is secure and locked, and there are cameras every thirty or forty feet outside. There's one right above the door Saunders broke. We've got him," I said, watching the street as a car rolled past before focusing on Costa. "Unless you've got an objection, I'll drive by Mr. Berry's house and see whether I can talk to his family before they hear about the shooting on Twitter."

Costa nodded. "Good luck."

I nodded and thanked him before walking to my truck. With so many bodies on the ground lately, it was easy to forget that each victim was an individual tragedy. Each victim had family and friends. In life, they had hopes and dreams. In death, they had nothing. Saunders had stolen everything that mattered from them. No matter what he had done, Mr. Berry didn't deserve the fate that had befallen him.

This needed to end soon. I didn't care if Saunders surrendered or went down in a blaze of gunfire. I wanted him out of commission. He had ruined enough lives.

Chapter 41

B lowing his boss's head off had been one of the greatest experiences of Glenn's life. Even twenty minutes later, he could picture the stupid, surprised look on Finley's face when he and Mary Joe walked in. He could smell the burnt gunpowder; he could feel the pressure of the trigger beneath his finger; and he could hear Mary Joe's encouraging words in his ear. He'd remember killing Finley for the rest of his life—however short that might be.

He squeezed Mary Joe's hand and smiled.

"You're in a good mood," she said, smiling at him and squeezing his hand in return and winking. "Get lucky this morning?"

The memories of the things he and Mary Joe had done made him smile even wider. They stood beside one another in the basement of Finley Berry's house. The principal's gun safe was open, and Glenn had laid the firearms on the ground in front of him so he could make his choice. He turned toward Mary Joe and drew her into a soft kiss.

"I wish we could stay like this forever," he whispered.

"Me too, but we've still got work to do," she said, nodding toward the firearms. "Have you chosen yet?"

Back to reality. He sighed and knelt.

"The AK-47 would work," he said. "It takes a 7.62 NATO cartridge, and Finley's got plenty. It'd do the job, but it's heavy and inaccurate."

Mary Joe knelt beside him and put her hand on the firearm.

"Accuracy doesn't matter as much when your targets are close," she said. "The good thing about the 7.62 cartridge is that it's likely to punch right through your opponent. If they're bunched up along a fence, you might hit two or three people with one round."

He raised his eyebrows and nodded.

"That's true, but it feels so boorish," he said. "The AK is all brute strength. There's no finesse."

Mary Joe narrowed her gaze at him and nodded.

"You're thinking the AR-15, aren't you?"

He nodded and ran his hand over the sleek rifle. "An AK-47 is great when you're in the field and might need to shoot through a cinder-block building, but we'll be shooting housewives in bathing suits. This'll be one shot, one kill. Given what Finley has, the AR-15 feels like the best choice."

"This will be fun," said Mary Joe, touching his shoulder and smiling. "Make sure you grab all four magazines. We don't want to run out of ammunition before we run out of targets."

Glenn nodded, grabbed Finley's four thirty-round magazines, and stuffed them into his pockets. Then he took the rifle and stood. Glenn had only met Finley's wife twice at holiday parties at work, but she had talked to him incessantly each time. He had hoped to find her in the house and shut her up, but she must have been out. It was a pity. At least he got one of the duo of dunces.

Before leaving, he put Finley's rifle on the rear seat of his car. Then he sat beside Mary Joe in front. He put his hand on her knee. She put hers on top and smiled at him.

"This is it," he said, his voice soft. "I'm not walking away from this one."

"No, you're not," said Mary Joe. "We've had a good ride, haven't we?"

"We have," he said, taking his hand from her and twisting his key in the ignition. He backed out of Berry's driveway and started the short trip to Sycamore Park and the public pool it held. As he drove, a red Dodge Ram pickup caught his attention. It was old, but its chrome front bumper and grill gleamed. Someone loved and cared for that truck. A blond woman sat in the driver's seat, but she was driving in the opposite direction on the road.

"Pretty girl?" asked Mary Joe.

"Yeah," said Glenn, shaking his head and focusing on the road in front of him again. "For a second, I thought that was your truck."

She reached over to touch his shoulder.

"I'm right here, sweetheart. You're not getting rid of me."

"I'm glad you're here," he said. "Let's finish this. I'm tired of fighting. I'm ready to go home."

Mary Joe squeezed his shoulder. "Soon every voice will grow quiet."

Finley Berry lived in a two-story brick home with a wide front porch and big dormers on the second floor. The grass lay across the front yard like a thick carpet, while someone had trimmed the hedges beneath the front windows into perfect cubes. The porch swing swayed in a lazy summer breeze, and the front door hung open. An uneasy pit grew in my stomach.

I parked in front of the house and kept my hand over my firearm as I crossed over the lawn to the front door. Nothing inside the house moved.

"Sheriff's Department," I called into the foyer. "Anybody home?"

No one responded, so I called again and waited. Then I heard a door shut.

"Sheriff's Department," I called for a third time as I removed my firearm from its holster. "If someone is in the house, please tell me now."

"I'm here. I'm Cassie. I'm the homeowner. Please don't hurt me."

Meaning she was Finley Berry's spouse. I holstered my firearm because it sounded as if she were on the verge of tears.

"I'm on your front porch. Is everything all right?"

"No," she warbled. "I'm coming up."

I waited another moment until a woman in her early forties stepped out of a side door and onto the tiled entryway. Her straight black hair framed a thin, pale face. When she saw me, she covered her mouth with both hands and trembled as she walked backward. She looked like a flower that had bloomed and then wilted. I didn't want her to fall, so I held up a hand.

"It's okay," I said, looking over my shoulder and stepping back. "I'm here to help."

She lowered her hands from her face, allowing me to see her quivering lower lip. Tears streamed down her cheeks.

"They weren't lying," she said. "If you're here, Fin's dead."

I drew in a breath and lowered my chin. "Who told you that?"

"Is it true?" she asked, wiping tears from her eyes. I said nothing, so she nodded. "You don't have to answer. I know. They killed him."

I held up a hand, hoping she'd answer my questions.

"Was someone here?"

"Yes," she said, her face crumbling as she blinked tears from her eyes. "It was Glenn Saunders. He works with my husband."

"Did you talk to him?" I asked.

She shook her head and ran her hands through her hair.

"No. I was doing laundry. They kicked down the door, so I hid. I didn't even see them, but I recognized Glenn's voice. He was looking for me. He kept saying he wanted to kill me, too, so he could have the whole Berry set."

I lowered my voice. "You're safe now. He's not here."

She said nothing and slid down the nearest wall. Then she brought her knees to her chest and sobbed.

"I know this is hard," I said, "but we need to talk. Who was this other person with Glenn?"

She didn't answer, so I repeated the question. Then she shook her head.

"Somebody named Mary Joe. She didn't talk, and I never saw her. I was hiding in the laundry room."

I snapped my head up. "Are you sure it was Mary Joe?"

She nodded and rubbed her eyes but said nothing. It could have been a coincidence, but it was unnerving.

"Can I walk through the house to make sure we're alone?"

She nodded, so I took the stairs to the second floor and pulled out my cell phone to call Agent Costa. After I told him what had happened, he agreed to call his boss and send help. Then, I cleared the first and second floors before searching the basement. There, I found firearms and boxes of ammunition strewn on the ground. It wasn't a huge gun collection, but it had two tactical rifles and three handguns.

I went back upstairs. Mrs. Berry still sat on the floor, but she had stopped sobbing. I cleared my throat, and she looked at me.

"Do you store all your firearms in the gun safe?"

She blinked and then closed her eyes.

"Yes. My husband was a responsible gun owner."

That was why Saunders had come, then. He killed his boss for his keys and then raided his gun safe.

"Can you come downstairs with me and tell me if anything's missing?"

"Can't I stay here?"

I softened my voice. "I know this is hard, but I need your help."

She shook her head but stood and walked with me down the stairs. When she saw the firearms, she sighed.

"The AR-15 is missing. There's at least one pistol missing, too, but I don't know which one."

"He wouldn't have taken the weapon without reason," I said. "Did he or Mary Joe mention where they were going?"

She said nothing, but she licked her lips as if she were trying to speak. I repeated the question.

"He said something about shooting housewives in bathing suits."

"Housewives in bathing suits," I said, frowning. I almost asked where he expected to find housewives in bathing suits, but then it seemed obvious as it hit me. I pulled out my phone and called Agent Costa.

"Finley Berry's wife is here. Saunders has a partner, and they took an AR-15 and pistol from the house. They talked about shooting housewives in bathing suits. They're going to a pool. Call your people and tell them to get to the country club on Pinehurst. I'll send my people to the public pool at Sycamore Park."

Costa paused. "You sure about this?"

"There are no guarantees in this business, but it makes sense. The pool's surrounded by a fence, and there'll be a big crowd. It's a soft target."

Costa swore under his breath. "All right. I'll call this in."

"Do that," I said, hanging up. I looked at Mrs. Berry. "I'll head out. You stay here. You'll be safe. Saunders isn't coming back, and uniformed officers are on their way."

She begged me to stay, but I was only three blocks from Sycamore Park. Saunders could have been there already. I had to stop this. I ran to my truck and threw it in reverse before flooring it out of the neighborhood.

While holding the wheel with one hand, I called my station's front desk. Jason Zuckerburg answered.

"Jason, hey," I said. "I've tracked down Glenn Saunders and need you to send every officer we've got to the pool in Sycamore Park. Saunders is well armed and dangerous. The bureau's sending officers to the country club. He's going to one of these two, and he'll kill a lot of people unless we stop him."

Jason typed. "How do you know this?"

"A witness heard Saunders talking," I said. "Who's the nearest officer?"

Jason grunted. "We're scattered around the county. We've got a team at the high school, we've got a pair of teams near the interstate, and we've got almost twenty people way out by the river for the Boy Scout thing. No one is near Sycamore Park."

I swallowed and nodded. "Send whoever you can and tell them I'll be on site. Then call the pool and tell them to get everybody inside the locker rooms. And do it now. Tell them to lock the doors once people are inside."

Jason paused. "I'm routing officers now, and I'm looking up the number for the pool."

"Thanks."

I hung up and tossed the phone to the seat beside me, hoping and praying I wasn't already too late.

Chapter 42

A t fifteen acres, Sycamore Park was one of the smaller parks in St. Augustine County's parks system. The town had set aside the land almost seventy years ago, making it the oldest park in town. Before Helen had disappeared, she had played in a girls' softball league organized by their church. Once or twice a month, the family would drive to the park so Helen could practice batting at the park's baseball field. Edward would pitch while Glenn fielded balls.

Helen never became a great softball player, but those were the happiest memories Glenn had of his father and sister. Edward had even smiled then some. Nothing had felt as good as making his dad smile. Those were the good years.

Glenn's dad stopped smiling after Helen was murdered. He killed himself two years after that. Today was about making that right.

Since he couldn't find a spot at the pool, Glenn parked off the side of the road near the playground. A man in his early twenties pushed a red-haired girl in pigtails on a swing. Freckles dotted her pale skin, and she laughed with the carefree joy of a child ignorant of the world's terrors. He hoped Mary Joe wouldn't make him kill her.

Mary Joe stepped out of her side of the car and waved to the little one. Glenn expected the girl's father to notice the beautiful woman waving at his daughter, but he only had eyes for his little girl at the moment. It was nice to see.

"Where should we set up?"

Mary Joe swept the park with her eyes. The park's landscape swept from a hill near its eastern entrance to a flat plain in its center to another downward slope on its western edge. A canopy of leaves and enormous trees covered everything but the pool and part of the basketball court. The trees would give him plenty of cover if someone shot at him, but they limited his view of strategic areas.

"Let's walk," she said. "We shouldn't stay still too long."

Glenn nodded and grabbed the duffel bag with his stolen rifle and ammunition from the back of his car. Mary Joe headed toward the pool. Hot sunlight broke through the trees, beating down on the blacktop parking lot in front of the pool and making the asphalt almost gooey. He smiled at a mom struggling to carry two small children and a giant canvas beach bag.

"It would be ideal if we could block the exit or collapse the locker rooms," said Mary Joe, her voice low. "We can't do that, though."

Glenn nodded and waited until the mom and her kids passed before speaking. "Even if some people escape, we'll have plenty of targets."

Mary Joe nodded and crossed in front of the pool's entrance on her way to the basketball courts. This evening, teenagers would line up to play, but in the heat of the day, the court was abandoned. They walked for another five minutes to the base of a slope on the park's eastern edge. Above them, a dense thicket of scrub brush and trees separated the park from the road, while the plain opened before them.

Mary Joe pointed toward a black gum tree about halfway up the hill.

"There's your spot," she said. "The tree trunk will give you concealment and cover from the front. The brush behind you will give you concealment from the road. If they try to approach you from the north or south, you'll have plenty of time to pick them off."

It was a good spot, so he nodded. The slope was about twenty degrees. Butterflies fluttered in his stomach, and his throat felt tight. He knew what to do and why he had to do it, but he felt the first twinges of remorse anyway. Mary Joe scampered up the hill beside him and gave him a sympathetic look.

"You're doing this for Helen," she said. "You'll see her soon."

He nodded and unzipped his bag. The black tactical rifle looked almost wicked.

"Will I see you again?"

Mary Joe looked out over the park. From their vantage, they could see clear to the batting cages on the park's western edge. She shook her head.

"No, but you know that."

He looked down to the pool.

"You don't exist, do you?"

She humored him with a smile. "No, but you know that, too."

He looked toward the pool. "Helen existed, though."

"At one time," said Mary Joe, her voice low. "She died, though."

"So what are you?" he asked. "A figment of my imagination?"

"I'm a wish made real," she said. "I'm here to help you."

"Then help me," he said.

Mary Joe nodded and reached for Glenn's hands. He allowed her to move him like a puppet. Together, they reached into his duffel bag and removed the rifle.

"Your targets are between three hundred and four hundred yards away," she said. "The wind and humidity are negligible. The conditions are right. Do this for your sister."

Glenn knew it all even before she spoke. He grasped the weapon. As he looked to his left, he caught the last image of Mary Joe fading away like smoke from a candle. He closed his eyes and held his breath as he listened. He heard nothing.

The voices he had lived with for so long had disappeared. He was free.

Glenn drew in a breath of sweet, fresh air and rested. Birds sang nearby. Insects buzzed. Children laughed and played. Somewhere distant, a kid thumped a ball against the ground.

He could run.

Helen was gone. His shadow had disappeared. No one would stop him. His car had a full tank of gas, so he could drive for hours. He could go anywhere. Without the voices, he could start over. He could stop hurting.

Only he wouldn't.

For years, he had pretended Helen had run away and then returned. But she hadn't. His beautiful sister had been a child younger than most of his students when she died. The woman he knew, the woman who had lived with him, was a dream constructed by his heart and given life by his grief-stricken mind.

Glenn had knowingly lived a lie for most of his life. His father had told him the truth before he died. An evil man had raped and murdered Helen. The police tried to build a case against him, but they failed. To make it up to the family, a relative of that evil man had made Edward's lifelong dream come true. She gave him the money to start his own business. It was supposed to be a fresh start. Instead, it became a punishment.

Edward quit his job at Pennington Hotels and opened his own furniture-making shop. Every day he had gone into work, and every day, he had known his daughter's blood paid for his dream. Edward had tried to be a good father, but Helen's death had broken him. He killed himself. Before then, though, he had passed the torch on to his son.

Unlike his father, Glenn was strong. He would finish the job his father never could. For years, Glenn had refused to face the reality of his task, but he couldn't ignore it any longer. The people of St. Augustine refused to give his family justice. Now, they would feel his family's vengeance.

Cold like he had never before felt swept over him. His hands steadied, and his heart hardened as he inserted a magazine and chambered a round. Glenn brought the weapon to his shoulder and looked through the scope. Even at four hundred yards, his targets appeared before him, fat and ripe.

Glenn adjusted the sight. He had no one to call out targets today, but he didn't need a spotter. Hundreds of targets lay before him. He chose a fat little boy in blue swim trunks and centered the reticle over his chest. Then, he took the slack out of the trigger but didn't fire.

"Now cracks a noble heart," he whispered. "Good night, sweet prince, and flights of angels sing thee to thy rest."

Since my truck didn't have lights or a siren, I kept my hand on the horn and my foot on the gas the entire drive to the pool. Most people got out of my way. I screamed at the recalcitrant few who impeded me, but there was little I could do otherwise. I reached the outskirts of Sycamore Park four minutes after I left the Berrys' house.

By the time I saw the pool, I was too late. Even from the park's entrance, I saw that blood had stained the water pink. My heart hammered against my breastbone, and my breath stopped in my throat. Cars occupied every parking spot in front of the pool's main building, so I braked hard and skidded to a stop on the roadway near the front entrance.

I opened my door and stepped out onto the running boards, frantically looking for our shooter.

Four shots rang out. My eyes shot to the north in time to see a lone man scrambling across a grassy field toward the pool. He held a black tactical rifle in his hands. After running fifteen or twenty feet, he slowed and brought his rifle to his shoulder. He was two hundred yards from me. If I fired toward him and missed—which was likely at that distance—I could hit somebody at the pool.

I couldn't let him shoot somebody, though, so I swiveled and fired twice at a nearby hill to get his attention. The rounds penetrated with a dull thump. Saunders lowered his rifle and turned toward me. For a split second, our eyes locked. He raised his weapon toward me.

I jumped back in my truck and put the car in gear. The lawyers wouldn't like it if I ran Saunders down with my truck, but he'd be just as dead of an impact with my bumper as he would be if I shot him. I floored the accelerator. My old truck roared to life, and the front tires hopped the curb. I bounced out of my seat and nearly hit the roof, but I held onto the steering wheel so I didn't fall.

"Come on, baby. Come on, baby. Come on, baby."

I kept repeating it as my tires tore into the countryside. Saunders fired. The sound boomed around me. A round smashed through my front windshield and thumped into the vinyl seat beside me. Tiny shards of glass hit my hands and tore into my cheeks, but the now shattered window held in the frame. I could hardly see, but I didn't dare slow down.

Saunders fired twice more. This time, the rounds pinged against the undercarriage near my feet. He was trying to hit my tires. I had momentum on my side, though. Even if he took out my tires, I'd take him out with me.

He fired again. Four shots, this time. They hit the engine block with four wrenching thuds. Detroit cast iron stopped the rounds, but already my old truck felt and sounded different. Something—the radiator, if I had to guess—whistled.

Saunders ran for a tree. I whipped the wheel and let off the gas. The back end of my truck fishtailed, and the wheels on my right side lifted from the ground.

"Please don't flip. Please don't flip. Please don't flip."

I held my breath and felt gravity pull me back to the ground. My wheels hit hard and bounced as my old truck slowed. I slammed my foot on the brake, bringing the heavy vehicle to a rest. The engine throbbed and then died.

Saunders darted from behind the tree and fired into the cab. I ducked low so he couldn't see me and jumped out of the driver's door as round after round slammed into the vehicle. The engine block gave me limited cover, but he had me far outgunned. This was a losing position.

My backup was coming, but they were still likely a few minutes out. Saunders could have brought two or three hundred rounds. My truck couldn't stop all of them. I balled my hands into fists and bit the knuckle of my left index finger as an idea coalesced.

"Joe, this is stupid," I whispered before drawing in a deep breath and shouting, "Glenn, I'm here to help you!"

As if to answer my request, he squeezed off four rounds. Each hit my car and made my ears ring and my gut twist.

"I know about Helen."

I gritted my teeth, expecting gunfire. Saunders didn't shoot, though. I peeked over the hood of my truck. He stood beside a tree about forty feet away with his rifle pointed in my direction. It was a good position. The tree gave him cover from my direction, and a hill behind him gave him cover from the rear. If I could get to his flanks, I could take him out, but I'd need help for that.

"Helen didn't deserve what happened to her."

Again, Saunders said nothing. Beads of sweat dripped down my forehead and into my eyes. My heart raced, and my hands trembled.

"I want to help!" I shouted again. "I know what happened, and I won't cover it up like they did before. We can find the guy who killed her and make sure he can't do it to anyone else."

"He's already dead," said Saunders, his voice a snarl. I winced.

"Killing innocent people won't help anybody," I said. "These are kids, though. They're like Helen."

I counted to ten and then twenty, waiting for his response. Nothing. I peered over the hood again. Almost instantly, Saunders's rifle boomed, and a round skipped over my head with a tight buzzing sound. I popped back down, gasping. My hands trembled. He had me dialed in well, so I doubted his next shot would miss.

"I can't help you if you shoot at me."

"I don't need your help. And the kids in this pool aren't innocent. Nobody is. Everybody in this godforsaken county has blood on their hands."

I didn't know what he meant, but it didn't matter. Already, I heard the faint warble of distant sirens. I needed to keep him talking for a few more minutes.

"Help me understand," I said. "Why are you doing this?"

"Because they deserve to die. And so do you."

He opened fire on my car. Rounds struck the other side. A tire popped, and glass shattered. The truck rocked on its shocks, but the engine block caught everything directed at me. Those distant sirens grew louder and louder until they seemed as if they were on top of us. Then, all at once, the shooting stopped. I looked beneath the truck this time, but I couldn't see Saunders. He must have gone behind the tree.

Moments later, the first cruiser turned into the park with its lights and siren blaring. Saunders opened fire. The front window shattered. I couldn't see who was driving, but he had no cover at all along the road. Saunders kept shooting, and the cruiser kept rolling down the hill until it slammed into a car parked alongside the road. After what had happened on the water tower, we knew Saunders could shoot. He had probably just killed one of my colleagues.

I sprinted north, away from the cover of my truck's engine block. The second cruiser screeched through the park's entrance, its lights blaring. Saunders opened fire once more. He was so focused on killing my colleagues that he didn't see me running. Once I had a clear shot at his back, I raised my weapon and squeezed the trigger until the weapon ran dry.

Half a dozen rounds caught him flush in the back. The weapon dropped from his hands as he fell.

A third cruiser and then a fourth came careening around the corner as I reloaded and ran forward. Saunders lay on the ground faceup. He was blinking. I kicked away the rifle and held my weapon on him. After everything he had done, I wanted to put another round in his skull, but it wasn't necessary. Blood trickled down his chin. If I thought I could save him, I would have called for an ambulance, but he was dying. People screamed all around me, but I focused on Saunders.

"Helen?" he asked, his voice hoarse. "Is that you?"

"No," I said. "I'm Detective Joe Court with the St. Augustine County Sheriff's Department. You're under arrest."

He tried to say something, but blood instead of words poured out. A uniformed officer ran to me, his weapon drawn.

"Joe, you okay?"

I glanced up to see Marcus Washington, one of our uniformed officers.

"Yeah," I said, nodding. "This guy's dead, but call for every ambulance you can get. We've got casualties."

Within moments, dozens more police cars arrived and ran toward the pool. The first wave of ambulances came shortly thereafter. Paramedics pulled Bob Reitz from the first cruiser Saunders had fired on. His skin was pale, but even from a distance, he looked alert. They strapped him onto a gurney and drove him away. A second pair of paramedics came to me, but I was fine, and Saunders had died.

It was over. Now, we had to tally the dead.

Chapter 43

When he saw me, Sheriff Delgado ordered me to go to the hospital so the doctors could check me out and make sure I wasn't in shock. Even in my condition, I saw what he was doing: He wanted me out of there before the media arrived. He needed a win, and I had given him the biggest win of his career. The Apostate was dead, and every news outlet in the country would run the story. I didn't care. I had done my job.

A nurse in the ER cleaned up my cuts, and a doctor examined me for shock, but I was okay. Mom, Dad, and Dylan—my brother—waited for me in the lobby when the doctors released me. I didn't realize I had needed a hug until the three of them crowded around me. Then, I broke down. They must have driven me home because the next thing I could remember was unlocking my front door.

Dad and Dylan went grocery shopping, while Mom and I sat on the couch in the living room. We didn't talk, but it was comforting having her there. After a while, Agent Costa picked me up so I could go over what had happened. For almost four hours, I answered questions and led a team of

FBI investigators through Sycamore Park to show them what I had done and when.

While there, I saw my truck. Bullet holes riddled the exterior. Saunders's shots had broken every window and shredded two tires. The ground around it smelled like diesel, most likely because a round had punctured the fuel tank. I was lucky to be alive even if my truck had driven its last mile.

We got lucky at the pool. The lifeguard staff sounded the alarm as soon as they received word of a potential emergency and were already starting to get people inside by the time Saunders fired his first shot. He shot a lifeguard in the shoulder as she tried to climb down from her stand. Thanks to the quick and courageous work of two other lifeguards, she made it to the relative safety of the locker room, where their supervisor—a part-time paramedic—kept her from bleeding out. Saunders shot at others, but he didn't hit them.

News crews from St. Louis, Kansas City, Chicago, Memphis, and half a dozen other locations parked everywhere around town. At a little before six, Agent Costa drove me home. I had dinner with my family. Dylan told me about a girl he was dating, and Dad told me about his first trip to a lumberyard. Mom held my hand under the table and said nothing the entire meal. I needed that.

Dylan had to work the next day, so he and Dad went home. Mom stayed with me and slept on the couch, which I appreciated more than I could say. I didn't want to be alone.

Over the next few days, the FBI's Behavioral Analysis Unit dove into Glenn Saunders's life with a gusto I didn't often see in law enforcement. They interviewed me half a dozen times and talked to all of his co-workers. He had no friends whom they could interview.

While the conversations might have provided insight, the real gems were his journals. Saunders had kept them since he was a teenager. The FBI agents were like kids visiting Disneyland for the first time. Never in my life had I seen so many psychologists so excited. I had spent enough time in Glenn Saunders's head for ten lifetimes, though. They could have him.

Delgado gave me a week off to recover. He also ordered me to see Dr. Taylor again for an additional six visits. I didn't know how much a therapist could help, but having someone to talk to wouldn't hurt.

On Friday, five days after the shooting in Sycamore Park, Agent Costa and Deputy Director Alexis Koch came to my house. Though it was only nine in the morning, it was already so hot outside I didn't want to mow the lawn. I made a pot of coffee and sat across from them in the living room with my coffee table between us.

"How are you feeling, Detective?" asked Koch, a smile on her face.

"Good, all things considered," I said. "I've been trying to keep busy. Are there still news vans on every corner in town?"

Costa looked at his boss before speaking. "A few. They haven't bothered you, have they?"

"No," I said, shaking my head.

"Good. We've been trying to keep them away."

I nodded but said nothing. After an awkward silence, my coffee maker beeped, and I stood.

"You guys like your coffee black or with cream?"

"Black is fine," said Koch. Costa nodded his agreement, so I left and poured three mugs of coffee, which I carried to the living room on a tray. For another moment, we were silent. Then Koch put her mug down and blinked.

"We've been reading Saunders's journals," she said. "We can't diagnose him posthumously, but our team thinks he was schizophrenic with full auditory and sensory hallucinations. He seemed to believe Helen was alive and lived in his spare bedroom. He was a sick man, but he hid it very well. None of his co-workers suspected he was ill."

I raised my eyebrows and drew in a breath. "Is that common among serial killers?"

"I wouldn't say it's common," said Koch, "but it happens. David Berkowitz—the Son of Sam killer—had schizophrenia. Richard Chase—he killed six people and drank their blood—was also a schizophrenic. If we had caught Saunders alive, he would have spent the rest of his life in a prison mental ward."

I looked down at the coffee table. "Why are you telling me this?"

"Because he wrote about you in his last journal," said Costa. "You never visited him at home, did you?"

I furrowed my brow. "No."

Both FBI agents nodded.

"He thought the two of you were in love," said Costa. "In his notebooks, Saunders described you as Mary Joe Saunders. We found some women's clothing in the house. We think it's yours."

"You can keep it, if that's why you're here," I said. "You can't wash away whatever he did with them."

Both agents smiled a little.

"We're wrapping up our investigation," said Koch. "Since you broke the case, we thought you would want to hear the firsthand story."

"Thank you, but I'm tired of death," I said.

"I understand," said Koch. She looked to Agent Costa, and the two of them stood. "We'll see ourselves out."

I nodded and allowed myself to sink into my couch as I thought through the rest of my day. I had some vodka left, but my fridge was mostly bare. I needed to shop. My department had let me borrow an unmarked SUV from our motor pool, but I wouldn't have it forever. That meant I needed to start looking at cars. I didn't know if I had it in me to rebuild an old truck again.

I was so occupied by my thoughts I didn't notice Agent Costa standing in my doorway until he cleared his throat.

"There's one more thing if you're interested," he said. He paused, and I nodded to let him know I was listening. "We found two letters in Saunders's house you might be interested in reading. They explain a few things."

"Email them to me," I said. "I'll read them later."

He nodded and pulled the door shut behind him as he left. After they drove away, I figured I might as well start my day, as simple as it was. Dad made an omelet for me the last time he visited. It tasted good, so I showered, dressed, and picked up groceries to make another. I also bought a bottle of good tequila. As I drove home, my phone beeped. I didn't bother looking at it until I parked in my driveway. Costa had sent me his promised email. I slipped the phone into my pocket without reading it before carrying my groceries inside.

I hadn't purchased a lot of food, so it only took five or six minutes to put everything away. Then, I focused on my phone. Costa had sent me photographs of two letters found tucked into a journal in Saunders's attic.

The first was a handwritten letter from Saunders's father. In it, Edward Saunders told his son he had made arrangements for him to live with an aunt and uncle in St. Peters, Missouri, and that he was sorry for what he was about to do. I didn't realize it at first, but it was a suicide note. I felt like a voyeur intruding on someone else's pain. The last paragraph made me pause.

I can't do this anymore. I don't deserve to be here. Helen's blood is everywhere in this town. Make them hurt for what they've done. Make them scream so loudly your sister hears them from heaven. Let her know you've done what I never could. Make them all bleed. Please.

Nothing would excuse what Glenn Saunders had done, but he hadn't been born a monster. A heavy knot grew in my stomach. I wondered what I would have become if someone had hurt Audrey or Dylan. I wouldn't have killed anyone, but it would have changed me—and not for the better.

The second letter came from Susanne Pennington—my neighbor—and she had addressed it to Edward Saunders, Glenn's father. In it, she said she could never apologize enough for what her husband had done and enclosed a check for fifty thousand dollars so Edward could open his own woodworking shop.

I closed the photos and called Costa's cell phone.

"Hey, it's Joe Court," I said. "I read through the letters you sent me."

"What'd you think?"

I paused. "I'm not sure yet. What's your read on them?"

"With Saunders dead, we've got to speculate a little. I read the notes you took when you interviewed Keith Fox, so I know about Antonio Mancini and Helen at the summer camp. We think Antonio killed Helen, but the county didn't have enough evidence to prosecute him. Instead, Stanley Pennington—the town's local big shot—and the sheriff beat Antonio half to death in a cell. With nothing to hold him on, they took him to the hospital and released him."

I knew that part of the story, so I nodded.

"And you think that's what the letters referenced?"

"Yeah," said Costa, his voice sounding a little surprised. "The locals had to let Antonio go after Stanley and the sheriff beat him up. To apologize, Mrs. Pennington wrote Edward Saunders a check. Edward felt guilty for accepting that check, so he killed himself and told his son to seek revenge."

Neither Costa nor I said anything.

"You think otherwise?" he asked, after a pause.

"I'm not sure," I said, sinking into a seat at my breakfast table. "I need to check on something. Can I call you back later?"

He said I could, so I hung up and searched my phone's call history for the number of Dr. Sheridan, our coroner.

"Hey, doc, this is Joe Court with the St. Augustine County Sheriff's Department. Are you in the office?"

"Yeah," he said. "What do you need?"

"A records search," I said. "I know that's a job for your clerk, but I think you'll find something problematic."

He paused. "Okay. What are you looking for?"

"Male decedent named Stanley Pennington."

I listened as he typed.

"We've got a record," he said after a moment. "I'm reading through it now."

Neither of us said anything. Then he cleared his throat.

"This is interesting. Mr. Pennington died in 1971, and the coroner conducted a partial autopsy. It lists the cause of death as heart failure, but it doesn't explain his manner of death. The document is typed, but there's a handwritten note on the top that says detectives should direct all questions to Councilman Darren Rogers."

I paused. "Did Darren Rogers ever work in the coroner's office?"

"I've never seen his name on reports before this," said Sheridan. "This is unusual."

"Everything about this case has been unusual, but I think I'm getting somewhere now. Thank you for this. It's helped a lot."

He wished me luck with whatever I was doing, and I hung up. A deep heavy pit had formed in my stomach, and my throat felt tight, but I had a job to do. I went to my closet and took my badge and a pistol from my gun safe before grabbing my keys and getting into my department-issued SUV.

The drive to my neighbor's house took less than a minute, but it felt longer. Susanne opened the door with a smile the moment I knocked. Then she saw the pistol on my hip, and her smile waned.

"You know how I feel about those things," she said, pointing to my gun. "Firearms are not allowed in my house."

"I'm not here as a friend. I'm here as a detective. We need to talk about your husband's murder."

She hesitated and blinked before shaking her head.

"No one murdered Stanley, honey. He had a heart attack."

"No, he didn't," I said, my voice sharper than I'd expected. "We can talk here, or I can drive you to my station. Either way, we need to talk."

She held my gaze for a moment, but then her shoulders slumped, and her eyes tilted down.

"What did you find?"

"The letter you wrote Edward Saunders," I said.

She nodded. "Then come in. I'll tell you the context."

Chapter 44

As Susanne led me inside, my gut felt tight, the muscles of my legs trembled, and my throat threatened to close at any moment. I hated everything about this. We sat down in her living room. I took the loveseat, and she sat in a chair to my left. The clock on her mantel ticked with each passing second. For almost a minute, neither of us spoke. Then I sighed.

"You once told me your husband was a bastard."

"He was," she said, her lips flat.

"I talked to a retired detective who knew him. He seemed to like him. Your husband gave scholarships to kids so they could go to summer camp to give them an incentive to stay out of trouble. That doesn't sound like a bastard."

She raised her eyebrow and then crossed her legs.

"That's your opinion."

I leaned forward. "Is it wrong?"

She said nothing, and I closed my eyes.

"I need you to talk," I said.

"You came here, Joe. Ask a question."

I balled my hands into fists and drew in a deep breath.

"You gave Edward Saunders fifty thousand dollars in 1971. That was a lot of money."

"To some people," she said, blinking.

"To almost everyone," I said. "What would that be worth today? Two hundred grand? Three hundred grand?"

She shrugged. "I don't know. You'd have to ask an economist. I was a schoolteacher."

"And Stanley, your husband, was a businessman," I said. "Back then, he was the biggest employer in the county."

"We brought a lot of business to St. Augustine."

I nodded.

"How'd he die?"

"Heart attack."

I stood up and paced.

"Did your husband know Darren Rogers?"

She tilted her head to the side and narrowed her eyes at me.

"Everybody knew Darren Rogers. He made sure of that. His daddy was the biggest landowner in St. Augustine County."

The hardwood floor creaked beneath my feet as I paced.

"In 1971, he would have been twenty-four, twenty-five years old?"

Susanne paused but then nodded. "Twenty-three, I think."

"Did he and your husband get along?"

She closed her eyes as she sighed.

407

"I suppose, but they didn't talk often. Stanley dealt with Darren's father. Back then, he was the important one."

Playing nice was getting me nowhere. I locked my eyes on her.

"Why was your husband a bastard?"

Susanne's smile turned cold. "There are aspects of my life I don't share, even with my friends."

I nodded. "But you already shared it with me. After you learned a man raped me when I was a teenager, you told me we were sisters. You told me everyone who has been through what we've been through becomes our sister."

She said nothing.

"In 1971, the country had no laws against marital rape. Stanley could do whatever he wanted to you. Your only recourse was to divorce him."

She blinked as her eyes grew moist. My heart beat faster.

"That's why he was a bastard. He didn't like hearing the word no, did he? Even if you went to the police, they'd only drive you home. Your husband was an important man in this county. I bet he had friends in the court system. I bet you couldn't even file for divorce. You couldn't escape."

A tear fell down her aged cheek.

"He was a bastard," she said, her voice low.

"Who else did he hurt?"

She sat there and fluttered her eyes but said nothing.

"Who else?" I asked, my voice harder. I waited a moment. "Antonio Mancini didn't rape Helen Saunders. He was gay.

That was why Stanley blamed him. Antonio was an easy target. By the standards of the time, he was sexually deviant. If he slept with men, he wouldn't hesitate to rape a little girl. Right?"

She still said nothing.

"Your husband raped you."

Her lower lip quivered.

"Helen Saunders was a sweet little girl raised by a single father who was doing his best to provide a life for his family. Her father worked for Pennington Hotels. He even built some of your furniture. You knew him. When I asked you about him, you pretended you didn't, but you lied."

Susanne looked down. I sat at the loveseat again.

"Stanley knew Helen," I said. "He saw her grow up. He saw that sweet little girl turn into a beautiful young woman. And she was sweet, wasn't she? Innocent, too. Probably naïve. She baked brownies for the police and firemen's charity bake sales and helped raise her brother. She was the closest thing her little brother had to a mom."

Susanne continued to look at the floor, but I watched a tear trickle down her cheek.

"Helen was a child," I said. "Everyone loved her. Your husband, in the dead of night, coaxed this sweet, innocent child from her cabin at summer camp and led her to a sandy beach. There, he ripped off her clothes and stuffed her underwear in her mouth so she couldn't scream. After he raped her, he drowned her and left her on the beach as if she were garbage."

She looked at me with tear-stained cheeks. Something profound passed between us. A sense of loss welled inside me at the pain I was causing my friend. Susanne's mouth opened, but no sound came out. Finally, she nodded. I held her hands as she cried. I softened my voice.

"Did you kill him?"

"He deserved it," she said, her eyes closed as she nodded.

The pit in my stomach grew.

"How did you find out?"

When she looked at me, the corners of her mouth curled upward.

"He told me over dinner one night. It was like he was proud of himself for getting away with it. He laughed at her and said Helen was stupid for agreeing to meet him out there. I'll never forget the way he laughed at that poor little girl."

I squeezed her hand.

"What did you do?"

"Nothing right away," she said. "But I waited. Two days later, he took a bath before bed—as he always did. I had this little yellow hairdryer back then. It matched the tiles in the bathroom. I cared about things like that. When I heard Stanley turn off the water, I walked in, plugged in my hairdryer, and dropped it in the bathtub, right on his chest. It didn't kill him right away, but the electricity paralyzed him. I left him, called the Sheriff's Department, and told the dispatcher I had just killed my husband."

I nodded. "What happened next?"

"Deputies drove out, but by the time they got to the house, Stanley was dead. I told the sheriff everything. He took me to the station. Their typewriter wasn't working, so I wrote what I had done on a piece of paper. I didn't ask for leniency. I killed my husband, and I was ready for my punishment."

I reached into my purse for a notepad.

"You didn't go to jail," I said. "What happened?"

"Darren Rogers came in," she said. "The station back then was small. I was sitting at a detective's desk, and Darren came through the front door. His daddy had just appointed him to the County Council."

I nodded. "What'd he do?"

"He and the sheriff talked. Then the sheriff drove me home and told me to stay. The next morning, Darren Rogers came by and told me he had a way to help me get out of trouble. I was thirty years old. He was in his twenties. I thought he wanted to sleep with me."

I scribbled down details.

"What did he want?"

"My husband's money," she said. "He didn't say it outright. He asked whether I'd be willing to put St. Augustine County first, and I said yes. Then he told me some men would be by later that day requesting development grants. If I put St. Augustine first, the county would take care of me. My legal problems would go away."

Put St. Augustine first. I had heard Rogers use the same turn of phrase when he wanted me to make a quick arrest in a murder investigation.

"What did you do?"

"I took meetings all day. Fourteen men came by with business propositions. I said yes to them all and promised fourteen strangers eight million dollars, no strings attached. When I finished with them, Darren Rogers returned and told me he needed money for two more projects. I built a pool in Sycamore Park and gave him a hundred thousand dollars so the county could throw a spring festival to celebrate the new St. Augustine. After that, he tore up my signed confession and told me I had settled my husband's debt."

"What happened with these grants?"

She smiled. "It took about six months, but I sold everything I owned. Jordan Reid used his money to create Reid Chemical. Ross Kelly used a million dollars and a land transfer to create Ross Kelly Farms. Jake Conroy used his money to renovate the Wayfair Motel and to open a restaurant and truck stop by the interstate. Most of the other places went out of business, but I hear Able Morgan's diner is still open. His nephew runs it now."

My stomach twisted.

"Yeah. Able's is still open. They make good milkshakes," I said. I paused. "Did Edward Saunders come to you at the hotel?"

"No," she said, giving me a quiet smile. "Edward was a good man. He was quiet and proud. When I commissioned our coffee table from him, he told me his dream was to own his own furniture shop."

Susanne paused before speaking again.

"Darren Rogers didn't bother telling Edward about the deal he cut, so Edward didn't know who killed his daughter. I told him the truth and gave him every dollar I owned so he could start over. I hoped he and Glenn would leave town, but Edward built his shop and followed his dream."

"He killed himself," I said.

Susanne nodded. "I know."

Neither of us said anything. I drew in a deep breath and stood. "I need you to come downtown with me and tell some of my colleagues what you just told me."

Susanne paused and held my gaze.

"Do you understand what you're doing?"

"I don't have a choice, Susanne," I said.

"You always have a choice," she said. "I killed a man who raped his wife and murdered an innocent young woman. Stanley and his friends destroyed everything good in my life and planted a poison tree on Helen Saunders's grave. St. Augustine has lived with that poison tree for so long, its fruit has become a part of who we are. If you tear it out, you'll tear out the heart of this county with it. Think about what you're doing."

I swallowed hard and tried to keep the tremble from entering my voice.

"Susanne Pennington, you're under arrest for the murder of Stanley Pennington. You have the right to remain silent. If you talk to the police, we can use whatever you tell us against you in court. You have the right to an attorney. If you can't afford one, the court will provide one for you at no charge. Do you understand your rights?"

She held my gaze for a silent ten count before nodding.

"I understand," she said. "Before you take me, can I use the restroom?"

"Of course," I said.

She stood and put a hand on my cheek. "I'm sorry I put you in the position to do this."

"Me, too."

She nodded and walked to the restroom. I thought I heard her talking to someone up there, but that may have been my imagination. When she came out ten minutes later, I walked her to my SUV and helped her sit on the backseat. Within five minutes, she trembled. I thought she was scared, but then I saw her dilated pupils and the now pallid tone of her skin. Moments later, her tremble turned to a convulsion as whatever drug she had taken worked its way through her system.

I flicked on my lights and siren and glanced at her in the rearview mirror, my heart now racing.

"You took something in the bathroom, didn't you?" I asked.

Her voice was hoarse and weak. "I couldn't let you destroy this place."

"Damn it, Susanne," I said, flooring the accelerator. "What did you take?"

"Everything."

I squeezed the steering wheel hard and clenched my jaw tight as I drove. Cars made way in front of me, but I couldn't drive fast enough. The tips of her fingers were blue as she clutched her chest. I radioed the hospital to let them know I was bringing in a suspected overdose, so paramedics and nurses met me in the driveway. They took her away.

I stayed in the car and covered my eyes as waves of anger, pain, sadness, and frustration washed over me. I wanted to cry, but I didn't have tears. Eventually, I went into the waiting room. The doctors were still trying to save Susanne, so I told the receptionist my name and position. She promised to keep me updated. I also called my station to let them know what was going on.

Then, I settled into a chair to wait. After an hour, the emergency room's exterior door slid open, and Darren Rogers walked inside. He wore gray slacks, a white shirt, and a red tie, and he carried a battered leather briefcase. The waiting room's harsh lights glinted off his slick liver-spotted head. When he saw me, he smiled and came forward. Every part of my body felt hot.

"Detective Court," he said, holding out his hand. "Congratulations on Glenn Saunders. You did it. You got the bastard."

I ignored his hand.

"Saunders won't hurt anybody again," I said. "I would have preferred an arrest, though."

Rogers smiled and lowered his hand as if he hadn't offered it.

"I hear there are big things on the way for you," he said, winking and lowering his voice. "I'm not supposed to tell you this, but the FBI requested your service record. You impressed them. I think they'll be offering you a place in the next class at the FBI training academy. You'll make a hell of a special agent."

"I'm not going anywhere."

My voice was so low I barely heard it over the ambient noise of the hospital. Rogers straightened and furrowed his brow.

"I don't mean to tell you your business, but you'd be a fool to turn down an offer from the FBI."

"Susanne told me about her former husband's death," I said. "Stanley Pennington raped and murdered Helen Saunders almost fifty years ago. My department covered it up and blamed an innocent man. When Susanne killed Stanley, you covered it up and engineered a deal. If Pennington Hotels went under, it'd take this county with it. Instead, you arranged for her to sell her company, stay out of jail, and donate her money to your friends so they could build their own businesses."

Rogers patted me on the shoulder and smiled. "You certainly have an active imagination, Detective Court. I'd love to sit and chat, but I'm here to visit a client."

"You own bars and restaurants," I said. "You don't have clients."

"My family owns a lot more than bars and restaurants," he said. "Besides, I'm a licensed attorney who provides discreet legal services to a select clientele. You can't keep me from my clients. If you'll excuse me."

I stepped back. "By all means."

He smiled again and walked past me toward the front desk. He spoke to the receptionist for a moment, and then a nurse in scrubs escorted him back to the treatment area. Rogers stayed inside for about five minutes and then left. On the way out the door, he tilted his head toward me.

"I'll see you around, Detective," he said.

"You will," I said. As he left the waiting room, a doctor in blue scrubs came from the treatment area and walked toward me. "How's Susanne?"

"You're Detective Court?"

I nodded. "Yeah."

"We did what we could, but any further intervention would only prolong her suffering. I'm sorry."

I opened my mouth.

"Did Darren Rogers do something to her?"

He paused.

"Mr. Rogers is Mrs. Pennington's attorney, and he let us know she had a durable do-not-resuscitate order in her will. It didn't factor into my decision to end life support, though."

My fingers tingled, and my body felt hot. "He was trying to kill her so she couldn't testify against him."

The doctor paused again. He opened his mouth and then closed it twice before speaking.

"I can assure you that Mr. Rogers didn't change the situation. Does Mrs. Pennington have a family I can call?"

"The Sheriff's Department will notify her next of kin," I said.

"Okay," he said, nodding. "If you or they have questions, let me know."

I thanked him, and he walked back into the treatment area. I sunk down into a seat and rested my elbows on my knees.

Since becoming a detective, I had fired my weapon multiple times in the line of duty, I had been abducted and tied to a chair, I had disemboweled someone with a knife hidden in the bottom of a contract murderer's shoe, I had seen children abducted and murdered. I had lost colleagues and now a friend. All this time, I had believed there was something wrong with me, that I was cursed, that I had brought this death and pain into my life.

It wasn't me, though.

It was this county, this town, these people. Darren Rogers and men like him had brought something dark to this county.

The people of St. Augustine had made me a detective. They trusted me to peer into the darkness on their behalf and to protect them from the monsters that lurked in the night. I hunted murderers, rapists, and predators who preyed on the weak. St. Augustine was my home, not by birth but by choice. I had made it my own. I had put down roots. St. Augustine was mine, and I didn't plan to give it up without a fight.

As I drove to my house, the impact of what had happened in the ER hit home. I had lost one of my only friends. My whole body felt numb. I wanted to sit in a dark room and drink until I didn't hurt, but as I approached my house, a young man sat on a rocking chair on my front porch. There was no car in the driveway. I parked and got out of my car.

The guy on my porch was in his mid-teens, and he had blond hair and blue eyes. His face looked familiar somehow. I wondered whether he was a sibling of someone Saunders had taken to his dungeon. I wanted to tell him to leave, but I couldn't do that to the brother of a murder victim.

"Hey," I said. "I appreciate that you came all the way out here, but this isn't a good time."

He looked at me but said nothing. He wore navy shorts and a sky-blue polo shirt.

"I didn't know whether you were real," he said.

"I'm real," I said. "Who are you, and why are you on my porch?"

He stood. He was taller than me but not by a lot.

"I'm Ian."

I waited a moment, but he didn't continue.

"Hello, Ian," I said. "Why are you on my porch, and how did you get here? There's no car in the driveway."

"Uber," he said. "I got your address from Brenda Collins. She's a lawyer."

I crossed my arms and spread my feet shoulder-width apart. It was a shooter's stance, but he didn't know that.

"Why did an attorney give you my address?"

"She didn't," he said. "Her firm's IT department doesn't update their software as often as they should. Her version of Outlook has an information-disclosure vulnerability. It's not important. I got your address from her."

I closed my eyes and sighed. "So you broke into her computer and got my address. Why would you do that, Ian?"

"Your mom was Erin Court, right?" he asked.

A cold spike traveled through me. My voice became iron.

"Why did you break into Ms. Collins's computer, and how do you know Erin Court?"

"Erin was my mom," he said. "She died when I was two. I wanted to meet you."

I studied his face and shook my head, but then I realized why he had looked familiar at first sight. He had Erin's eyes.

I brought my hand to my mouth as a fluttery feeling took hold in my stomach.

"You're not lying," I said, my voice barely above a whisper. He nodded. "I have a brother."

"And I've got a sister. I was hoping you'd be taller."

"Me, too," I said. After everything that had happened to me over the past few weeks, after all the death I had just seen, I didn't think I had a smile left in me. And yet, the corners of my lips turned up. "Let's sit and talk."

***

I hope you liked THE BOYS IN THE CHURCH! The Joe Court series continues in THE MAN IN THE METH LAB! It's a great mystery, and I think you'll really like it. You can purchase it directly from Chris Culver [store.chrisc ulver.com], and at Barnes & Noble, Amazon, or other major retailers.

Or turn the page to get a FREE Joe Court novella....

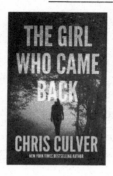

You know what the best part of being an author is? Goofing off while my spouse is at work and my kids are at school. You know what the second part is? Interacting with my readers. About once a month, I write a newsletter about my books, writing process, research, and funny events from my life. I also include information about sales and discounts. I try to make it fun.

As if hearing from me on a regular basis wasn't enough, if you join, you get a FREE Joe Court novella. The story is a lot of fun, and it's available exclusively to readers on my mailing list. You won't get it anywhere else.

If you're interested, sign up here:

http://www.chrisculver.com/magnet.html

As much as I enjoy writing, I like hearing from readers even more. If you want to keep up with my world, there are a couple of ways you can do that.

First and easiest, I've got a mailing list. If you join, you'll receive an email whenever I have a new novel out or when I run sales. You can join that by going to this address:

http://www.indiecrime.com/mailinglist.html

If my mailing list doesn't appeal to you, you can also connect with me on Facebook here:

http://facebook.com/ChrisCulverBooks

And you can always email me at chris@indiecrime.com. I love receiving email!

C hris Culver is the *New York Times* bestselling author of the Ash Rashid series and other novels. After graduate school, Chris taught courses in ethics and comparative religion at a small liberal arts university in southern Arkansas. While there and when he really should have been grading exams, he wrote *The Abbey,* which spent sixteen weeks on the *New York Times* bestsellers list and introduced the world to Detective Ash Rashid.

Chris has been a storyteller since he was a kid, but he decided to write crime fiction after picking up a dog-eared, coffee-stained paperback copy of Mickey Spillane's *I, the Jury* in a library book sale. Many years later, his wife, despite considerable effort, still can't stop him from bringing more orphan books home. He lives with his family near St. Louis.